Lace

and

Blade

5

Edited by

Deborah J. Ross

This book is a work of fiction. All characters, names, locations, and events portrayed in this book are fictional or used in an imaginary manner to entertain, and any resemblance to any real people, situations, or incidents is purely coincidental.

LACE AND BLADE 5

Edited by Deborah J. Ross

ISBN-13: 978-1-938185-64-9
ISBN-10: 1-938185-64-1

Trade Paperback Edition

February 14, 2019

A Publication of
The Marion Zimmer Bradley Literary Works Trust
PO Box 193473
San Francisco, CA 94119-3473
www.mzbworks.com

ACKNOWLEDGMENTS

Introduction copyright © 2019 by Deborah J. Ross
"Sea of Souls" copyright © 2019 by Robin Wayne Bailey
"Clockwork Unicorn" copyright © 2019 by Doranna Durgin
"The Custom of the Country" copyright © 2019 by India Edghill
"The Bottle" copyright © 2019 by Steven Harper Piziks
"Fire Season" copyright © 2019 by Anne Leonard
"Ascent" copyright © 2019 by Shariann Lewitt
"Til Death Do Us Part" copyright © 2019 by Pat MacEwen
"Allons" copyright © 2019 by Gillian Polack
"Spire Witch" copyright © 2019 by Marella Sands
"The Ferryman" copyright © 2019 by Dave Smeds
"The Ghost of Lady Rei" copyright © 2019 by Adam Stemple
"The Golden Fir" copyright © 2019 by Harry Turtledove
"An Interrupted Betrothal" copyright © 2019 by Lawrence Watt Evans
"Water Bound" copyright © 2019 by Julia H. West

CONTENTS

INTRODUCTION

by Deborah J. Ross

Since I began editing this series back in 2008, much has changed. The field of fantasy literature has flourished while publishing has undergone one upheaval after another, and the tastes and sensibilities of readers have also evolved. I myself, as editor, writer, and reader, have grown. So too has the underlying concept of the anthology series.

In the beginning, Vera Nazarian, publisher of Norilana Books, came up with the concept of "lace and blade" as a subset of sword and sorcery fantasy; by this she meant elegant, romantic, swashbuckling tales with rapier wit as well as actual steel blades. She described it as "exotic and beautiful high fantasy and period fantasy, including fantasy of manners, ancient historical fantasy; where duels of sharp wit and steel are as common as duels between the sheets; where living jewels flash in earlobes and frothy lace defines the curve or wrist and the hollow of throat; where erotic tension fills the perfumed air with frissons of anticipation and romantic delight; where hearts are broken and resurrected by true love, dangerous liaisons decide the fates of kingdoms, and courtesans slay with a kiss."

In my introduction to that debut volume, I wrote:

"The wind was a torrent of darkness among the gusty trees.
The moon was a ghostly galleon tossed upon stormy seas.
The road was a ribbon of moonlight over the purple moor,
And the highwayman came riding—"
Alfred Noyes, The Highwayman, *1906*

Something in these deeply romantic words tugs at our imagination, stirs our dreams. Is it a yearning for adventure and passion in our own lives? Do we resonate with the underlying mythic images? Is it pure escapism? Or...do we, in some wordless manner, recognize the truth that our hearts whisper if only we can listen: that life itself is filled with mystery, with wonder, with paradox that can be lived but not analyzed?

The book you hold in your hands began thousands of years ago, when Homer sang of the anger of Achilles and Odysseus matched wits with Circe. It owes a debt to the many writers and editors who, over the centuries, translated eternal archetypes into exciting, engaging stories.

All of this still holds true, and it seems to me that the more dire straits our world finds itself in, the more our hearts crave uplifting stories, especially fantastical tales where hope and longing take physical form. Fantasy uses archetype and metaphor in deeply resonant ways. It follows its own emotional logic and has its own internal structure, its rise and fall of tension, its conflicts and twists and moments of perfect resolution. It is no accident that fiction often feels more "true" than "real life" events. One reason for this is that fiction relies on an orderly sequence not just of plot or events but of psychological and spiritual development. Good fiction invites us to grow—and to hope and dream and heal—along with the characters. It leaves us changed; it enlarges our innermost vision.

Some of the stories in this, the fifth volume, can be described as the high or period fantasy Vera envisioned, although they step (nay, leap headlong!) beyond the constraints of Western European courtly drama. Others take us to realms that are purely the products of the imaginations of the authors. From the earliest volumes of *Lace and Blade* to this one, non-Western European settings and non-stereotyped love stories have embroidered the original concept with added richness and diversity.

In every one of these anthologies, themes have emerged so that the stories resonate and enhance each another. I am not sure whether this is an example of the synchronicity of great authors, or the way these themes arise from our times, or simple coincidence, but it delights my editorial heart. The debut volume contained not one but two tales of Spanish highwaymen. Here, for instance, you'll find unique but complementary visitations from spirits of water and fire. I arranged the stories as a journey that made intuitive sense to me, one that's based on my own taste. Not every story pleases every reader equally, of course. In the spirit of play, I encourage you to allow your own inner editor to emerge. Pay attention to how the previous stories influence your experience as you go along. If it is true, as I believe, that every time we love, we become more capable of loving, then every time we fall in love with a character or a story, our hearts open just a bit more to the next. Even if this isn't always true, it's a lovely conceit that invites us to the dance of dreams unfolding in these pages.

— Deborah J. Ross

THE FERRYMAN

by Dave Smeds

Dave Smeds has authored novels (including *The Sorcery Within* and *X-Men: Law of the Jungle*), screenplays, comic book scripts, and articles, but is best known for his short fiction. His work has graced the pages of *Asimov's SF, F&SF, Realms of Fantasy,* and a plethora of anthologies, including most particularly the *Sword and Sorceress* series and the *Lace and Blade* series.

Of "The Ferryman," Dave tells us it seemed only natural to him to get around to composing a tale set entirely upon a river. The Kings River of the southern San Joaquin Valley runs along the edge of the farm where Dave grew up. He spent many an hour partaking of a pastime for which the waterway has become renowned—floating on tractor inner tubes below the bluffs and oak trees, beside the willows and muskrat burrows. He vastly preferred this to swimming in lakes or at swimming pools, where his natural lack of buoyancy continually threatened to pull him under. He writes, "You can drown in a river, too, of course, but all you have to do is manage to tread water for a short time, or hang on to something like those inner tubes, and the current will deliver you to land. What seems like an ending instead becomes an adventure, and your story continues."

As Erom drifted down the river, the mists appeared. Once again, he had been summoned.

He played his usual game, trying to predict what his landfall would be. He dipped his fingers over the side. Not long after his gondola was enveloped by the murk, the water temperature shifted from bracing to inviting. Seconds later a dragonfly whisked past, wings bright with the color and iridescence of a southron species. In the shallows off to the left, ibis sedge whispered in the breeze, a snakelike susurrus warning him to venture no closer, because even a craft as buoyant and flat-bottomed as his could be stranded.

He sighed. His destination could only be Allistoya. Land of goats and olives, distinctive only for the long tenure of its ruling dynasty. As a young man—before he had ever met an immortal, much less become one—he had blundered through Allistoya.

Even then, he had not liked the place.

The pier loomed, a dark outline in the greyness. Soon he could make out the stone waterfront and its gibbets, a newly executed trio of men suspended from the nooses around their necks.

His frown tightened. Just once he would like to take on a passenger at a normal dock, where commerce took place, where fishermen dangled their lines, where drunken sailors zigzagged to their berths singing bawdy songs.

The crowd caught sight of him. They called out, not to him but to one another. They began taking their positions, some in order to get the best view, others creating the gantlet down which the condemned person must travel.

The assembly was larger than the last time he had been summoned to Allistoya. When had that been? Not more than half a year.

Did they have nothing better to do?

He poled his way in until his port gunwale bumped gently against stuffed burlap. He tossed up his fore and aft mooring ropes, and teenage boys fastened them to the cleats.

No one spoke to him. Few were even willing to make eye contact. A pair of stewards brought the usual wooden chests of supplies and tribute, lowering the containers to him by means of pulley and tackle. He stowed the items, taking the opportunity to put away his cloak, his fur-lined boots, and his gloves, reducing his ensemble to a sleeveless shirt and knee-length breeches, as suited the climate.

The convict emerged from the holding house on the waterfront's upper level. For once it was a woman—the first female to be tendered into his custody in a dozen trips, and not what he had expected from Allistoya. A peppering of grey moderated the raven blackness of her hair, but she was not beyond childbearing age, or so he judged from the steadiness of her gait and the smooth lines of her neck.

She began her descent down the ramp. A pair of wardens flanked her on either side. Another followed. All three had their swords drawn, ready to cut her down if she tried to flee. Erom saw no hint she would attempt to do so.

By now, the people had formed into their long lines. The woman proceeded between them down the center of the pier. The wardens remained at the shore end, leaving her both unescorted and unshielded.

As ever, some onlookers jeered or shouted, cursed or spat. An urchin threw a fistful of mud—or something as brown as mud—and spattered her prison smock. A gap-toothed crone flung a bucketful of fish offal, striking so true the mess drenched the target from neckline to waist.

The promenade of the guilty had been played out before Erom thousands of times. Not once had he derived pleasure from being its witness. He did not turn away, though, because something unusual was going on. Yes, there was cruelty in play, but no one scattered broken glass on the planks in front of the convict's bare feet. No one tore open her garment. Some observers were somber. Others, anguished. A few even went so far as to glower at the wardens. Erom wondered if an attack would break out, no matter that the law's representatives were armed and armored, while the common folk were empty-handed.

No such incident developed, and in due course, the woman reached the end of the pier.

"Zeranna of Fallen Oak, you are condemned to the river," the magistrate intoned, waving a sigil-stamped order. "Step aboard, and be gone."

Another huge pair of wardens stood near the high official, available to enforce the declaration if need be, but Zeranna continued to show no resistance. She went to the wooden ladder to do as commanded.

An elderly woman near the end of one of the rows stepped forward. She held out a covered wicker basket.

Zeranna smiled at the grey-haired matron and took possession of the basket.

To Erom's surprise, she was allowed to keep it. The magistrate and the wardens did not interfere.

Down the ladder Zeranna came. Two steps, then she poised on the third. Erom held out his hand. She took it, and with a light hop, began her exile.

She seated herself near the prow, basket in her lap, facing the river rather than the realm and people that had spurned her. The boys on the pier loosened the ropes and tossed them down. Erom poled out into the current.

"Do not speak of whatever you did that brought you here this day," Erom stated once they were out of the hearing of those behind them. "Especially do not tell me you were falsely accused."

"How weary you are of those words," she responded.

Erom could not recall an occasion when the first conversation out of the mouth of one of his passengers contained any measure of sympathy, yet that was what he sensed from her. Perhaps she was an actress.

"Most who cross the water with me believe I must have the ability to moderate their sentence in some manner, but I am only the ferryman. The river will decide where you are to go. What you might say to me, and whatever I might think of it, will not alter the destination."

When he had been new to his incumbency, hearing his riders' tales had been a diversion. Who else did he have to talk to? What more natural way to pass the time? But long ago, the stories had begun to ring too familiar.

Zeranna did not comment. She kept her eyes forward, spine straight, as if declaring she was steeled for whatever hell or desolation she was bound for.

They floated on, he making the occasional adjustment with his pole whenever the portents warranted, she waiting on the bench, hands poised on the basket.

Beyond the immediate vicinity of the boat, the vista was unchanging. Just fog. Yet to Erom, a great deal was happening. Pressure nudged from one direction then another. Thresholds were crossed. Voices spoke to him inside his head, most in whispers too soft to decipher, or in languages he had never learned, but the god-touched part of him understood.

Zeranna was detecting none of that. Inevitably she wearied of the featurelessness and turned around. She opened the lid of the

13

basket.

"Would you like some bread?" she asked. She pulled out a braided, glazed loaf.

He shook his head.

"Do you even consume food?" she asked.

"Of course," he replied.

"Obviously not much."

Her gaze tracked up and down his body. He imagined himself as she must be seeing him. "Push a pole in and out of river mud every day for seven hundred years, and this is the result," he told her.

In truth, he had not eaten in a number of hours, and the aroma was seductive, but he had noticed the purple discoloration below Zeranna's eyes and the unsteadiness of her hand as she had lifted the lid of the basket. Each of these things told of how long she had been subsisting on prison fare, and of how little of that she had been given.

"Very well," she replied. She turned her attention back to the bread, and suddenly it was as though she were in her own home, invisible to anyone's scrutiny as she paid court to the first mouthful. Erom felt as though he were intruding on a private moment.

She swallowed. She smiled the most peaceful smile he had seen in a hundred years. And then she began eating more.

"You're sure you won't have any?" she asked.

He found himself raising his hand. He poised his thumb and forefinger slightly apart.

She plucked out a shred and gave it to him.

The morsel clung to his teeth, moist and chewy, rich with the flavors of flour, yeast, cardamom, and especially of butter. He knew he would find nothing of this quality when he opened his supply chests.

"It was so good of Basha to think of me," Zeranna said. "Her baking is the equal of my own grandmother, and I told her so." She took another nibble, and closed her eyes while she savored it. "Though now I think even that compliment was insufficient."

Her placid mood disappeared as a long, disturbing moan pushed its way out of the mists and rolled over them.

"What is *that*?!" Zeranna blurted. She nearly dropped the remainder of the loaf.

He had no comforting answer. "The wretch you hear is the victim of a contagion. We are approaching the Writhing Shore. Few who dwell there escape its touch. The curse is in the soil itself."

"Is that where I am to go?"

"No. We are only passing by."

A bluff loomed, boulders and shrubs and hanging vines still colorless through the veil of mist but discernible enough to show what they were. Less defined were the large beings that shambled along the top. Links of chain clanked on packed dirt. A stench wafted down that combined the taint of sewage with the fetor of death.

"The wharf is around that bend. The passengers I have delivered there are uniformly vile. Often they are evildoers spared from the gallows only to protract their punishment—make them suffer more for what they've done. I am glad to know you are not that sort of person."

They continued on. The moans and cries began to fade away.

"Has anyone ever jumped overboard to avoid going there?" Zeranna wondered aloud.

"Of course. They drown. The river makes sure of that. If you wish to imitate them, I will not stop you."

"That's not why I asked," she said. "I was just curious."

He caught her glancing at the scars on his abdomen and his throat. She did not ask the corollary question. Obviously there were passengers who attempted to take control of his boat. Just as obviously he had prevailed.

In another quarter hour, Erom lifted his pole from the water. The current was pulling them along more assertively now. The slosh and slap of rapids became increasingly audible.

"Brace yourself," he urged.

The mists hid the cataract until they were nearly upon it. Abruptly the vessel tipped beyond the edge of the shelf of the terrain and lurched down through billows of water, past boulders and over swells. Droplets rose higher than their heads as they splashed into a pool, but they were only moderately soaked. After two lesser plunges they safely reached the end of the turbulence and proceeded into a new stretch of level river, the waters now chummed with flotsam and foam.

The mists peeled away, revealing a sunny sky liberally adorned with clouds. The heaviest of the silt sank out of sight and the water became clear enough to reveal the clam banks and sunken logs. In the far distance the banks were wooded and reedy, a boundary of green just defined enough to confirm that they were still on a river and not on a gulf or bay.

There was however no sign of the cataract down which they had so recently pitched and heaved. It was part of some dimension they no longer occupied.

Zeranna shaded her eyes from the glare and took in the vista, smiling as a trout jumped, mouth wide, at a low-cruising chevron of gnats.

"This is certainly better," she commented. "Not gloomy at all."

"The mists are present when we are shifting between realms. At the moment we are fully in whatever place this is. I don't know that it has a name. I have been here many times but have never noticed any sign of inhabitants. We will go with the current until we are called elsewhere."

"How much time is this trip going to take?"

"Another day at least. Perhaps a week."

"A week?!"

"Possibly. I don't yet know."

Zeranna regarded the fish guts congealing on the front of her smock.

And she wilted. It caught Erom by surprise. Her attitude had been so stoic, but now she dropped her chin and surrendered the air in her chest. Her hands went slack over the basket.

He wondered how long her imprisonment had gone on. Long enough, apparently. She slipped from the bench and gathered into a lame-pup coil on the nearby stack of folded canvas. She did not close her eyes, but if they were focused upon anything, it was nothing more than the grain of the inner hull in front of her face.

She was still there, limp and listless, when his vessel ground against sand. Erom tossed a mooring lasso over a tree stump and pulled it tight.

Zeranna sat up. Her brow furrowed.

"I don't understand," she said.

She studied the scene as if expecting to see more than was there. It was, he conceded, not much of a place—an island twenty paces across, fifty paces long, just an outcrop of rock rising no higher than whatever tree the stump had once been part of. Its one structure was a blockhouse of plain masonry brick, the top open to the sky.

"That is the bathhouse." He gestured at the fish guts and mud spatters on her smock. "While you're cleaning up, I'll rinse that in the river."

She blinked.

"You do want to wash, don't you?" he asked.

"Of course."

"Best be about it, then. We've another leg to complete before sunset."

He hopped out, stalked up the incline, and swung wide the door of the bathhouse.

Inside it was just as he remembered, though it had been nearly a decade since the river had happened to guide his vessel to this particular waystation. The interior was a single chamber. Its main feature was a broad hollow of granite, waist deep. A subterranean channel of the river kept it full, the overflow draining away through a gap in the bottom of the downstream wall. A hot spring bubbled at the crest of the rocks in the upper corner of the enclosure, its steaming overflow trickling down, leaving an occupant of the tub able to seek out the place where the temperature was the desired mix. On the wall hung a net with several large cakes of soap that smelled of cedar oil. Two towels hung nearby, and several washcloths lay on a chiseled shelf.

He heard the scuffing of bare feet on stone as Zeranna came up behind him.

"This seems...impossible," she said.

"In the world we came from? Nearly so. But I assure you it is no illusion." He turned to find her holding a folded skirt and blouse.

"Where did you get the clothes?"

"I made them, once upon a time," she replied. "They were in the basket. Under the bread."

"Your friend Basha thinks of everything," Erom said.

He stepped out of the bath house.

"You're not going to watch?" Zeranna asked.

"You want me to?"

"No."

"Then why would I watch?"

"My jailers always watched."

Erom felt his cheeks redden. He faced her squarely, and spoke as plainly as he could. "You are not my prisoner. You are my responsibility." He placed the door against the jamb and pressed until the click of the latch confirmed it was secure.

After a period of time, he heard sounds of sloshing and rinsing. Her cheerless prison garment came sailing over the upper rim of the bath house and landed on the rocks. Erom picked it up with a wand of driftwood and tossed it into the brush at the end of the islet. He then retreated to the mooring.

Finally the door opened and Zeranna emerged.

Her clothes fit loosely on account of the weight she must have lost, but they had been made for her and still flattered her shape. She was transformed. She had gone in as a dungeon wretch and come out as a person.

"Better?" he asked.

"Much," she said.

"Then we are done here." He held out his hand to assist her into the gondola.

The waystation vanished behind them as they drifted down the mid-current of long, lazy bends of river. Eventually Erom's attention was drawn to a pair of crimson herons standing on a barely submerged sandbar. The birds were tossing a small frog back and forth to one another, never eating it. He knew then to get out the steering oar and guide his vessel toward the west bank. The mists thickened around them. A quarter hour later they dissipated, revealing a far narrower version of the river bracketed between sheer cliffs of layered rock. After an hour navigating the twists and whitewater of the channel, he saw and heard a bashhorn ram calling across the water, mocking the cave panther impotently eyeing the flock from a ledge on the opposite face of the canyon. The measure and pitch of the ram's bleats told Erom to drop his anchor and remain in place. The mists wrapped 'round. When they cleared, he and Zeranna found themselves along a placid stretch of river framed by cinnamon dunes and a verge of crocodile shoals.

He contemplated a bevy of day bats that fluttered along, feasting on the insects that cruised in the thermal layer some ten to twenty feet above the water. Finally he was satisfied with the portent, and nudged the gondola in that direction.

Throughout it all, Zeranna had watched him as much as she had watched the scenery. "You really *are* guided," she commented. "You don't choose which way to go."

"Why should that seem odd? I am a ferryman, not a pirate."

When the sun was low in the west they came to a place where he had stopped many times over the centuries—a large island suitable for a night's shelter, in a domain where they needn't fear intrusions by lions or pythons or any other dangerous creatures, especially humans. Erom gathered driftwood and lit a cookfire, leaving it to Zeranna to steward the coals and position the kettle while he brought the supply chests ashore.

When Zeranna saw the ample selection of food, she brightened. Erom, not having been as deprived of late as she, was more critical.

"We'll want something fresh as well," he said.

He climbed a coconut palm and cut down a pair of fat, round nuts. He halved them and set them down on a flat rock near the firepit. Next he foraged in the willow brambles at the upstream end of the island. He returned with a clutch of quail eggs.

It was Zeranna who cooked the meal. He saw the meaning the act held for her and did not interfere, though that went against his habit of self-reliance. To avoid fidgeting he went back to the coconut grove and strung hammocks, making sure both were anchored to thick, sturdy trunks and positioned where nothing would fall on either of them while they slept.

Zeranna did not challenge his wordlessness. Already today he had said more aloud than he typically did in a month. He could tell she had more questions, and was grateful she held them back.

After they had eaten, he spread a large blanket on the sand and settled down to admire the starry sky.

She approached, stood nearby, and likewise gazed upward. The glow of the embers was ample enough to reveal how fascinated she was at the plethora of strange constellations and the tiny red moon hanging near the zenith. He decided he could bear a little conversation, after all.

"In a short while another moon will rise. It's half again as big as the one that hangs over Allistoya, and more argent."

She sat down next to him. There was ample room on the blanket, but he tensed at the proximity. Occasionally in the past, when he was mired in loneliness or desperate for physical release, he had given in to overtures from passengers of his ferryboat. He did not want that now, no matter that Zeranna possessed the sort of unpretentious, villager's-wife appeal he had never been able to resist in his wandering-rascal youth. The overtures seldom had honesty behind them. They were inevitably a form of attempted bribery by convicts who had not fully accepted he could not improve the terms of their sentence.

Zeranna however did not impinge upon the remaining gap between them. She looked at the sky, not at him.

And one thing more. She relaxed. Even in the dimness, he could see it. She was not on guard against him.

He had forgotten how it felt not to be feared, or distrusted, or treated as a means to an end. He wondered if she even realized what a gift she had given. That was the true bribe, in part because she did not mean it as one.

Finally she spoke. "You seem quite at home here. On the river."

"I appreciate its virtues," he answered, "but I long for the day when I cast off my mantle and leave my boat for good, even if that means my bones will finally grow brittle, and my skin become fissured and stained."

"That sounds like regret."

"I do not regret that I am here. Of all the things I have done, that was necessary. It is just that I am weary and look forward to my rest. I regret that I am not stronger."

"That is my regret as well," she said. "That I was not stronger."

All at once, he knew her fate. The river whispered to him, and he knew it as if the magistrate had written it on the parchment.

"What is it?" she asked.

"What is what?"

"You seem different."

"Do I? Pay it no mind."

She let it go. She did not press. Again, a gift.

He leaned back, pillowed his head over his folded hands, and savored the peacefulness. The promised moon crested the horizon and its luster spread across both sky and water.

They were five days on the river all told, and part of a sixth. Gradually Zeranna ceased to brace herself each time the mists pulled back to expose a new realm. When the places were ominous or forlorn, as so many of the lands were that Erom and his boat visited, she studied their natures carefully and seriously, and asked what sort of transgression might have consigned her there. When the places were benign or beautiful, she immersed herself in the moment—fashioning a cowl for herself when they found themselves in bright glare, inventing names for the creatures they saw that were unfamiliar even to Erom, and at his suggestion, learning to fish.

Day by day, her body showed fewer signs of deprivation. The hollows below her eyes filled in and the shadows disappeared.

Day by day, her mood brightened earlier and stayed that way longer. Her questions turned to easy, conversational subjects.

Day by day, she grew stronger.

At last, the river decided she was strong enough.

"In a few hours, if I am able, I will deliver you where you must go," Erom announced on the morning of the sixth day.

"What do you mean *if* you are able?" she asked.

"Today we go the hard way. I cannot be certain either of us will survive it."

"I wasn't certain you *could* die," she said. "Not while you wear your mantle, as you put it."

"I have been spared the touch of old age and disease, but

21

nearly everything else that can kill a man will kill me."

"Do not take this risk on my account." She touched him on the arm. "I would not be the cause of your death."

"Thank you for that," he replied. "But I will do as I must."

Zeranna became very still and quiet. She nodded. The corners of her eyes moistened. But as she had at the beginning, she took her place on the bench near the prow and faced whatever was to come.

They had spent the night in a stilt hut in a mangrove delta. In any normal world that would mean they were at a river terminus, but that was of no consequence. The tide came in and the gondola was pushed into the river mouth and upstream. The mists gathered. When they vanished again, Erom and Zeranna were somewhere in the heart of a great continent where a tributary river, itself vast and wide, poured down as a hundred-foot-high waterfall.

"Now it begins," he said. "I want you to buckle in."

She did as ordered, fastening the safety strap around herself and checking to be sure it was securely attached to its rung.

They proceeded along the waterfall. He waited for the omen. It came in the form of a family of otters. The sleek creatures raced past them and abruptly vanished into the cascade. Erom pushed his pole as hard as he could, pointing the gondola at the same spot.

They were drenched. Zeranna was nearly washed off the bench and he nearly knocked from his feet, but momentum took them through the barrier and into a cavern.

Only a small portion of daylight filtered through the liquid wall, but as their eyes adjusted they made out the tunnel mouth at the back of the grotto. The otters perched on rocks to either side, their chorus of "hah hah hah" barks inviting them forward but far too happily, as if they knew what sort of joke was being played.

The opening resembled a maw. Zeranna leaned away from it, and drew in a sharp breath.

"Yes, that's our path," Erom said. "The gullet of the titan. We will be underground for some time."

No sooner had the tunnel closed around them than the passageway slanted downward. The boat picked up speed, plunging them into acute darkness. The vessel struck one wall or another nearly every moment, the vibrations of impact suggesting the hull might not be strong enough to hold out in the long run. The echoes made plain how closely the walls were crowding in.

Zeranna screamed. Erom would have liked to imitate her, but he needed all his concentration. Though he had no more ability to see their surroundings than did she, he could hear the voices in his mind, guiding him now with outcries instead of whispers. He obeyed without question. He struck out with his pole to shove them away from an obstacle. *There!* went the projection that would have skewered his craft. He dodged. *There!* went the stalactite past his ear that would have knocked his head off if he had not shifted.

Finally he ducked all the way down as far as he could. He pressed Zeranna low as well. The rock ceiling whipped by just over their heads.

And they were in daylight again, thrust out of a mountainside a dozen feet above river level and into the air over a vast pool. They plunged nearly to the gunwales before they popped back up.

Zeranna rubbed her bottom and winced, but otherwise appeared to be unhurt. "Will there be any more of *that?*" she asked.

He sighed. "To be frank, we are in a far more dangerous place now."

She turned to see what he was pointing at. She gasped. Looming into the horizon was a volcano. From a gap in its crater wall a massive flow of bright orange lava was descending inexorably in their direction. It was already more than halfway down, and appeared to have the speed and volume to make it all the way.

The water was too deep for his pole. Erom switched to his rowing oar. He aimed them toward the place where the pool became a narrow river that flowed along the base of the defile that divided the mountain range. "The molten rock is not what worries me. It will take a few more hours to arrive. But ahead of that are heavy gases. They will fill this little valley and push all the lighter, breathable air beyond the reach of our lungs."

"Did we truly have to come this way?" she asked.

"Yes. Don't despair. I think we will make it."

He was afraid he was exaggerating their chances, but it wasn't as though they could scoot back up the gullet of the titan. He put his back into his rowing, and when the channel grew more shallow, got out his pole and propelled them along with as much velocity as his stamina, experience, and sense of self-preservation could provide.

His effort was just good enough. He was finding it hard to draw breath—and not because of any exhaustion on his part—when the mists closed in.

They came out of the fogginess into a scene nearly as grey because of the overcast sky. The river on which they found themselves was wider than the one that had flowed beside the volcano, but still narrow enough that its current was powerful.

That was unfortunate, because their way was against that current. Worse still, the river was thick with calved-off glacier ice. Many of the chunks were larger than his gondola.

Erom had no doubt of the direction. On a bargelike slab of ice ahead was a troop of seals hooting at them even more enthusiastically than the otters at the waterfall.

Weary as he was, he had no choice but to drive forward, because even a brief lapse would shepherd them in the wrong direction. Within minutes, in spite of the chill air, sweat was beading on his brow. Every bit of progress was hard won. The ice prevented him from choosing the ways of least resistance.

The seals were amused, and followed them much of the way. Finally the mists enclosed them again. The current's viciousness ended and the ice vanished. His ordeal was over.

He combed back his damp hair with his fingers. He drank an entire flagon of water. His shoulders burned from the over-exertion. His palms were blistered.

Soon the water was not just ice-free, but warm. A dragonfly whisked past. The murmur of ibis sedge wafted their way from the unseen shallows to one side.

"This is it," he said.

The mists faded back, slowly revealing a pier whose outlines were familiar not just to Erom, but to his companion.

"How did this happen?" Zeranna asked.

"This is the river's judgment. Your presence is still needed among your own people."

As the waterfront loomed near, her chin began to tremble.

Erom had witnessed seven thousand passengers at the end of their crossings. He had seen fear. What Zeranna was exuding was not fear. It was resolve. Whatever endeavor had caused her to be condemned, whatever transgression she may have committed, justice was still possible, and she would pursue it.

The wharf was unattended except by a pair of ravens at a gibbet, picking at the remains of a hanged man's face. Erom was heartened to see it so forsaken. After all, why would folk want to linger at a charnel gallery? As for Zeranna, she seemed relieved to have no observers of her homecoming.

He eased the gondola to the end of the pier and took hold of a dangling rope.

"Go quickly," he urged.

She did precisely that, clambering up the ladder. From what he could guess, it was only after she reached the deck of the pier that she believed the river would in fact restore her to Allistoya.

She beckoned. "Will you not come with me?"

The invitation was a lance through the heart. "The river needs its ferryman."

"Does that have to be *you*?"

"The ferryman before me was...lacking. For as long as I can manage, I will serve. The river always knows where a traveler should go, but it can't always get them there without help." He flexed his left arm; his elbow had started to throb. "As you saw, sometimes the way is fraught."

Zeranna blinked away tears, but a smile blossomed on her face. "There once was a silly girl who thought the worst thing that could ever happen to her was to hear a good man say he would not go with her."

A good man. He tried to be.

"I will not say good-by," she added. "I think perhaps we will meet again."

"I would like that," Erom said. "But I think they will hang you before they let you ride with me again, given how ineffective a banishment it was this time."

"Then we will count on the river running dry."

She laughed. And with a sprightly step, she marched up the pier and onto the ramp toward whatever destiny awaited in the land of olive trees and bleating goats and a dynasty that had ruled for too many generations.

He laughed, too, and with new vigor suffusing his wracked body, he poled out into the regathering mists.

Even when Zeranna and her homeland were lost to sight, Erom's smile lingered. Long years he had endured. Every once in a while it was worth it.

ASCENT

by Shariann Lewitt

Shariann Lewitt fell in love with all things Japanese as a young girl, the result of her father being stationed in Okinawa during his Army enlistment. She had been mainly fascinated by earlier and more mythic eras in Japanese history until her most recent visit to Kyoto, when she saw the plaque marking the geisha house that hid several officers of the Meiji Rebellion. That period, being both foundational to Japanese history and modern, is extremely well documented, so she has barely begun research on the subject and has probably gotten a lot wrong. When not consumed with historical research or writing, she teaches at MIT, lives in the greater Boston area, and tries not to drive like a native most of the time.

Legend says that a powerful *kami*, Ishimaru, has a shrine in a remote place of great beauty above a waterfall. But to reach it, a supplicant must climb the rock face of the waterfall as a test of sincerity. At a pool above the falls, this *kami* can bestow a great gift, fit for a swordsman of only the most perfect warrior heart. While only the chosen swordsman (or woman, for the *kami* and the sword have chosen women in the past) can touch the glorious *katana* known as the Guardian of Heaven, those so chosen are invincible.

So the legend says.

But now a new era has arrived, a time of trains and steamships and guns. Of foreigners.

A time when people wonder why the Son of Heaven is kept prisoner, why some *samurai* claim rule when the Emperor is the descendent of Amaterasu, the Sun Goddess herself. A time when whispers have become louder and even fishermen and serving girls and weavers cannot escape them.

A time when old legends die. A time when old powers shiver as new strength breathes through the land. A time of change.

When he came to the ascent, Toshiro recognized it immediately though it was far more beautiful than he had seen in his dream. The high, narrow waterfall dove into a rock-lined pool beneath. Two ancient willows bent over the pool, their lowest branches trailing into the placid water belying the fury of the falls above. Cherry trees lined the stream that trickled from the pool over the boulders that jutted from the water. In the dream, the *sakura* blossomed in abundance and made the whole scene pink and white froth to match the frothing waters above.

Just over the waterfall, framing the moment of sunrise, rose the red *tori* gates that marked his destination. Toshiro arranged the bag slung over his shoulder so that it lay on his back and went to climb, hoping the hand and foot holds that appeared so conveniently in sleep came in the real world as well.

As the setting was both the same and yet more beautiful, so the climb was the same and yet more arduous. The largest outcroppings and a few roots of the most ancient trees remained, but some had slick surfaces from the damp that made his straw sandals slide. Finally, regretting the expense, he kicked them off one at a time. In his dream his muscles did not ache and his legs reached further because he had attained his full growth and manly development that, at sixteen, seemed as much a dream as this place had been. He sweated and panted as he placed one foot above the next, boosted himself higher to catch the next handhold, and tested it before trusting it with his weight.

Toshiro wanted to stop, to rest, to forget the whole endeavor. Perhaps his father had been right all along. Perhaps brewing sake and marrying Mariko and giving his mother grandchildren would make him happy. Right now that seemed very possible, definitely more possible than finishing this excruciating climb.

Then he looked down, and down was far, far away. He got dizzy and immediately looked at the rock face in front of him. Just the next handhold. Just the next place to put his foot, he need not think beyond that. He could rest and breathe whenever he chose, he told himself. He could hang on this secure anchorage until he felt ready to for the next move.

What had he come here for? He had come to earn his destiny, to take it from legend, to prove to the *kami* he deserved the reward. Taking the ascent slowly did not qualify him for glory.

But glory required sense and good strategy, he remembered. That must have been from the dream because he had never attended a sword academy or even spoken to a *samurai* except to fill an order. And even then, he only spoke to a retainer who took care of household affairs.

Sense required that he climb sensibly. He had little enough experience, for not many waterfalls and cliffs appeared in Edo, and when they did he had no time away from his pick-ups and deliveries. At least those had made him strong, lifting the barrels of sake and the empties to return, pulling the wagon through the streets alone since his father had hurt his back three years since.

He thought. He searched for the next foothold, then handhold, heaved himself up and rested. Repeated the action. Perhaps he rested longer. He did not have to be home in time for supper. The *kami* had been there forever and could wait a few moments more. Toshiro took his time and climbed forever next to the magnificent waterfall. Only the rock face and the water existed, the smell of the damp earth and pine. All of life combined in this one moment, and Toshiro understood that this, this single minded focus was the moment of combat. And that it, too, had all the beauty in the world.

Ishimaru watched his approach with both immense desire and great detachment, for it was a *kami* that had lived at this shrine for perhaps a thousand years. Stories circulated among the greatest warriors about this shrine and the gifts this *kami* could give, but it was said that this one was capricious and bestowed its favors strangely. Sometimes it chose girls, or even those not *samurai*-born, instead of famous swordsmen. Sometimes it chose none at all, though many came to seek its favors.

Some said that it lured its victims to their doom, for not many survived their encounter. Many fell to their death from the rock face. Others were found with their swords by their sides or in their bellies beneath the serene willows that dipped into the pool below.

Some died beneath the red *tori* without a mark on them. The *kami* took and tested and chose its own. All *samurai* knew the *kami* was dangerous and cruel, and the people of nearby towns knew it as well.

But Ishimaru did not know, for it was a *kami* and did not think as men. It simply yearned for that which completed it, that singular form of honor, of greatness of soul, of purity as pure as the water spirit of the *kami* itself. It never lured so much as sought, it never tested so much as yearned. And now as it watched Toshiro approach it hoped with all the power of the waterfall, with all the depth of the pool, with all the laughter of the stream, with all the indifference of its spirit nature.

Toshiro climbed forever, but the sun had not reached zenith when he pulled himself up over the edge and onto the paved floor of the shrine itself. A small path had been laid between between the maples that led to the red *tori*, which now towered over the landscape at the heights of giants. The path led to the still lake that fed the waterfall, but here shimmered like a mirror and, indeed, the red gates plunged into its depths as deeply as they rose above. Stepping stones led from the path to a tiny island in the lake, perfectly situated for an altar and just the right size for a shrine.

The whole shimmered, flawless and glistening a little too precisely, all the borders of the leaves and trees a little too brightly edged with light, the water like September sky. He had not quite seen this place in the dream, though he had dreamed it was here, waiting for him.

Before he went any further, he took off his everyday kimono of white and indigo patterned cotton. With great respect, he took a sip of water from his flask and then wet a small towel from his bag and washed off the worst of the sweat and dirt from his face. Washed away the blood, too, from his palms and his feet. When he was as clean as he could manage, he took out his good black kimono with the crane painted in silver on the entire left side. This kimono, too, was made of cotton, but a much finer weave, and had clearly been painted by a master. He put it on and tied the belt carefully.

Then Toshiro tied his hair up in some approximation of a

warrior's topknot, though he knew he had no right to this style. As he could not shave the top of his head in any case, he untied his hair and let it loose. But that felt wrong as well, so he tied it behind his neck so it hung neatly down his back. He took out his flute and closed his eyes for a moment, hearing in his mind the tune he would play. He played the flute quite well, or so the neighbors said, and someone had even suggested that he might join a troupe of musicians. But he had already had the dreams and knew where he must go.

Here. Dressed in his very best. And coming to the *kami* who had called, Toshiro played the flute, with incense and a gift in his bag. So the notes of the flute pierced the stillness of the shrine as he set foot on the path, as he followed the stepping stones out into the lake and as he approached the altar. His stomach clenched but his breathing remained steady as he played for the *kami*, whether it was prayer or entertainment he did not know.

He had not died. So far.

The final note of his tune faded and he laid the flute on the altar. He took the incense he had brought with him and the flint striker he had brought as well, and lit the stick over the stone. After good, thick smoke rose, he swept it over his face two times, three, before he clapped firmly to announce his presence to the *kami*.

Not that Ishimaru had been unaware of his presence, oh no. The *kami* watched with pleasure as the boy had made the attempt to wash and had changed his clothes. So very many men of high status and renown had come to this shrine. Many had tried to call to Ishimaru from the pool at the bottom of the waterfall (Ishimaru refused to accommodate them—it required that they climb for any favors) and, finding nothing, went out and said that the stories of this *kami's* power were only just that. Stories. That any power had died long ago.

Other seekers, who wanted more, or perhaps had felt a shimmer of power, took off their rich armor and had made the climb (if they could, for some were older or unaccustomed to climbing) but then strode on the path to the altar without appreciating the great beauty of the shrine or honoring the *kami* by cleaning themselves.

Certainly none had changed clothes, very few had washed, and Ishimaru had never heard the sounds of a flute before. Once, long ago, a maiden had come singing through the night. The *kami* had loved her and favored her with many gifts, but that had been so very many Emperors ago. The *kami* had not heard music since.

All, of course, burned incense. Any person approaching a shrine must burn incense; that was the ritual, along with the strong, evenly spaced claps. As were the requests written on colored papers tied with red string to the single willow tree on the altar island. Most had been written in very fine calligraphy and one or two had even had poetry written as well. The *kami* had enjoyed those.

But this supplicant, now, this one Ishimaru recognized. This one the *kami* had seen before. But even in the before times, the *kami* had not known that the boy could play the flute so nicely and would observe so very many proprieties that grown men of high rank ignored.

After he had finished his firm claps, Toshiro waited a proper amount of time. Not that he knew how long, but he simply waited until he felt—something. And then he opened his bag again and pulled out a single, perfect white camellia.

He had stolen the flower from a garden just as he had turned off the road. He would have taken one from home, but home had been many days away and his offering would have wilted, rendering it imperfect. He also took out a packet of cooked rice with a slice of pickle wrapped in a *shiso* leaf, which he had obtained quite honestly at the Shinto shrine where he had inquired for directions to this one. The food was the usual offering, but he had wanted something more, something special, for this *kami*, and when he saw that one lovely camellia he could not resist.

His offering laid on the altar, Toshiro stood straight, bowed his head and waited.

He did not know what he expected. He did not know why he had come, precisely. Only that he had needed to come, that the dreams had driven him.

The dreams had been with him all his life. As a very young boy they had been simple. He had been in the beautiful forest and seen the waterfall and the two willows, and high above the waterfall the red *tori*, and his heart had yearned to go there. He had seen the sun rise through the *tori* and he knew that this was Amaterasu, the Sun Goddess, blessing all of Japan with her immortality, her eternity.

When he became older, a sword had entered the dreams, a sword he could never touch because he was not *samurai*. A sword that glistened with the kiss of Amaterasu, that she had sent down to guard the children of her grandson, the Emperors of the Dragonfly Islands.

And when he became older still, he became confused. Because while only *samurai* had swords and said they served the Emperor, they really served the Shogun who kept the Emperor prisoner.

Toshiro didn't know exactly how he knew these things. They were in the air, like the scent of burning leaves, like the chill on a winter morning. And they came wordless in the dreams that had become more frequent as he had grown older. More frequent, and more compelling, so that he could no longer ignore them waking.

The dreams became more specific, too. He had seen this place since had been too young to speak clearly, but now he knew the direction and the roads, the name of the nearest town and the shrine where he should ask for the final directions. He could draw a map should he need one, so firmly had it been burned into his mind.

He knew exactly what he needed, how long the journey would take, and how much money he would require. Well, that part came from being a merchant's son. Unlike a *samurai*, Toshiro could handle money. He knew what cheap lodging cost for a night and how much a landlord would charge for a bowl of soup. He knew how much he could take from his mother's pantry as well.

Since he worked, Toshiro had a few coins of his own. Not quite enough, so he arranged with his father's client who owned a bath house to stack the wood and prepare the fires overnight while the man who usually did this work healed from an injured ankle. No matter how deeply the dreams compelled him, Toshiro knew how to make a plan and prepare.

"If you do not prepare, you fail," his father always said. "Honor be damned."

Toshiro squirmed when his father damned honor. His only desire was to live by it alone, as the great heroes of legend had done. But this was a modern age, and legends had faded. Gunships in Yokohama Harbor had killed the gods. All the boys he knew laughed at him as he talked about plans for his pilgrimage.

"Make a pilgrimage to Edo Castle instead," his friends said. "It's right there on the hill. You can see it from here. See if you can find some fine *daimyo* to serve. Or better, as a customer." And they had laughed at Toshiro the dreamer.

But they did not dissuade him. So he counted his money and bided his time. When old Hiroki slipped and hurt his ankle, Toshiro overheard the bath house owner complaining to his father when the owner came to adjust his order. And Toshiro had stepped outside and suggested, most politely, that he could fill in for the man's night work until he was fit to return. The bath house owner looked Toshiro up and down and muttered that he looked a bit skinny for the job, but hired him on the spot.

Two weeks of extra work brought him more than enough for his journey, though he got very little sleep. The dreams became less difficult, as if the fact that he now planned seriously meant that whatever sent them trusted him to be on his way. Toshiro had never questioned the dreams, the calling, or why he was drawn.

Now, waiting at the altar with his head bent, he wondered, "What next?" Where did this lead? Or did it lead nowhere, just to here and back again to his father's shop in their hometown, back to Mariko and the life that threatened to strangle him?

He waited. The water shimmered and he saw it first in the reflection of the lake before he dared look up.

Between the red *tori*, drifting a little above the water, a glorious man waited for him holding—a sword.

Not a man, Toshiro reminded himself. A *kami*. And, as he looked up and upon the shining creature, he could see very clearly that this was no man at all. For he appeared to be made of dancing water, his hair the blue of the still lake and his eyes the brilliant shimmer of the waterfall. He drifted closer to Toshiro, and Toshiro could see that he glistened, as if he were covered in mist. And his clothes were made of fog, or of silks that drifted into fog at the edges.

The sword, as well, shimmered as a thing made of water. The *kami* held it out and smiled. "You may take it, Toshiro. It belongs to you."

"But I am not *samurai*," Toshiro protested.

"I know," the *kami* said. "Take it and you shall be more than samurai. For I am above them and so shall you be. And She who made it is above us all." With that the *kami* glanced skyward and Toshiro shivered. "Take it and see."

The *kami* touched a foot to the island and became more solid. His coloring, still strangely water-like, warmed enough for Toshiro to think that he might be partly a living thing. When he put the sword into Toshiro's hands, the *kami's* hands still were damp and cool and too smooth, as if he had been carved of stone and polished, and moistened by morning dew.

Toshiro took the sharkskin hilt of the *katana* in both hands, as he had seen *samurai* do in prints he and his friends had stared at as young boys. And something went through him. The sword itself had been a warrior for the reign of a hundred Emperors. It had a soul that sought a mate to wield it, for it would only serve in the defense of the Son of Heaven.

All of that knowledge spread through Toshiro's body as well as his mind, as if his muscles adjusted to all those who had previously been given the honor of this weapon, and he merged with them. He remained Toshiro, himself, and yet he knew...he could see back in time as if through previous incarnations. And his body moved through the fighting *kata* as if he had been trained from boyhood.

"Are these my previous incarnations?" Toshiro asked.

The *kami* shook his head. "I do not know. But the sword seeks its soul mate, as all of those before have been. So, perhaps. But that is of no import. Now is all that matters. Only now."

Time runs differently in the world of the gods and the *kami*. Now became forever that Toshiro stood with the sword in his hands. Now flickered for the barest instant, and yet he saw the past of the sword, and he saw Ishimaru within the being of the sword, its keeper and guardian, but something greater and something less as well. From all the past lives of those who had held this sword he understood the *kami*, too, a spirit being of immense soul.

"But to take the sword is to return the sword. And you must take a sacred vow, to the sword itself, and to Amaterasu and to her

35

great-grandson, the Emperor."

"With all my heart," Toshiro replied.

Sorrow shadowed Ishimaru's eyes. "It is not easy. You must return the sword here, to this shrine. Even if you fall in battle, you must return the sword. Or you will never be reborn human for a thousand years."

Toshiro looked deep into the *kami's* eyes. To love the sword was to love the *kami*. Toshiro breathed—a century, a second, he knew not which. And he saw his own death. It was too early for the cherry trees to blossom in the shrine and that was his only regret. "I make this vow. To you, and to Amaratasu, and to our Emperor himself. I shall use it in his defense, and I shall return it."

The *kami* now stood entirely on firm ground. It still retained its spirit nature and looked inhuman. The stone-white skin and sky-blue hair remained, but now Toshiro opened his eyes and saw a creature that captured all of his desire.

Impertinent though he knew it was, he could not resist reaching out and touching that magnificent snow-soft skin, which was as smooth as ice and cool to the touch, far more like stone under water than living flesh. And he ran his fingers through the blue hair, which rippled far finer under his fingers than any hair should by rights.

And the *kami* came to him and Toshiro felt its stony flesh warm, though only slightly. "What are you?" Toshiro asked. "Are you man or woman?" Though in truth he did not much care.

"I am both. I am neither. I am *kami*. I can be as your heart desires."

"My heart desires you as you are."

The *kami* took him to the edge of the lake, and the cherry trees burst out in white and pink blossoms that fell and made a bed for them as soft as any cloud, and a blanket that floated as the waterfall mist. And in the morning Toshiro rose at the bottom of the waterfall with the glorious sword and the memory of a promise.

Toshiro returned to the world to find a battle raging and himself no more a gangly boy but a man at his strength, for time in the world and time with a *kami* flow differently. Before he had climbed the waterfall he had heard whispers that those loyal to the Emperor wished to bring him to power and replace the government of the Shogun. Toshiro, as a very young man (or a boy, as his parents would have it) thought all decent Japanese would agree that the Emperor should rule alone, but had not thought he would enter into such affairs. He was a merchant, not a warrior or a scholar. He had no part to play in the world of the great and powerful.

His father refused to care about politics at all. "That is for the high and mighty. Whoever wins or loses, we sell *sake*."

When he found his way back from the waterfall to the inn in the town where he had eaten his last meal before his ascent, he learned that the Emperor's forces had defeated the Shogun, but that the Shogun's last forces had four great warships and were headed north to defend Hokkaidō.

Toshiro, who thought he had left the shrine without a yen, found a full purse in his bag. He ordered a full meal and ate with relish, though he found it odd that the people around stared at him and the man who served him did so with far too much deference and perhaps fear. Toshiro finished the last grain of rice and his tea, and set off on the journey north to meet the Emperor's troops.

He arrived in Hokkaidō in early winter, a battlefield enfolded in a depth of cold he had never imagined. The men-at-arms around him came from another age, for they wore what appeared to be Western uniforms and carried long guns. Toshiro wore his black kimono, not even armor, and carried the sword.

And yet, the men made way for him, either stared or looked aside as if he were not an ordinary man, the son of a *sake* seller. Toshiro had not quite noticed the change in his hands, in the color of his skin, for he had become as white as the most sheltered maiden. On a noble lady perhaps it might look natural, though most would suspect powder. On a fighting man with a sword that sang when it crossed the wind, the pale color indicated a more ghostly origin.

And since Toshiro did not care to look into a mirror, he did not realize that his eyes had changed color. No longer warm and deep brown, they had become blue. Not the sparkling waterfall blue of the *kami's*, but the deeper, threatening blue of the sea before a storm, of steel ready to strike.

These were modern men he had joined, who embraced technology and diplomacy, who wanted to emerge into the modern age and shed the enforced antiquity of the Bakufu. They did not believe in heroes and legends, in magical swords or *kami* or spirit gifts. The only thing they believed was that the Emperor was divine, and even then, they might temper that within some greater modern notion of pantheistic deity informed by the Rights of Man.

These modern men with their modern weapons and Western clothes had to confront Toshiro, who walked out of a painting of the past with a sword that sang legend. Who attacked an enemy also equipped with the most modern killing machines with only this relic of an ancient past and—cut them down. With his single and singing sword he ran again and again into gunfire, into machine gun nests, and emerged with his blade drenched in the blood of the last of the *samurai*.

So the Emperor's troops, officers and men alike, looked upon him with respect and fear, but kept their distance. They did not want to know who and what he was. They did not want the past to become part of the future they had risked everything to bring to birth.

And yet, his courage inspired each of them. They glanced at him and then glanced away. They did not speak of him, did not give voice to the superstition they feared but could not ignore. It gave them heart, to know that a spirit world did exist and that the Emperor was indeed descended of the divine. To have proof before them that the world of the gods and spirits had sent something sacred, a sword, a legend, to uphold the rights of the Son of Heaven. This one man, who was not quite a man, proved all that they had given up for the birth of the modern age.

And so Toshiro fought alone. No one spoke to him except for the briefest necessary comments. Still, he felt no loneliness, for the sword and the multitude who had come before him remained with him. They whispered to him while he ate, and the sword sang as he fought. At night as he lay down he felt Ishimaru's arms around him and the *kami's* too-cool skin pressed against his own, and he felt far more delight than he could have found in any of the camp followers who offered services for a fee.

They fought through the winter, through the snow and ice

where soldiers could not find purchase on the slick ground. The winter turned late to spring and Toshiro thought of the time when the camellias bloomed, later here in the north, and then the time of the cherries, and still the enemy held out.

Toshiro's skin, though strange, could be wounded, and he collected battle scars, but no infection took hold.

Summer solstice came and went without notice, for they were tired. So were the defenders of the fortress. Surely they knew they had no way out, that they must surrender or die in the end, but in any case their cause was lost.

Mere days after the solstice, when the heat threatened to bake the soldiers in their Western style wool coats, Toshiro heard a whisper from the sword. He had taken it from the scabbard to clean it once again, and a single ray of early dawn touched the blade. It blazed red and gold, reflecting light into the air as if flames licked the sun herself. He tilted the sword and directed the light to the battered fortress and saw the light burn against the stone, up the tile roofs. And there it stayed, heating the heights where the last defenders of the Shogunate stood watch and it burned their eyes.

"Now," Toshiro roared, and without thought raised his sword and ran forward alone. The guns atop the fortress remained silent as he covered half the distance, three quarters, as the men who had been temporarily blinded found replacements.

Forward he ran, brandishing the sword, and the Emperor's men followed him with their modern weapons trained on the heights. Only then did the enemy start to lay down covering fire, but by then the Emperor's forces had the upper hand and were able to break through the gates.

Toshiro thought he was dying. He didn't mind that; he had known that he would die in Emperor's cause and live in the memories of the sword. But he had made a vow and he did not know how to fulfill it. Honor demanded that such a vow be fulfilled no matter what the circumstances, even beyond death. The sword, the sword might know...

He tried to think, to close out the noise around him, the shrieks of the dying and the screaming of the guns, the stench of cordite and his own body now dying and days without a bath. How could he return? It was a long, long way to the shrine, and he would have to leave the battlefield. After dark, he thought. After the victory. Surely he could survive that long. He had enough money to hire a boat to take him all the way south. That would be faster than the road.

At nightfall, he tried to rise and found he could not walk. He could barely crawl for he had lost not only so much blood, but had suffered a solid bullet hole straight through his thigh so his leg refused to move. In the moonlight the field was still. The dead lay thick on the ground, hundreds of men who he could not recognize in the dark. He refused to look, searching only for a stick to help him hobble upright to the shore, to someone who, for good pay, would take him back south.

He found an officer's stick and made his way. The pain shot through him with each step and yet he could ignore it and go on. No one noticed him, not the villagers who had come out to plunder the dead, nor the victors who had set watch against such pillage. Perhaps the magic of the sword cloaked him, he thought, and gave him the energy he needed.

South, he thought. He had to leave Hokkaidō and get to Narita, to the shrine. The image of a boat rose in his mind. Yes, a boat would take him, would not sap what little strength he had left.

Certainly the sword had found them passage on a large fishing boat happy to take his coin to transport him, for he himself could barely drag himself to the dock. He remembered none of the discussion that must have happened with the captain to secure his berth, though he did recall some surprise at finding far more coin than he thought he should have to pay for the trip. But then, his mind was fogged and he forgot things like how much money he had or when he had last eaten, for he felt no hunger. So long as he grasped the sword in his hand Toshiro felt warm and safe, and at peace, for the sword wanted to return home and knew that he was taking it.

Perhaps he slept as the boat rocked him on the water, for he had no memory of the passage. He knew what awaited when he reached land, the long road to the shrine, the climb up the waterfall, but Toshiro could not think of those things on the water. He thought only that he had done his duty and that made him smile. He thought that he would see Ishimaru, and that gave him comfort. He touched the hilt of the Guardian of Heaven, and that sang him to sleep.

He did not worry about the journey. And so when the fishing boat left him off he found himself in a luxurious inn in Osaka. After the many months of battle, Toshiro lay on a soft, clean futon covered by a quilt like a cloud. Just as he woke, a lovely maid in a lilac kimono scratched gently at the *shoji* screen and asked if he would like some tea and soup.

He had not felt hunger in so very long and called out to her to tell her no, but she put the tray just inside the door and left anyway. Even from where he lay the food smelled enticing. Toshiro could not remember his last meal. He rose carefully from the futon, surprised to find that his wounds troubled him far less than they had before. His leg still hurt and he had some pain, but he had some hope that he would be able to reach the shrine.

He ate the noodles in the broth and they tasted finer than any he had ever tasted. Then he sipped the rich broth and he could feel the strength enter his body. The tea was finer than any he had ever tasted.

For a moment he wondered if he had died and entered the afterlife, but he saw the sword on the rack in the corner and touched it, and heard the multitude within it. Surely if he were with the dead he could not hear the dead, his companions for months, as he had before.

The maid came to collect the dishes and Toshiro asked about a bath. An inn this fine must have its own bathhouse, and so this one did. He hesitated, and then took the Guardian of Heaven with him into the steamy bamboo enclosure. He had forgotten how scrubbing with such finely scented soap felt.

He removed the bandage from his leg and washed the deep wound as best he could. It still wept, though the many holes in his chest and left shoulder had dried and scabbed over. After he rinsed off with water, but before entering the hot tub, Toshiro found a long length of linen, clearly a clean bandage, which he wrapped around his thigh.

And then he released himself to the embrace of the hot water, letting the heat relax him and take away the fears along with the

41

dirt. The fear that he would die before he fulfilled his vow. The fear that he was too weak to climb the waterfall. The fear that he would never see Ishimaru again.

He dried himself, his face and his hair, and put on the fresh indigo *yukata* the inn provided. And then Toshiro returned to his room, where his futon and quilt had been aired, and slept again.

The next morning, Toshiro left the inn. A clean black kimono with a white painted crane, so much like his old one, hung on a pole ready for him to put on. His bag contained only enough to buy some soup and tea, and a few shrine offerings along the way, which made him smile.

He was still weak and wounded, still in pain. But now he had learned there was no shame in prudence if it meant achieving the goal. And so he walked the path as he had earlier climbed. A step at a time, resting as often as he required, thinking only of the next step as his goal. Only one at a time. He need go no further. Sometimes he rested for what seemed like an hour from one step to the next, sometimes he dragged himself the smallest distance and counted it victory. Sometimes he crawled.

The sun set and he slept, afraid that he might not wake and he would leave his promise unfulfilled. But when the sun rose he woke and felt a little better than he had the day before.

He ate dried fish wrapped in *nori* that he had brought from the inn and enjoyed the taste. The food gave some strength and he resumed his journey.

Toshiro heard the waterfall before he saw it, which gave him heart and drove him onward.

And then he burst into the light where the frothing waterfall danced into the pool below. The two willows still dipped their branches into the stream and the cherry trees, now green with deep summer, lined the banks. Above, he could see the red *tori* and his heart lifted with joy. In his thirst, he thanked Ishimaru and asked permission to drink from the pool. Feeling it granted, he cupped his hand and sipped the fresh water.

Suddenly he felt strong again, and whole. He had never been wounded, never shed his blood. He was healed, whole, given new being, with the full power with which he had left the shrine so long ago—and such a very short time ago.

The climb, which had once been terrible and which so recently he had feared as impossible, had become easy. He almost bounded up the cliff face, delighting in the spray. Rocks and roots reached out to hold him up and push him onward, the climb no harder now than to walk up a staircase. He reached the top and the shrine quickly.

Once there, Toshiro washed in the water of the lake. He felt that Ishimaru would permit him, given that the road had been so hard. A clean kimono had been laid out on the edge of the path, this one silk in shades of deep blues and a sash of deep red and gold. He walked again to the island altar, where he saw the camellia he had left as an offering, still fresh and perfect along with his flute. Now he laid the *katana* next to them.

And Ishimura appeared before him, flowing water, white and blue as before. "Beloved," the *kami* said, and held out his hand.

"Beloved," Toshiro replied. "I have kept my promise."

The *kami* smiled. "Of course. The sword always choses true. It calls only those of the purest honor, the greatest heart. How could I ever not love you?"

And with that, the *kami* drew Toshiro into his embrace, and Toshiro encompassed the *kami* as well, for he was no longer unblooded or a boy, and he had become just a little bit of a spirit thing himself. And they lay down together and made love, and the cherry trees bloomed and made a bed of white and pink softer than the clouds.

"Will you live with me forever?" Ishimaru asked.

"Always, my love."

And so the *kami* drew Toshiro again onto a bed of cherry blossoms, froth of pink and white over the mirror still waters of the lake, and they returned to the water which was the kami's true home and stayed together forever.

On the morning of the 27th of June, the men of Emperor's forces walked the field of Hakodate to gather and bury the dead. One among them found a single body in a black kimono with no armor, shot to ribbons, unrecognizable except for his strange ocean-steel eyes. They searched for his sword but could not find it, nowhere near him.

"If anyone has stolen it, he will be executed and the sword will be given to that warrior's family. They deserve it," one of the commanding officers said gruffly.

"But do we know his family?" a younger officer asked. "Do we even know his name?"

And the men of the Emperor's forces realized that none of them knew his name or family, and many thought he was perhaps not entirely human. But they buried him with honors and marked his grave with "He Was True to the Emperor to the End."

THE GOLDEN FIR

by Harry Turtledove

Harry Turtledove is an escaped Byzantine historian. He says he has made a "poor but none too honest living" writing fantasy, science fiction, and, when he can get away with it, historical fiction. He lives in Los Angeles with his wife—fellow writer Laura Frankos—and three overprivileged cats. Three daughters and two granddaughters round out the brood. If you like, he can annoy you on Twitter @HNTurtledove.

The day the branchrot struck the Golden Fir, the Queen began to die. Were both stricken in the same hour? In the same minute? In the same heartbeat? No one ever knew, not for certain. People in Valnia needed a long time to—probably—narrow it down to the same day.

Had the Valnians needed a little longer still... Had they needed a little longer still, this would be a different tale.

Queen Hovsefa was in an audience chamber in the palace, hashing over a trade treaty with the minister who'd dickered the terms and the mage who would make sure the Gastarok didn't cheat...too much. Hovsefa was bored as bored could be. She started to yawn. She'd been doing that for a while now.

Commoners saw the palace. They saw the satins and velvets and furs. They saw the gold and jewels. They wished they were Queen—or, if men, Queen's Consort. They didn't see all the hard work that went into ruling even a medium-sized monarchy like Valnia.

Hovsefa was often tempted to shirk it. Her ministers could take care of things, and tell her afterwards that they had. Or they could *not* take care of things, and tell her afterwards that they had. She'd never know the difference if she didn't do the work herself, or not till too late. Tales where the Queen found out too late commonly weren't tales with happy endings.

So she listened to the minister, and to the mage. The Gastarok were born smugglers. All their neighbors knew that. Blocking spells and truth spells made smuggling harder. The mage—her name was Purvasa—explained how much good they were likely to do.

Quite a bit but not really enough, was what it boiled down to. As Hovsefa got older, she realized that was what almost everything boiled down to. The Gastarok would be able to cheat some. They wouldn't be able to cheat as much as they wanted to. The world would go on.

This time, Hovsefa didn't just start to yawn, she went through with it. She coughed, too, coughed and coughed and had trouble stopping. Her mouth tasted of something harsh and hot, as if she had a new-minted copper in there.

Blood, she realized. She also realized that coughing to the point where your mouth had blood in it couldn't be good news.

"Are you all right, your Majesty?" Purvasa asked.

The trade minister—her name was Ariam—had better sense. "You're *not* all right, your Majesty," she said. "That's blood on your lips. You should call a healer, or a priest."

Ashta the healer held the Queen's tongue down with a flat tool of brass and peered into her throat with a small, round silver mirror soldered to a brass handle. Hovsefa endured it as best she could. She gagged, but she didn't quite heave. "Well?" she asked when the ordeal ended.

She saw at once from Ashta's face that it was not well. "You have a growth," the healer said reluctantly. "I have seen these cases before, and read of more. They do not have a fortunate prognosis."

"What can you do?" Hovsefa Asked.

"I have root elixirs. I have poppy juice when—uh, if—the pain grows severe," Ashta said. "Prayer may do more than I can. You should have time to make, ah, the arrangements that seem best to you."

"You're telling me I'm going to die." How easily the words came out amazed the Queen. She might almost have said, *You're telling me my eyes are brown.*

"Everyone is, Your Majesty."

"But I'm not ready!" Hovsefa had just celebrated her half-century. Her black hair held a few threads of gray, but only a few.

"No one is, Your Majesty. Do see a priest. Prayer and sacrifice can work wonders. Now and then, the goddesses and gods *will* dole out a miracle."

Hovsefa knew as well as anyone else that most of the time the goddesses and gods wouldn't. She visited a priest anyhow. Though Kashkar was a man, he had a name for quiet discretion. He was tall and stout, his salt-and-pepper beard almost hiding the silver buckle that closed the belt on his midnight robe. He gravely listened to the Queen. Then he said, "Your Majesty, what prayer and sacrifice may do, rest assured they shall do."

"However much that is. Or however little," Hovsefa said.

As Ashta had before him, Kashkar spread his hands. "We can but entreat, Your Majesty. What comes of our entreaty lies in the laps of the goddesses and gods."

"I know." Hovsefa wanted to cough again. She didn't—that time.

On the far side of the Blue Mountains from the city of Great Valnia lay the Vale of Meshov. Valnia's neighbors often called it the Misty Monarchy, sometimes in scorn, more often with a hint of grudging awe. Fogs and mists were a part of life in Valnia, sometimes a part of life its mages could use to their advantage and their foes' woes.

Even in Valnia, the Vale of Meshov had a name for mistiness. The Veil of Meshov, some named the usual weather there. The Vale was full of pines and firs and spruces and larches, many of them with moss of one kind or another dripping from their branches, watered by the ever-swirling fog. In the dim, attenuated light, the sides of the mountain valley were dark green, darker green, blackish green.

All but the Golden Fir, the tree that had been Valnia's chief talisman the past three centuries and more. Did not the Golden Fir grace the monarchy's banner, with a crown no more golden above it to show that Valnia *was* a monarchy? The priests said the fate of the tree and that of the monarchy were somehow tied together, though even they did not presume to say how.

In the hot sun, under a pitiless bright blue sky, the Golden Fir might well have been blasted brown by too much light. But the hot sun came not to the Vale of Meshov. Even the pale sun was often but faintly glimpsed through the clotted vapor.

Such weather let the Golden Fir thrive. When the sun did peek through, poke through, the mist, the tree's tall cone seemed so bright a gold as to be almost a sun itself. Then the pilgrims dropped to their knees in prayer and awe. But few were those so blessed. Most saw the Golden Fir through the fog, darkly.

Gazrik was one of the tree's attendants: one of its younger attendants, as the beard still lay soft and downy on his cheeks. Like his senior colleagues, he kept other trees from encroaching too closely on the Golden Fir, and also policed up the twigs and needles it shed. A pilgrim would pay much to go home with a tiny twig from the Golden Fir. Pilgrims would, and pilgrims regularly did. What they paid went into feeding, clothing, and housing the woodsrangers.

Because the Golden Fir had been so strong and healthy for so long, the attendants gave it less attention than they might have. Years drifted along as they took the Golden Fir for granted. If not for Gazrik, too many years might have drifted along before anyone noticed the creeping rot.

Gazrik did notice things. Noticing things about the Golden Fir and the surrounding wood was the one part of being an attendant that he was really good at. He also noticed things that had nothing to do with the tree, so many of them that he regularly annoyed his seniors.

The Chief Woodswarden , in fact, had more than once almost called him in and ordered him not to point out so many things that might be better. He made extra work for himself, which he didn't seem to mind, and for the other rangers, which they did. Only the fact that Gazrik had never yet noticed—or, at least, had never yet mentioned—anything that didn't need attending to made the Woodswarden stay her hand.

Gazrik was looking for shed twigs and even shed needles under the Golden Fir when he chanced to look up at the tree. He'd done that countless times before. He'd always seen what he expected to see: the great symbol of Valnia's continuing health and prosperity. As long as the tree thrived, so would the monarchy.

Maybe it was that the sun shone brighter than usual that particular morning. Not brightly, not in the Vale of Meshov, but brighter than usual. Or maybe Gazrik didn't look at the Golden Fir as a symbol that morning, but only as a tree.

When you looked at something as a symbol, you saw what you expected to see. A symbol would be no symbol if it weren't what was expected to be in that place. When you looked at a tree that was only a tree, you stood some small chance of seeing what was really there.

He saw a great thick branch thrusting out from the trunk, smaller boughs thrusting out from the branch, lesser branches thrusting from the boughs, and twigs thrusting from the lesser branches. All the twigs were glad in the yellow needles that made the Golden Fir so famous.

No, all save one. The needles on that one were black and shriveled and dying.

A frown pulled down the corners of Gazrik's mouth. He stood so close to the blighted twig, his eyes almost crossed. He needed to be sure he saw what he thought he saw.

All too soon, he was. He looked on other branches and boughs and twigs. Most of them looked as they should have. A few, a very few, were diseased like the first one he'd spied. Even in that wood full of spicy forest scents, the Golden Fir smelled uncommonly sweet. The handful of blackening twigs smelled like dead, rotting meat.

Gazrik waved to another ranger who was doing something—or perhaps doing nothing—not far away. "Some pox or pestilence has afflicted the Golden Fir!" he called, his voice shrill with alarm. "I'm off to tell the Woodswarden . Keep everyone as far from the tree as you can till I come back, with her or without her."

The other ranger called something after Gazrik as he hot-footed off. Agreement? Doubt? Fear? He never knew. He was gone too fast to let the words catch up with him.

Zavena's hut—Zavena being the Chief Woodswarden —lay a little more than a mile from the Golden Fir. She looked up in surprise when Gazrik burst in on her. She was used to interruptions from rangers, but not from rangers all panting and sweaty and wild-eyed like this one. "What's gone awry?" she demanded, cutting to the heart of things in three words.

He sketched a salute. He could remember the proprieties, could Gazrik, when he thought that might serve his need. "Mistress," he gasped out, "Mistress, the Golden Fir is diseased."

Of itself, Zavena's left hand twisted in a sign to turn aside evil omens. "You're sure?" she asked sharply.

"Mistress, I am." Gazrik spoke in detail of what he'd seen and smelled.

She rose from her fragrant cedar wood seat. "I will see this with my own eyes," she said. It was not that she feared Gazrik was mistaken. No, worse: she feared he wasn't. "Go back there with me, quick as you can."

He'd already run the fastest, most desperate mile of his life. Now he ran another one. Zavena was in good hard trim herself, but found she was dropping behind. He stood by the tree, hunched over with his hands on his knees, when she came up. Even if she was in good hard trim, she hadn't run like that for a while. Her heart sledged inside her chest.

Gazrik went over to the Golden Fir and pointed to the very first blighted twig he'd spied. "Here, Mistress. Here and other places."

Zavena used her sleeve to wipe sweat and mist from her stinging eyes. She examined the twig with the same helpless horror Gazrik had felt. Her eyes stung again, this time from tears. She fought down absurd anger at Gazrik. Why couldn't he have been wrong for once?

"Mistress, you know many more things than I do," he said, and she only wished that were true. "What do we do now? What *can* we do now?"

"We send to Great Valnia," Zavena answered. "The one thing I know about this is, it's beyond anything I know. Maybe someone there will have some notion of what to do, or if we can do anything." She wished she hadn't come out with that, but it was true.

Queen Hovsefa did not die right away. The mages' spells and the healers' elixirs left her feeling better than anyone should have whose remaining earthly business was putting her affairs and those of her monarchy in order.

They did most of the time, anyway. When she looked in a mirror, she saw more and more clearly the bones that always lurked below skin and flesh. It was as though they were pushing out. In fact, she was pinching in.

As much as she could, she stopped looking in mirrors.

That helped some, but not enough. Once, for a little while, all the medicaments and all the magics wore off at the same time. Until more took hold, she had no doubt whatever about how sick she was.

Most important, of course, was the succession. She and her consort had had a son, but he was not in the line. It was almost a shame; for a young man, he had good sense. But she did not intend to flout law and custom. The choice had to come down to one of her three girls.

Pasksha, the eldest, was, well, the eldest. Jrayl, the middle daughter, already had two girls of her own, so she offered stability. Erisha, the youngest, most reminded Hovsefa of herself at the same age. The next obvious question was whether that was a recommendation for or against her.

While she felt strong enough, Hovsefa kept up with matters of state as best she could. She learned of the Golden Fir's trouble, though, not from some memorandum but from one of the mages who were doing what they could for her. "It would be terrible," the woman said, "if Valnia lost sovereign and symbol at the same time." She went on with the charm. When she could speak of other things again, she added, "We will all do what we can to keep this from ever coming to pass."

"Yes," the Queen said abstractedly. Then her gaze sharpened, as it had a way of doing. "Someone will have come from the Vale of Meshov to bring this news to the Mages' Guild." The sorceress did not deny it. Hovsefa went on, "Arrange for that person to come before me. I will hear more of this."

"As you say, Your Majesty, so shall it be," the mage replied. Hovsefa nodded. One of the better things about ruling over even a middle-sized monarchy was getting what you wanted when you wanted it.

Except more years, she thought. *That seems unlikely now.*

When Gazrik appeared before her, he looked alarmed and amazed in about equal measure. "Your—Your Majesty," he stammered. He sounded the way he looked: as if unsure whether he'd meet the headsman next.

Hovsefa smiled. She hadn't had anything to smile about for a while. "Tell me what you know about what's befallen the Golden Fir," she said.

"Yes, Your Majesty," he said, and he did. He didn't try to honeycoat anything; as far as Hovsefa could tell, he didn't simplify anything, either. He knew a lot—the Queen couldn't imagine anyone knowing more about trees in general and the Golden Fir in particular—and he gave forth with it in long bursts punctuated by pauses for thought. The more he talked, the more he lost the nerves with which he'd entered the audience chamber.

I must make sure Erisha meets him before he goes back to the Vale of Meshov, Hovsefa thought. Like herself, her youngest was also the kind who liked to, who *needed* to, know things. And a Princess' Consort (perhaps even a Queen's Consort) who was good for something more than regular gushes of seed might prove a pleasant novelty.

Out of the blue, Hovsefa said, "You know I've been taken ill myself." She listened to her own words in astonishment. She hadn't intended to tell him that. She didn't think she had, anyhow.

His eyes went wary. "I've heard...a little," he said, picking words with care. "I didn't...want to believe it." But believe it he did, plainly. He understood what he was looking at when he saw her.

"Believe it. It is true," Hovsefa said.

The young man bowed his head for a moment. When he raised it again, he was alert as a hunting hound. But he chased an idea rather than a stag. "Do you suppose there is any connection between your, um, illness and the Golden Fir's?"

"I don't know. That hadn't occurred to me," the Queen said slowly. "I don't think it occurred to anyone. Until you thought of it just now, I mean." *I definitely* need to make sure Erisha meets him, she thought.

Gazrik looked amazed again, in a different way this time. *Amazed at other people's blindness*, Hovsefa judged. She knew that feeling herself. Erisha, she suspected, was also more familiar with it than she wished.

"I can't imagine why not," Gazrik said, and the Queen believed him. He hurried on: "The Golden Fir is the image of the monarchy. Your Majesty is the personification of the monarchy. Doesn't it stand to reason that what goes wrong with the one may also go wrong with the other?"

"May..." Hovsefa echoed. "But what if it does not? What if what stands to reason nevertheless proves untrue?"

"Then we try something else, your Majesty," Gazrik replied. "What else can we do in that case?"

Die, Hovsefa thought. *Me and the Golden Fir both.* But she held the dark thought in. Speaking words of ill omen might do no harm, but surely it would do no good.

Gazrik had ridden alone down the long, winding track from the Vale of Meshov to Great Valnia. He'd had a warrant that let him eat and sleep at caravanserais without spending his own silver. The serai-keepers sent him sour looks when they fed him, but feed him they did. Another warrant let him change horses at the stables of the Royal Post. The stablemistresses gave him less trouble than the serai-keepers; they lost no money by helping him on his way.

He traveled back from the capital to the fog-shrouded forest in considerably greater state. Three mages rode with him, two women and the male apprentice to one of them. They were the best Valnia had when it came to dendromancy. Gazrik loved to listen to them. No matter how much he already knew, he heard things about trees he'd never dreamt of.

A squad of jingling horsemen in chainmail and iron helmets also traveled with him. Some carried lances, others compound bows. The men all had hard, watchful faces. So did their captain, who might have been beautiful if she weren't so grim. She frightened Gazrik more than a little.

He knew the guards weren't there to protect him, or even the mages. They'd come to ward Princess Erisha, who was going to the Vale of Meshov to see what the dendromancers could do. "I'm my mother's eyes and ears in this," she said.

"Her image, too," he answered. When Hovsefa was young and

healthy, she would have looked a lot like Erisha. They both had long, oval faces. No gray yet streaked Erisha's dark, curly hair. Like her mother's, her brown eyes were large and knowing. Erisha's nose seemed less a prow than Hovsefa's, but sickness didn't gnaw at her vitals.

She stood on little ceremony. She had two servants with her, but tended to her gelding herself. And she eyed and talked to Gazrik with an amused speculation he didn't begin to understand. She plainly took after the Queen not least by having both sense and wit.

"I pray what we do in the forest will help her," the princess aid. "I don't know what Valnia would do without her." Erisha's mouth twisted. "I don't know what my sisters and I would, either."

Gazrik's father had clutched his chest and fallen over dead when the forest ranger was only nine years old. Thinking of him could still make Gazrik's eyes sting now, fifteen years later. "It's like an arrow wound," he said. "Scarring fills up the hole, but it's still there. It never goes away. It hurts less after a while, and you don't think about it all the time any more, but it's still there. It ups and bites you at the oddest times, too."

Erisha sent him that speculative look again. It annoyed him, because he knew he didn't know what she was speculating about. She was a Princess. He couldn't come right out and ask her. He didn't think he could, anyway. He'd been raised, first by his mother and father and then by his mother alone, to respect the royal family as long as they ruled Valnia well, which they did.

When his parents were raising him, they hadn't imagined he would ever meet the Queen or travel with one of her daughters. His father had been a charcoal burner, and started teaching him tree lore as soon as he could understand it—which, considering the kind of small boy he'd been, was very early indeed. He'd always cared more for living trees than for their blackened remains, though.

But even a charcoal burner's son who was succeeding as a ranger in the holy Vale of Meshov, a ranger trusted to care for the Golden Fir itself, normally would not expect to become acquainted with his sovereign and her family. Nor would he have looked for the tree to sicken, much less at the same time as the Queen.

Life wasn't what you looked for. Life was what you got. He'd learned that when he was nine, when his father's death rubbed his nose in it. All you could do was try to go on.

Hovsefa did not care for Ashta's decoctions of poppy juice. She needed the healer's strongest draughts now, and even those did not do all she wished they would. They clouded her wits, too, as if she were only vaguely tethered to the real world, and they clogged her bowels so badly, she had to take purges with them if she wanted anything at all to pass through. Sometimes even the purges didn't work well enough. Sometimes they worked too well.

She could not do without the poppy any more. Without it, she could feel the thing in her throat as a fire that was consuming her.

She carried on as best she could. She never thought of doing anything else. As she always had, she wondered about the future. But even that curiosity contracted; she feared she had less and less future to wonder about.

She did continue curious about what Erisha thought of Gazrik on their journey to the Vale of Meshov, and what Gazrik thought of her youngest daughter. The latter likely mattered less. What Erisha wanted, she had a way of getting.

Other lands' envoys couldn't very well help noticing Hovsefa's decline. Wishes for her continued good health came in from monarchies that probably meant them and from others that just as probably didn't. She thanked everyone as even-handedly as she could. She had nothing against hypocrisy in moderate doses. Hypocrisy was a lubricant that helped people and countries get along. As long as it didn't drip off and stain the furniture, she recognized its utility.

Some days, though, she simply had not the strength to present herself as a Queen was supposed to do. She stayed in then, letting her ministers handle things as best they could. Since she did not choose fools to counsel her, the women's best was apt to be good enough.

More and more, she wanted to melt her mirrors. But she would have known how scrawny she was getting even without her image. Sneaking food past the thing in her throat got ever harder. Soups, puddings, gels... Even those gave her increasing trouble.

It wasn't as if she had much appetite. "I've seen this in other such cases," Ashta said. "It's called cachexia."

"I don't care what it's called." Hovsefa's voice had gone husky and soft. Using it at full volume was liable to bring on bleeding. She continued, "Does giving it a name help you do anything about it or just recognize it?"

"I think you would be worse, Your Majesty, if I were not doing everything I know how to do," the healer replied.

Hovsefa nodded. Ashta had been straightforward with her. "At least you didn't say, 'I think you would be dead,'" she remarked.

"No, your Majesty," Ashta said. But *Not yet* was in her eyes. The Queen could see it. It might even be *Not yet, but pretty soon.* On bad days, Hovsefa thought that way herself.

Not long after the healer bowed her way out of the royal bedchamber, a messenger from the Mages' Guild came in. He handed Hovsefa a half-sheet of parchment sealed in wax with what she recognized as the Archmage's personal seal. The wax the Archmage used was specially enchanted not to stick if anyone but she herself affixed that seal.

"What's inside came to her by crystal from the Vale of Meshov. No one but she has seen it." The messenger nervously plucked at his whiskers. He wasn't used to playing even a small part in dealings of such weight.

Hovsefa read, *We are commencing. Goddesses and gods grant us success.* She folded the half-sheet again and told the messenger, "Thank you."

He bowed almost double. "Is there a reply, Your Majesty?"

"Tell the Archmage to tell them I wish them good fortune. That's all," Hovsefa said. The messenger bowed even deeper and hotfooted away. The Queen wondered whether the message mattered or not. Before too long, one way or the other, she'd know.

Not for the first time, Princess Erisha exclaimed, "It's so beautiful! It's so marvelous! It's so perfect!"

Gazrik turned away so she wouldn't see him smile. Everyone who saw the Golden Fir for the first time sounded like that. He had himself, and he was as sensible and pragmatic as any young man was likely to be. He judged that Erisha was the same kind of young woman, and young women went further along the road to sense and pragmatism than young men were ever likely to. (It was no accident that men filled out the ranks of common soldiers in Valnia's army.)

But Gazrik's smile quickly slipped, for he had to answer, also not for the first time, "Your Highness, it's not as perfect as it ought to be. It's not as perfect as it was when I set out for Great Valnia." Saying that last pained him like whiplashes, pained him like scorpions, but he said it because it was so.

Erisha frowned. At first, he thought that was because she'd told him to stand on no ceremony and he'd disobeyed her. Instead, she said, "I see it perfect with my heart. I want to see it perfect. I *need* to see it perfect. If I see it whole and perfect, I see the monarchy whole and perfect." She lowered her voice. "If I see it whole and perfect, I see my mother well."

"Yes." Gazrik didn't know what to say after that. The branchrot had spread alarmingly while he was gone, and he hadn't been gone that long.

No pilgrims crowded round the Golden Fir to venerate its connection with the monarchy. The rangers were keeping them away with persuasion, with barricades across the paths, and occasionally with fists and clubs—some pilgrims were uninclined to take no for an answer. In a way, Gazrik sympathized with them; they'd traveled far along hard roads to reach the Vale of Meshov. In another way, though... For all he knew, a pilgrim had brought the branchrot from outside the Vale. The Golden Fir needed no more disturbance now.

Nor did the mages trying to cure it. Achitobel, Babika, and Babika's apprentice Sebukht examined the Fir as a whole. They examined both healthy twigs and those that were blackened and putrefying. They peered with their unaided eyes and through lenses and crystals of various shapes. Whenever they touched a diseased twig, they dipped their fingers in raisin brandy afterwards, to take away the taint.

They cast spells and muttered to one another over what the results meant, and over whether the results meant anything. No flashes of lightning, no great glowing nimbuses... It was less dramatic than Gazrik had looked for. He said as much to Sebukht; he didn't have the nerve to speak to Babika or Achitobel. They had fully mastered their calling...and they were women. Talking with another mere man felt much less intimidating.

Sebukht's crooked smile said he understood. "When I first got into magery, I looked for fireblasts and demons, too. Excitement, you know what I mean?"

"Oh, yes." Gazrik's head bobbed up and down.

The apprentice chuckled and shrugged. "Mostly, it's not like that. Once in a while, but not mostly. It's a little of this, a little of that, compare the two, see what the difference tells you, then try something else."

"Like any other trade or craft, then," Gazrik said.

Sebukht laughed out loud. "By the gods and goddesses, you sound like my mistress. Achitobel is always saying that. She says any trade *is* like that. She says tiger-tamers are bored putting their beasts through their paces."

"They are till something goes wrong," Gazrik said.

"That's right," Sebukht said. "So the idea is to make sure nothing goes wrong. Ever. That's true with tigers, and with magecraft. Tigers can't eat your soul, only your carcass."

Gazrik hadn't spent much time worrying over the state of his soul. Why would he have, when he was neither mage nor priest? "And you wanted to learn this because...?" he asked.

"Some people write songs. They can't do anything else," Sebukht said. "Some people make chairs as if they were born to it. I suppose some people love picking their way through the trees in the fog." He cocked a bushy black eyebrow at Gazrik.

"Well, you've got me there," Gazrik said with a wry chuckle. "What's the proverb? 'Each cat her own rat,' that's it."

"There you go. Magecraft is my rat, all right. I'll go as far as I can in it. As far as this lets me go, anyhow." The apprentice plucked at his beard, which was thicker and fuller than Gazrik's.

"What can you do?" Gazrik said. They both shrugged this time. You couldn't do much. The world ran the way it ran, not the way you wished it would. The man who clawed and scrambled his way to the top at anything was a prodigy. Everyone knew women were the clever, sensible sex. Even when a man showed signs of cleverness and sense, women often didn't want to see them or refused to see them because they were so unexpected.

"What can I do? I can slide off with some of the purifying brandy, that's what—enough to let us both forget our worries for a little while, anyhow. How's that sound?" Sebukht said.

"I like the way you think," Gazrik said, and so the deed was done.

Thanks to the crystal messages the dendromancers sent, Hovsefa knew they would soon try a spell to heal the Golden Fir. She knew it had to be soon, too; she could tell she didn't have a great deal of time left. Before, feeling the sand run through her hourglass that way would have terrified her. It seemed almost a relief now.

They hadn't told her exactly when they would ensorcel the Fir. Healing it involved healing her, and they wanted no interference between its troubles and hers. She knew that, when she was in full health, she would have insisted on having every detail ahead of time. But, when she was in full health, the question wouldn't have arisen.

As things turned out, she knew to the heartbeat when the magic started. It wrenched her out of uneasy, poppy-juice-soaked sleep: the only kind she got these days.

For a moment, she thought she was in the Vale of Meshov, staring at the marvelous light that seemed to pour from the Golden Fir on a rare day of bright sunshine. She'd visited the Vale and seen the monarchy's talisman, though never on a day like that. Days like that came seldom there, with years between them.

Then she realized the buttery light poured not from the Golden Fir but from herself. Her skin was shining like a gold coin in the sun, filling her bedchamber with radiance.

She felt hot. She felt cold. She felt stretched and pulled and twisted in ways for which neither Valnian nor any other language she knew had the proper words. She felt lifted on high, though she still lay on her silken coverlet. She imagined—or maybe it wasn't imagination, but a true vision—she could see Valnia and all the surrounding realms as if they were a map below her.

She felt...dropped.

Falling forever, she smashed to earth, all without leaving her bed. The glow that had come from her winked out more abruptly than a snuffed candle, plunging the bedchamber into blackness. And this blackness seemed somehow darker than any she had known before. She imagined—or maybe, again, it was a true vision—things she could not see, did not ever want to see, stirring there. She imagined them creeping closer, readying themselves to drag her down into the dark from which there was no returning.

"Not yet," Queen Hovsefa said hoarsely. "Goddesses and gods curse you, mortality—you can't have me yet."

Something—luckily, not something very big—burst in the thing that clogged her throat. Blood filled her mouth. She reached for the silver bowl on the stand by the bed. She realized she could dimly see it: the darkness was just darkness now, not the impenetrable stuff it had seemed a moment before.

Hovsefa spat. She rinsed her mouth with wine from a cup beside the bowl. She spat again. She sipped a bit more wine. Greatly daring, she swallowed this time. The wine burned like lye when it touched the growth, but it went down.

She wasn't cured. Nor was the Golden Fir. She felt its illness as she felt her own. And she felt that Gazrik knew what he was talking about when he said Queen and monarchy were connected. As they had thrived together, so now they failed together.

All at once, Hovsefa was cold, cold as if a midwinter's blizzard howled round the royal castle. Scrambling under the coverlet seemed to take all the strength in her. And it helped much less than she wished it would have. She huddled and shivered and wondered whether the night would end or she would. When consciousness slipped away again, she had no idea whether it would come back. She was even less sure she wanted it to.

Achitobel and Babika sprawled in failure under the branches of the Golden Fir. They were both so worn, they could barely breathe. Sebukht staggered around like a man too drunk to stand straight. Gazrik judged the apprentice was less battered than the mages only because they'd thrown more of themselves into the magic—and what they'd thrown, they'd lost. Gazrik wondered if they would, if they could, ever get it back.

"Goddesses and gods!" Sebukht groaned, over and over. "Goddesses and gods!" He seemed to have forgotten how to say anything else. But Valnia's much-loved goddesses and gods had proved conspicuous only by their absence.

Erisha set her hand on Gazrik's arm. The touch made him start. "What are we going to do now?" the royal princess asked. "What can we try next?"

She'd watched the magic with him, watched it struggle, falter, and die. The question pulled him at least a little out of his own gloomy funk. "'Till you spoke," he said slowly, "I hadn't thought there might be anything else we could do."

"There must be!" Erisha's voice was fierce. "If the Golden Fir perishes, my mother..." She turned the subject, at least a little. "It mustn't happen! The monarchy can't bear it!"

Gazrik was only a woodsranger. What he knew of state affairs would fit on a skinny pin's head. Yet even he could see Valnia would be worse off without an experienced hand at the steering oar. And would the monarchy even be Valnia without the Golden Fir?

He gathered himself, as much as he could. "You're right. We have to keep working," he said, and then, "Sebukht! Hey, Sebukht!"

The apprentice's eyes went wide and wild, as if he were amazed to be reminded he owned a name. He probably was. "What?" he asked. By the way he said it, nothing could possibly matter.

But Gazrik persisted. Persisting was something else he was good at—and Sebukht was only an apprentice, and only another man. "If this spell is out the window, what can we do next?"

"Sleep," Sebukht said. "Sleep for a week, or a month."

Gazrik shook his head. "We haven't got that long. The Golden Fir will be dead by then."

"So will my mother," Erisha added quietly.

Sebukht tried to pull himself together. Gazrik watched him try, and watched him fail. Then the ranger's gaze swung back towards Erisha. "I wish your mother could have come here," he said. "I've thought all along that it's no accident the Queen and the Golden Fir are failing together. Something tells me they should *be* together."

"She couldn't make the journey," Erisha said. Gazrik nodded; he understood that. But the princess hadn't finished yet: "Her blood flows in my veins. I am here in her place, if that does any good."

"If it..." Gazrik's voice trailed away. His eyes widened. He sprang forward and planted a big, smacking kiss on Erisha's cheek. At another time, that might have got him sent to the mines. Now both he and the princess hardly noticed he'd done it. He grabbed Sebukht, pulled him aside, and spoke to him in a low but urgent voice.

"What?" Sebukht said, and then again, "What?" Then he said, "You're out of your mind." Gazrik talked right through him. Sebukht said, "Maybe you aren't out of your mind. Maybe. But the mages won't be fit to work again for goddesses and gods only know how long, if they ever are."

"Do it yourself, then," Gazrik said. "Once you see it, it can't be that hard. And we don't have time to waste."

Sebukht's eyes swung toward the Golden Fir. It seemed less golden, more blackened than it had before Achitobel and Babika tried their spell. His mouth thinned to a downturned bow. "Well, you're not wrong," he said. "I'll try. Nothing I do can be worse than doing nothing. But I have to have *some* sleep, or I'll be worthless as a counterfeit gold piece stamped from lead and gilded."

"Tell me what is going on, please." Erisha spoke with the irritation of a highborn woman unaccustomed to men talking past her.

"Sleep first," Sebukht said. Gazrik nodded. He and Erisha had cast no spells there in the dark of night, but they'd been up as long as the apprentice and the dendromancers. Erisha started to argue, but yawned instead. She laughed sheepishly, spread her hands, and gave in.

It was dark again when Sebukht woke. By then Achitobel and Babika had roused enough to lurch away from the ground under the Golden Fir. It was only too plain, though, that they were badly wounded in spirit. They might heal, or might not. For now, they were out of the fight.

After watching Sebukht plow through three men's worth of food, Erisha said, "*Now*, please." Yes, she knew she was a princess.

"It's simple, really," said Gazrik, who knew no more of magecraft than he had to. "We'll use a healthy bit of the Golden Fir to cure the Queen, and we'll use your healthy blood—which, as you say, is also your mother's—to cure her. By your leave, of course." Erisha nodded at once.

"It's not so simple, really," said Sebukht, who would have to work the charm, "but we'll try it anyhow."

Gazrik searched long and hard to find and cut a perfect, tender, untainted twig from the Golden Fir. Once the whole tree had been perfect. No more. But he came up with (he hoped he came up with) what he needed.

Sebukht used the same knife to cut Erisha's finger. She never flinched as her blood dripped into a silver vial. When the apprentice judged he had enough, he bandaged the wound. He mixed the blood with brandy and healing herbs, then divided it into four portions.

He built four small fires under the Golden Fir, one at each cardinal direction. He lit them, north and south, east and west. He dropped some of the mixture into each in turn. The flames flared green. He genuflected and chanted and genuflected again while fragrant smoke rose up to mingle with the ever-present mist and fog the Fir.

As he incanted, Erisha ate the twig. She made a face. "Resin," she said, "like they put in wine, only more so." She chewed and swallowed till it was gone. Then she asked, "Now what?"

"Now we wait," Gazrik said. "And we hope. Hope is all we have left."

Hovsefa rolled over, stretched, and woke up. A morning sunbeam had slithered past the window hangings to tease her eyes open. *I could do with some breakfast*, she thought.

She ran a hand through her hair. Her arm was so thin, she could see the bones. Sweat matted her hair, the way it did most mornings. It was as if she broke a fever every night. One night, perhaps, the fever wouldn't break, and then everything would soon be over.

63

She took a deep breath. Halfway through, she stopped in astonishment. Poppy juice or no poppy juice, breathing had hurt for some time now. This morning, she just... breathed. And she was...hungry? That felt as odd as breathing without pain. For a while now, she'd been eating from a sense of duty, like a potter feeding the furnace under her kiln so her bowls would turn out the way she wanted.

"This is—strange?" Hovsefa's voice was still raspy and rough, but talking didn't mean a dagger in her neck, the way it had since her illness took hold. She simply talked. As if from very far away, she remembered doing that. Because it didn't hurt, she tried it again: "Over in the Vale of Meshov, they've managed... something."

She rang the bedside bell. A servant rushed in, relief and worry scrambled on his face: relief that she *could* still ring it, worry that she wouldn't be able to much longer. She'd seen that expression so much, she hadn't noticed it for a while, not till now. "Your Majesty?" he asked.

"For breakfast, a big bowl of barley porridge with some salted pork bits thrown in to give it body," Hovsefa said. "And, I think, a cup of sweet red wine. They say it builds blood."

The man stared at her. "Your Majesty?" he said again, disbelieving.

"You heard me, Yovsep. Tend to it." Hovsefa was still Queen. Though weak, her voice remembered she was Queen. When reminded that way, so did Yovsep. He bowed jerkily and fled.

With a smile, Hovsefa sat up and stretched again. It might not be such a dreadful day after all.

Gazrik carefully descended from the Golden Fir. He wore a silly grin. He had for some time now. The branchrot was fading, dying back day by day. All the new growth—and there was a lot of it, startling at this season—seemed fresh and free from disease.

As soon his feet touched the ground, Erisha rushed up to him, threw her arms around him, and kissed him square on the mouth. His arms folded around her, too. The kiss went on for some time.

"What was that for?" he asked when they finally broke apart. "I mean, it was very nice and everything, but what was it for?" *Nice* understated things. The kiss had lasted long enough for him to respond to it. He shifted his robe a little so as not to embarrass himself.

"Well, part of it was for saving the Queen, who happens to be my mother. And part of it was for saving the Golden Fir, which happens to be the most important *thing* in the monarchy," Erisha said, as if to a none-too-bright child. Gazrik's ears heated; a different part of him cooled. Then the princess added, "And part of it was because I wanted to. There! Does that make you feel better?"

"Some," Gazrik admitted reluctantly. Everyone always said men were the ones who needed pumping up because they got down on themselves so easily. He hated acting the way everyone always said men acted, but here he was, doing it.

"Good," Erisha said, and kissed him again. If she wasn't doing it because she wanted to, she could have taken her act onto the stage. After a while, when her lips had drifted away from his, she asked, "Because you save my mother and the Golden Fir, how would you like to be Princess's Consort? Maybe Queen's Consort one day; I don't know."

Gazrik's jaw dropped. He dug a finger into one ear. "I think I must be going mad. Did you just ask me if—?"

"That's right." She nodded briskly. "Mother told me to see how you shaped while we were traveling and working to save the Golden Fir. I think you shaped better than anyone dreamt you could."

"Then...this was her idea?" Gazrik didn't think he liked that.

Erisha made an impatient noise. "She said to be sure I liked you, too. I like you, Gazrik." She kissed him one more time.

You wouldn't do that with somebody you didn't like, Gazrik thought dizzily. Still, he asked, "Could I...leave Great Valnia sometimes and come back her to the Vale to see how the Fir and the woods are doing?"

This time, Erisha laughed. "Of course you can, silly. Consorts have a lot of time on their hands. If you have a hobby that keeps you happy and out of mischief, that's nothing but good. So—is it all right?"

What if I say no? he wondered. But he knew what she would

answer: *I'll find someone else, then*. He would have to find someone else, too. He had no idea how she would fare with a different partner. He had the feeling he couldn't do any better; never mind rank, she was one of those uncommon women who didn't seem offended by the notion that men might know things and think about things, too.

"It's fine," he said.

"Good." She gave one more decisive nod. Things had worked out the way she wanted. When you were a woman, they commonly did.

ALLONS

by Gillian Polack

Dr. Gillian Polack is a writer and historian, and describes herself as "rather Australian." She studied the French Revolution as an undergraduate, then advanced to the Middle Ages for her next couple of degrees: this story has been lurking a long time. Gillian still does a bunch of research (some of which is not terribly obscure) but she mostly writes novels (*Langue[dot]doc 1305*, *The Wizardry of Jewish Women*, *The Time of the Ghosts*) that use history, science fiction, fantasy and Australia in more or less equal measure. She has recently published a short story collection, *Mountains of the Mind*.

Jeanne would rather she were not in the Marais. It was dirty and it was damp and it was dangerous and it was far too close to the Bastille. For Gregory, however, it was perfect. It was close enough to all the things he needed.

"Why bring me to Paris at all?" she asked. "Why don't you go about your business of spying while the Estates-General meet and leave me safely in Calais? You don't need a woman in your life."

"I need to prove my French connections," he said. "And don't call me a spy. It's wrong."

"You mean someone might hear?" She mocked him in his own language. The whole household spoke English from habit, because Aunt Florence refused to speak French. Whoever was the senior family member present determined the language and right now it was Gregory. "I'll shout it on the streets unless you tell me the real reason we're here."

"Why did you come if you didn't want to?"

"We have a perfectly good house a half hour from here. Why the Marais? Why me?" She looked him directly in the eyes, which she knew he hated. She heard the rustle of his clothes as he showed his discomfort. She could look him in the eyes and he could not return the favour. She hadn't been able to see him since she had turned twenty-one and it didn't matter a jot. Except to Gregory.

"Tell me," she said.

"You won't like this," he replied.

"So it's dangerous."

"Maybe," and his voice turned shifty.

"Tell me." Jeanne made her own voice firm. She would never put power into it, not with Gregory, but she let him know she could. That sufficed.

"I need you to do me a drawing."

"I could do that from anywhere," she pointed out.

"This is Paris," he said. Jeanne wanted to be very sarcastic at that moment, but she decided to refrain. There would be time for sarcasm. "The drawing will be of something here, and I cannot follow it up."

"You want your blind sister-in-law to do all your work?" She definitely let her sarcasm shine through. "What have you done?"

"Late in May, when the Estates-General wasn't meeting on tennis courts and making oaths to change your nation, there were a lot of soldiers here."

"There still are," Jeanne pointed out.

"Yes, but I also had a lot of friends here. We had all been to Versailles and come back to Paris and were maybe a bit drunk."

"Maybe a lot drunk? Does everyone know your hobby?"

"No one knows that part of me. And it is not a hobby. What they do know, all those soldiers, is that I am very good at insulting them."

"Teach me some of it. My English is dull and it bores me. I could use those words."

"No. I will not. You are a lady and I was very rude."

"So rude you need me to do your work for you."

"I shall dress up as your servant. You will have your very own Berthe with you. Wherever it is."

"If I do this for you, you will teach me your English words."

"I will never teach you such foul language."

"Then," said Jeanne, very calmly, "I will never do you that

drawing or collect you your object. Find other means."

Jeanne heard nothing for two whole minutes. Gregory was so very quiet. She suspected that he was running his hands through his hair.

"You give me no choice."

"I need paper and charcoal," she demanded.

"Already on the table," his smooth tenor voice was smug.

"What am I looking for?"

"A letter. Signed by King George. I can't tell you what it says, but it needs to disappear. If you could create fire from a distance that would be better."

"She's gone, my sister. That was too hard a gift to bear."

"I miss her. My tempestuous wife."

"We all do. Why did you bring her up?"

"I don't want to risk you. I don't. I was...meandering. Dreaming."

"And that means you miss her."

"Maybe."

"Let's get on with this, then, so that you can leave Paris and not think of her. You can take me home, then cross the Channel."

Jeanne sat down at the table. She picked up the charcoal and smelled its dusty odour. She always started a sketch with the scent of charcoal. She then identified the limits of the page with the tips of her fingers. When she was ready, she thought of the English king and his manner and called forth the scent he'd worn when they had met, bay touched by juniper. Her left hand drew and her mind dwelt and soon the picture was done.

She had known Gregory since she was fifteen. No, longer. The families were friends. It was when she was fifteen that he had married Marguerite and that they had become firm friends. Of all her relationships, this was the only one that had not changed when she had come into her gifts and when she had paid for that with her eyesight. It did not change now. Before Gregory picked up the page, he gently washed the charcoal off her fingers.

"Where are we going?" Jeanne asked. "Can you tell?

"I can," Gregory sounded surprised. "It's not too far from here."

"By 'not too far from here' what do you mean?"

69

"Rue Saint-Antoine, near the Bastille."

"No, no, and no." Jeanne was scared. "The Marquis is in the Bastille. Even meeting you here, in the Marais, is too close to him. I did not sleep last night. When the carriage pulled up into the dankness of this district, I thought of him. He is evil, that man."

It took time, but Gregory persuaded her that the Bastille was still the giant fortress she had known as a child and the Marquis would not abuse her ever again and...

"I need to tell you," Gregory started, ponderously.

"I know that tone of voice. What have you been hiding?"

"Two things," Gregory offered, his voice a silver platter. "The first is that Necker is no longer Finance Minister."

"I knew that. He gave a speech that lasted for hours and made half the Estates-General fall asleep. The first time they meet in so many, many decades and he makes them fall asleep with lists and descriptions of money. Besides, no-one trusts him. That was days ago."

"Today, then. Today is the problem."

"What happened today?"

"That new militia stormed Les Invalides. That's why I am urgent. I want us gone before nightfall."

"Are we packed?"

"Berthe is packing your things now. You didn't bring much. I would leave from here if I could. If I could leave that letter, I would," Gregory never sounded regretful, Jeanne told herself but today...he would rather go. He would leave the work he came here to do and just go.

"What actually happened at Les Invalides?"

"I really do not know any detail. All I know is that it should not have happened and that I would rather we were out. Being near the Bastille is not good, for people are assembling outside."

"What do you know that you're not saying. Tell me!" While she demanded, she stood up and turned to Berthe, who had quietly entered the room. She allowed herself to be prepared for outside. "I will wear full mourning," she told her maid. "We were half there–but full mourning will be safer, I think. And there will be only one basket for you to carry. This is the first time in two years I am glad for the dignity of mourning."

"Les Invalides had its usual arsenal, but they moved the explosives to the Bastille. I think that the crowds are going to follow the agitators. As I said, crowds at the Bastille. Although they won't be there yet. We have time."

"There are already people there," offered Berthe. "We should go into the Bastille for safety."

"We should not," spat Jeanne. "I will never go near that bastard. Not even in a castle with walls and locks between us."

"So we will collect this thing and leave."

"Without coming back here?" Jeanne wanted to be clear.

"Now that's a fine idea. I wish we could do that."

"Why can't we?"

"Englishman and walls," he said vaguely.

"You speak perfectly good French," she retorted. "Remain my servant."

"He has no papers," said Berthe dubiously.

"I have papers for myself and servants."

"You will humiliate me," said Gregory, delighted.

"Of course," said Jeanne.

The house they were looking for was too close to the Bastille for Jeanne's comfort. What de Sade had done to her was impossible, unforgettable and undeniably nasty. That was the problem inside Jeanne. Outside, the streets sounded different.

Jeanne asked for a running commentary. Gregory refused, but Berthe told her everything. Berthe told her about the crowds, that the street they were walking through was filled with people who didn't belong in this part of Paris. They weren't carrying trays and selling snacks or small household goods. They were carrying garden hoes and they were carrying muskets and they were carrying, "Everything," Berthe summarised. "Everything that can be turned into a weapon. And they're all walking towards the Bastille. Dozens of people."

"More than dozens," added Gregory, unhappily.

"And we're just walking through them?"

"Not at all," said Gregory, his arm guiding her in a straight line. "They move aside for you, very courteously. You are a lady, and blind, and wearing mourning."

"This is odd," said Jeanne.

"I've never seen anything like it," Gregory admitted. "I've seen crowds and I've seen weapons, but never like this. Ordinary people doing something very strange. We need to move quickly."

It didn't take long to reach the house Jeanne had drawn, but it felt like a long time. Far too long. The air had all the oppression it carried every July, and the people, all the people, were carrying anger. Hot anger. The city smelled hot, too. Warm stones. Hot shit. The scent of people, tumbled and emotional, growing stronger by the second. Paris was on a precipice.

"Do you still have a country house?" she asked.

"I have houses in the country, yes."

"I may accept your invitation after all. Just for a little. I would like to be out of the country for a few weeks. Can you feel it?"

"I cannot. No one has these skills outside your family."

"Witch hunting," she mocked.

"Maybe partly that," he said, seriously. "What do you feel?"

"I want to get away. Far away."

"Marry me," he said. "When we get to England. Do what your sister never could. If you aren't Catholic and we hide your special abilities—"

"Then there's only my blindness to worry about. You don't want to marry me, however," she said.

"This is the house in the picture," interrupted Berthe.

Gregory knocked on the door for Jeanne and explained that his lady would like to speak to the master. He used his best Parisian French, a perfect accent and a hint of street slang.

"He's not home," Gregory reported back, "but his wife will welcome you. And of course I want to marry you. Your sister was a necessary arrangement. You are the centre of my life." He said this while he led her inside, as casually as if he were arranging a meal.

The lady of the house was disturbed. Jeanne decided not to reassure her. The crowds on the big road nearby made her home, so close to so many soldiers, uncertain.

"I'm sorry to disturb you," she began. She looked in entirely the wrong direction until Berthe gently faced her towards her hostess.

"May I offer you..." and the woman's voice trailed off. She had no air in her lungs and no happiness in her voice.

"That is very kind of you," Jeanne replied, "But really, none of us should be out in these crowds. I would like to get home very soon and to bar the doors. My manservant saw muskets in the crowds outside."

"I did," said Gregory's voice, sounding properly subservient.

"I am looking for a letter," Jeanne said.

"A letter?" The voice sharpened.

"It is the oddest thing, and you're the seventh house I've tried."

"You should have sent a servant. All the letters my husband has received since he left Paris are on his desk. I see no reason to read them until his return."

"The letter is a love letter from the English king. It was sent to your husband to be delivered. It should not be delivered."

"And you're telling me what it is? I don't believe you." The voice was now flat and uncommunicative.

Jeanne lazily exerted her power. "I do not know what is in it. I only know who it was from. And that it will destroy a French family if it is discovered that their fair daughter is involved. Give it to me." Jeanne turned and her eyes looked directly into the woman's. Jeanne couldn't see the women's face, but the woman could see her eyes.

"I'm sorry," she said, nervously. "I'm so sorry. I'll get it at once. Excuse me."

"Be ready to hurry," Gregory said. "She's going to send a servant out to call someone."

"We're always ready to hurry," said Jeanne, acerbically.

The conversation was interrupted by a door slamming, then another one, then by the lady of the household.

"Take it and leave. I've read that letter and it's nothing to do with French innocence. I want no part of this. I do not want my husband plotting against our king and I do not want a reward for my son. I do not want my family involved at all." She thrust the letter towards Jeanne. Gregory intercepted it and cast an eye over it. He gave it to Jeanne. On her way out the door, Jeanne slipped it into her sleeve. There were better places to store letters, but she wanted to move quickly.

"Thank you," said Jeanne. "We shall leave."

It was a half mile to their place in the Marais. Gregory took a look at the drifting crowd and turned them in the other direction. "If something happens," he said, "Get to the nearest gate. There's a carriage outside."

"Of course there is," said Jeanne, resignedly. The three were walking quickly, but Gregory was close enough to her so that she could hear every word of his murmur. "I have the papers."

Berthe kept up her running commentary. This was despite the men who cursed at them for walking in the wrong direction and who bumped into them.

"It's not only citizens of Paris," she said. "The men who tried to walk over us just now were *Guardes Françaises*. There are a lot of them. They all look bold and angry and as if they won't listen to anyone."

"We need to walk faster." This came from in front of her. Gregory had moved from her side and was directly protecting her. "Hold any part of my clothing you can." He gave them barely long enough to fumble and find something and then strode on.

It didn't take long for Jeanne to find out why they were hanging onto bits of clothing as if they were lost children.

The first time someone bumped into them she heard Berthe cry, "The basket!"

"Leave it!" said Gregory, his voice almost vicious. "We must get out of this."

The next time someone bumped into them, Jeanne heard the whisk of knives. Gregory was going to fight their way out, if he had to. And he did. The knife thudded and hit and Jeanne and Berthe stood still until Gregory was finished.

"I daren't look," whispered Berthe, loudly.

Jeanne checked her sleeve for the precious cargo. It wasn't long before Gregory said, "Clothes," and gave them even less time before he strode off.

The citizens were not silent, even though Jeanne and her people were. They were shouting to each other. Jeanne listened as she walked.

"Surrender," she said, urgently, to Gregory, leaning forward as she walked. "They want de Launay to surrender the Bastille."

"They're damned trouble." He kept walking as he talked. Every syllable was short and shouted and full of worry. Very English. Something inside Jeanne smiled at the thought. "Don't get swept back in the direction of the Bastille."

"We need to hold on tighter," Jeanne shouted, finally. She was so careful with her language. She could not use 'witch' or 'magic' or anything that suggested she had power. They were words that triggered wrath. "If de Sade is freed and he sees me–he will say something and the crowd will take me down."

Gregory took a step to the side and linked his left arm with hers. "Hold on tight."

They pushed and they marched and they reached the gate. Berthe shoved and Jeanne walked straight ahead, hoping that the road was clear, and every now and again she heard Gregory's knife. She had no idea if it was any use at this stage, or if it made him feel safe. The strides became shorter and more tired.

Finally the crowd became less oppressive and less noisy. It was still difficult to move forward, for they carried so much emotion and so much fear.

Gregory stopped and the women stopped with him. Jeanne almost toppled from the speed. "The letter," he said, "Do you still have it?"

Jeanne checked again. "Of course I do," she said.

"Not far," said Gregory. "The crowd now is people trying to leave. It's going in our direction."

"It's not only men who are carrying weapons," said Berthe.

"Don't even think it," retorted Jeanne.

It became like wading upstream, which Jeanne had not done since she was a child. No one walked in a sensible fashion. More people were turned back at the gate than progressed through it. People bumped into other people and cursed and swore and there was no happiness. She turned to Gregory, "If you teach me how to swear in English I'll marry you," she said.

"When we're in the carriage, I'll kiss you," he answered. "For I'll keep you to that."

Towards the gate, their progress slowed. It was still like forcing one's way upstream and there were still bumps and bruises, but the stream was made of treacle. Eventually, they reached the gate.

Jeanne brought out her papers.

"You can go through, but not your servants," the armed guard said.

Jeanne's inner journey slowed and stumbled. The carriage waited for them and her future waited for her. She would not play the stupid blind woman who needed help. Not this time. Maybe she should have allowed Berthe to grab a hoe from someone from the street. She herself was going to fight. Right now.

She looked across at the guard. "I will not leave without my people," Jeanne stated, clearly, then she let her eyes flash with green and with red and with blue. "Let us through," she ordered, using that power she swore she would never use again after the Marquis had abused it so vilely. "Now."

He stepped back in fear, and the three walked through, together, linked and strong. This was nothing like the last time.

"The carriage is here." said Gregory and they veered and twisted around people until they reached it.

Once they were in it, Gregory kept his promise and kissed her. Then he held her closely until they both felt safe. Her whole world smelled of Gregory and dust and of the fading warmth of Paris.

THE CUSTOM OF THE COUNTRY

by India Edghill

India Edghill would like to say she was raised by either a tribe of great apes or by a pack of wolves, and went around the world with Auntie Mame, who taught her to *live, live, LIVE*—as well as how to mix a perfect dry martini. Alas, that would be quite untrue, as India is merely a writer of historical novels (so far, mostly set in Ancient Israel) and fantasy short stories (set everywhen from India to Darkover to Imperial Russia), India's love of history has resulted in the acquisition of far too many books on far too many subjects. A former resident of the beautiful Mid-Hudson Valley, New York, India and her Cavalier King Charles Spaniels now live in the beautiful Willamette Valley in Oregon.

The roots of "The Custom of the Country" lie buried in *Annals and Antiquities of Rajasthan, or, The Central and Western Rajpoot States of India,* by Lieutenant-Colonel James Tod (1782-1835). At one point in the approximately 1500 pages of extremely tiny Victorian type, Tod tells the story of Krishna Kunwari. She was a Rajput princess, and the struggle over who would gain her in marriage led to tragedy. A secondary influence was the fact that India in the 1700s was a hodgepodge of feuding kingdoms, and the once-mighty Moghul empire was crumbling. European soldiers of fortune found India a great place to swash buckles and hunt jewels beyond dreams of avarice. A number of the freelance generals married Indian women, and in at least one case, that woman wound up running his military company after he died. These two stories inspired "The Custom of the Country"–although Edghill created a happier ending for my Rajput princess than Krishna Kunwari got.

"Four things better than all things are—
Land, and women, and horses, and war."

Rajput Proverb

The zenana walls were so high that even if a man stood upon an elephant's back, he could not see over the painted stones. Behind the smooth thick walls coiled a serpent's lair of dark hallways and small rooms perfumed with the scents of jasmine and of dust. Latticed windows spied only inward; none opened onto the world beyond the palace. The high-born women of the Rajput kingdom of Kalipur kept strict purdah.

But in some places the ornate lattices half-hid one of the zenana gardens. There a brighter light would force its way through the tiny openings of a carven screen, promising sun and air. Illusion; the gardens also were prisons, deep-walled traps for heat and shadows.

Within one of the small zenana gardens, a princess walked. Each step she took was as calm and measured as the one before; as calm and as measured as each step of her life had been since the day that she was born, as it would be until the day she died. Step by predestined step, along an unchangeable narrow path.

In that garden, she could see the sky past the zenana walls. And sometimes, if she were lucky, she could see eagles soar far above her, fierce and free in that pale hot sky.

She was born the year the Emperor Aurangzeb died; the year hopeful jackals and competent wolves began to feast upon the still warm remains of empire. Her father, the Rana of Kalipur, saw opportunity in the disintegration of the Moghul rule, and so, although she was only a girl, she was named Jayashree Devi—"Our little goddess of victory." Perhaps the name would please the gods, and besides—"She is only a girl, after all—if the Moghul returns, who will care what a girl was named? Does she look to be pretty, ayah? I have no use for a daughter who is not pretty!"

"Oh, no—she will be ugly, lord, ugly as a mangy monkey!" The ayah spoke swiftly and loudly, for this child promised rare beauty. But the gods had already been tempted—and the gods loved to play. No one heard the soft whispering wind as Lakshmi Herself laughed...

By the time the little princess could stand upon her own feet and not fall, it was clear she would be the zenana's fairest flower. By the time she could walk alone and no longer hold her ayah's skirt, it was clear she would be the rarest beauty in Kalipur. And by the time she was five years old, even her father could see that he possessed the most precious gem in all Rajputana.

The Rana of Kalipur studied his little daughter, and smiled. For such a bride—bred of the pure line of a thousand kings and beautiful as the goddess Lakshmi—for such a girl, only the richest and most powerful suitors need apply.

The princess's price was paid by the Maharajah of Malior—the largest bride-price ever paid in Rajputana. Malior sent gifts to his bride—jeweled slippers and saris woven of Benares gold; chiming clocks from Europe and painted vases from China. And quiet amid the flashing gold and flaming gems, a rope of black pearls coiled thick and heavy within an ivory box.

She stroked the pearls that coiled, warm and glossy as a serpent, about her throat. Captured night strung upon a silken cord, each pearl as large as a ripe cherry, as perfect as a full dark moon. A king's ransom; a heavy weight upon a girl's small shoulders.

Black pearls for Kalipur's black pearl. The name caught the zenana's fancy; soon she was called nothing else. And the name originally bestowed upon the Black Pearl faded from memory.

The horoscopes of bride and groom had been cast. The lavish gifts to both groom and bride had been made; the outrageous bride-price paid. The wedding day was set; the guests invited, the feast prepared. And early on the morning of the wedding day, her mother told the Black Pearl that she was not to be the Maharani of Malior after all. The bridegroom who had paid so much to possess her was dead.

"Must I give back my pearls, then?" the Black Pearl had asked.

She was sorry she was not to marry the man who had sent her pearls to match her eyes, but her father saw a rich opportunity for a double profit from his Black Pearl. He had no intention of returning the bride-price to Malior if he could help it, and the throne of Malior was now uneasily held by the late king's young brother. It did not seem likely he would hold it long.

The Rana dismissed Malior from his thoughts, and let it be known he once again was accepting offers for his Black Pearl.

A month later, she was to be dressed for her wedding to the Rajah of Nildekhand—

"A great savings, for all the preparations are made already," as her father told her mother gleefully.

Her father had patted her head, and demanded to know if she liked her new bridegroom's presents as well as those of the last. The image of an obedient daughter, she lowered her thick lashes modestly over her dark eyes, and stooped, supple as a cat, to touch her father's feet.

But she did not answer him in words, and later, as she paced back and forth in her garden, she heard an eagle scream high above her. She looked up at the small neat square of blue sky, and for the first time wondered what sort of world lay beyond the impassable zenana walls.

Garlands of marigolds once again draped the zenana's courtyard; the sacred fire had been kindled anew beneath the wedding canopy. Her wedding garments of scarlet silk blazed flame-bright; diamonds and rubies burned like sullen coals beneath her veils. A living treasure, so heavy-laden she could barely stand.

But stand she must, though her legs trembled under the weight of her gem-encrusted skirts. She could hardly see through the veil and the curtain of rosebuds tied before her face; she was pushed and prodded through the role she must play.

Stand here. Bow to a shadowy figure in cloth-of-gold who was her bridegroom. Lift a garland and place it about his neck to show she accepted this stranger as her husband. The bride must consent.

Bracelets heavy as shackles weighted her arms; she fought the weight, trying to lift the chain of marigolds high enough to place about the man's neck. He had bowed to her in turn, but not low enough, and her hands trembled so that she could not lift it any higher—she would drop the garland and who knew what disaster that would cause—

"Stop!" A cry from nowhere; a man's voice, shouting. She was never quite sure what had happened after that. Her mother hustled her away, hidden within a group of shrieking women whose stiff silks rustled like a nest of disturbed cobras. She was locked in her room, and there was nothing to do but wait. After unmeasured time, she let the wilting garland of marigolds fall upon her lap. She stroked the black pearls looped about her throat, comforted by their smooth warmth.

This time it was her ayah who came to tell her what men had decided to do with her life.

"It was the Maharajah of Malior—the new one—*your* Maharajah's brother—" Ayah shook her head, and began to remove her Pearl's wedding finery. The jewelry was laid upon the bed as solemnly as if each earring, each ring, each bracelet, were a dead queen. "*He* strode right into the zenana courtyard and let out a great cry of outrage—"

"Why?"

"Why? Why because he says you are *Malior's* bride, not Nildekhand's. That your marriage contract was with Malior, and as he inherited all else that was his brother's—" Here Ayah lowered her voice to a dramatic whisper, "—you, too, are his and must marry him," she went on, briskly unpleating the careful folds of the Pearl's fire-red wedding sari. "So there is to be no wedding at all— at least, not today, little one."

"Where is my mother?"

"Weeping her eyes out for shame." A most proper activity, Ayah's tone of satisfaction indicated.

"And my father?"

" Why, I suppose he is talking with the priests. They must decide, I suppose—for who has ever heard before of a scandal like this? *Ai*, who knows what will happen now?"

The man who pays my father most will marry me, the Black Pearl thought, and looked at the crumpled marigolds of her marriage garland. When she was alone again, free of the burden of her wedding garments, she took the garland and draped it over the ivory Ganesha who sat patiently upon a small shelf.

Ganesha, the elephant-headed one; the kindly Remover of Obstacles. Hoping the god would understand what she asked when she herself did not, she arranged the rope of fading marigolds carefully around the ivory statue. Then she stepped back and pressed her hands respectfully together, palm-to-palm before her face. *Help me, O Ganesha, O Kindly One. Grant me what I do not know even know how to ask.*

In the flickering lamplight, the statue seemed to smile at her, even as the scent of dying flowers lingered, spice-sharp, on her henna-painted fingers.

Anyone who knew anything at all of men—which the Pearl did not—would have known what would happen next. Inevitable as birth, marriage, death.

War.

The new Maharajah of Malior demanded his brother's bride. The Rajah of Nildekhand refused to give her up. Neither would yield, and the father of the Black Pearl dared not decide between them. The first battle was fought before the gates of her father's city.

It was a struggle bloody but inconclusive; the rivals withdrew to bind their wounds and plot their strategy. To gather up men and arms, and to fling them once more against the opponent. To fight, and maim, and kill.

Beyond the walls of garden, zenana, palace, armies raged across three lands, ravaging like starving jackals. Over her—or so they said.

For their own pride. It was a voice in her mind that spoke, a chill clear voice that she heard more and more often as she grew older.

Four years now the rulers of Malior and Nildekhand had fought like mad dogs. As their men died, they hired others to replace them. That was almost all the zenana knew about the matter; what, after all, had women to do with war?

Nothing save to give their sons to be slain for men's folly. Nothing save to die themselves for men's honor. That was all, now. The days of fighting queens were long past.

Four years. Even men grew tired of the war, and the prize over which they struggled grew older. But within the zenana, the war was insubstantial as song. Meaningless reports garbled with each retelling whispered through the zenana's cloistered halls until stories of hot battle and ghastly slaughter had as little reality as fairy tales.

Ten thousand men rode this way and slew ten thousand more; ten thousand men rode that way and cut ten thousand throats.

Then a new rumor slid through the zenana: "*Nildekhand has a feringhi now. Feringhi are cunning as cobras and fierce as tigers—the war must end soon—soon, soon, soon—*"

O Kindly Lord Ganesha, let them be right. I do not care who wins; only let them end it soon!

"*Ai,* my Pearl—" Ayah, hurrying for once, flustered. "Your mother sends for you—come, and quickly—"

Her father was there, and her mother was weeping.

"My daughter—" Her father pretended to cough, and would not meet her eyes.

"Oh, my daughter, my daughter!" her mother wailed, and flung her arms about the waiting Pearl, clutching her to tear-wet silks.

"Be silent!" her father commanded. He sounded relieved to have something weaker than he to seize upon. "Be silent, unless *you* wish to tell the girl."

Her mother released her and pressed the end of her veil to her face. Puzzled, the Pearl touched her mother's arm softly, and continued to look straight at her father.

Under her gaze, her father seemed to lose power again; he fumbled at his sash, pretending his dagger was insecurely settled. Then it seemed the knot of the sash was loose. She waited, implacably patient, listening to her mother's muffled weeping.

Finally her father could pretend no longer. "My dear child—" He still did not look at her; his gaze was fixed upon his own hands. "Terms have been set for peace."

Peace at last? "I am glad," she said. *And who is the victor?*

"You have always been an obedient daughter." Her father looked at her now, a quick sliding glance at her face, and then his eyes fled away again.

"Thank you, Father." Again she waited.

"Life is hard," he burst out at last. "But you are a princess of Kalipur, and our blood has flowed pure and unstained through the veins of a thousand generations of kings—"

And of queens. She remembered the tales of royal women who had fought for honor upon the battlefield, and those who had died for honor upon the *sati* pyres.

"—you will understand, and do your duty to your father and your country."

Her mother sobbed again, a sound the veil could not muffle, and her father turned angrily. "If you cannot keep silent, woman, go elsewhere—or you tell her yourself, if that is your wish."

Not turning, her mother shook her head; her father looked disappointed and uncomfortable. Then he straightened his shoulders as if preparing to strike out against a foe.

"I must tell you, my daughter, what has been decided."

"Yes, Father." She stood with modestly downcast eyes, waiting to be told the name of her husband. To the victor, the prize. And she was the prize, the Pearl, the cause of a four-year's war. *Will my husband think me worth the price?*

"Neither Nildekhand nor Malior will yield, and neither can win. But another year's war will ruin all of us—a girl cannot understand the reasons, but I, your father, tell you this is so."

She nodded, grave and assenting.

"But neither will yield his claim to you." He stared at the floor, then continued in a rush of words. "Since neither king can claim victory, neither can claim you. I cannot stop this madness—if I give you to either, the other will set himself against me to the death. So—they insist that neither have you—for honor's sake–so the price of peace is—"

"That I must die." She spoke as calmly as if she had always known this, and she did not permit herself so much as a muscle's quiver of reaction. To die for honor—that was a time-hallowed act, a royal privilege. But this death was sinful, for she belonged neither to Malior nor to Nildekhand; their honor was not held in the hollow of her hands.

Her father nodded; her mother seemed to crumple into a small helpless figure bound within gold-heavy silks. "Yes. Then the fighting will cease, and men go back to their own countries—"

"And what of Kalipur?"

Her father sighed heavily, plainly relieved that she had neither screamed nor wept. He stepped forward and put his hand under her chin, lifting her head. His eyes shone with unshed tears. His fingers were over-fleshed, soft. The fingers of a merchant; a peddler who had sold her thrice over.

Now he loses his merchandise and I can be sold no more. His tears are for that, when they should be for his honor. Now she knew why her mother—the woman who would walk proudly to the fire to join her husband if he died before her; the woman who had raised her daughter in the ancient precepts of Rajput honor and duty to face her own destiny unflinching—wept so, crushed beyond bearing. *She mourns Kalipur's lost honor.*

"You will do what must be done?" her father asked, and she heard fear running beneath the words, noxious as the sewers that ran beneath the palace floors. "Remember, you are my daughter."

She stepped back, away from his touch. "Yes, Father. I will remember that." She walked away from him, towards her weeping mother, and taking her mother's hands, knelt before her. "Mother, do not weep. What else are we women raised for, but to sacrifice ourselves? What is our duty, but to cherish honor?"

Her mother's eyes were reddened from much weeping, and tears had dragged streaks of kohl down her face. She drew a deep breath and smoothed her hands over the Pearl's cheeks.

"My daughter—" she whispered, the words barely loud enough to reach her daughter's ears. "Oh, my daughter—" Unable to say more, she bent and kissed the Pearl's smooth forehead, while the words she could not say sang between them. *My daughter, we both know this is wrong; it would be better to burn the city and all in it to ashes than submit to this shame. But we are only women, and my duty is to my husband and yours to your father. I cannot save you—but I love you.*

The Black Pearl smiled up at her mother, then kissed her hands and bent to touch her feet. *Yes, Mother; I know; I understand. I love you.*

Her mother brought the death cup, carrying it in steady hands. "I could not surrender this task to another. I brought you into this world, and I will be with you as you leave it." Her mother's eyes were dry, now; emotion no longer marred her proud face. "Drink, child—and do not be afraid. What I have brought you is strong and swift."

The Pearl took the goblet from her mother's quiet hands and looked into the golden bowl. Her future lay there, in the dark crimson liquid that shifted, oily and sluggish, as she tilted the cup towards the lamplight. Then she looked for the last time at her mother's face.

"I am not afraid, Mother. But this I would do alone."

For a moment her mother hesitated, then smiled and laid her hand against the Pearl's cheek. "You are a true Rajput, my daughter. You will be reborn as a great queen."

Just before her mother closed the door, the Black Pearl spoke to her for the last time. "Mother—tell my father I will remember to the last beat of my heart that I am his daughter."

Now she was alone, gold and poison balanced in her hands. She lifted her death, touched the goblet's rim to her soft red lips. A wave of scent filled her nostrils; sweet heavy perfume masking a sharper odor.

Do not hesitate. Drink it quickly, that way will be easiest— She was not afraid; she trusted her mother's word. The poison would kill swiftly. But her lips refused to open; her hands to tilt the cup.

Why must I die? demanded her inner voice; no longer a whisper. The silent words rang clear and pure as crystal bells. *Why must I die for their greed?*

Slowly, she lowered the poison-cup from her lips. The truth was that she was not dying for Kalipur's honor, and she was not bound to die for that of Nildekhand or Malior. *Even if they possessed any, which they do not. They may call themselves kings, but not one of the three of them is fit to touch the dust under a dog's feet.*

Anger kindled, began to burn slowly through her bones. Three men expected her to redeem their greed and folly, to purify their soiled honor with her death, for she was a Rajput princess and the golden chains of honor bound her. All her life she had worn those chains proudly, knowing them the unbreakable symbol of her lineage and destiny.

But now honor was inconvenient. So the men flung honor's chains aside themselves, while demanding that *she* cling to its cold brass links. *Cowards.* They owned not even so much courage as she—and she, as she had been told all her life, was only a girl.

And so must lack brains and courage and honor. But she lacked none of these, and she would not die for their—convenience. *I will not do it.*

"I will not," she said, and the whispered words seemed to echo around her like ghosts. Something that had waited, eternally patient, through the years, flared into hot new life within her.

"I will not." The unthinkable spoken. As if summoned by defiance, new thoughts beat wild wings against her mind's closed shutters, broke free. *I need only walk out of the zenana. That is all. Who knows my face beyond that?* Though men had fought and died to own her, beyond the zenana walls who knew the Black Pearl's face?

She set down the poison cup and touched the rope of black pearls coiled about her throat. Then she opened a chest and pulled free a shawl—cream Kashmiri wool, woven in swirling northern designs. Flung about her, the shawl hid the red silk she had dressed in with such proud care earlier that evening, and in which she had awaited death carried in her mother's hands.

Red garments for a wedding; for a pyre. For the closing of one life and the opening of another.

She gathered up two things only before she walked out of her room forever. The smiling ivory Ganesha.

And the wine-cup full of poison, carried in her small cool hands.

Her father's own dishonor eased her path. She was alone as she had never been before; no ayah to tend her, no women to guard her through the night.

The hour was late; the few people she saw were asleep across doorways or hastening to their own beds. No one paid any attention to one shrouded woman carrying a cup.

Soon she passed beyond that portion of the zenana that had been permitted her, and now unfamiliar corridors stretched dim and endless ahead. Ganesha was a small comforting weight against her waist, but the wine cup grew heavy in her hands.

Rooms, courtyards, doorways; she lost count of the number of steps she took. Scent of coriander and ghee: the zenana kitchens, empty. She walked on, through clean-swept cooking rooms until she came to a wide wood door. Unlatched and swung open, it revealed a tangle of alleyway and rubbish heap beyond. The Pearl wrinkled her nose and stepped through the doorway.

Then she paused. A virtuous woman made one journey only out of the zenana in which she had been born: as bride, she was carried from her father's house to her husband's. Such a woman wore red all her days, and her husband lit her funeral pyre and mourned the mother of his sons. Ill deeds in this life or the last earned the disgrace of widowhood, a shame redeemed by a second, shorter, journey to the fire.

Somewhere in the palace a gateway stood guard between the zenana and the world. Red handprints adorned the gateway walls, pressed there by *satis* before they walked through that gate to the fire. The handprints were the only sign left that a woman had once lived, and been faithful. Once, when she had first been betrothed, her mother had taken her to see the *sati* wall and lay flowers in the dust below it. The bright scarlet dye did not last; the newest handprints upon the gateway wall were already faded roses. The oldest blurred into the wall's time-smoothed stones.

I am not a widow. Or a bride.

And this was not the *sati* gate. *But it is my gate, to my life.* She tilted the cup, poured crimson liquid over her hand, and tossed the cup aside. Then she pressed her wine-wet hand against the whitewashed surface of the wall beside the kitchen door. When she had counted seven, she pulled her hand away and wiped it clean upon her shawl.

Now I am nothing. Soon all I shall be in the Kalipur palace is a memory, a ghost. A handprint on a wall.

She straightened her shoulders and raised her hands to her veil and flung it back, uncovering her face and hair. Head high, she walked, slowly and deliberately, through the kitchen gate, out into the wide world. She did not bother to close the gate behind her.

After a dozen paces, she stopped and looked back. The mass of the palace huddled dark against the paling sky; a golden wine-cup rolled gently back and forth over the lintel of the kitchen gate.

And a handprint gleamed, lurid and crimson, upon the kitchen wall.

The *feringhi*-general was the ugliest man she'd ever seen. He was huge, all odd rough features and stark muscle. His face and hands were burned red as demon masks, but elsewhere his skin was white, pale as ivory in moonlight. His hands too were huge; large enough for one of them to close around her slim golden neck. Scarred hands, oddly warped and misshapen, as if once broken and never well healed.

Most startling of all, his massive body was covered with hair. Short wiry hair, red as that tousled about his angular face, a fire's shimmer over chest and arms and broad shoulders.

He is a demon; a fire-demon. When she had been a child, her ayah had filled her ears with tales of them—hill-demons who would eat her up if she were not good and did not do *puja* to the gods.

But she was not a child now, and, looking up into the *feringhi's* eyes, she knew he was no demon. Strange eyes golden as a tiger's; pale as fire's heart. But a man's eyes, for all that. In her short secluded life, she had not met many men, but still she knew one when she saw him.

Feringhi or demon, he is a man, and my father is not. This—*this* was why she had sought him out. She knew nothing of him, but he could hardly own less honor than the three kings who had bartered her life for their safety.

The *feringhi* stared at her with those eerie tiger's eyes. "And who might you be, pretty one?" His voice was as ugly as his face and body, harsh and rumbling; a tiger's growl. "I warn you, if you're a whore, you're too expensive a toy for me."

Anger burned her face. "I'm no whore, *feringhi*."

"No?" He splashed more water onto his broad pale body. "What, then?"

A lifetime's schooling in the womanly arts enabled her to answer him calmly. Meekly. "Lord, I am she for whom your master has gone to battle."

Perhaps the *feringhi* had been lessoned in a school as strict as her own; he showed no emotion at her words. "So? You're the Kalipur princess they call the Black Pearl?"

"Yes."

The *feringhi* stared at her again, his eyes hunting her face, her jewels, her body. At last his gaze came to rest on the black pearls looped about her throat. "I've heard of those pearls," he said.

"They are more renowned than I," she said, and stroked the necklace.

"The Kalipur princess—what the devil are you doing here? What trick is this?"

"It is no trick. I came because—because—"

"Well?" he demanded as she faltered.

She called desperately upon Lord Ganesha and answered, "Because your name was whispered behind zenana screens. It is said you are a great warrior."

"There are many great warriors. Why come to me?"

For a moment hot shame flooded her, yet she knew she must tell him the truth. And so she began to speak in a small clear voice, telling this *feringhi* soldier of her betrothal, and how it had led to war between Malior and Nildekhand.

"...and so they girded on their swords and rode to war, and the victor was to wed me." As she spoke, she realized she had fallen into the words and rhythms of the old tales, the songs of love and war and honor told over in her childhood. She paused, and tried to find her own words; when she did, they seemed flat, unsatisfactory things. "They went to war over me—over my marriage."

"Over you? Little girl, no man ever went to war over a woman in all the years of mankind. And don't tell me about Helen of Troy."

She had no idea what Helen might be, or Troy either. "Why, then?"

"Land. Money. Why else do men fight?"

"For honor." That was what she had been taught from her birth. But her father had sold honor for true gold and false peace.

He laughed, a full-throated sound that boomed like thunder. "Honor? These warriors you laud aren't so honorable they won't hire *feringhi* to do their fighting for them. I don't know about their kind of honor. Mine's for sale. My only honor is to stay bought."

She thought for a moment, examining these new ideas as if they were strange jewels. Then she smiled, and shrugged. "Well, they went to war. And now they are tired of it, and have come to terms."

"Have they, by God?" Suddenly his voice was very soft, his words falling into the air between them like a tiger's heavy footfalls in the dust.

He did not know. The knowledge slid swift and sure into her mind. *Nildekhand did not tell his hired general that the war is over—and so has given a weapon into my hand.*

"Oh, yes," she said. "For since neither can slay the other, and can agree on nothing else, they say that *I* must die to end it. My own father told me so, and my own mother handed me the poisoned cup." Scorn curled her lips in a derisive smile. "Do you think Nildekhand will pay you now, *feringhi-sahib?* Is your honor still bought?"

There was a pause; the only sound was the tent walls sighing under the wind's touch. At last he said,

"And what of *your* honor, Rajputni? Where is the poison cup now?"

"Gone." A spreading stain upon the dust; a handprint upon a kitchen wall. She shook away the clinging memory and lifted her chin. "My father flung his honor into the dirt; I will not lick it clean for him."

He smiled then, quick and grim. "So, then. Yet here you stand, and I've only to hand you over to the Rajah of Nildekhand and he'll pay in full."

"Will he? Yet he did not tell you that truce had been called, and the war ended."

"It's not ended yet. But grant your point—what is it you want of me?"

When she had come here, she had not known. But she knew now. She knew *him.*

For all the blaze and ripple of fiery hair, he was not hot, but cold. Ice to her fire, and within him a core of cold tempered steel that called to the honed ruthlessness of her own soul. Here at last was a blade fit to match hers; a flash of steel caressing steel. His tiger-eyed gaze was hot challenge: *take up my gauntlet if you dare.*

Excitement pressed behind her heart and beat hard through her racing blood. *Yes. Yes, I dare.*

Smiling demurely, she lowered her lashes, regarding the carpet beneath her dusty feet, knowing herself the perfect image that all men must desire. She chose and discarded elegant poetic words, sensing they would have no effect upon this harsh man.

"You," she said at last, her voice soft as a dove's. "I will go with you, *feringhi-sahib.*"

"Will you, by God?" He sounded neither delighted nor overawed by his good fortune. "And what the devil makes you think I'll have you?"

Stunned, she hardly dared move or speak. She had never once considered that he might hesitate, or refuse. Of course he would want her; all men did. It was why she stood here offering herself to this alien warrior. "But I am the Black Pearl of Kalipur. I am the daughter of a hundred kings—descended from the Sun and the Moon."

"And what's that worth to me?"

What is it worth? For fourteen years it had been enough that she existed, pure and perfect. *What am I worth? What have I to offer? Am I nothing but my face and body?* She had been taught that was enough; that was all she was.

But it was not enough for this strange man with his keen eyes and broken hands.

And it is not enough for me. The knowledge welled up like pure water from a deep new well. *Not enough!* Now it seemed to her that she had always known this. It was this knowledge that had made her restless in her bones, denied her contentment. To be a plaything was not enough.

To be a pawn was not enough.

But what else was she? A woman; what was a woman worth? *Nothing*, her world insisted.

No. I am not nothing. And neither is this man, this feringhi. I need him. But what can he need from me—? And then she knew the answer.

"I offer myself," she said again. "Marry me, lord—you desire power. For that you must own knowledge." The words flowed with swift certainty; this was right. This was the way. "You have knowledge of one world only—the men's. But there are two worlds. And I—"

"Can get into those cobra pits they call zenanas," he finished for her.

"Even so, lord." Fourteen years of training commanded her to lower her eyes, meek; to whisper timidly. Five minutes' experience of this man warned her that only boldness would serve her now. And after all, was it so hard to look a man in the eyes after she had walked alone and unveiled through an army's camp?

So saying to herself, she lifted her chin, held her head as proudly as any conqueror as she looked straight into his tiger's eyes. Sword against sword, and no retreat.

"That is what I offer you. Now," she said, and her voice was cool as water flowing through a zenana fountain, "what have *you* to offer me?"

He stared at her a moment, then laughed. "By God, you're a cool one! But a fair question enough. Well, then, I will lay my cards upon the table." For a moment he was silent, then he began, "I'm a Pole—if that means anything to you. My family's noble—if that means anything either. And were wealthy, once." He began to pace the tent, restless now as a caged tiger.

"Once you could ride ten miles in any direction and your horse's hooves still tread my family's lands. My family's lands for ten generations back. Yes, that's nothing to you lot—you and your sun and your moon and your thousand-year family trees—but trust me, it is a great deal in Europe."

He paused, and she, obedient to the unspoken command, asked what had happened that had sent him here. Men were most pleased when talking about themselves. This *feringhi* was a man, after all. *A man, and no demon. Perhaps he is a demon-man.* Her skin tensed with an odd thrill, as it did before a storm broke.

"I'll not bore you with the details, girl. But from what happened I learned one thing. Never surrender."

Seeming meek, she bowed her head, as if accepting divine degree.

"But it seems you know this already."

She raised her head again and looked into his eyes. Now they seemed more green than gold, and his lashes circled them in pale fire. "Oh, yes, lord. This I know already."

"You Rajputs," he said. "You're all stark mad. It's what I like in you." Teeth flashed strong and white; a tiger's smile. "After all, we none of us live forever."

"No, lord. But I will not die today."

"All right, then." For a moment he seemed elsewhere, his strange, changeable eyes staring into unfathomable distances. "Very well, girl, I'll marry you."

She touched the thick snake of pearls wrapped black and luminous about her golden throat. And smiled, remembering ancient law. If a man does not marry his daughter within the first six months after she becomes a woman, she may choose her own husband.

It is four times six months since I became a woman, Father. Since you will not decide upon a husband for me, I will. And I choose a feringhi, a barbarian foreigner. A man whose sword and honor are sold to the highest bidder, just as I was sold. But this man holds to his oath, as you did not, Father.

Whose honor is then the purer?

The Brahmin priest flatly refused to perform the ceremony. *"Nahin;* I cannot do it. Impossible."

"I do not like that word," the *feringhi* said. "How impossible, priest?"

With a patronizing smile, the priest began to recite the reasons. "This is a girl of high caste—and you are a *feringhi,* casteless. It would be pollution."

"Would it, now?" he asked softly. "Well, that is not reason enough for me, priest. Try again."

The priest's smile remained serene, his voice condescending. "A girl must be given in marriage by her father—where is he?"

The Black Pearl did not wait for a man to answer; she stepped forward and said, "My father is not here, nor need he be. For he did not marry me within the time allotted by Manu's law, and now I may choose a husband for myself. So say the *shastras."*

"Is that true?" the *feringhi* demanded.

"The woman misunderstands," the priest began, refusing to look at the girl. "Women know nothing; understand nothing. True, it is written that a man must give his daughter in marriage within a certain span, but it is also written that a woman must always be ruled by men. How can a woman understand the true meaning of the sacred words?"

Her man turned toward her. "Is that true?" he repeated, and she inclined her head.

"Yes, lord. Once all princesses chose their husbands so. I have only to place a flower garland about the neck of the man I choose, as did Sita and Draupadi in the time of gods and heroes."

"This is not the time of King Rama," the priest said to the air above her midnight hair, "nor are you Sita. You are only an immodest, unwomanly, ignorant girl. Women are fools," the priest stated with great condescension.

"So are men," the *feringhi* said. "Is there such a ritual, priest?"

Plainly uneasy, the priest hesitated before answering. "Once, perhaps, but that was in another time, and the rite of *swayamvara* is no longer—"

"Have you a flower garland, girl?" her bridegroom asked, looking into her dark eyes.

"I have this," she said, and lifted the rope of black pearls from her neck. She held out the string of pearls in small steady hands; the foreigner smiled.

The top of her proud head came barely as high as his heart; he bent low before her and she slid the pearls over his head. He turned to the frowning Brahmin. "Well? Will this ease your qualms, priest?"

The priest drew himself up and began to speak with great dignity. "This is unseemly; I cannot countenance such an act." Refusing to look at the girl, the priest went on condescendingly, "Nothing is prepared, there is no sacred fire. No horoscopes have been cast—and if they had been, surely they would not match." He shook his head. "No, the thing is impossible—"

"It is not impossible, and I see no difficulties." The foreign warrior drew his sword. "Do you, priest?"

The priest paled. "But lord—the horoscopes—"

"This is her horoscope." He coiled the black pearls around his scarred hand. "And this is mine." He lifted his sword an inch. Sunlight gleamed along the finely honed edge of the blade. "Read them carefully, priest—they match, do they not?"

The priest stared at the shining sword blade, and gulped, and made his swift decision. "Yes, yes, they match—never in all my years have I seen so compatible a pair!"

"And I see a fire there—" He nodded towards a cooking fire a few tents away. "So. The horoscopes match, and the fire is lit?"

The priest bowed to the inevitable. *"Hai, haiji,* great lord—"

"Then we will be married now." He did not resheathe the sword, but carried it; the naked blade burned silver fire.

The priest did not argue further, but began hastily to chant in Sanskrit and fling pinches of colored dusts into the cooking fire's yellow flames. When it came time for the bride's veil to be tied to the groom's sash, the priest, desperately eager to finish the ceremony with his skin intact, hastily improvised. The Black Pearl of Kalipur and the *feringhi* warrior took their seven steps around the sacred fire joined by her black pearls looped about his sword's hilt.

"So," her husband said as soon as the seventh, the irrevocable, step had been taken, "that's done, then?" Barely waiting for the priest's anxious assent, he turned to his bride. "Time for us to be off. Can you ride a horse, girl?"

"I have never set foot beyond the zenana courts before this day, lord." She forced herself to meet his eyes boldly. Her new lord was not a man uncertain of his own power, and hence eager to rule others; he would demand obedience, but not submission.

"You can't ride, then. Come along, girl—and stay by me. The kings won't like this, and the wind will have whispered the news to all the world before the sun's much higher."

The speed with which the *feringhi*-general and his men broke camp and were ready to ride astonished her. Even so, before her new husband had set her upon a horse the three warring kings rode up, their cavalry behind them.

"Come to wish me well on my wedding-day, have you?" the Black Pearl's husband asked.

These were not the words they had expected to hear; Malior

and Nildekhand looked horrified and her father outraged.

"You cannot! Her bride-price—" her father began, and stopped. But he had already betrayed himself past redemption.

"How many times must her bride price be paid?" Malior demanded.

"How many times can he play one of you fools off against the other? So far he's made a good living out of *not* marrying her—but that game stops here."

"Yes, it stops here." The Rajah of Nildekhand spurred his horse forward and stared down at the Black Pearl as she stood beside the *feringhi*-general. "The war is over, foreigner. Go now, and take your soldiers with you."

"Gladly, Highness—when I've been paid what you promised."

Nildekhand smiled and touched his stallion's glossy side with a blade-sharp spur; the horse tossed its narrow head and edged closer to the Black Pearl. The stallion's iron-shod hooves danced perilously close to her bare feet.

She did not move.

"We have settled our differences," Nildekhand said. "There is no work for you here, *feringhi*." Nildekhand ignored the Pearl as if she were a shadow in the dust.

"Then she's my ten percent of the plunder you owe me. You can keep your men and their horses."

"*You* cannot marry a Rajput princess!"

"I already have. Go ask the priest, if you doubt my word or my wife's. If you can catch him."

The Black Pearl followed her husband's lead. "Yes, we are married—and who knows better than you, father, that it was my right to choose my own husband now?"

"How can you shame yourself and your family so?" demanded her father bitterly.

"It was not hard, when I remembered that I was your daughter." She said the words unsmiling; her angry pride solaced by the high color that rose into her father's cheeks and the way his gaze slid away and would not meet her own.

Under the accusing eyes of Nildekhand and Malior, her father tried to salvage what he could. "And you, *feringhi*—if I give you my daughter—"

"No need. I've taken her already."

"She is a princess of Kalipur; her bride-price is higher than any but a great king can pay." Defiantly refusing to look at anyone but the *feringhi*-general, her father continued, "And she brings no dowry with her."

"No?" Her new lord reached out and lifted the rope of black pearls that lay across her breast. He weighted the black pearls in his hand; a few wayward stands of her hair drifted like dark smoke across his skin. "She comes with dower enough. As for a bride price—I leave your city walls standing. But if you ask more, O seller of daughters—" He flung a handful of coins into the dust before the Rajah's horse. "Let that content you."

Without another word he closed his hands about her waist and lifted her to his horse's back. For a moment they looked straight into each other's eyes. In the sunlight his tiger eyes blazed copper fire; his hands burned upon her skin as if branding the marks of his fingers upon her flesh.

It was written in the Sacred Laws of Manu that a woman's husband was her god. This was a god she could follow joyously into fire. She smiled as he swung easily up before her.

"Hold tight," he ordered. "If you fall off, I'll not come back for you."

"If you come back for me, I'll slit your throat and then mine!" Laughter bubbled up in her, rich and potent as wine. She had honor in her bones and a strong man in her arms. What matter that they faced three armies? This was how a Rajput should live and die.

"Now," he said, and raised his sword high. Sunlight flamed over the blade, blindingly bright. "We go." The sword swept down and the stallion leapt forward. For the first mad moments she clung desperately, struggling for balance. Then she found it, pressed against her man's broad back, as the stallion hit his full stride.

His troop reached full gallop with what seemed impossible speed, aiming its mass of horseflesh and cold steel at the center of the waiting host. She could see nothing but the riders galloping beside them, golden shadows in the stifling dust. Tightening her grip to the utmost, she braced herself for the shock of impact.

With shocking suddenness the horsemen barring their way gave ground. Shouts and jangling harness and startled faces— Her father desperately spurring his horse out of their headlong path—

Then they were past the three kings and their baffled warriors, riding hard to the west. Once she looked back, but all she could see behind her was dust turned to a veil of fire by the rising sun's rays.

The *feringhi*-general led his troop well up into the hills west of Kalipur before permitting them to stop. "An hour." He turned in the saddle, lithe as a cat, and plucked her from his stallion's back. A twist of his arm lowered her to the ground, her bare feet slapping firmly onto warm rock. Then he swung down from the saddle to stand beside her.

She looked up at him, tilting her head far back to look into his eyes. "We stop here, lord?"

"We rest here. Then we ride again." He did not ask whether she were strong enough to go on.

He does not treat me as if I am no more than a beautiful doll. A strange thought; all thing seemed possible now.

"Well, that was folly," the *feringhi* said, and laughed. "Well, girl, are you satisfied with your bargain now?"

All things are possible now. She drew a deep breath and dared once more. "I am satisfied. May I know your name, lord?"

He smiled. "Rufin Kosciusko. And yours? Don't tell me you were named the Black Pearl."

The knowledge that she at last belonged to a man of valor and honor glowed within her like fire's heart. She stooped to touch the dust on his feet, and when she straightened, she looked into his eyes and smiled.

"My name is Victory. And I ride where you do, Rufin," said the Black Pearl.

CLOCKWORK UNICORN

by Doranna Durgin

Doranna Durgin is an award-winning author (the Compton Crook for Best First SF/F/H novel) whose quirky spirit has led to an extensive publishing journey across genres, publishers, and publishing lines. Beyond that, she hangs around outside her Southwest mountain home with horse and accomplished competition dogs. She doesn't believe in mastering the beast within, but in channeling its power—for good or bad has yet to be decided. She says, "My books are SF/F, mystery, paranormal romance, and romantic suspense. My world is the Southwest, and my dogs are Beagles!" She's best known for the Changespell Saga, and her most recent book completed the Reckoners trilogy.

About "The Clockwork Unicorn," she writes that it started simply—a title, popping in out of nowhere—and quickly grew into a complex world that might just get its own book someday. Because, she asks, who *doesn't* want to touch a unicorn horn?

"Is that the most recent list of the dead?" Jensa Mirchen op Dahr, newly appointed Principle of Welfare, held out her gloved hand to receive the thick, crisp sheets across the polished sheen of her work podium, the rustle of her clothing loud in this muted office of thick carpets, closed curtains, and rich wall hangings.

Senior Recorder Cindra presented the pages with the two-handed gravity they deserved, her ink-stained fingers closed a little too tightly around their red edges. "Categorized," she said, her gaze sweeping surreptitiously across Jensa's outrageously copper and barely contained hair, the jewels of her home-crafted hair comb, the pale freckled complexion of the outer north. Not a heritage often seen here, never mind in high office. Never mind a Null at that. "Ague numbers from our executive, market, hand labor, farmstead, and elder populations. As we hoped, the worst of it seems to be past, especially here in the city."

The senior then cleared her throat with deliberate delicacy. No one these days coughed with vigor, of course, nor made any such obtrusive throat sound. "As usual, the rolls have not yet been gathered from the ranges. I still contest we should strike them from—"

Jensa clapped her hands, a sharp motion faintly muffled by the gloves. Half gloves, supple and thin and perfectly fitted, exposed fingers allowing her the precision necessary to handle pen and paper, seals and aether wax and glue and ribbons. "Do not finish that that thought, Senior. Not as I sit in this chair."

In point of fact, she wasn't sitting behind the tall podium. But the Senior took her meaning well enough. "I mean them no ill," she allowed, a quick flush staining cheeks almost dark enough to hide the color. It was a quick recovery from a woman still coming to know Jensa. *Principle. Null.* And now her superior. "Just that they do not truly seem to be part of us."

"The border folk were placed there against their will during more shameful days," Jensa said, reaching for the papers. "Some here find it all too convenient to forget that their sacrifice helped build our interior."

She knew the words the senior didn't dare, those parroted by so many as the subject came up. *They should ask for less from us; they should make more of themselves. They should be more like us.*

But Jensa knew what it was to be an outsider. She would brook no slight to others simply for who and where they were.

She flipped to the last page. Ah, yes. Farmstead, elder, and ranges. And indeed that latter, a region of superstitions and folk magics no longer countenanced in their inner realm of quickly developing industries and aether-driven clockworks, remained without entry.

She arranged the stiff pages, tapping them crisply against the desk. "We respect all our dead," she said with finality. I need those numbers. Without them, we cannot assess containment."

Senior Cindra folded her hands at the flat, decorative purse hanging just left of her belt knot. It held only one item: the aether-stamped key of her office. Perhaps the feel of it grew her courage. "All the same," she said, even as her gesture indicated her compliance, "they might try harder to fit in."

Jensa offered the lanky Senior a bemused stare. Cindra, too, wore the gloves of office, her skirt panels meticulously arranged, her shirtwaist blouse obscured by the patterned scarf of her family's colors. She finally found dry words of response. "I'm quite sure the matter is foremost on their minds."

Cindra looked back a moment too long for respect, then opened her hands to gesture departure. She had barely turned away when a great shout filtered through the grand rotunda and the immense open doors beyond.

It was a clash laced with thick border tones, as if in response to their conversation. Cindra dashed defiance over her shoulder. *You see? It's one of them now, and just listen to that fuss!*

Jensa ducked around the podium, laced boots loud on the polished floor outside her chamber. She dodged the frozen old clockwork unicorn and pedestal, out-pacing Cindra with ease. Nor was she the only one rushing to the Rotunda entrance, where steep steps fanned out in patterned stone bordered by intricately groomed garden plots.

Steps not usually smeared with the blood of a whirling fight.

For the first instant, Jensa couldn't resolve the three entangled figures, two armed Rotunda guards and the third figure who seemed to be more than holding his ground. But as Jensa brought herself up short, he assayed a quick block and flipped a short blade in his grip, smacking the pommel between his opponent's eyes.

A furious scream with no apparent source rang out, and the next instant Jensa knew why—the second guard had recovered from a stumble and come up from behind to slam her truncheon at the man's pale-haired head, her blade then whipping up to catch at the loose cloth of his light, shapeless coat.

Down he went, still in motion, bowling through the two guards and up the steps. Only then did he allow himself to stagger, catching himself on the top step.

"Nieko, Nieko, Nieko!" The screaming voice rang out, shrill and high and full of both anger and terror—and belonging to the little girl who emerged from the small side shrubs to dash across the steps. She brandished a tiny knife at the guards even as she clutched the man's coat and wailed his name. *Nieko, Nieko!*

No, not a coat. A brown-patterned border wrap, to match the border burr in his shout. And a fierce little border girl, hair bright even under a clouded sun, protecting her guardian with tears gleaming and teeth—such as she had—bared.

"As I said," Cindra muttered tightly, her hands clasped in front of her key purse as though it needed protecting.

The guards, though, hesitated—not quite taking on the little girl and her little knife. Jensa grasped the moment to speak sharp command. "Stand down!"

The guards complied, evincing a relief that seemed more related to their battered appearance than any innate discipline. Jensa left the cool shadows of the Rotunda, sweeping a stern gaze across the man, the stained steps, the guards, her demand implicit in her expression.

The ranking guard stepped forward. She looked as harried as one would expect, here in the Central Rotunda where citizens behaved with decorum. "He failed to respect legitimate requests and then resisted escort."

The girl's voice sounded no less young now that innocent, righteous fury replaced most of her fear. "You're a liar!" She wrapped her arms around the man's neck, which did not look to be exactly what he needed.

But his head was obviously clearing, for he placed a quelling hand on her gold-blonde crown. "Laella," he murmured, revealing the voice, deep with a burr, that had started it all.

"They were *mean!*" the girl persisted. "They *pushed* him!" Her words were all the harder to understand for their slight lisp around missing front teeth, and Jensa mentally shifted her age estimate downward.

"Oh, now—!" the guard said. She hauled her partner to his feet; blood ran a thin trickle from the lump on his forehead and down alongside his thin brown nose and his black eyes didn't quite focus. "We did no such thing. We searched him, as is our right."

"*Pushed*," the girl insisted. "Called names!"

Null! Freckle face! Torch-head! Jensa was well familiar with the guard's defensive expression, just as she could still feel the sting of being outcast. And still, the guards had a right to search, even though they did it seldom.

"No matter, that," the man said. He gently tugged the girl's arms free from his neck and stood, his posture weary—although something in his expression yet mirrored the girl's recent defiance. "But leaving my girl here, I would not do."

Jensa struggled with an instant's confusion before she understood: the guards had meant to escort the man away and leave the child behind on her own.

"It would have taken only moments to record his particulars!" the woman objected. But the thought of Jensa's own small niece in the same circumstances sent a small chill down her spine.

Recorder Cindra snorted in dismissive disdain, still in the doorway with the cluster of junior recorders and a small scandalized clutch of ungloved aides. "Detain them both, then. This has gone far beyond simple *resistance*."

"In that, you are right," Jensa said. They were perhaps not well-matched, she and this Senior. "Guards, stand down. This citizen has come far; let us show him some kinder welcome. Come inside, then, sir, and tell me how we can serve you."

If the girl heard the rustle of appalled response, she gave no indication. She lifted her arms to the man as he scooped her up and then relaxed against him in full confidence, her arms around his neck both secure and possessive. "My gear," he said, nodding at the bundle of rucksack and rolled bedding beside the bush that had hidden the girl.

"We will bring your gear," Jensa said, giving the senior guard a look to make it so. "Come inside. We will hear you."

Jensa hadn't meant to use the formal phrasing, the one that obligated her to a full hearing. And yet she could hardly have done less. Not with the desperation settled over these two, and what the man had endured simply to be here.

They trooped in past the clockwork unicorn, a thing of instant captivation to the girl no matter that no amount of aether—undiscernible to a Null, a warm trickle to all else—could induce the thing to move. The girl would have touched its gleaming metal, stroked its articulated joints, perhaps even raised her finger to a prick of its dull, canted horn. The man had shifted her to his other hip with effortless familiarity and they passed by the dysfunctional old piece even as an errant shaft of light from high windows burnished it bright.

But the clouds quickly came over again, and Jensa shook away her distraction. She shooed the lingering onlookers away and brought man and girl to her chamber, pretending not to notice the girl's captivated reaction to the thick carpet. There she saw them supplied with tea and tiny meat pastries, settling them in the little reception space beside the window and drawing the curtains to reveal scattered clouds above the geometric patterns of the long raised garden beds.

The girl was already wolfing down the pastries. The man slowed her with a glance and she chewed with hands over her mouth to hold back the overflow.

The man himself ate and drank nothing as Jensa sat. "I am Principle Jensa Mirchan op Dahr," she said, sitting her padded chair with formal starch. "I oversee assessment of the Quick Ague impact, but I have some influence in other matters. Speak to me of your presence here."

"I am Nieko of the border." He sat straight, but without her formality. His words were more refined than before, but still colored by his isolated region. "This is Laella. We have come far." He looked aside at Cindra. "Perhaps too far."

"Please." Jensa indicated the tea. "Refresh yourself. And speak to me."

He pulled his wrap back from his wrist in a practiced gesture, spanning the teacup rim with his fingers to pluck it off the table. He tipped back the entire contents, swallowing once and seemingly unaware of Cindra's disapproving *tsk*.

But Cindra's reaction turned to a gasp at the sight of the tattooed dots spiraling around the tanned skin of the man's exposed wrist, and she went so far as to point. "So many!"

He ignored that to set the teacup down firmly enough to ring against the table mosaics. "Tell you? An' you should already know! I come because the ranges are dying, and the city does nothing!"

As Jensa searched for words of response, Laella had time to wipe her mouth on the back of her wrist, take the teacup with both small hands, and gulp several generous swallows before sitting back with a sigh. Another few moments and she'd be asleep.

Nieko twitched the girl's shawl to cover her more completely. He looked not better for the libation and rest, but as if such things had disagreed with him.

She found only an unimpressive response to his impassioned words. "We sent herbs and physicks. It is as much as we do for those here."

"An' the ranges be not here!" he said, a wild temper flaring in tired eyes. "We are rock and wind and stinging rain, we have but goats and scant greens and roots. Those who watch the borders cannot forage; those who are sick cannot forage. Those who have not foraged do not live!" He stood abruptly enough to startle Cindra into another overdone gasp, pacing a few short steps away and turning sharply to stand behind his chair, both hands on the back of it and tightening down.

For that instant, Jensa thought she might indeed have erred, bringing this man into a place of city refinement and city expectations. Then the clouds crawled away long enough to pass a shaft of sun over Laella's face, an exhausted little mien already in deep sleep.

Nieko's face softened at the sight of her, but not his words. "You sent us there—you and yours. You thought us too superstitious, too unruly, and you gave us to the ranges so we could watch for you. *Fight* for you." He jerked his sleeve back again, this time putting the spiral tattoo on deliberate display. *"Die for you."*

A voice spoke from the doorway. The woman guard again, along with the Junior who'd clearly fetched her. "Principle, is all well?"

Jensa cleared her throat. "Perfectly fine," she said. "Feel free to stay, but do not interfere." She turned back to Nieko with a tighter composure, gesturing at the tattoo. "Are those not the marks of kills?"

He stared back without comprehension, then marked understanding with a short and humorless laugh. *"Kills?* You think I prowl the ranges in search of hapless travelers?" He lifted Laella's small limp hand, turning it outward so Jensa could see the single black dot there. "Do you think this little one *kills?"*

Jensa sucked in a breath, off-balance again. *What, then?*

Because everyone knew that the range folk were unruly and untamable, an insular clan that had been sent away to prowl equally wild hills, killing as they could and would and keeping the border safe as a result. They belonged there; they thrived there. Conditions might not offer luxury, but kept them challenged, away from the inner regions.

They did not caress the carefully braided hair of a young one, nor argue eloquently, if roughly, for their own cause.

"The marks represent encounters survived," he said, answering her unspoken question. The intensity of the moment had taken something from him; he no longer bristled with energy. "Smugglers and bandits and those who must climb past us to reach you. Or sometimes just something with claws and teeth. We have no need to go *looking* for kills."

Jensa looked at that pale thin wrist, smeared with the grime of the road and dotted with survival. "No little wonder she went after that guard."

"Neither are hurt." He said it flatly, a dismissive honesty. "I took care for that."

The woman watching from the doorway looked away in annoyance. Jensa eyed the man, seeing in him the same hunger displayed so clearly by the girl, the same tightness in his features and the grey tinge of his face. She saw desperation—and something unexpected along with it. A hint of command.

"You are no mere patrol officer," she said. "Come here with his sister."

"Niece, if precision is needful." He looked down on her sleeping form with a flicker of grief. "Orphaned."

"And you—"

"Range chief."

The guard winced and withdrew more completely, suddenly no longer looking eager to finish what had been started between them.

Jensa quelled the urge to rise, lift her morning cloak from its hook beside the door, and lay it over the girl. It might disturb her. "Your needs are not within my purview. But I will speak to those who can act."

Nieko said, that flat tone again, "If I do not return with

preventions and supplies, my people will die." *Those who might still yet survive.* And then he coughed.

It surprised him; it doubled him. His hand pressed his side and Jensa saw with equal surprise that the brown wrap had covered a spreading blood stain.

He had protected the guards from his fierce competency, yes, but they had held no such compunction in return.

Which of them was barbaric, then? she wondered, but he coughed again, wracking and sudden, and his eyes rolled back in his head. No one was close enough—or even tried—to soften his fall.

"Contagion!" Recorder Cindra cried, dropping her pen on the podium and springing aside—as if that would help.

"Summon the physicker!" Jensa commanded. "One word of his cough to others, and I will have you permanently dismissed!"

Cindra fixed a startled gaze upon Jensa until understanding flooded in, resentment with it. She bustled for the door. Jensa turned her attention to the guard. "You. Come inside."

The guard shook her head, a mute protest.

"Do you think you haven't already been exposed?" Jensa moved to the man's side, expecting and finding the break of Quick Ague sweat at his temple and throat. She flipped the wrap aside and tugged away the stained shirt. The wound was a shallow thing, the slice of a moving blade; stitches would tidy him up. The Quick Ague, with its high, burning fevers and body-sapping tremors, posed far more risk. These two had no resources to spare. "Come just inside the door, and close it. Either our physicks work to protect us, or they don't."

The woman complied with palpable reluctance, craning her neck to peer at the wound from the farthest possible position beside the door. Satisfaction entered her voice. "Ahh, so I did get through."

"Yes," Jensa snapped. "Right after he forbore to kill you, no doubt."

The woman recoiled into silence. Jensa carefully placed a pillow under Nieko's head, all the while hoping the girl would not rouse from what had become a merciful sleep.

Within moments the physicker arrived, a deep-complexioned

man bearing a bulging leather satchel. He confirmed they were each fully dosed on their protective physicks and briskly donned his gloves, hood, and thin, lace-closure coat. Jensa moved aside and gave him space to swiftly assess his new patient.

"Stitches," he grunted, eyeing the wound. "Insignificant." He touched here, prodded there; checked the man's body heat and quickly found the classic red spots inside his eyelids. "His condition is extremely spare. I hope for little but to isolate the contagion to our sickroom." He glanced at the girl, who was rousing. "She will come with us until this is over, one way or the other."

He held out his hand; Jensa belatedly realized she'd become his assistant and pushed his bag within reach. He extracted a small vial and popped the cork, waving it above Nieko's nose. "He must walk to the sickroom. There we will stitch his wound, and that is all anyone has to know."

"I understand," Jensa said. They would avoid panic in the rotunda; they would contain the Quick Ague in all ways.

And more than that, she understood that the physicker expected his new patient to walk just far enough to die, taking his niece with him.

Jensa had not believed that Nieko would indeed be able to stand, never mind cross the inner rotunda to the stairs leading below to the sickroom. He did it with one arm draped over the girl's shoulders and a buffer of space around them, one step after another and no one the wiser that his unsteadiness came from contagion and not the injury that had soaked the side of his shirt, the one left so deliberately exposed so all could see and assume.

She had not, with unexpected sadness, expected him to live through the night. But even as she arrived early the next day, taking his cause to her fellow Principles, she received word that he was swallowing broth. Laella had been started on prevention physicks, and raised brows everywhere with her appetite.

Jensa had also not expected to be fighting her own battles. But Principle Adderick looked down a rather long, thin nose with a patronizing false patience and said, "The ranges have always been considered outside our purview. We have no support measures set aside for them."

Jensa perched stiffly on the edge of his reception chair, her teacup untouched. His chambers dripped with private hangings and golden service scarves, ostentatious to her eye. "Outside our purview in what way? Are they not of us?"

"Yes and no." He waved his hand in an airy, presumptive gesture. "We sent that clan off generations ago; they have had no interest in rejoining us. They prefer their wild life."

Jensa asked, "How do you know?"

"I beg your pardon?" But he didn't, not truly. His narrowed eyes told her as much; his mouth pressed flat, paling the deep olive skin around his mouth.

She set the teacup down, not quite as firmly as Nieko had done the day before. "I can't even curate the simplest of death rolls for that area. When was the last time we included them on a census circuit? Do we owe them nothing for the protective role they play?"

The man snorted. "My dear," he said, though she was no such thing to him, "What do we owe them for giving them what they wanted all along? Freedom from our ways, and from responsibilities to the city? How many of us have the option to live exactly as we please?"

Her mouth dropped open; she took a moment to close it, most firmly. Freedom was fighting for one's life at every turn, in the roughest of circumstances? Freedom was serving as a buffer between the border dangers and the inner farmlands and city?

"Do not romanticize them simply because they created your clockwork unicorn before they left," Adderick advised, misreading her great restraint for invitation. "After all, look how quickly it ceased to function." He glanced at the overflowing basket of his own office symbol, sitting just inside the doorway. On each hour, burnished food goods disassembled and reformed—from fruit to root vegetables to grains, all fairly sparkling with the vigor of the driving aether.

Jensa rose abruptly enough to startle him into disapproval. "Thank you, Principle. I appreciate your time. I can see that I'm asking the wrong questions of the wrong person, for which I'm sorry."

It was meant to be an insult. He was meant not to understand that, and he didn't. He simply nodded as if the apology was his due, and remained seated as she took her leave.

"The ranges?" Principle Chiren shook his head. Behind his podium, his office symbol shifted from a pristine city badge to the bright sun over the rotunda, sparking with aether. A fan of swords would come next; Jensa had seen it before. Chiren's walls held few damping curtains to interfere with the weapons on display, and a crisscross of forged bars filled the tall, narrow window.

Chiron didn't bother to patronize her. He was matter-of-fact, and matter-of-factly puzzled. "They want nothing of us," he told her. "Our garrisons have never been welcome in that region."

Jensa had little doubt. Garrisons were hosted by the locals they ostensibly supported, and the ranges quite evidently had nothing to spare.

"I understand," she said, quite carefully. "But right now they need our help, as we might help any of our distant farm communities. They are depleted. These are not ordinary circumstances."

Chiren tapped a tall set of drawers, the sort that held regional incidents filed one to each small card. "We have no reports of incursions in the area."

"You don't think it will be too late to respond at that point?" *Too late for the ranges, certainly.*

Annoyance darkened his coarse features, drew his heavy brows together. "Do not presume to school me, Principle Jensa."

"No," she said. "No, of course not."

Of course not.

The following day, things went no better with Principle Idela, who could have released stores of prevention physicks. "Those people have their own ways," she said. "They wouldn't take our physicks even if they had them."

"But they're *asking*," Jensa said, with little hope at that point.

"One single person is asking," Idela said. "An exile, for all we know."

A range chief.

But she didn't say it. Idela clearly wouldn't understand the significance of it, just as Jensa herself might not have done so days earlier. When she still thought the spiral tattoo to be a boast, not a memorial.

She returned to her own chambers wanting nothing more than a quiet cup of her favorite tea, sitting in the broad, padded sill of her window and looking down over the precisely patterned gardens and their new blooms of the season.

This day, she thought those gardens might seem a little *too* precise. A little *too* constrained.

But Recorder Cindra waited for her there, laden with newly completed rolls. Beside her stood the physick, displaying a harried expression that made Jensa think he'd only just arrived.

"Ah," he said. "Very pleased I didn't miss you after all."

"Is all well?" Jensa doffed her principle's scarf, a thing of bright watercolor hues meant to represent the all peoples of their regions. Or now, as she understood in a new way, the peoples of their *inner* regions. "Surely he has not now taken a turn, having survived these two worst days?"

"No, no, not at all." But the physick's face held more resignation than relief. "He could indeed still take a sudden turn, but he is recovering to this point. The girl is also well, and has absorbed the physicks well. She has been through all the entertainment mechanics suited to her age—it truly is a shame she isn't..." he stopped. "Well. She is what she is. As are they both."

"I don't understand." Although she did, in a way. She was a Null. She'd heard such words before. She felt a quick flutter of trepidation.

He cleared his throat. "I'm afraid there's a cost when determined advocacy brings a situation to the wrong Principle's attention. Understand, I had no say in this. But the decision is made. The man will not be allowed to leave the city."

She couldn't immediately absorb that information. The sudden rustle of scrolls at her back reminded her of Cinda's presence. "Leave those," Jensa said of the scrolls. "We will tend them later."

Cindra's mouth flattened with protest. She deposited the scrolls in their basket and departed, her desire to stay and listen a palpable thing.

Jensa waited for Cindra's heels to clip-clop to her own little alcove before she said, "Surely they don't mean to imprison him? That initial scuffle was instigated by the guards, and—as you know—he went out of his way to avoid injuring them."

His expression filled with grim regret. "Not imprisonment. Simply not allowed to leave. Not *him*. The girl, they say, might or might not be farmed out to a community that needs more hands in the wake of the Quick Ague."

"They would *separate* the two?" She could not immediately fathom the callousness.

The physick took a few quick pacing steps, then sharply reversed course. "I told them it was too early to discuss it with him," he muttered. "He's at a very delicate stage of the disease."

"What do you mean?" Jensa's voice was fainter than she expected.

"Still active," he explained, seizing the question with evident relief. "In these first days there's often a quick, apparent recovery, but such advances are fragile, and relapse is common."

"No," she said, interrupting him without meaning to. "To *discuss* it with him? They're telling him *now*? On his sickbed?"

The physick frowned, turning his jaw line into jowls. "They want the restrictive anklet on him now, while he's too weak to protest."

"But *why*?" Jensa cried, and then had to wave away the concerned attention of the guard who had passed close enough to touch the unicorn horn, as many did—once, it was said, the device had offered a protection. "Already they refuse to help him. Why *keep* him?"

The physick looked at her with a kind of pity. "Because he would report their failure to help. They can't afford range defection—or worse, an uprising." He scowled in the direction of his treatment rooms, across the rotunda and down. "This way, they suppose, the ranges will think he died on the road. Or simply abandoned his task."

"Then they don't know him," she said promptly, already knowing him better than that. "And I don't think they know the ranges, either."

"If they need help so badly, will they spare someone to come looking?"

Jensa looked at him in open scrutiny. "You believe him."

"I believe we do his people wrong," the physick allowed. "But then, unlike others in these chambers, I have been outside this city in the past decade. And I think they will pay for—"

A high, full-throated scream of fury rang though the rotunda, echoing through the vast dome. The childish words were just as furious, spat out in a jumble that would have been unintelligible even without the rough range curl. A male shout of protesting alarm, a quick tumble of furniture—

Jensa ran to the chamber doorway to see Nieko and his charge emerge from the physick stairway. She wore new city clothes, trousers and cinched tunic, with Nieko's wrap bundled around and all but obscuring her. He still wore his bloodied shirt and tough trousers, his boots unlaced. Metal glinted in his hand, a thing he held as though it might ward off all comers.

The girl's little knife.

No doubt they'd taken his long range knife. No doubt they'd thought themselves safe enough.

A cluster of Principle Seconds, equally panicked and affronted, emerged in his wake. Someone blew a high whistle of alarm and guards came rushing—and by then, Nieko was halfway across the rotunda, fever still strong on his cheeks and brow, his bright hair a sharp contrast to those behind him and his strength a thing he surely could not maintain.

"He'll fail," the physick murmured. "And he's given them the excuse they need to contain him." Not just the anklet, but true imprisonment. "If he lives, I should say."

Jensa thought Nieko and the girl were running for the exit. She was wrong. The unicorn outside her door spat sudden startling sparks and shards of gold light—and when her vision cleared, there he was.

Right there.

He snatched her arm, whirled her around, and pressed up behind her, the little knife right at her throat. His hands burned her skin with Ague heat, and Laella pressed incongruously against her leg.

"Been taking your preventions?" he asked against her ear, a warm and ticklish sensation. "No mind if not. We're about to get plenty of it, and my blade back, and then we'll all go."

She craned her neck, a futile effort to evade the blade. Her fingers scrabbled against the loose shirt and corded muscle of his forearm. *Spiraled tattoo, winding up that arm...a man who survived...* He would not easily release her.

Sparks shone again in the corner of her eye; she flinched against him without meaning to and almost missed his final words, complete with their apologetic tone. "You'll travel with us just for a while, then," he said. "Until we lose those who will follow." His voice also said he didn't doubt he could do just that, and she found herself believing it.

But—

"Nieko!" the girl said, wonder in her voice. "It shines!" She took a step away from them—a step closer to the clockwork unicorn, which did more than shine. It *moved*. And it finished, finally, that awkward frozen step—joints moving smoothly, haunches lowering slightly, head turning toward them as if it sensed who had woken it.

Jensa thought of the faint hazy glow around the old unicorn, that which she'd then thought to be passing sunshine, and knew. They'd come from the ranges, and they'd woken it. And now the clockwork unicorn *moved*. Soundlessly, smoothly, naturally—with metal no longer dull.

Had her predecessors ever known, she wondered, that the mechanic was not built on city aether, but on the unfamiliar energies sourced from a people not their own? Or had they just forgotten along the way?

More than one astonished curse sounded from across the rotunda, where those giving chase had skidded to a stop and now hovered in confusion, too startled by the unicorn's movement to proceed.

But they were not slow to notice that the girl now ventured away from the safety of her uncle's protection.

"Laella!" Nieko's voice sounded low and urgent, but Jensa felt renewed weakness tremble through his arms, enough of a shudder to press the knife against her skin. A warm, instant trickle of blood slipped along her throat. He steadied himself. "Laella!"

Laella stretched to her tip-toes, her finger extended; the

clockwork unicorn lowered its horn as if drawn to her, the air brightening in a distinct line between finger and point-of-horn, shrinking as the distance closed, and then, at the touch—

Jensa flinched from that flash of energy; the others cursed anew. Laella's giggle filled the air. When Jensa blinked away the spots, she saw nothing but that gap-toothed grin on an excitement-flushed face. Not quite so sharp-boned as Jensa remembered. Not quite so grim.

"I'm so very sorry," the physick said quite abruptly, coming upon them from behind—there where Nieko had forgotten about him, or perhaps never even seen him. He used a tightly rolled scroll to rap Nieko sharply on the wrist and wrested the knife away from a grip that had already weakened. "I truly am."

Nieko staggered into the door frame, bringing Jensa with him. Laella leaped to his side, a bundle of renewed energy still largely hidden beneath the oversized wrap. Just as quickly, the hovering guards dove in to grab at him, rough hands tearing Jensa free and bruising her more than Nieko ever had. Fingers tangled in her hair, pulling away combs and leaving it to tumble down, bright and outrageous.

As the moment passed and all stood panting, Jensa swiped hair from her face and pointed at the clockwork unicorn with a trembling finger. It had risen into a rear, powerful metal haunches engaged, forelegs striking out, head twisting in defiance to sling its metal strands of mane into the air.

And the horn...

The horn, it *glowed.*

But Nieko sagged in the grip of not one but three guards. The physick muttered concern, already fetching his bag. Cindra peeked out the entrance to her work alcove, her gaze openly torn between Jensa's dishevelment and the suddenly active unicorn. The *living* unicorn, with its horn no longer a thin spire, but an edged blade.

Laella saw it, too. She tugged her uncle's sleeve, got his bleary attention.

"No," said the physick sternly. "Let it be, man. There is a point beyond which I cannot help you, if we have not already reached it. Your heart is pounding, is it not? It cannot sustain this!"

Nieko looked at him only briefly, and then it was to Jensa he spoke. "There is a *point beyond* when that matters little," he said, trembling and flushed from the spiking Ague. "I must do what I came for." He laughed, a mere expiration of breath. "Even if not what any of us expected."

The guards cursed as he surged up between them, twisting away as he landed blows both precise and effective. But he faltered too soon, among his niece's cries and the guards' shouts and the physick's dismay. Cindra entered the fray, smacking randomly about with her great stout ruler. Laella tugged at her uncle, crying, one hand reaching futilely for the suddenly rising horn.

Only Laella herself knew what she'd felt upon the touch of that horn, a thing once more shining to a blinding degree. Only Nieko knew why he would risk death, a very certain death, to reach the clockwork beast.

Jensa didn't have to know. She just had to be what these supplicants needed. *Null.* Empty, with no impediment coursing through her body.

As Nieko sank back down, gasping horribly, Jensa stepped into the gap between man and unicorn and held out a hand to each.

His hot, dry fingers closed over hers. The clockwork unicorn instantly bent to her, the blade-horn a fiery, blinding brightness. She closed her hand to the sharp slice of metal, flesh giving way.

Her body jolted with unfamiliar energies, raw-edged heat nothing like the aethers that sometimes slithered around her but never *through* her. The guards dropped Nieko and stumbled away, taking Cindra with them, and Nieko's weight hauled her downward—but only for an instant. He took a great whooping breath, and another, and then his grip on her hand closed with new strength. New determination. A new shine she could *feel*.

When she could see again, he stood beside her—flanking his niece and the unicorn and Jensa—her bloodied hand now fallen away from the startlingly liquid machinery that had so quietly, so unassumingly, been the symbol of her office.

No one moved. No one had the nerve, seeing what Jensa could also see so well.

Nieko, standing with the same innate strength he'd had upon arrival.

Not unmarked by his time here—a spot of fresh blood on his

shirt, a flush still high on his cheeks—but with vigor. More vigor than he'd brought with him, and no one had forgotten the outcome of that tussle on the outside steps.

The unicorn turned its head to him, stretching a mobile neck. Bowing.

Presenting the horn.

"*This*," he said, extending a hand without quite touching the bright metal. "This is what we have been missing." He looked at those who would have captured him, held him, kept him from this moment. "Even we had forgotten what our people did here, ere you drove them out."

Jensa wrapped a fold of her skirt panel around her bleeding hand. "What *is* it?"

He took a step closer, no longer particularly concerned about the guards, going so far as to pass the little knife to his niece. "I believe you would call it a repository." The flowing metal creature remained bent, presenting the horn. "An endowed form to gather and dispense the aetherless ways that your people no longer recognize, but that mine know how to use."

Only now did Jensa see that the newly sharp device wobbled at the base. She somehow wasn't surprised when it fell neatly into Nieko's hand, the grip shaping to suit him.

The unicorn stood, lifted its neck into a proud arch, and rose slowly into a powerful levade—its movements slowing, its bright shine fading. Solidifying. *Emptied.*

Nieko turned from her, but somehow his hand—strong and calloused and no longer furnace-hot—had found hers. He held the glowing horn-knife aloft so those who had never quite dare approach could see. "In rejecting us, you rejected this. It is all I take from this place, and you may live on with your physicks as best you can." He pushed the knife into the empty sheath at his belt and rested his hand on Laella's thin shoulders. "If you want the use of this, you may come to us. Bring such gifts as you think will suit."

Jensa found herself murmuring, "As should be."

"You," he said, turning to pin her with his gaze, raking her from what seemed to be the inside out. "*You* need bring only yourself."

She cleared her throat, met that challenge head-on. "As I

indeed might."

Nieko's hand closed around hers with a hint of pressure, then slid away. He strode out of the Rotunda as if it had been his own, the little girl at his side and the cure sheathed securely between them.

Jensa lifted her hand and found it healed.

SPIRE WITCH

by Marella Sands

Marella Sands writes that she likes to travel, and in 2018 was able to do some fun things like watch a village cricket match in Cerne Abbas, Dorset; search the Jurassic Coast for fossils; visit the Phallological Museum in Reykjavik; and stand in the crack between the Eurasian plate and the North American plate in Thingvellir National Park, Iceland. She, like most writers, has more writing projects on her desk than are really good for her sanity.

The dying woman had a surprisingly strong grip.

Niffrel kept hold of the woman's hand, unmindful of the late afternoon heat or the acrid smell of the slums that filled her nose and stung her eyes. Her attention was on the woman, who lay on a thin blanket under a small wooden eave someone had attached to a crumbling building. The building itself housed several large families; at least two babies were currently crying, and there had been more crying when Niffrel arrived a few minutes ago.

"Please..." said the woman in a voice barely audible.

Niffrel didn't know exactly what the woman wanted, but over the past several years, she'd sat with enough of the dying to have some idea. People usually asked for the presence of loved ones; or a blessing from Mita, the goddess of mercy; or, more practically, water.

This woman had rejected water and had shaken her head when Niffrel asked if she could send for someone. That left a blessing from Mita as the most likely request.

"Mita, extend your comforting embrace to our sister and welcome her into the love and light of your bright fields where mercy and compassion await everyone who comes to you with a

120

humble heart. I pray for your mercy and kindness in this, my sister's hour of need." Niffrel rarely knew the names of the people she met under these circumstances, but Mita knew everyone, so Niffrel didn't see that it made any difference.

The woman sighed and her grip went slack. A wave of sadness, but also peace, passed over Niffrel. She didn't know if the feeling came from the woman, from within herself, or from Mita, but she was grateful for it. The feeling seemed to underscore that this life had not gone unnoticed or unmourned. As nameless as this woman was to Niffrel, she had had a name, and a past. Someone had raised her. Someone had loved her. And now, someone had marked her passing.

Niffrel laid down the woman's hand. Someone would be here soon to take the body away; the slum, often called the City of Sighs, policed its own streets, at least most of the time. City guardsmen rarely entered the filthy streets and narrow alleys. Lately, patrols of the Tetrarch's own personal guard, the Vanguard, had become a frequent sight, though they never did anything but observe.

No one knew why they came. Everyone simply stayed out of their way.

Niffrel moved away and sidled into a narrow space in between crumbling hovels and looked around for one of the thousands of spires that dotted the city. In the more affluent areas of town, they were large and soared hundreds of feet into the sky. Here in the slum they were often only a few feet across at the base and thirty or forty feet high. Some glowed a pale blue or green at night, and a gentle orange or red during the day, while others were pink or deepest violet. But many in this day and age were dark. Legend said they had once all been brightly lit in all colors of the rainbow, so that the city glowed all day and all night, truly deserving its ancient name of Visanya, the City of Light. These days, the city housed a few extremely wealthy families, some neighborhoods with some affluence, and otherwise was full of the poor and near-destitute. Many of them had been born in the City of Sighs and would die without ever leaving it. Others had come to Visanya looking for a better life, but had ended up in one of the crumbling hovels, begging or stealing what they needed to survive. A few businesses that dealt mostly in barter could be found in the slum, but they were pale imitations of the kind of establishments that catered to the wealthy.

"Hey, you there, where are you going?"

Niffrel turned slowly, expecting the man with the imperious voice to be clad in the peacock blue of the Vanguard, but he wore the drab brown of the city watch. They were in the slum even less than the Vanguard. What was he doing here?

"Yes, sir?"

"What happened here? Did you kill this old woman?"

Niffrel stifled an urge to put him in his place. She had left any authority or ability to order a city watchman around when she'd run away from her father's mansion six years ago.

Before she could respond, a beggar standing in the shadows nearby said, "She sat with the old woman as she died. It's her way."

"The City of Sighs sees enough death without adding more on purpose," she said, grateful for the man's support. The people of the slum were accustomed to seeing her on her missions of mercy and often shared with her whatever they had. This was the first time someone had ever spoken for her, though.

"So you picked her pocket, then?" The watch was apparently not impressed by either Niffrel or the beggar.

"No, sir."

The watchman knelt by the woman and patted her body. At her waist, he found what he was looking for; a small purse. He held it up and poured out a few iron coins, the smallest of the city's denominations. Three iron coins could barely buy a crust of bread these days.

A man in crimson robes stepped out of the shadows. How had she missed him? His black hair fell to his waist and was covered in a hairpiece laced with tiny silver bells that tinkled as he walked. He was immaculately clean but, to Niffrel's surprise, didn't evince even a shred of disgust at walking through the filth of the street. Behind him came several more of the city watch.

"Come, boy," he said. "I would talk with you."

Blessed Mita, what now? She wanted to get away from here, but she couldn't very well run from this man for no reason. Other city watchmen stepped into the alley; Niffrel counted seven. The crimson-clad man had certainly brought enough protection to keep him safe in the slum. But why was he here to begin with?

The beggar darted back into an alley, no doubt unwilling to face such a crowd of armed men.

"I won't hurt you, boy," said the rich man dismissively. "In fact, I'll pay you." He held out a handful of copper coins, so new they were almost blindingly bright in the afternoon sun.

Niffrel couldn't refuse. What waif in the City of Sighs would turn down money when they had nothing to hide? She inched forward.

The man did not throw the coins at her feet as she expected, but waited for her to get close enough to hold out her hands. He poured the coins into her palms and Niffrel quickly pocketed the money. "What does the lord wish to know?"

"First, the lord would like to get out of this wretched alley." He waved at the watchmen. "Get the body to the burial ground before it makes the area stink any worse. You, boy, come with me." He turned and strode away without a backward glance.

Two of the city watch remained, staring at her. She bowed her head and hurried after the man. She didn't dare run with the man's money now that she'd taken it; the watch would chase her down.

The man led her to the edge of the slum where the streets became wider and the foot traffic less dense. Niffrel avoided these streets most of the time; she was too dirty and clad too shabbily to pass for anything but a street urchin. She only came after dark to see if she could find scraps to eat or something someone had lost or dropped that she could barter in the City of Sighs for her next meal or a place to sleep.

The man went to a small café and took a table on the street. The café was fronted in the glazed multi-colored tiles for which the city was known. This particular building was all orange and yellow; daytime colors, warm tones designed to appear friendly and appealing to passers-by. No doubt the back of the establishment was plain adobe; only in the wealthier neighborhoods could people afford to have the glazed tiles on all sides of the building. Here, it was enough show some beautiful tile just at the front.

A pale man with short blond hair and reddened face, no doubt the proprietor, popped out of the establishment immediately. He didn't even give Niffrel a glance. He bowed to the man. "How may

I serve you, lord?"

"Whatever's in your pot. A bowl for me and one for him. A bottle of your best wine, and two loaves of bread from that bakery down the street." He laid two square silver coins on the table, more than enough for a day's worth of food. "And I expect we won't be disturbed."

The proprietor scooped up the coins efficiently and bowed. "Everything will be as you wish, lord."

Niffrel was impressed. If her brothers had tried something in this neighborhood, they would have flashed gold coins around, and been robbed of everything, even their lives, by nightfall. This man had brought much more practical sums of money that were enough for him to accomplish what he wanted, and even to show extraordinary generosity, but not so much to tempt anyone to commit murder. Now that she was paying more attention to him herself, she noticed he had a simple silver chain around his neck and only one ring, a tiny silver-colored band on the little finger of his right hand. It was not flashy enough to warrant a daylight robbery.

She would have to be careful. This man was smart, and she had no idea what he wanted. But she didn't dare speak to him unless spoken to first. Sometimes, that was hard. She'd grown up as imperious as the next highborn daughter, but six years surviving hand-to-mouth in the City of Sighs had trained her to keep her wits about her. She'd perfected the art of appearing to belong in the slum. Even her accent marked her as a resident of the poorest neighborhoods.

The man merely watched the people going by on the street until the proprietor returned with a tray containing their food. A waiter brought out the wine and two tin goblets. The goblets were plain, marked only by the owner's stamp on the base. The man across from her waved the proprietor away when he would have poured the wine, and then poured it himself.

Niffrel's stomach growled at the sight of hot food. She had rarely been able to get anything like this since coming to the City of Sighs. Even when the people in the slum cooked their food, it was often boiled scraps or the remains of something thrown out of a wealthier household.

But her hard-won caution kept her from diving into the stew right away. She couldn't afford to offend the man and have him send her away before she could eat. A little more patience was all that was required.

"So," said the man at last. He cut one of the loaves in half and handed it to Niffrel. "Do you sit with the dying often?"

She shrugged and took the bread. It was soft and still warm from the oven. She savored a bite before answering. "Sometimes. There is a lot of dying in the slums, but Mita is merciful to those who show mercy. It is not a hardship to hold a hand for a few minutes once in a while."

"Mita? Not a name I hear much at home," he said as he ate a bite of bread. "Zuran rules the elite households, and he is not a god who seems concerned with things like mercy. But I'm glad I found you. I'm looking for just such a person."

Niffrel's appetite disappeared but she kept eating. Who knew when she would eat again? "Why?"

"I'm seeking out a woman who may be the key to getting this city back in its proper order. I have heard of a woman who doles out mercy and then is seen going to the spires and touching them. They say the spires glow brighter under her hand."

Niffrel's heart stopped beating for a moment. That was indeed what she did. She wasn't sure why; it seemed natural to offer some kind of prayer at the spires after sitting vigil at a death, and it had become her habit. It was true that the spires glowed under hands but she had always assumed they glowed for everyone. It was just that she was the only person she knew who was brave, or foolhardy, enough to touch them.

"What you can't know is that, if you look at the old records in the city vaults, you will find that the city used to be much different. Poor people were few. The spires shone so brightly they rivaled the moon and the stars. Zuran's prosperity brought greatness to the city, but so did Mita's gentleness and compassion. This city was the jewel of the continent; a shining light that spread wonder and awe to every port where her ships traded. In those days, there was more than just the Hands of Zuran and the High Council to advise the Tetrarch. There were the Eyes of Mita: men and women who had a gift of mercy from the goddess herself."

125

Niffrel nearly choked on her stew. "I never heard a story like that!" At her own house, her father and brothers talked about Zuran blessing their trade deals and watching over their shipping interests. They had only mentioned the spires to wonder if they could be torn down to make room for more warehouses. Mita's name had never been mentioned.

"You wouldn't have, in the City of Sighs," he said. "But for obscure reasons lost in the moldy pages of mouse-gnawed tomes, the Eyes of Mita were banished from the city. The spires were blocked off so no one could touch them anymore. And the Hands of Zuran held both ears of the Tetrarch instead of only one. The rich got richer and more prosperous, but the poor got more numerous and the spires faded. Now, over half of them never even glimmer, even to reflect the moon. And the City of Sighs grows every year. Soon, the blight that has infected the city will reach even the Tetrarch and his coffers, but by then it will be too late. Visanya will have consumed itself from the inside."

Niffrel simply sat, numb.

The man ate more of his bread and gestured for her speak. "Well, boy, what do you know of a woman who sits with the dying and, perhaps, has something to do with the spires?"

Niffrel shook her head. "Nothing, lord. The dying are often comforted in their last moments by a friend or family member."

When she had first arrived in the City of Sighs, Niffrel had assumed that everyone in the slum merely looked out for him or herself. She hadn't understood the complex web of relationships people built around themselves, and how intricate the dance of daily survival was and how important it was to have a network of friends if family wasn't an option.

Not that there was no crime in the City of Sighs, but there was less than she had expected. People watched out for their own in the slum. The friends she had made in the City of Sighs might not be the lifelong true friends of the romances she'd read as a child, but they could be counted on for help as long as they knew they could count on you in return. Some days, that was the thin line between a meal and hunger, or a homespun shift and nakedness.

Even now, she noticed a small boy across the street whose mother she had nursed when the woman was ill after the birth of

126

her last child. The family had nothing to give her, but it was comforting to know the boy was keeping an eye out to give witness to what might happen to her, if nothing else. In the City of Sighs, people might not have the means to help much, or often, but that did not mean they didn't want to. They did what they could. They were more family to Niffrel than her own family had been.

"What do they call you, boy?"

"Wren." No need to keep that to herself; her street name would mean nothing to the elegant man across from her. She had chosen it because the small brown bird might have be beautiful for its voice, but it was drab to look at. No one looked at a wren twice.

"I am Temmeril noh-Vanji," he said. "You may continue to call me lord. Technically, Lord Vanji is my father, but such technicalities are important at court, not here."

Niffrel's gut twisted into a painful knot. Vanji? They were the main trading rivals of her birth family, the Jurahs. Niffrel voh-Jurah had been raised to be proud of her name, and suspicious of anything associated with the Vanjis. Never trust a Vanji her father had said often enough.

And then he'd plotted to marry her to one.

Learning he'd been in negotiations with the Vanji and planned to trade her to them in return for access to a route across the mountains to the ruby mines had terrified her. That had been the first moment of her life where Niffrel had realized her wishes and her family's wishes were not necessarily the same, when she had truly understood how much power her father and brothers had over her. By the time the contract had been finalized, she had stashed away as many coins as she could without arousing suspicion, stolen a patched dress from a household servant, and slipped over the household wall on a moonless night. By morning, she'd cut off her hair. By the next morning, she'd been robbed of many of her coins. She'd learned early how to become invisible under nondescript clothing and to hide the small sums of money she could beg or steal.

The next six years had been difficult and painful, but at least she wasn't married to the enemy in exchange for rubies for her father and brothers.

"I'd be willing to pay more for some information," said the

Vanji who sat across from her. "If there is a woman who could bring the worship of Mita back to the Tetrarch's court, she would be invaluable. She could help change the world. I thought I could find her by having men guard the spires, but there's no way to watch them all. Instead, I've paid people to keep watch for anyone who will sit with the dying, figuring anyone who would do that might know the woman I'm looking for."

"No one has anything to do with the spires," she said. "You can't eat them or trade them or sleep under them."

"Very practical," he said. "But I must find this woman."

"Whatever these Eyes of Mita were, no one I know has ever heard of them."

"Perhaps by another name? To the poor, they were called Spire Witches."

Spire Witch? That was a term Niffrel had heard once or twice after she'd touched a spire and it had glowed under hand. She hadn't given it any thought.

"Why would you sit with the dying in the first place?" asked the Vanji man. "What good does it do you?"

She stared at him, unable to find the words. How could one not? She'd tried avoiding it sometimes, if she were tired or felt ill, but her heart wouldn't let her pass by. As a child, she'd been unable to leave a dying sparrow to flop around the Jurah gardens; she always tried to help. Her brothers had teased her mercilessly and she'd learned early to keep wounded animals from them, lest they kill the animal in front of her and laugh at the sport.

She'd rarely saved one; she had no training in healing and had no idea what to do. But being with the animal as it died had filled her with a sense of purpose, a way of belonging to the world, that nothing else did. If she could do nothing to help, at least she could be present. And that seemed to count for something. In the poorest of neighborhoods, she'd found that her sense of doing something important was magnified every time she sat with a dying person. Passing by was not an option.

Besides, she'd gotten a reputation. People now sought her out, even paid her sometimes, if they had a spare crust of bread or a small iron coin. Niffrel didn't like taking things in exchange for her vigils, but the beast of hunger could not be denied. She did have to eat.

"I...I don't know," she finally said. "It feels right."

He gave her a strange look and cocked his head slightly, which made the bells in his hair tinkle. Well, her brothers and father wouldn't have understood doing something because it was right. They only understood their ledgers and the wealth they could accumulate.

"All right," he said, apparently willing to abandon that train of questioning. "Then tell me about the spires. They're supposed to be inaccessible. In the wealthier areas, the Vanguard maintains the walls around them."

She shrugged. "The barriers around a few in the City of Sighs have come down over the years. Who would repair them here?"

She looked up into the black eyes of the Vanji lord. He was staring at her intently. Suddenly, he leaned forward and rubbed her close-shaven scalp, a look of shock on his face. "I've been calling you boy but you're a woman!"

Niffrel froze a moment, panicked to be found out so suddenly. She resisted the urge to bolt and instead bowed her head. She didn't even try to hide her trembling. "Please, lord, you may call me a boy if you like, and I will surely give you more information about the woman you seek if I ever see her."

"But how do I know it's not you?" he asked.

"I am no one," she said. "No one the great lord need notice."

"Lord!" shouted one of the guards in the street. "We are..."

A sickening thud silenced the man. Niffrel spun around, prepared to run, even if the heaviness that had moved up past her gut into her chest made her feel as though a weight was pressing on her lungs, preventing her from breathing deeply, let alone help her escape.

The street was filling with blue-clad men with the peacock symbol of the Tetrarch on their chests. The Vanguard. Though they had been in the City of Sighs recently, they had always remained aloof, just observing. Today, they were focused, daggers drawn, ready for violence.

"We must go," said the Vanji lord. He grabbed her arm.

The Vanguard man nearest them shouted and ran toward them. Niffrel reached for her own knife and would have backed away, but the Vanji pushed her down and stood over her.

The soldier thrust his dagger at the lord, who tried to parry, but was hampered by Niffrel at his feet, and the table at his back. The proprietor chose that moment to pop outside.

"Holy Zuran," said the proprietor. He disappeared back into his shop. "The Vanguard!" he shouted. "The Vanguard! Everyone out!"

Niffrel pulled her own dagger and thrust it upward into the soldier's side where the leather pieces of his armor had been tied together. The man screamed and wrenched himself to the side, pulling the handle of the knife out of her hands.

Niffrel stood up and looked over at the lord. He was holding his side and staring at the blood leaking out around his fingers.

Niffrel grabbed him and shoved him into the restaurant. She pushed him through the milling customers, who seemed confused as to which way to go. It took longer than she wanted to get to the back, through the kitchen, and into the nearest alley, but if the customers had gotten in her way, they'd probably be in the Vanguard's way as well.

Niffrel would take advantage of whatever time they had managed to buy. She pushed the Vanji down several more alleys and made a confusing set of turns before allowing him to stop. Before he could say anything, she said, "Shut up. Put on my robe." She pulled off her outer robe and helped him get it on. He groaned when she tied it tightly around his waist.

"Maybe that will put enough pressure on the wound to slow the bleeding long enough for us to get away," she said. "Once we've found somewhere to hide, we can take a better look at that."

He looked at her mutely, and then nodded. He threw his arm around her shoulders and she helped him down the street, praying to Mita that she could hold both of them up. Her own legs could have been made of rubber, and she felt as if she were breathing around a rock in her chest. She began to see the shimmering of the spires in front of her, as if they beckoned her, or were driving her mad. That hadn't happened before.

But she had no time to wonder what was happening beyond moment-to-moment survival.

Carefully, she made her way back to the slum several blocks

from the restaurant. She didn't know the more affluent neighborhoods enough to have hideouts in mind, but she knew the City of Sighs well. If she could make it to one of her bolt holes, the two of them should be safe for a while.

Finally, they reached the tiny space under a small workshop where Niffrel holed up in bad weather. The city was usually blessed with heat and sun but a few days a year were rainy and cold. The thick adobe walls of the buildings suffered with the sudden introduction of so much water, but usually held and dried out well enough. Still, one had to find somewhere to get out of the rain, and that was difficult.

This street was higher than the others and water ran off into the other buildings, but this one was always dry. Even underneath, the ground remained hard-packed and untouched by moisture. It was safe to hide here even in the worst storm.

Niffrel pulled the man into the crawlspace and placed baskets across the entrance. As long as the Vanji lord had not dropped too much blood in the streets on their way here, they should be able to hide.

"Why are you helping me?" he asked as she laid him on her thin blanket. "Why didn't you run away?"

She undid the belt and pulled the edges of the robe back. Half-dried blood stuck to her hands as she fumbled with the layers of his clothing. Finally, she gave up trying to see the wound. "I don't know. I've never been able to pass suffering, even that of an animal. My brothers mocked me for it."

"And you are the Spire Witch."

"I don't know what that is," she said. The man had continued bleeding. She pressed her hands down on the wound and he grunted. "I'm afraid we will be unable to stop the bleeding but I'll try."

"You must leave the City of Sighs and go to court," he said. "You must help restore the balance in the city."

"What's that to me?" she asked. "I'm just Wren. I'm no one."

He sighed. "It is just as well. I had hoped...but no more. My hope was in vain."

"Hoped what?"

He closed his eyes. His voice was barely above a whisper.

"There was a girl, so beautiful, so kind. Her family and mine were enemies, but I loved her from afar. I saw how she treated the donkeys that brought supplies to her family's kitchen. I watched her play with kittens. She fed songbirds from her hands. She was unlike any other girl my mother had urged me to marry. They were all vain creatures, cruel to their servants and thinking no further than their next dress or hairstyle. This girl made me think of the Eyes of Mita of old: compassionate, full of mercy. I told my mother I would marry her, or no other. It was not easy to get my parents to agree."

"How could you watch this girl?"

"My family owned property near her family's primary residence. I could watch her from the roof of the building."

"And so you married her?"

He shook his head once. "She disappeared. I thought her family had sent her away, or killed her, to keep her from me, even with the marriage contract finalized. But then, a few weeks ago, I heard of a woman in the City of Sighs who cared for the dying and I heard the rumors of a Spire Witch. I thought...I hoped...but no. Now it's clear the Tetrarch is also keeping track of the rumors and wants to kill any Spire Witch that appears in the city. If my love had come to the City of Sighs, she would have been dead at his hands long ago. You cannot be her."

Niffrel wanted to run away and hide somewhere even more difficult to find than this crawlspace. The Tetrarch himself wanted her dead? That was why his guards had been in the slum? They were looking for her?

But even more unsettling, this was the man her parents would have married her to? This was her fiancé? "What...what was the name of this woman?" she asked.

"Niffrel voh-Jurah," he said. "She has haunted my dreams since I first saw her. Now I can finally join her in death. Flee, little Wren. You can't be found with my body."

"Where can I flee so that the Tetrarch can't find me?" she asked helplessly.

He moaned but did not answer.

Niffrel's eyes were caught by his silver chain, which had snaked out of his robes and lay over his left shoulder. Attached to it was a pendant of pink crystal.

It looked like the kind of material the spires were made of. Niffrel put her hand on it and it immediately glowed brightly enough to light up her small crawlspace.

A warm tingle ran up her hand to her spine and made her tremble slightly. It felt good to hold this crystal. It felt right.

The crystal itself seemed to pull at her, cozening her mind with calmness but also a sense of purpose. She was supposed to do something.

But what?

She stared at the crystal for a few moments, but her mind was blank. Then an old ditty sung by the children of the City of Sighs came to mind. *Crystal lights, crystal nights, always warm, something bright. Sickness flees, darkness weaves, every morn, sadness leaves.*

Sickness flees? Could she do something for this man with the crystal?

She held the crystal tightly in one hand and pressed down on the bleeding man with the other. What could it hurt? The pool of blood seeping out of Temmeril's robes and staining the dry ground beneath him gave witness that his time was running out.

If Temmeril had a chance, it would be through her, with the help of Mita.

Niffrel tried to empty her mind. Another vision of the spires rose before her eyes, accompanied by a strange scratching at the inside of her ribcage. That she had felt before, when she touched the spires, but had never understood it. Now it seemed like something inside her wanted to get out, to find expression. And the crystal could help her do that. She grabbed on to the feeling and felt it pulse warmly throughout her entire body.

The feeling rose in her chest and seemed to flow into her arms. Without thinking about it, she placed the hand holding the crystal on the wound and put her other hand on top. Now a desperate, almost joyous, rush of power flung itself through every nerve and ran down her arms and into the crystal.

All around her, the pink glow spread outward from her crawlspace, into the street beyond.

Temmeril jerked but made no sound.

As the feeling ebbed, Niffrel relaxed. She felt weak, but whole and at peace.

She looked down at Temmeril. He stared at her with wondering eyes.

"What did you do?"

She blushed and shook her head. "I don't know. I just remembered something, and hoped I could help. I used the stone you wear."

Slowly, he sat up, though the effort made him shake. "My grandmother gave that to me. She said it was my inheritance from her grandmother, and that I should always wear it, and so I have. I thought it a mere memento." He felt his side where had had been stabbed. "But...I think...I think the wound is gone." His eyes were wide with wonder.

"But you still lost a lot of blood," she said.

The face of the owner of the building popped into her crawlspace. "Wren? What is going on? What was that light?"

Niffrel became aware of a commotion on the street.

"I think we need to go," she said. She turned to her friend. "Get everyone off the street! The Vanguard are hunting me and they will have seen that."

"The Vanguard!" The owner abruptly disappeared. Niffrel heard him running into his shop screeching to everyone that the Vanguard were nearby.

More commotion and the sounds of panic. The street would be full of frightened people looking for somewhere to lie low. That might confuse anyone chasing her and Temmeril for a short while. They needed to make good their escape now.

"Come," she said. She tugged on his arm. "We have to go now."

"I can't," he said. "I'm too weak."

Anger made her pull at him harder. "You'll come now!"

The aristocrat in him arose out of the wounded man he had been and his eyes flashed with anger as well as fear. "Who are you to order me?"

She should probably say something humble, something he would expect from a street urchin, or something simply to soothe his rising panic. But she had no patience to spare. "I think I'm the Spire Witch who just healed you and doesn't want to see you cut down. Now get up and let's get out of here."

Niffrel half-dragged, half-cajoled Temmeril out of the crawlspace. By now, the street outside was darkening as the sun dropped down behind the western mountains. Unexpectedly, the spires in the City of Sighs glowed a bright pink, just like the stone in her hand.

"What is this? The spires have never all been the same color before," said Temmeril.

"I don't know; I'm just worried they're pointing out our location to the Tetrarch's men," said Niffrel. "We need to be gone."

"I agree, but I'm afraid I'll have to lean on you."

"Stop talking and start doing."

Temmeril threw his arm around her shoulders and, true to his word, he leaned on her. Heavily. Niffrel's knees nearly buckled, but she managed to stay upright. They wouldn't get far if he was no stronger than this. He could barely hold up his own weight, let alone move.

But the street was already filling up with blue-clad men with the peacock symbol on their chests. One of them sported a gold badge on his shoulder.

"You, there. Spire Witch!"

Niffrel realized she and Temmeril weren't getting away. She removed his arm and let him slump wearily to the street. She stood between him and the gold-badged guard.

"Call me what you like," she said. "What crime do you accuse me of?"

"Being a Spire Witch is enough," he growled. "The Tetrarch's orders are to cut any witch down without trial. The sickness you carry could infect everyone in the city."

"Sickness?" That was Temmeril. He didn't stand, but he raised his head to look at the guard. "Captain, what sickness is this? Spire Witches never spread illness."

"It's...it's what they do," said the captain. "They heal others by taking the sickness into themselves, and then dispersing it to the city. They are evil! Better for one person to die than for the city to do so."

"Is that what the Tetrarch believes, or just what he tells you?"

asked Temmeril. "It sounds like nonsense to me. I was stabbed by one of your men, and now I am whole. She healed me."

"It doesn't matter how the magic does what it does," said the captain. "Only that she needs to die to protect the city."

"To protect the Tetrarch," said Niffrel. "He keeps his throne by killing anyone he thinks could oppose him, when no one even has! It never occurred to me to question his right to the throne, until now. But if he murders innocents, he isn't worthy of either Mita's mercy or Zuran's prosperity."

"He is the Tetrarch," said the Captain. He raised a hand and pointed to his men, then to Niffrel. "Kill her."

The men nearest him stepped forward, then stopped. "Captain..." said one in a hoarse voice.

Niffrel turned around. Behind her stood the citizens of the City of Sighs. The father of the boy she'd cradled after a horse had kicked him in the head. A woman she'd given a few coins to so she could feed her children just one more day. A child who had once given her a pretty rock in exchange for a blessing from Mita. The shop owner. The boy who'd watched out for her when she was at the restaurant with Temmeril. Her eyes filled with tears. She could not hope that they would actually fight the Vanguard, but they were standing up.

"There needs to be more healing around here, not less," said the owner of her crawlspace. He stepped out of the crowd. "You'd kill Wren because she can heal? What have you done in your life that's worth a tenth of what she's done?"

The Captain's hand tightened on the handle of his knife. "It doesn't matter. I have orders. Anyone suspected of being a Spire Witch dies. The rest of you can die, too, for all I care."

"Do you have enough men to bring us all down?" More people stepped out of the side alleys. A young man who had been thought to be dying, but who had recovered while Niffrel sat vigil with him. The beggar from earlier this afternoon. An old woman who had once given Niffrel a coin for a meal. And more. Dozens more. People she had helped over the past six years. A sob escaped her. She was grateful, but also terrified. These were her friends. They couldn't put themselves at so much risk for her. They shouldn't.

The spires nearby pulsed their pink glow and the street began dancing with light.

"I don't think Mita will appreciate you striking down her servant," said Temmeril mildly. But despite the calmness in his voice, Niffrel heard desperation. Let the spires glow if they wanted; all the captain had to do was order her death again and nothing else mattered. Slum dwellers had no recourse, no court system to help, nothing in the laws to protect them from the Tetrarch's men.

But Niffrel was not a street urchin. She was unused to thinking of herself as one of the elite, but she was. She could claim that now, and it might buy them time.

"Captain," she said in her old upper class accent, "I am Niffrel voh-Jurah. You may not execute me without a signed order from the Tetrarch himself, giving my name and spelling out the manner of my execution. If you cut me down here and now, my family will have your head by tomorrow's dawn."

That was probably a lie. Her family had surely disowned her the moment they discovered her missing and the marriage contract inconveniently already signed with a bride unavailable. On the other hand, they cared for their reputation, and for a lowly captain to have killed a Jurah on the street would not sit well with her father.

"My family, too," said Temmeril. "She is my fiancée. The marriage contract may be years old but it is still valid, and it is signed by my father and hers."

Niffrel looked down at him. He stared back up at her in awe, as if surprised he hadn't seen the highborn girl under the street urchin. Well, she looked a lot different now, and he had believed her dead. She had gone from a long-haired girl with silken dresses, jewels at her wrists and neck, and bells in her hair, to a shaven gaunt creature in a homespun robe who could pass for a boy. She looked nothing like the woman she had been raised to be.

But she was exactly who she was supposed to be. Spire Witch. Now that she'd gotten used to the term, she liked it.

The captain licked his lips nervously and looked at the growing crowd. "I have no guarantee you are who you say you are," he said.

"I vouch for her," said Temmeril, "and I am Temmeril noh-Vanji. This is my affianced bride. You threaten her at your own peril."

Niffrel's heart was in her throat. Would the captain stand down? He didn't have to. She counted six men with him, but he no doubt had others behind her, or stationed in the alleys. If he gave the word, there would be a massacre. The people on the street might be armed with short knives, but they weren't trained and would get in each other's way. The guards would cut them down despite their best efforts to defend themselves and her.

The pink radiance danced across everyone's faces. The crowd muttered in appreciation; the captain swatted at the lights as if they were flies. The disgust on his face grew stronger.

He was going to order the massacre.

"Run!" shouted Niffrel in desperation. She grabbed one of Temmeril's arms; the shop owner grabbed the other. People on the street ran in between Niffrel and the captain as the captain screamed something unintelligible at the top of his lungs.

Niffrel could not stop to wonder what he said. She had to get Temmeril away. Uncaring as to which direction she picked, she simply ran forward and hoped there was some way to get Temmeril to safety. The pink sparkles in the air got stronger and brighter.

The more the lights danced around her head, the more she realized she was approaching a spire. Suddenly, she realized that had been her destination all along. The spire called to the stone in her hand. They were one and the same. All the spires communicated with each other. Every piece knew every other piece.

They were family. They were community. And they welcomed Niffrel into their midst. She rushed toward the spire, unmindful of the filth in her way or the half-destroyed adobe barrier that had meekly separated the spire from the people in the city for far too long.

The people around her seemed to sense what was needed. Together, they pulled at the crumbling adobe and ripped the barrier down. Young people, old people, children carrying younger children, they all crowded around the spire and touched it.

And it glowed with a brightness almost like the sun except it did not hurt to look at it. Instead, it was welcoming, dazzling.

Niffrel turned to face whatever fate awaited. She felt the

pulsing of the spire light in her bones and knew it was hers, not to control, but to consult, and to beseech. The spires were not her servants; she was theirs.

She reached out her hands.

"No, Wren..Niffrel!" shouted Temmeril.

But she couldn't pay attention to him right now. The captain and his men stood in front of her.

"The city has been waiting for Mita's return," she said in a voice her own, but oddly not. "You will not stop this. Nor can any Tetrarch."

Niffrel spread out her hands and the power of the spires flowed through her into the street, into the buildings, into the very soil beneath her sandaled feet.

Grass and trees sprang up from nothing, or perhaps from long-dormant seeds that had been waiting for just such an invitation. Joyous songbirds flew into the square and circled the people with song. The feral cats of the streets came to watch, eyes narrowed, tails cocked in approval.

It was as if the city had held its breath, and now was reborn.

The people around her gazed at everything in awe, but without fear. The pink light gave a sense of rightness that Niffrel could not explain, and did not need to. Everyone could sense it. The city had been missing some part of its soul for centuries, and this was the first step toward reclaiming that.

The light died, leaving the street full of new trees and flowers blooming from every alley. The birds alit in the branches of the trees and kept up their song.

The captain's men had fled, but he stood his ground. Or, no, he was being held. Tiny vines had emerged from the soil and wrapped themselves around his ankles. His eyes were full of fear.

"Go," said Niffrel. She gestured and the vines released him. "No one will harm you."

The man fled.

Niffrel turned. Temmeril had managed to stand on his own. He stared at the spire, then at her, in awe. "Mita?" he asked quietly.

She laughed. "No, I'm just Wren. Niffrel, if you prefer. Your fiancée. Maybe your wife. Maybe not. We are going to have to get to know each other before I agree to marry you."

"I think...I think that would be wise," he said as he surveyed the changes in the street. "Everyone in the city is going to have to get used to the idea of Mita's return, and what it means for there to be a Spire Witch again."

"Witches," she said. "I can't be the only one. The barriers that keep people from the spires need to be torn down. We need to find the others and then figure out how we can begin healing this city."

Temmeril looked up at the spire. "I can almost hear it speaking to me."

"Maybe you're a Spire Witch, too," she said. "Maybe that's why your grandmother gave you the stone. Maybe that's why you noticed a silly girl who was nice to donkeys all those years ago."

"Maybe," he said. "Or maybe they will speak to me just because I love you."

"We'll have time to discuss that," she said as she grabbed his elbow. He might be standing, but he was shaking so hard she had no doubt he'd fall without assistance.

A donkey watched them from the shadows. Niffrel gestured to it and it came to her. "Here, get on this beast," she said to Temmeril. "We'll go to your father's house. We'll talk. And we'll see what tomorrow holds for us."

"Yes," said Temmeril. "But I already know what it holds for me." He kept a hand on her shoulder and his eyes did not look away from her as they made their way down the street toward the Vanji household.

Niffrel didn't look back; the spire was in her mind now and she could see it more clearly in her thoughts than she could with her eyes. She would find others like herself and the city could be, would be, healed. For the first time in her life, she realized exactly what she was to do.

Thank you, Mita. The city is yours again.

And yours, came an answer. *And everyone's.*

Niffrel smiled.

THE GHOST OF LADY REI

by Adam Stemple

Love comes in many shades and flavors, from the tremulous awakening of two young people to the abiding loyalty between teacher and student. Each of them has the power to transform, to condemn, or to redeem the lives of those it touches.

Adam Stemple (adamstemple.com) is a Minneapolis writer, musician, web designer, and poker player. He has written eight novels and one poker book. Ken'ichi and Master Shichiro appeared in two stories previous to this one in the now sadly defunct Paradox Magazine.

All arts are the same, Master Shichiro once told me.

"To the samurai," he said, "Archery and swordsmanship, calligraphy and flower arranging—they are all one."

I never saw any relation between skewering an enemy from a thousand *shaku* away and placing cherry blossoms in a bowl, but I was merely a servant—and a rather poor one, at that. If Master Shichiro said that cutting someone in half was the same as writing them a letter, who was I to argue? A good servant—or even a foolish one who wishes to be good—doesn't argue. An even better servant emulates their master when they can, and brings honor to their master's house. As I was useless with anything more lethal than a thrown rock, and doubted my ability to put pen to parchment or peony in a pot, I decided to try my hand at another artistic pursuit: poetry.

My relative success in this endeavor was a source of much discussion at Master Shichiro's hilltop abode.

> *despite tender care*
> *spring's promise is unfulfilled*
> *rabbit tracks in the garden*

141

"What does that even mean, Ken'ichi?" Master Shichiro said, emerging from the house. "If you're going to torture me with your doggerel, the least you could do is make it comprehensible." He was a large and imposing man already, and with a topknot adding to his height, a thick beard and wild eyebrows framing fierce eyes, and two big swords at his waist, he was positively terrifying.

The fact that I'd seen him kill more than two dozen men didn't make him any less so.

I stared down at the ruins of my cucumber patch. "It means we will have to go into town for vegetables."

"No matter." He held up a scroll that had been messengered up the hill to us that morning. "We go to Lord Yoshimune's castle anyway."

"Excellent news!" I said aloud. My thoughts, however, were less charitable. Our last visit to the castle had been when Lord Yoshimune had ordered my master to kill himself. Their relationship had been a bit strained since then.

This could hardly be worse, I thought, looking up at Master Shichiro and trying to read his expression. I was utterly unsuccessful. *Could it?*

Master Shichiro tucked the summons into his belt next to his katana and oversized *wakazashi*.

"Come, Ken'ichi. We shan't keep the *daimyo* waiting."

My mind was a-roil with too many memories of our last visit to Yoshimune's castle to appreciate the beautiful trip down the mountain. Summer was just past its peak, and the flowers bloomed all the harder for the sight of so many of their brethren rotting on the ground. The air was redolent with their perfumes—and the smell of their decay, as well—a reminder that life is so sweet in part because it ends so quickly. Or, if you were *bushi* like my master, a reminder that death was the only moment all men shared, and how you faced it was what made you samurai.

Dark thoughts for a pleasant afternoon, and I decided to shake them off with conversation. Besides, philosophy was not a luxury afforded to someone of my station.

"Master Shichiro," I asked, looking up at him astride his horse.

"What do you think Lord Yoshimune wants of us?"

Master Shichiro frowned down at me. "Us? I am certain he wants nothing of you, Ken'ichi."

"Apologies, My Lone and Solitary Master. What does he want of *you*?"

Master Shichiro smiled as if at a small and very stupid child. "Me? Why, he wants nothing of me."

Sometimes—and I admit this only now, as my former master is long departed and his legacy quite secure enough to withstand an old poet's minor slighting—sometimes talking to Master Shichiro was akin to pounding one's head against a giant boulder.

"Of course, Most Repetitious Master. Forgive my denseness, but if he wants nothing of either you, me, or the both of us together, why has he summoned us?"

I believe nothing made Master Shichiro happier than confounding me with his predictions. When he explained them later, he would always make the predictions appear as if even the basest fool would have reached the same conclusion if he'd but thought about it for a moment or two. But every time one of his seemingly random utterances came to pass—and they always did—it would seem like magic.

So it came as a complete surprise—and as no surprise at all—when he cackled aloud and said, "He has summoned us to travel to Edo, of course!"

Then he urged his horse to a trot, signaling the end of the conversation.

One could say that Edo, the capital of our entire island nation, is bigger than Mizushita, the capitol of Ichiwaza, Lord Yoshimune's small, bog-ridden province. One could also say that an eagle is bigger than a hummingbird. Both statements are true, but neither captures the true essence and enormous nature of the gulf between the two. The basest streets in Edo were wider than the main thoroughfare of Mizushita. The hovels were as large as Lord Yoshimune's palace. The Great Lord Tokugawa's castle—when we could see it through the press of people—looked big enough to need an entire city's worth of soldiers just to man the walls. And unlike Mizushita, where you could go days without seeing anyone wearing a sword, Edo's streets and taverns were brimming with samurai. Some wore the colors of local Lords, while some, like Master Shichiro, wore the colors of Lords from the outer provinces. Still others were lordless Ronin wearing no colors at all. And whether serving or not, every samurai was eager to either make a name or increase the luster of the name they already owned, and none of them brooked even a hint of disrespect from anyone. It took the merest sideways glance to cause swords to be drawn, and a split-second and a flash of steel later, one man was dead and another's reputation was one kill greater.

Dusty streets were a common problem in every city, but it was said that Edo's air was the best in the empire: samurai blood kept the streets wetted down no matter how dry the weather.

Master Shichiro took us to the market, where merchants hawked their wares for coin, and singing collectors chanted "let's exchange, let's exchange," as they offered children cheap toys for bits of scrap metal. I was hungry after our long journey and was relieved that we headed quickly to the riverside fish market and its many food stalls. The smell of tempura made my mouth water and I gobbled down the fish Master Shichiro purchased for us so quickly that I couldn't have said whether it was eel or icefish.

"I don't care how many times you explain it, My Wise Yet Impenetrable Master, I do not understand it," I said, pausing briefly to lick the last of the tempura oils off my fingertips. "How could you possibly have known we would be sent here?"

I waved my arm to indicate the massive expanse of Edo, forgetting how crowded the market was and almost struck a man in the nose. Luckily, the nose—a rather large example of the species—belonged to an umbrella repairer, not an itinerant samurai, and I was frowned at severely instead of immediately missing an important appendage.

"Ah, Ken-ichi-san," Master Shichiro said, his voice muffled by a mouthful of fried fish. "It is as simple as seeing the sun going down and knowing that night will soon be upon us." He took another large bite of his fish which rendered his next few sentences incomprehensible.

"I am sorry, Master, I did not catch that."

He swallowed noisily and pointed to a stall selling *kasutera*, indicating I should buy some. I grabbed two pieces of the spongy cake, and Master Shichiro flipped the gap-toothed merchant a coin. "I said that a mystery is merely a road that one only knows the beginning of. One must travel that road until it ends. If it ends prematurely, than you must have missed a fork and you backtrack until you find it. Go down enough roads and one will inevitably lead you to your answer. Try it."

I thought hard for a moment while he took a big bite of his *kasutera*. "Well, our road began with Yoshimune's summons..."

"No, idiot," Master Shichiro interrupted. "Try your cake."

I took an obedient bite. It was an excellent example of the barbarian delicacy, eggy and light and honeyed to just the right sweetness.

"Mmmmrph," I said loquaciously. And, "Mmm, mmrph, mmm."

"Ahh," smiled Master Shichiro. "finally some true poetry from you." He ate the last small bite of his piece and went on. "Yoshimune would not summon me to his castle for anything except a truly dire emergency. And anything of that nature in Ichizawa, I would have had word of long before we heard from the *daimyo*." As head *yoriki* of Ichizawa, it was up to Master Shichiro to investigate all crimes in the province and if necessary, capture those responsible and bring them to the *daimyo* for punishment.

"Mmmrph," I said, still speaking of my cake. The second bite had been even better than the first, and I was dismayed to see that I had only a very few bites left.

"Indeed," Master Shichiro answered me. "So, it was a summons from someone else, and furthermore a personage who could order a full *daimyo* to do his bidding. And to do it in secrecy as well." Master Shichiro pushed through a crowd of merchants that partially blocked our way, and they bowed and thanked him for the sharp blows that he delivered to their shoulders and arms with his sheathed sword. The gratitude was heartfelt; another samurai may not have kept his sword sheathed. "The secrecy was the final bend in the mystery's path. Nothing inspires secrecy and intrigue like an Imperial Court. The summons must have come from Edo. And Edo is as likely to come to Ichizawa as the Emperor is to bow to Ken'ichi-san. Therefore, Ichizawa must go to

Edo."

With a truly great sadness in my heart, I took the last bite of *kasutera*. "As always, My Most Perspicacious Master, I am awed by your reasoning. One question remains unanswered, however. Who are we to meet in the Bountiful Lotus Offering tonight at the Hour of the Rat?"

Master Shichiro stopped in the street and a young messenger who had been traveling far too fast and a little too close bumped into him. The youth blanched to seashell white when he saw the giant samurai he had accidentally struck and fell fully prostate on the ground, groveling with hopeless abandon.

Master Shichiro ignored him. "Ken'ichi, if I had not seen the briefest moments of insight and intelligence from you in the past, I would believe you had been dropped on your head as a child. Repeatedly." He let out a world-weary sigh. "Who in Edo would know the name of a lowly *yoriki* in the glorified piece of swampland that is Ichizawa?"

The answer came to me at once, and suddenly I, too, suspected maternal clumsiness in my past.

"Of course, Lord Mat—"

"Do not say the name!" Master Shichiro snapped, then lowered his voice. "He has done much to keep both his involvement and our arrival a secret. It would not do for one servant's flapping lips to undo in a moment what took a great lord weeks to accomplish."

I nodded mutely, but said the name to myself. *Lord Matsudaira.* Not only was he the only great lord I could think of who had visited Ichizawa, he also had reason to know my master's name:

Master Shichiro had solved his niece's murder.

Despite his constant attempts to educate me in his methods, I could never claim to have half the intuitive mind that Master Shichiro had. Still, upon arrival at the Bountiful Lotus Offering I could state with some authority that the *izakaya* was not a regular destination for Lord Matsudaira. Or his samurai. Or his samurai's servants. Or the peasants who removed his servants' night soil.

The Bountiful Lotus Offering was a midden heap. Only a midden heap smelled better. The light of the weak lantern hanging by the tattered curtains that led inside showed a half-dozen drunks sleeping in their own excrement outside. This seemed to be the source of most of the smell. However, the walls were stained with filth as well, some of it certainly more excrement, some of it possibly dirt, and lots of it probably blood from those who forgot their manners inside the establishment and had to get "helped" outside. Though what form of manners were to be expected in a place such as this, I had no idea.

Master Shichiro stepped over a snoring drunk and marched forward. I stopped him with a touch on his arm. "Master," I said.

He stopped and raised an eyebrow at me.

"Forgive me for even suggesting that I walk before you in anything. But I must go instead of you."

"And why is that?"

"Because of what you said earlier about secrecy. Please forgive me again, but you are a well-bred, highly-trained, gigantic samurai who would stand out in that establishment like a barbarian in a Shinto temple."

Master Shichiro frowned, thinking. "I could remove my swords."

Shaking my head, I said, "Then you would be a well-bred, highly-trained, gigantic samurai who had no swords. An even bigger curiosity."

Master Shichiro smiled. "A *naked* barbarian in a Shinto temple?"

"Precisely, My Master of the Disturbing Image."

"Hmmmm." He thought a moment, then pointed to a thin alley across from the Bountiful Lotus Offering where the overhanging roofs of the buildings on either side kept even the moon's thin light from penetrating the darkness. In a neighborhood thick with deeply shadowed alleys, this was a paragon of the type. "I shall wait for you there. I shall be..." He paused for a moment of uncharacteristic confusion. "What do the ninja do when they sneak about in the night?"

I thought about that. "I believe they skulk, Master."

"Yes, that is the word. *Skulk*. I shall be in that alley *skulking*."

"For the first, and most likely, only time, My Forthright Master."

He nodded, and moving swiftly for a man of his size, entered the alley to skulk. Trying desperately not to breathe through my nose, I stepped over the drunks and up to the tavern door. Touching the curtains with as little of my hands as possible, I pushed them aside and stepped only partially into the Bountiful Lotus Offering, which seemed every bit as dark as the alley that Master Shichiro waited in. And though I was certain that at most times there would be a great deal of skulking going on in here, tonight the three denizens desperate or stupid enough to drink in the Bountiful Lotus Offering were gathered in plain view around a person who was obviously a great deal of both. Because if she wasn't both desperate *and* stupid, a delicate young woman with fine features, a thin waist, and a neck like a preening swan would never find herself in the Bountiful Lotus Offering.

"Careful, Takeshi," said one of the three men, a ragged man with a tumor nearly the exact shape of a peony blossoming on his left cheek. "She might have a dagger tucked up under her kimono."

"Well," said a hunched creature, presumably Takeshi, who wore a *kosode* worn so thin as to be nearly as invisible as his conscience. "I'll just have to check then, won't I?" He flicked the girl's garments up and despite the many layers of kimono she was wearing, I turned away before seeing anything untoward.

I turned back as she shrieked in fear. "Ruffians!" she cried, "I am under the protection of..."

Strangely, she stopped herself before saying the name of her protector, but the third man in the group, idly scratching his nose with a worn stump where his left hand used to be, explained that it hardly mattered. "Even if a lord's protecting you, he probably has a price for our death, anyway."

Takeshi cackled and reached for the girl's skirts again. "Add another maiden to our account."

I stood frozen in horror. *If a lord's protection means nothing,* I thought, *what good is the assistance of a lowly servant? Especially one who is roughly as deadly as your average field sparrow?*

"Better let me do a full and proper search," the man with the tumor said.

And if I signal Master Shichiro to help, our attempts at secrecy will be destroyed, and he may not get here in time anyway!

The girl waved at Takeshi's hand in a vain attempt to ward him off, and he laughed, serving her a hard slap across the face.

"Quiet now, little one," he said. The oddly gentle words turned foul in his mouth.

The sharp crack of palm on cheek finally snapped me out of my terrified reverie.

Even the field sparrow is dangerous, I thought, *when faced with insects.*

They were brave and contemptuous words, but they brought me no closer to rescuing the girl, who I was suddenly certain was the person I was to meet. *Why else would she be in this pile of night soil?* This, too, was a rare and brilliant thought, but also failed miserably to effect a rescue. But despite all that, I was buoyed to be thinking once more instead of worrying uselessly. I had been in tough scrapes before. Admittedly, the scrapes were most often entered into with Master Shichiro right beside, or more usually, a fair distance in front of me, which tended to skew the odds of victory sharply in my favor. Still, I was able to think quickly in dire situations, and this was no exception. No sooner had I regained my bravery, then a plan came to me and I strode fully and manfully into the room.

"Katsumi, you murderous bitch!" I shouted. Four heads swiveled to look at me. "I've caught you at last." I waved my arms in a parting-the-seas motion. "Step aside, boys. She's as deadly as she is beautiful."

The three men moved back, but only a little. "Deadly?" the one-handed man said. "Her?"

"As the plague."

They moved away a little more, yet still looked ready to put my claims to the test by attacking the girl, and me besides. But the girl was as quick-witted as a spirit-fox. And not a half-bad actress, either. In a pure venom tone completely different from the scared girl's voice of mere moments ago, she hissed at me, "Ichiro! I almost had these fools. Like I had your five men in Takayama." That moved them back. They scuttled like roaches to put chairs and tables between them and "Katsumi."

"Let's take this fight outside before any innocents get hurt." *Not that there are any innocents but her in this viper's pit.*

The Bountiful Lotus Offering's owner, who hadn't seen fit to interfere with a proposed rape and murder, chose that time to pipe up from behind the bar. "Yes, take it outside. I won't stand any fighting in my place."

"Quiet, coward," the girl said. "I can kill you before he reaches me."

No response came to that, and the girl began moving toward me. I backed out the curtains as if cautious of her approaching too close, keeping my eyes on the now four men who watched us carefully. Then she was outside and the curtain fell back into place quickly. Her eyes, so fierce when she was playacting in the tavern, were now wide-eyed with fright once more. A red mark, evidence of the blow she'd received, was forming on her cheek.

"Thank you, great lord," she said.

Happy to play the great lord for a moment, I gave her my deepest bow. "Ken'ichi, Beautiful One, and it is my honor to serve." I would have said more, perhaps, but I had forgotten a key thing about the nature of most rogues and scoundrels the world over: they may be unwilling to *fight* in a great battle, but they will almost always want to *watch* one. The girl's three attackers and the tavern-keeper as well piled out of the *izakaya* in time to see me bow and offer my service.

"Hey," said Takeshi dimly. "They're not fighting."

"What *are* they doing?" said the one with the tumor.

The one-handed man, who seemed the ripest vegetable in a rather raw bunch, made several intuitive leaps and shouted a remarkably intelligent order:

"Get them!"

I answered with an even more intelligent order to both the girl and my feet:

"Run!"

Grabbing the girl's hand, I set word to deed and sprinted toward the dark alley across the way. She was light and swift and leapt over the drunks with ease. I was neither light nor particularly swift, but I ran far faster scared than our pursuers did angry, and we entered the alley well ahead of them. They failed to follow up the one-handed man's sole intelligent thought with a second one: the reasonable assumption that one shouldn't follow unknown persons who most likely want to do you harm into a deeply shadowed alley in a neighborhood that turned a deaf ear toward screams in the dead of night.

Master Shichiro's katana was a two-body blade, and he nearly proved it on the first pursuers into the alley, cutting the first clean in half and severing the spine of the second with a single stroke. The third's mouth continued to emit a fearful screeching for the briefest of moments after the head it belonged to was separated from the body. The tavern-keeper was a fat little man and the slowest of the bunch. He was bringing up the rear and when he saw the three men cut down, managed to turn his bulk around and start to waddle swiftly back to the relative safety of the Bountiful Lotus Offering. Master Shichiro needed only two long steps forward to grab him by the hair.

"Do we need to ask him anything, Ken'ichi?" he said.

It was a grim question, especially since the tavern keeper hadn't taken a direct part in the attack. But Master Shichiro hadn't asked me whether he was good or bad or my opinion on the relative value of human life. He'd asked me a direct question, and I gave him a direct answer.

"No," I said.

To my master's credit, he did not make the man suffer. Three strokes in less than a second: two across the back that split the kidneys and snapped the spine and a final one to the neck that left another head leaking into the now blood-muddy street. Master Shichiro looked to the door of the tavern to see if anyone else would exit it, then peered left and right before flicking the blood off his blade with a practiced motion.

"You are Master Shichiro," said the girl. Apparently she knew who she was supposed to meet. "And I am Hitomi. I have much to tell you."

"I imagine so," Master Shichiro said, sheathing his blade. He glanced around again. "I suggest we move to somewhere a bit more palatable for the telling."

"My mistress's brother told me to meet you here," she said.

Master Shichiro nodded. "And you have done so. Follow me now."

The girl hesitated. "He was insistent on this location."

I decided to speak up. "The alley is close enough to the

Bountiful Lotus Offering. If the purpose of the order was to meet Master Shichiro secretly and obtain his services, then you have accomplished half of it and must come with us to accomplish the other half." I put voice to something I had always known but somehow never had the words to speak until now. "Blind obedience is a credit to the servant; clear-eyed obedience is a credit to the master."

She looked at me straight on then and I began to see why her parents had named her Hitomi. Her eyes were wide and clear, the pupils a magnificent dark brown with flecks of magenta that shone even in the near absence of light in the alley's mouth. "And you are obviously of great credit to your master, kind Ken'ichi."

My parents should have named me Usagi, for I was transfixed by her gaze like a rabbit by a snake. Some useless part of my brain thought, *I wonder if I should get snakes to guard my cucumber patch*, while another, and possibly even more useless part thought, *she is the most beautiful creature that has ever spoken to me.*

I heard Master Shichiro chuckle, though whether at my discomfiture at her kind words, or the thought of me being clear-eyed, I did not know. He said, "Neither of you will be a credit to anybody if we do not move away from here now."

I nodded, shaken out of my second reverie of the evening. "Back down the alley, Master?"

"No," he said. "I find that skulking does not suit me."

"I would never have thought that it would, My Straightforward Master."

As we crossed over the drunks a third time, all still sleeping soundly despite the chases and murders going on around them, I gave Hitomi my hand for assistance. Judging by how easily she had leapt over them earlier, she had no need for my hand, but took it anyway. And not until after we were past the human obstacles, not until after the area improved and the streets were less strewn with possible obstructions, not until we finally sat with Master Shichiro at a fine table near a fire and discussed our plans in Edo, not until then did she let it go.

"So," said Master Shichiro, "I shall recap." He pushed his sake toward me and I surreptitiously moved it out of his reach. Master

Shichiro couldn't fully enjoy his sake while working. Unless that work happened to be singing loudly and off-key, vomiting noodles into strangers' laps, and arguing with tavern keepers about the quality of rice wine that he had obviously stopped tasting hours before. But there was hardly ever any call for that type of work.

"Lord Matsudaira has one son, and he had two daughters," Master Shichiro pointed at Hitomi, "One of which is your mistress." Hitomi nodded. I noted how the firelight made her black hair shine like the iridescent feathers of a blackbird. "The other has been murdered. Lord Matsudaira, knowing I solved his niece's murder, wishes me to solve this one as well."

He raised one eyebrow at Hitomi and she nodded again. "Yes, great lord."

"That is very interesting," he said, and reached for where his sake used to be. He sighed as his hand closed on empty air and said, "But it is also mostly horse droppings."

Hitomi gasped. "Lord?" she said, her voice quavering.

"Matsudaira has no reason to like me, and even less reason to call on me. His resources for solving a murder here are far greater than I could bring to the task. The only reason to call upon me is that I am completely unknown in Edo. Therefore, Matsudaira wants this investigation hidden from the emperor and the Imperial court, and I do not believe I can be involved with that deception." He stood abruptly. "Ken'ichi, we must go."

I've thought back to the next few moments a thousand times, always thinking that if I had said nothing, and just followed my master's orders like a good servant should, than at least one tragedy would have been averted. But the cost to avoid that tragedy, as great as it was to me personally, would have been paid with the lives of personages of far greater station than me, and so, in the end, there is no doubt that I did the right thing.

This knowledge has never been of any comfort to me.

"Hitomi," I said, trying her name out in my mouth and liking the taste of it. "I am sure you're not supposed to tell us any more. But I am also certain you know more than you are telling. My master will leave now if he knows no more, and your mistress's sister will go unavenged." She looked at me wide-eyed and trusting, but scared to overstep her bounds. "To be clear-eyed is occasionally to see more than your master or mistress. Are you sent here to recite a script, or to enlist our help?"

She looked from me to the towering Master Shichiro. When her eyes met mine once more she seemed to have come to a decision. "Lady Ryoko was kidnapped. She was murdered after Lord Matsudaira refused to do what they wanted."

Master Shichiro gave me an almost imperceptible nod and sat back down. "Who are they?"

"That's what we don't know," Hitomi said. "And Lord Matsudaira cannot tell anyone what they want him to do, or he will be ordered to kill himself."

"What do they want him to do?"

She spoke to Master Shichiro, but looked to me to answer when she was done. "I am entrusting you not just with my mistress's life, but with the life of her father. And more besides."

I nodded gravely. "You will find no one more worthy of that trust than Master Shichiro."

"And you, Ken'ichi-san?"

I smiled. "I am as trustworthy as my master tells me to be."

She tried to smile at that, but was too nervous about what she was about to reveal. Speaking in a voice so low I could barely hear her, she said, "They want him to kill the emperor."

"We must warn him!" I cried, and tried to leap to my feet, but Master Shichiro's hand on my shoulder held me down.

"Quiet, Ken'ichi. The emperor is in no danger." Master Shichiro took his hand away. "Lord Matsudaira would commit *sepukku* before he would harm even the emperor's dog. That is why the need for secrecy. If word of this plot reaches the emperor or the shogun, the easiest way to prevent it would be the suicide of Matsudaira."

"His sword was in his hand when his wife came up with the idea of contacting you," Hitomi said. "She had already lost a daughter. She didn't want to lose a husband, too." She stopped for a moment, looking shy. "There's something more, but I don't know if it means anything."

"Go on."

"Lord Matsudaira has been traveling a lot lately. And I have heard his wife crying late in the evening when he is gone."

"Indeed," Master Shichiro said. Then he was quiet and I recognized his deep thinking face: eyes looking up and to the right, brows drawn together, bottom lip protruding ever so slightly. Hitomi opened her mouth to say more, but I laid my hand on her arm and shook my head once. Her arm was surprisingly warm. I felt the heat of it all the way into my chest, and I suddenly had trouble breathing.

Master Shichiro broke his silence. "I have it." He frowned. "It is imperfect and unfinished and more will die than I would care for, but I have no time for anything more elegant. With every passing moment the likelihood of Lord Matsudaira ending the matter with his small sword increases." He stood and held his hand out to Hitomi. "Come, child. We must talk. Ken'ichi, procure us rooms for three nights."

"Rooms, Most Frugal Master?" I accentuated the plural.

He nodded solemnly. "Yes, you will have your own room on this occasion."

Accustomed as I was to sharing a room with a man who snores like a Ussuri brown bear, this was a rare pleasure. I didn't dare ask what I had done to deserve my own room for fear he would reconsider.

"I shall be working the rest of the evening," Master Shichiro said, nodding toward his abandoned sake. "Don't let that go to waste." Then he led Hitomi from the tavern.

After arranging the accommodations, I sat and sipped the sake, thinking about Hitomi. I decided that to describe her neck as swan-like was ridiculous. She was far more graceful than a swan. Her hair was spun silk died as dark as midnight, her eyes dark jewels mined from exotic barbarian lands. Her waist was slender as a reed, her feet dainty as the sweet scent of cherry blossoms in bloom.

She was also walking back into the tavern.

"Ken'ichi-san?" she called.

Perhaps it was the sight of her again, or more likely the sake, but I swayed a bit as I stood to motion her over to the table. As she came forward, I noticed her eyes were red and her pale cheeks were blotched with more than just the mark where she'd been struck. She had been crying.

"Hitomi," I said, "Whatever is the matter, Master Shichiro will fix it."

"He cannot," she said. "It is not broken. It is as it must be."

I motioned her to sit but she stayed on her feet. "I do not understand."

She shook her head. "Oh, Ken'ichi, there is nothing for those like us to understand. Lord Matsudaira has left Edo at Shichiro-sama's suggestion. Whoever has threatened Rei will know he intends not to kill the emperor."

"But Master Shichiro will protect her." It wasn't a question.

"He said it is very difficult to protect the hare if the fox is willing to die to reach it." She sighed and looked at me with an odd look in her eye. "But he has protected her already."

I didn't know what she meant by that, and she didn't give me much time to think about it.

"Ken'ichi," she said, reaching out to me, "show me the room your master gave you."

I took her hand in mine. It shook a little. Or maybe it was my hand that shook, it was hard to tell. We didn't speak again till we reached the room. It was a plain room, merely a mattress and an oil lamp, but even if it was appointed like the palace of the Chinese emperors, I would have had eyes only for Hitomi.

I tried to say her name, but she put her hand to my lips. With her other hand on my chest, she pushed me fully into the room. My legs were weak and buckled at the edge of the low mattress. I tried to turn my fall into a graceful sitting down, but was only partially successful. I looked up at Hitomi, her features in shadows—all but her dark eyes that reflected the lamp's light back at me.

"Ken'ichi," she breathed slowly, seeming to test each syllable. Then she went on in a rush of words. "I would like you to court me properly. I would like to serve you tea. I would like you to take me with you when you return to Ichiwaza and I would enter your master's service and help you grow cucumbers in your garden. I would like—"

She interrupted herself with a small cry.

"Hitomi," I said, starting to stand, but she dropped to her knees before me. Our faces were at the same level, separated by a mere hand's-breadth. One tear glowed gold on her cheek.

"But I cannot have any of those things," she said. "For I only have an hour before I must return and do my duty."

She leaned forward then and I went to meet her, and our lips touched in a hesitant kiss. She tasted of honey and cherry blossoms, and I must have tasted like sake and six days of travel, but she didn't seem to mind, and the kiss soon turned fierce. Our tongues found each other, and our hands, too, and when we broke apart for a moment her face was flushed with more than a slap and a recent crying bout.

"Give me this hour, Ken'ichi," she said, "and ask nothing more."

I could refuse her nothing at that moment, of course, but still, I balked at this instruction. "But I do ask for more," I said. "I want it all: the tea, the courting, the help in the garden. I want tonight, tomorrow night, and all the nights to come. I have never—"

"Stop! Say no more, my sweet Ken'ichi-san." She was openly weeping all of a sudden, and I couldn't understand why. I would have asked, but her lips were entangled with mine again, and I couldn't speak. After that second kiss, I tried once again to profess my devotion, but she said, "One hour, Ken'ichi, and nothing more." Her voice was so fierce that I finally relented and gave myself over to that one beautiful hour.

The kimono is a complex garment of many layers and folds. Normally, it takes a fair amount of time to drape it correctly over one's body and tie it into place. I swore it took Hitomi mere moments to get dressed after our hour was up.

"I will ask again, you know," I said, smiling up at her. We'd filled the whole hour with all a man and woman could do to please each other, and still had time to lie in pleasant torpor and gently caress each others' faces. "For tea and the rest."

She looked down on me, and this time allowed herself a small smile instead of a tear. "You will not have the chance, my dear Ken'ichi. But always remember, I am clear-eyed and obedient, and I did my duty."

I had no idea what she meant at that time, and momentarily wondered if I should be angry. "This was doing your duty?"

"No! This moment was only for me."

I smiled at that, even as I disagreed with her: "And for me as well, dear Hitomi."

She knelt down and gave me one last kiss, lingering for a moment with her hand on my cheek, then she was gone in a rustle of silk, leaving behind only a slight scent of honey and cherry blossoms.

They killed Lord Matsudaira's daughter, the Lady Rei, the next afternoon.

She was walking through the market with Hitomi by her side. I tried to get Hitomi's attention, but she wore a strange hooded garment that obscured her features and she kept her eyes to the ground like a good servant. Master Shichiro kept us a fair distance away, as well.

"If the Lady Rei is in such danger," I asked Master Shichiro, "why doesn't she travel in a curtained palanquin? With armed guards."

"Quiet, Ken'ichi," Master Shichiro said. "You distract me from my search for assassins."

"Why doesn't she stay at the castle? Why aren't we closer? How can we—"

"Ken'ichi!" he hissed, and I shut my mouth and allowed him to search for assassins undistracted.

And he did seem to be searching: eyes constantly moving, watching the crowds, the shadows, the rooftops. But when the attempt came, it was I who saw the black-cowled man draw a bow from atop the roof of a noodle house opposite the market.

"Master," I cried, pointing at the bowman. Then, "Hitomi! Watch out!"

Hitomi dove into the shadows, but Lady Rei merely turned slowly and looked at me. I never saw her face, because I was darting forward and looking up, trying to get myself between the incoming arrow and its target. I was surprised Master Shichiro hadn't beaten me to it, but I *had* spotted the assassin first. I doubt it would have mattered if he'd passed me by; I was still yards away when the arrow entered Lady Rei's breast. I pushed forward to see what could be done to save her, but Master Shichiro grabbed me by the shoulder.

"It is too late, Ken'ichi. Let us be after the bowman!"

I turned and followed him as he ran over, around, and practically through the people who crowded the street. We crashed into the noodle house and wooden bowls clattered to the ground as startled diners jumped out of the way. I was right behind him on the stairs, and practically in his shadow when we burst onto the roof. We needn't have hurried however, the assassin lay in a widening puddle of his own blood, his throat cut.

Master Shichiro examined the body while I looked over the roof's edge to the scene below. Matsudaira samurai were flooding the street now, gathering round the body and facing outward to guard it. Seemed a bit late to me, but I was no samurai and could hardly be expected to understand the intricacies of martial behavior and the way of the *bushi*.

"Ken'ichi, come look at this."

I tore myself away from the sight of Hitomi holding Lady Rei's hand gently as she died, and went to look at the dead assassin.

"What do you see, Ken'ichi?" Master Shichiro asked.

I looked down at the dead assassin. He was swathed in dark clothing and wore a black hood. His bow was a few feet from his left hand, and a dagger with a bloody blade lay just next to his right.

"I see a ninja who, after performing one of the most cowardly deeds even his kind are known for, has taken his own life to avoid capture."

Master Shichiro nodded. "Exactly as you were meant to. Look again."

I did as instructed, but saw nothing different. One dead ninja.

"He didn't kill himself?"

Master Shichiro shook his head. "There is no sign of a struggle, and clearly he was a martial man. He would have made at least some defense."

"So he did kill himself." Then it hit me. "Why would a ninja kill himself?"

"Precisely. The few moments it took us to get up here would have been plenty for even a moderately skilled magic man to fade into the populace." Master Shichiro nudged at the ninja's jacket with his toe. "And the only weapons he carries are the bow and the dagger. Usually it's a miracle these men can walk without clanking, their garments are so filled with weapons."

"So he's not a ninja?"

"No." Master Shichiro scratched his ample beard. "But still, it was a skilled shot. One arrow, one kill. He was a samurai."

"So he was following his lord's orders."

Master Shichiro looked at me, smiling. "Very good, Ken'ichi. We'll make a *bushi* of you yet."

"Oh, I doubt that very much, My Very Hopeful Master."

He frowned. "I was joking, of course."

"Without a doubt." I looked at the dead, disguised samurai. "But who is his lord?"

Master Shichiro flipped the man over with his foot. Peered at his back for a moment before stepping over to me and looking over the edge. Matsudaira samurai had loaded Lady Rei into a palanquin and were escorting it out of the square.

If they'd done that in the first place, I thought, maybe this would have turned out differently.

"I do not know who his lord is," Master Shichiro. "But I shall find out tomorrow."

"Tomorrow? Why not tonight?"

"Because tonight we must prepare for the funeral."

When Master Shichiro said we, he must have meant just him, because he tucked me into my room and left for the evening. I tried to spend the time thinking about Lady Rei's murder, but instead I spent it dreaming about Hitomi until my heart ached with the missing of her. The hours crept at a snail's pace and every time I thought it must surely almost be morning I would look outside and see that the moon had barely moved. I hadn't thought it was possible to miss someone so completely that you had known for just over a day. I even had the decidedly uncharitable thought that now that Lady Rei was dead, surely Hitomi's duty to her was done and she could come back to Ichizawa with me.

I forced myself to ignore that nagging thought and thought instead of Hitomi's eyes and her soft neck and the little bird cries she let out as we had made love. I also thought about how different she had seemed in the market before her mistress's death. How differently she moved when she was fully in the role of servant. Much stiffer than her normally graceful self.

She must be a very devoted servant, I thought, *to give herself so completely.*

I was humbled by it, and swore to be a better servant to Master Shichiro, if only to make myself more worthy of her love.

Love.

It was the first time I had used the word, but I had no doubt that love is what we both felt. I would tell her of my love the very next time I saw her, and I was certain any and all obstacles to our being together would be instantly swept away. I finally fell asleep with that happy thought on my mind, and slept soundly through the night until the sun was alarmingly high in the sky and I heard Master Shichiro calling my name.

"Coming, Most Forgiving Master," I said, scrambling into my clothes and rushing to attend to him. He was already up and had dressed himself, which should have sounded an alarm somewhere in me. But I was still too full of the sweet, unending promise of new love to sense danger anywhere.

Master Shichiro rode to the funeral in silence, obviously deep in thought. I walked beside him, thinking about nothing but dark eyes and darker hair, and the smell of honey and cherry blossoms. My mood lasted until we reached the temple.

It was a rich one, and tall, stretching high into the Edo sky, the swooping corners of each story making it look like the whole building was poised to take flight. The gate was as wide as Master Shichiro's whole house, the statues guarding it nearly two stories in height. Inside the ceilings stretched nearly as high, and light from the high windows died in thick incense smoke before it reached the floor. There were buddhas and bodhisattvas tucked into every shady corner, and you couldn't look in any direction without the serene eyes of Siddhartha gazing upon you. It was an impressive space, especially dressed up as it was for the funeral of a lady of one of the exalted families.

No funeral is a happy affair, and one for a noble girl who had died horribly and too soon was a tragic scene indeed. Grim-faced samurai in the colors of the Matsudaira guarded every entrance, their hands never far from their sword hilts. They filled the temple as well, eyeing all but the closest family members with suspicion. Of those, there were few left: the mother sat weeping uncontrollably, while her sole remaining offspring, Lord Matsudaira's son, Daiki, held her hand and whispered consoling words in her ear. Of Lord Matsudaira himself, there was no sign.

Neither was there any hint of Hitomi. I was distressed by this in the extreme, as I wanted—no, I *needed* to tell her of this great love that was now practically bursting from me. But I had never buried my master and had no idea what terrible stress she was under, or what her duties required of her.

Oh, by the ever increasing myriad Shinto deities, I thought, *what if she intends to kill herself to be with her mistress?*

This thought consumed me as the funeral began. I swiveled my head back and forth throughout, trying to get a glimpse of her.

I shall stop her if she tries, though the whole might of Matsudaira stands against me!

Obviously, I wasn't thinking clearly.

The Soto Zen priest completed his first *sutra* and began Lady Rei's ordination as a Zen monk so she could receive the rest of the funeral rites. He gave her a new Buddhist name, a *kaimyo*, so that people could say her name without raising her ghost.

Just at this moment, a loud murmur began at the back of the temple. I turned to see what was happening. A girl, clothed all in funereal white except for a red patch of fabric over her heart, was moving slowly through the crowd. Her hair hung long and tangled about her shoulders, obscuring her features, and her arms were extended weakly before her, elbows tucked close to the body. The finger of one hand pointed loosely forward.

"Master," I said, tugging at his sleeve.

He shrugged me off and continued staring intently at the bereaved mother and her son.

I turned back to the figure now, and for just a moment my heart leapt.

Hitomi!

But the girl in white continued forward, and the resemblance dropped away, leaving a very different girl coming toward me. She was beautiful like Hitomi, if a bit older, and she shared her fine features and graceful swan's neck. But her nose was a bit more hawkish, and her eyes not so dark, and she was far more lordly in carriage. Swathed in white silks so long they trailed well past her feet, it appeared almost as if she were floating. The patch over her heart wasn't fabric at all, but a thick red stain, and finally it hit me:

"Master Shichiro, it is Lady Rei!"

For indeed it must be, or at least her ghost, this floating *yurei* with a mark on her breast where the death blow had struck.

Apparently, the *kaimyo* had failed to keep her ghost from walking.

"I know," Master Shichiro said. Which was an awfully strange thing for him to say since he hadn't so much as glanced over his shoulder. But I was too busy staring at the first ghost I had ever seen for that small oddity to strike a chord.

Lady Rei's ghost came ever forward in a slow drift, and the crowd parted before her. She was close enough now that I could see her face through the tangle of her hair; there was a deathly white cast to her features that matched her silks. Pointing at her mother and brother, she said one word in a low, rasping, groan:

"Why?"

I turned away from her to look where she pointed and saw her mother drop to her knees. She was weeping and crying and saying something over and over but too softly to make out.

"Why?" the ghost repeated.

Her brother, Daiki, dropped to his knees as well, his face nearly as white as his sister's ghost. He began gibbering incomprehensively as well, but louder than his mother. She increased in volume to compete, and soon they were both near shouting. But not a word could be understood.

I couldn't be sure, but as I turned back to look at the ghost, I swore I saw her glance at Master Shichiro...

...who gave her a small nod and a 'keep going' gesture with his left hand.

I stared at him until he hissed, "Put your eyes back in your head and pay attention, Ken'ichi. The murderer is about to be uncovered."

"Why?" the ghost inquired again.

Only it's not a ghost, is it? I thought to myself. *Master Shichiro has engineered this entire scene to make the murderer reveal himself.*

I turned back to Lady Rei in her ghostly garb, now eager to see what would come next.

"Why?" she asked a third time. This only served to goad the two grievers to increased volume and incomprehensibility. Finally, sounding a bit aggravated, she shouted, "What?"

I thought this petulant outburst might tip them to her fully corporeal status, but they were too far gone with fear, grief, or guilt to notice the ghost's change in tone.

Daiki stopped shouting immediately; the mother, a moment later. She spoke first, however.

"I am sorry," she said.

"I am sorry, as well," Daiki said.

Lady Rei said nothing. This time I was certain she glanced at Master Shichiro imploringly.

Apparently, he felt it was time to help out a bit, and asked, "Sorry for what?" He spoke in a tone that always got me to obey, and it didn't fail on the two Matsudairas.

"I should have protected you," Rei's mother responded immediately. "I should have demanded your father protect you. I should have let him kill himself. I—"

"Enough," Rei shouted. She turned to her brother.

I hadn't thought it possible, but he turned even whiter.

"I, too, am sorry," he said.

"Why?"

"I...I should have protected you."

"Why?"

"I...I am sorry," he was visibly shaking now.

"Why?" Rei shouted. I winced as she stepped forward, audibly stomping her foot on the floor. Any pretense of ghostly floating had to be gone after that, but Daiki was close to the breaking point and again, didn't notice.

"I...I..." he stuttered.

His mother, tears finally dry, looked over at her son. "Why do you hesitate? Tell her why you are sorry, Daiki-san."

I could almost see something break inside him. Something that he'd held close and hard for too long finally gave way, leaving him bereft of even the terrible anger that must have driven him.

"I did it for you, mother," he said in a voice that would not have been audible if everyone in the temple hadn't been holding their breath and straining to hear.

"What?" she spat at him. "Did what for me?"

Daiki looked up at her and I saw the anger return to war with sadness and regret in his eyes. Anger won.

"Father dishonored you!" he shouted. "I heard you crying when he was gone. I followed him." He stood now, hand on his sword hilt. I don't think he knew he'd put it there. "I saw him with her!"

Daiki's mother shook her head in disbelief. "No. This was a plot...this was to kill..."

"No, mother. I only wanted him gone." Daiki took a step toward her, but she stepped away. "He would have left you. And how long before his new wife had a son, and we had nothing?" He was pleading now, but his mother was shaking her head silently, her mouth frozen in a small O. "With him gone, we would have everything, and you could be happy again."

His mother looked about to speak, but suddenly Daiki was engulfed by a screaming, white-robed whirlwind as Lady Rei leaped at him, fingernails gouging great furrows in his cheeks. He didn't try to defend himself, even hugged her closer. Her fingers found his eyes, and I thought she would blind him, but Master Shichiro chose that moment to intervene, striding forward and pulling her off with one great arm. She struggled fruitlessly in his arm for a moment, before going nearly lifeless. He beckoned me near, and laid her into my arms. Anger and sadness fled her features as unconsciousness set in, and I could see how much the emotions aged her. She was much younger than I'd first thought, and again, I was struck by her resemblance to Hitomi.

I looked up from Lady Rei to see Daiki dropping to his knees. His cheeks bled ferociously, and he looked as if he were weeping rivers of blood.

"And now you have nothing," his mother said quietly, speaking obviously to Daiki but looking instead at the large golden Buddha behind the altar. "Not even your honor."

Daiki said nothing. Instead, it was Master Shichiro who spoke.

"You can regain your honor, Daiki-sama," he said.

Daiki looked up at Master Shichiro like a man dying of thirst looks at a rain cloud. Still on his knees, he took his sheathed katana from his sash and slid it across to Master Shichiro. Then he drew his wakazashi.

Master Shichiro retrieved the katana and walked behind the kneeling Daiki. "I won't let you suffer," he said.

Daiki shook his head. "I must," he said, then jammed the short sword into his belly.

Master Shichiro acquiesced to the Lord Daiki's wishes and didn't take his head until the middle of the third cut.

"Amazing, Most Knowledgeable of Masters," I said. "When did you know it was the son who had done it?"

Three Matsudaira swordsmen who must have been involved in the plot had pulled their own *wakazashis* and followed their young lord into death. The remaining samurai cleared the crowd out after the suicides, and now the only living people in the temple were a few warriors, Master Shichiro, myself, and Lady Rei, who lay unconscious still, with her head in my lap. Her pulse was strong however, and her mother was off searching for water to revive her.

"When I heard that 'they' wanted Lord Matsudaira to kill the emperor, I knew that the plot had to be to kill Matsudaira himself." Master Shichiro snorted. "Anyone who knew that loyal old bull would know that he would kill himself a thousand times before harming the emperor. That narrowed it down. And then I knew it was Daiki at the *izakaya,* when we were told that it was he who had set the meeting there. No Matsudaira wife has ever given birth to an idiot. And even an idiot would know that a meeting in that...*establishment*...was more likely to end in all the participants dead than in vital information being passed along." He glanced back at the front of the temple briefly, almost fearfully. Then spoke quickly. "Come we must go."

"I hate to contradict you, My Hasty Master, but I have a lap full of exalted family daughter here, and if I let her head hit the temple floor, mine might follow swiftly after." Master Shichiro frowned down at me but said nothing. "Why the elaborate ruse though?" I asked.

For some reason, he glanced again toward the front of the temple where not-Rei's body lay. "Time was of the essence.

Matsudaira would not be put off indefinitely, and I didn't know when they would make an attempt on Lady Rei. And it is difficult to accuse someone of murder when they can order you to kill yourself. Far better that they reveal it of their own accord."

It was easy to see the truth in that. I would have asked him more about his methods, but Lady Rei's eyelids fluttered and opened. She looked up at me, and much to my surprise, called me by name.

"Ken'ichi," she said. Her voice no longer rasped. "Hitomi spoke of you." She reached a hand up and brushed my cheek. "You do have very kind eyes."

"Hitomi!" I cried. "How could I forget? Master Shichiro! Mistress Rei! I know this comes at a terrible time with the tragedy in your family, and I am a terrible, unfeeling fool to ask. But Master Shichiro is in a hurry to leave, so I have no time to wait for a better moment." I took a big heaving breath and dove back in. "I wish only one thing in this world and that is that you please allow this most humble, most undeserving servant to take the beautiful Hitomi with us when we leave here. I would like her to..." I had plenty of breath left and a lot more to say, but I trailed off; Rei's eyes had left mine and turned to Master Shichiro with what looked like pure hopelessness in them.

"He does not know?" she said.

Master Shichiro gave a great heaving sigh. "I had hoped he never would."

"Know what?" I asked, but neither Master Shichiro nor Lady Rei answered. They didn't need to. I was struck by a memory of Hitomi as I'd last seen her, her skin still aglow from our lovemaking, telling me, "I am clear-eyed and obedient, and I did my duty."

I suddenly realized how very stupid I had been.

"You planned it all along, didn't you?" I said to Master Shichiro.

He didn't say anything. Didn't deny it either.

I slipped out from under Lady Rei. Stood up. Started walking hesitantly toward the front of the temple and the altar where the body lay. I didn't want to reach my destination and have my fears be proven, yet one step followed another like the inevitable flow of the Shinano to the sea. Eventually, I reached the body.

She wore a plain white kimono and a single square of white silk lay over her face. As I pulled the silk back, I thought I could smell cherry blossoms and honey over the incense the priests burned to cover the stench of death.

Even knowing what I would find, the sight of Hitomi's face pale and stiff with death drove a dagger into my stomach. I felt the pain of it as surely as Lord Daiki and his three men had such a short time ago.

Hitomi! I screamed silently. I was too shocked to speak, too hurt to move. All I could do was stare down at her frozen features—so recognizable, and yet so different, death robbing her of everything that gave her features form.

Hitomi. I tried to say it out loud this time, but I only let out a kind of animal growl. I was beyond anger, beyond speech. I turned away, a wounded creature ready to lash out, and I saw that Master Shichiro had managed to come up behind me unawares. Here then was a target for my rage. He had planned the act. He had executed it. He had killed Hitomi as surely as if he'd fired the bow himself. Without thinking, I howled and leaped at him like a rabid wolf, aiming to bury my very teeth in his neck.

He fired a short, two-fingered strike to just below my breastbone that knocked all the breath out of me. I didn't even see him move, but he was suddenly behind me with a giant forearm locked across my windpipe.

I couldn't even whimper as he choked me unconscious.

I woke tied to the back of Master Shichiro's horse like a spare pack.

"Ah, you're awake," he said, turning in the saddle to look at me as I squirmed.

I tried to answer him, but discovered I was gagged. My hands were also bound. I glared up at him uselessly.

"Let us talk," he said.

He stopped the horse, and loosening the rope that held me to it, lowered me gently to the ground, till I was kneeling on the road. Then he led the horse a short distance away to some sweet grasses and let it graze.

Deal with one dumb animal before the next, I thought.

The sun was getting low in the sky and we were a fair distance out of Edo, judging by the lack of traffic on the road. I must have been out for some time. Master Shichiro returned and stood looking down at me for a long moment. Then he sighed and sat down in the dust of the road, crossing his long legs underneath him like a giant, bearded Buddha.

"Ken'ichi," he began, then stopped. "Ken'ichi-san. I had to restrain you, and do so quickly." He waved vaguely at the ropes binding me. "If I hadn't, you would have said or done something foolish that would have forced me to kill you."

I couldn't argue with that. As I recalled, when he'd struck me I'd been in the middle of the extremely foolish act of attacking Takawara Shichiro, master of blade and bow, a samurai who had fought with Ieyasu in the Summer Campaign and killed Sanada Yukimura at the battle of Tennoji, and defeated at least twenty-five men of varying ranks in arranged duels, and Buddha-knows how many others in duels less formal.

"I had hurt you badly already, when I had no wish to," Master Shichiro said. "I certainly didn't want to make the wound mortal."

He paused and looked off into the distance for more than a few moments. I could neither speak, nor even move about effectively, so I waited patiently for him to speak again. It wasn't as if I had another option.

"Do you know what samurai means?" he finally asked. It was a strange question, and one he didn't wait for me to answer. "To serve. I am as bound to my master as you are to yours, perhaps even more so. It brought me no joy to hurt you so, but I had no choice. My duty was clear, and I performed it as best I could. As did Hitomi."

The sound of her name pierced me again, and I struggled uselessly at my bonds. Master Shichiro watched impassively until I subsided, then went on as if there had been no pause.

"And I will tell you one more thing before I untie you. And then if you wish to suicide by attacking me, I won't deny you. You have earned a warrior's death if you wish it." He grabbed my gaze and held it, searching for I know not what. He must have found it, however, because he gave me a firm nod and continued.

"Hitomi volunteered," he said. "Yes, it was my design, and yes, it involved the death of a servant. But I did not choose her. I saw the looks you gave each other, and had no wish to cause you grief. I argued for someone else in the household. Hitomi argued for herself. She was of a similar build. She knew the Lady Rei's habits. And she was a talented actress. We didn't know when or where the attack would come, and we needed to be ready. We had to act soon, and Hitomi, through impassioned and reasoned arguments, convinced me to send her to her death."

Master Shichiro unfolded to his full height, then stepped behind me. I heard a blade hiss out of its sheath and felt the bonds confining my wrists fall away. I didn't move.

"She asked only for an hour with you," he said directly into my ear, "and then she returned to do her duty."

He moved back around in front of me, *wakizashi* still naked in his hand. He lay it on the ground before me, point out toward him. Then he took three steps back and did something I had never seen him do before, and would never see again: he bowed to me. A warrior's bow, his eyes never leaving mine. Then, with one hand on the hilt of his katana, he awaited my next action.

Still kneeling, I worked the gag out of my mouth clumsily, my hands numb from being bound. I opened and closed them a few times to work the blood back in. Then I picked up the *wakazashi*. It was a Yasutsugu blade, part of a *daisho* given to Master Shichiro by Iyeyasu himself after the Siege of Osaka Castle and was barely shorter than Master Shichiro's katana, making it seem a full sword in my smaller hands. I tried to hold it as I had seen many samurai hold their weapons: right hand up under the guard, left further down with space between them. It didn't feel natural, but there was no reason it should have; I was no swordsman.

I took a step forward.

Master Shichiro shifted into a defensive stance, bending a knee slightly and pointing his toe in a different direction. He would do me the honor of pretending I had a chance of putting up a fight.

I took another step forward. There were cherry trees by the road, and I tried to sniff them in the light breeze. All I smelled was the dust of the road, and the horse musk that clung to my clothes.

A third step forward and I was within reach of Master Shichiro's blade. He had no need to draw yet, of course; he was swift as a snake, and could respond to any attack I launched from this distance with ease. If I wanted to defeat him, he would have to be much closer. And asleep. And as firmly tied as I had just been.

To serve, I thought. I served Master Shichiro, he served his *daimyo*, his *daimyo* served the exalted families, and they served the emperor. The emperor served only the gods. And who did the Gods serve? Buddha, himself, most likely, who may very well serve someone as well. I had a vision of the Buddha's wheel of life as a wheel of service, and the whole balance of the world required that we all serve in turn.

In the end, I thought, *we are all subservient to each other.*

It made no sense, but neither did it feel wrong.

I took a half-step forward and dropped to my knees, holding my hands palm up with the *wakizashi* laid across them.

"Clear-eyed and obedient," I said. "She listened to me and died. I will listen and live."

Master Shichiro took the sword form my hands and sheathed it. "A good choice, Ken-ichi-san."

I shook my head. "If I had a choice, my blood would be darkening this road even now." I looked back toward Edo, smoke from its many fires blending with the evening clouds. Some of the smoke was sure to be from Hitomi's cremation. "I have no wish to live without her."

"But you do your duty."

Nodding, I said, "I do my duty."

Master Shichiro reached down and pulled me to my feet. I walked behind him over to the horse, who made only a little protest as Master Shichiro yanked him from his grazing.

"I find I am cramped from riding," he said. "I shall walk beside you for a time, Ken-ichi-san." He glanced down the road. "There. We'll walk beneath the cherry trees for a bit. Perhaps the smell of cherry blossoms will clear the air between us."

"And honey," I said softly.

"What?"

"Nothing, Master," I lied, and walked not beside him, but two paces behind, as befitted my station. He set a pace that wouldn't tax either of us and we settled into a smooth rhythm. The cherry blossoms still on the trees were indeed sweet, but I had trouble smelling anything but the decay of those that lay dying on the ground.

It was a long walk home.

THE BOTTLE

by Steven Harper

Steven Harper is the pen name for Steven Piziks, a name no one can reliably spell or pronounce. He sold his first short story way back in 1990, and his keyboard has been clattering ever since. So far, he's written fifty-some stories and twenty-some novels, including *The Silent Empire* series and *The Clockwork Empire* steampunk series. He's also written movie novelizations and books based on *Star Trek, Battlestar Galactica,* and *The Blacklist.*

Steven also teaches English in southeast Michigan, where he lives with his husband and son. When not writing, he plays the folk harp, tries to stick to weight-lifting, and spends more time on-line than is probably good for him. Visit his web page at http://www.stevenpiziks.com.

The fire had already engulfed the first and second floors by the time Raymond got there with the bottle. Flames poured from several windows and greedily licked their way up to the fourth floor. Heat flowed over Raymond like liquid metal, and heavy, pungent smoke stung his eyes. People shouted and screamed from the upper stories. Women in mutton-sleeve blouses frantically fluttered white handkerchiefs like dove's wings, and men wildly waved dark bowler hats. Another group of people huddled at the edge of the roof, clearly afraid their choices would soon be to burn alive or risk a seven-story jump to the street.

Two different fire crews had already arrived, one with a horse-drawn water wagon, the other with a pump cart pulled by four husky firemen. Between them, the crews had more than a dozen firemen, and all of them were fighting with each other. Fists flew and flesh smacked flesh and angry shouts filled the hot, smoky air while the firemen figured out who was supposed to fight the fire. Another set of men had formed a bucket brigade and were gamely pouring water on the flames as best they could, but it was like emptying a teacup into a volcano. An older man leapt out of a fourth-story window and landed badly. Raymond heard the wet snap of bone, and the man lay still. A pair of women rushed to help him, but he was clearly dead.

Raymond ducked behind one of the fire wagons where he was out of sight and uncorked the bottle. It was a small glass bottle, green as a cat's eye, with nicks and scratches all over it. Orange smoke flowed from it, swirling and mingling with the smoke from the fire. It flowed around Raymond, and he could feel it sliding over his skin like a caress. At last, the smoke coalesced into the form of a man. The man was young, perhaps two years older than Raymond's twenty, and he was shockingly handsome. Coal-black hair worn a little long, with a bit of curl at the ends. Smooth, sun-darkened skin, fine as powdery sand. Thick, serious eyebrows. A long, clean jaw that accented his long, clean build. And electric blue eyes that contrasted sharply with his skin and hair. He wore the same fashionable beige sack coat and trousers Raymond did, with every crease razor-sharp and every line tailored to show off his build. A matching brown bowler topped his head. His name was Kaden. He pressed his fingertips together with a foxy smile Raymond still couldn't read, even after two months.

"I am here, master," Kaden said.

"Don't call me master," Raymond said, not for the first time. Another wave of heat rolled over them both. Where Kaden was swarthy, Raymond was fair. His red-blond hair matched the conflagration before them, and his eyes matched the cat-green bottle. The broad muscles of a laborer filled out the razor-edged sackcloth, and his hands were square and strong.

"What is your wish?" Kaden asked, and glanced at the burning building. "Ah. I can guess. Still, you have to ask. And you have to pay."

Brother Lawrence's voice slid through Raymond's head. *Only Lord Jesus can forgive your sins, but only you can stop from sinning.*

"I know," Raymond said. He took a long, thoughtful breath. "I wish—"

"Don't forget the rules," Kaden interrupted.

The breath rushed out. Always the stupid rules. They were unyielding and absolute, and Kaden had explained them in excruciating detail the first time Raymond had opened the bottle. Raymond had to make at least one wish every day. Raymond could never repeat a wish. Making the same wish with only minor changes, such as wishing for five dollars one day and six the next, counted as repeating. Raymond couldn't use a wish to get out of wishes.

And Raymond had to pay for every wish within the hour.

Unlike the djinn in the stories, Kaden also had a number of limitations. He couldn't create anything out of thin air, or wipe anything out of existence. He couldn't resurrect the dead, or drain the oceans, or move mountains. He couldn't undo previous wishes. And he couldn't give advice about what wish to make.

Fortunately, wishing for something beyond Kaden's capabilities didn't count as breaking a rule; it only meant Raymond had to make a different wish. This, at least, was a bit of good news. The day Raymond actually broke a rule, Kaden had said, Raymond's soul would belong to Kaden forever. Until then, there was no way to be rid of Kaden or the bottle. The fairy tales said a djinn was supposed to do anything you wanted, but having one at your beck and call had turned out more a curse than a blessing. After only two months, Raymond was starting to run out of wishes, and he was perversely a little glad that they had happened on a fire that could take up today's wish. Then he felt guilty about feeling glad, and then he felt glad about feeling guilty, and then he wondered how long this could go on.

"Waiting," Kaden said, and another man poised to jump from a window.

"I wish the fire was out," Raymond said.

"Yes, master." The air blurred and Kaden was gone. Fire brigade buckets snatched themselves from the people who carried them, sped into the building, and emptied their contents into the flames. The pumps on both fire carts sprang into action. The hoses flailed about like headless serpents, miraculously sending jets of water through the doors and windows. People gaped. Only Raymond, who knew what to look for, saw Kaden's impossibly fast form rushing from task to task. He watched with undisguised admiration, and then he crossed himself three times—once for the feelings Kaden roused in him and twice for the payment he knew Kaden was going to extract. Kaden moved so fast, there were a dozen, fifty, a hundred of him everywhere at once. In seconds, flying water overwhelmed the flames. They died hissing and vanished, leaving only charred, wet wood and steamy smoke hanging in the air.

A moment of silence marched by. Then the assembled people broke into a babble of cheers and excited conversation. The word *miracle* was repeated several times. The fire-fighters stopped fighting and boiled into the smoky building to help the residents outside. One lady became mysteriously faint and had to be carried out in a fireman's strong arms. Raymond envied her, and then stared at the ground, angry at himself for it.

You have to be a good boy, or no one will want you, said Brother Lawrence.

And then Kaden was standing beside Raymond with the fox's grin that always made Raymond a little breathless. He was sure that Kaden knew this fact, and that Kaden grinned all the more for it. The gesture created an oil slick of desire and guilt in Raymond's stomach.

Kaden raised an eyebrow, another trick only a djinn could do properly. "Satisfied, master?"

"Stop calling me that." Raymond poked him in the chest. The fine sackcloth glided under his fingertip.

Kaden cocked his head. "How many times am I going to call you master before you realize I won't ever stop calling you master? Master."

A matching smile quirked at Raymond's mouth. The guilt tried to hold it back, but the elated rush of ending the fire and Kaden's undeniable charm were impossible to resist, and the grin spread across his face.

"Ah! There it is." Kaden tapped Raymond's cheek, and Raymond felt the heat from his touch. "Like sunlight emerging from the clouds."

Raymond looked into the startling blue eyes for a long moment. His heart beat like a snare drum. The eyes drew him forward, and he leaned in a little. Kaden abruptly stepped back and fanned the air. The moment broke. "Or maybe it's the smoke. Do we have to stay here, master?"

Raymond flushed. Of course. Their arrangement was one of magic and convenience, payment and contrivance, nothing else. He was a fool and a pervert to think it could be otherwise. He glanced at the ruined building. "We should wander off now."

They strolled away from the ruined building and the increasingly large crowd around it, the bottle tucked under Raymond's arm. Raymond caught Kaden's eye, and a bit of laughter bubbled out of him. Kaden grinned back.

"You enjoyed that," Raymond observed.

"I did," Kaden confessed. "My other masters were always selfish when they wished. You...you think of others. And you let me stay outside that damned bottle. These last two months have been...refreshing. Freeing."

Raymond glanced down at the bottle. "How many masters have you had?"

"You're the third."

This caught Raymond off-guard. "You've had only two besides me?"

"I'm not as old as I look."

"What happened to the other two?" Raymond couldn't help asking.

"One made the same wish twice. The other didn't pay in time." Kaden gave a little cough. "They broke the rules, and their souls are mine."

The matter-of-fact tone chilled Raymond, and he lapsed into silence. Kaden noticed. "It's not always a bad thing to give up your soul," he said quietly.

"How could it be anything else?"

Kaden didn't answer. They kept walking. New York City was at her finest today under a crystal blue sky and gentle October sunshine that had yet to turn to winter's slushy torture. Sleek horses pulled buggies, carts, and open-topped carriages, and people in all styles of clothes bustled about. On Fifth Avenue, a newsboy waved a paper and shouted some new detail about the upcoming execution of Charles Guiteau, who had assassinated President

177

Garfield last year. Food shops and restaurants filled the air with a hundred smells of cooking and fresh produce, while the street tossed up scents of horse manure and animal sweat. In the distance, the graceful spires of the newly-completed St. Patrick's Cathedral speared the sky. It was a neighborhood Raymond knew well—he had spent his entire childhood in the diocese's orphanage, which now lay in the shadow of the new cathedral. He still lived here as a man, though his current quarters were rather more comfortable.

His corner came up. They could either turn down 56th Avenue toward home, or keep going up 5th toward the cathedral. Raymond pursed his lips and glanced in both directions, momentarily caught and undecided.

Kaden plucked at his arm. "You have to pay for that wish, or the penalty charge will tear your heart out. So to speak."

You have to be a good boy, or no one will want you, said Brother Lawrence.

And no one had wanted him. Raymond had lived in the orphanage from the day he'd appeared on the doorstep as an infant until the day he turned sixteen and Brother Lawrence had found him work as a groundskeeper in the parish cemetery. All his life, Raymond had watched other boys leave the orphanage with new parents, and all his life he had wondered why no one had wanted him. When his voice broke, longing for the other boys stole over him like his own shadow, and he began to suspect why no one wanted him. Raymond had never confessed this longing, not to any of the boys, not to Brother Lawrence, and not in the confessional. He wasn't a good boy, and the guilt made him heavy.

And then one day he had found a green bottle on a new grave in the cemetery, and everything had changed. Kaden did everything—*was* everything—Raymond had wished for, but in a twist handed to him from a perverse universe, Kaden was a slave who only enjoyed Raymond's company because he was required to. Given a chance, he would take Raymond's soul forever. And not one scrap of this changed the thrill Raymond felt whenever Kaden emerged from the bottle. Raymond both dreaded and delighted every time he loosed the stopper and made himself both enslaver and slave.

Raymond hung at the corner a moment longer. Guilt, always the guilt, towed him toward the cathedral, while other feelings towed him toward home.

"Where are we going, master?" Kaden touched Raymond's arm. Raymond's breath went away.

"Let's go home," Raymond said finally. "And stop calling me master."

Raymond's apartment in the Reilly Building took up the entire third floor. Plump, lavish furnishings with an Oriental aesthetic crowded the walls atop thick Persian rugs. A grandfather clock heavily filigreed in gold ticked in the corner of the parlor. It reported that Raymond had wished the fire out forty-five minutes ago. Time was running thin.

"Where, master?" Kaden's voice was low.

"Stop calling me master." Raymond turned down the flat's main corridor. Kaden followed. They passed a room piled with scarlet rubies, some as big as apples and oranges. Another room overflowed with jade jewelry in a jungle of grassy green. Yet another room was stacked with castles and towers of paper money, bank bills, and stock certificates. Each was the result of a wish, and now that the boy who had grown up in an orphanage in the shade of a cathedral had so much wealth, it all amounted to nothing.

Raymond's bedroom was more stark than the rest of the flat, done up in simple mahogany furniture. Dark silks covered the enormous bed, and a pair of high-backed leather armchairs set off a marble fireplace. Raymond took one of the chairs. Kaden stood over him, and Raymond felt the djinn's breath hot on his forehead. Kaden's heat crackled across Raymond's skin, and the air caught in his lungs. His groin grew tight, and he stared fixedly out the window. The steeple of St. Patrick's made a razor peak that scraped the heavens and weighed his guilt.

"Master?" Kaden said. His tone was brisk. Business-like.

Raymond replied, "Go."

With swift fingers, Kaden opened Raymond's trousers and slid them down. Raymond's erection came free, and Kaden's mouth engulfed it. Raymond gasped at the wet warmth and sliding sensation. He wanted to touch Kaden's head, run his fingers through his hair, but Raymond's fingers clutched instead at the arms of the chair, and he kept his eyes stubbornly pointed at the cathedral spire. He wasn't allowed to enjoy this. It was a transaction, a requirement to save his soul. But the soft, wet pressure that swirled around his hardness became a relentless pleasure that propelled him up and up under wave after wave. He tried to hold back, kept his eyes on the steeple to make the payment without the pleasure, but his body betrayed him. As Patrick's bells tolled the first of twelve solemn notes, Raymond cried aloud and the spending began. Raymond's body shook under the intensity, and his vision dimmed. The final toll fell silent, and Kaden took the final drop of essence in payment. Then there was that moment of tender, penitential pain as Kaden's tongue slid free.

"Thank you, master," Kaden said, rising. "You've paid in full. May I go?"

Raymond didn't want him to go. With shaking fingers, Raymond released the stopper on the bottle. Kaden dissolved into orange smoke that swirled a caress around Raymond before rushing into the bottle. Raymond pressed the stopper into place and sat back on the chair for a long time.

Eventually, he got up, pulled his clothes back into order, and wandered through the expansive flat. Glittering piles of treasure and countless stacks of bills looked back at him. The place was empty. Raymond was tremendously, impossibly wealthy, but a lifetime of poverty hadn't shown him what to do with any of it, especially when he had to make daily wishes that gave him more, more, and still more. He supposed he should join high society and find rich friends, but didn't know how to go about it, and as an orphan, he had no family. All he had was an apartment filled with worthless valuables.

His feet took him downstairs and outside. Tomorrow he would have to make another wish. In what was becoming an awful habit, Raymond started thinking ahead. He couldn't wish for more material goods—Kaden had brought him everything Raymond could think of. Kaden couldn't enchant anything, so there was no point in wishing for flying carpets or magic rings. Raymond had already traveled to Rome and learned from Kaden that he could only make one wish to go somewhere and another to return home.

Everything after that counted as a repeated wish, so more travel wishes weren't possible. Maybe he could wish to be less damned lonely.

The great bells tolled one o'clock, and Raymond found himself in front of St. Patrick's cathedral with Kaden's bottle in his hand. He had walked there while he was thinking. Raymond closed his eyes. He'd made his payment for the day. Perhaps it was time for other things.

The cathedral loomed over him, both stern and comforting. It was a Tuesday, so few parishioners were in evidence. As an orphan and altar boy, Raymond had spent countless hours in St. Patrick's, serving at the altar, sweeping the floors, and polishing the pews. As an adult, he had attended mass faithfully. But that had ended two months ago, when he had found Kaden's bottle.

As Raymond mounted the marble steps, the bottle trembled under his arm. The trembling grew more violent the closer Raymond came to the great doors. Raymond ducked into an alcove, checked against anyone seeing him, and popped the stopper. Kaden's smoke rushed out of it and he coalesced so close in the cramped alcove that his lips nearly touched Raymond's forehead. Despite their earlier activities, Raymond felt his body respond, right there on the cathedral steps.

"Where are you going, master?" Kaden demanded.

"I haven't been to... I haven't visited in a long time," Raymond said.

An agitated look crossed Kaden's face. "You know that the priests in this place have power of their own, and they don't like...my kind."

The first part of that statement hadn't occurred to Raymond. Still, if priests had the power to turn bread and wine into flesh and blood, they must be able to work other miracles. A strange hope flickered in him. He'd been coming for confession. Maybe he could leave with freedom.

"What kind is it that don't they like?" Raymond asked. "Djinn?"

"Anyone they can't control," Kaden said. "Anyone who breaks their rules."

That seemed a strange remark. Kaden himself was obsessed

181

with rules. "What rules did you break?" Raymond said.

Kaden's eyes took on a faraway look. "Djinn aren't born, you know. We're created. Cursed to serve."

"Cursed?" This was something Kaden had never mentioned before, and Raymond hadn't thought to ask. Until the djinn had said Raymond was only his third master, Raymond had assumed Kaden was ancient, like a fairy tale djinn. "What do you mean cursed?"

Kaden sat on the steps, his hands between his knees. "I was a man, just like you, until an Imam became angry at me. He said that since I corrupted the souls of others, I would now collect the souls of the corrupt, and since I had given payment to those I corrupted, I would now have to take it from them. I am as bound by that Imam as you are by these priests."

"What on earth did you do?"

Kaden leveled him a hard look. "The Imam caught me...giving payment to his eldest son while I drank from that bottle you're holding."

"Oh." Raymond flushed.

"That was two masters ago," Kaden finished. "My first master wanted to see America, so he wished himself here. He ran out of money, and without remembering he had already made a money wish, he wished for more. That ended him. I was trapped in my bottle for years before my second master opened it. He was more careful, and used me for nearly thirty years. Wicked, horrible man." Kaden shuddered. "But as he got older, he became careless. He became enamored with an attractive whore a third his age and wanted to impress her. After spending himself with her, he wished for me to give her a gift. I delivered to her a golden nightingale that sang when you twisted its tail. On our way home from her house, I reminded my master he would have to pay within the hour. When he was young, he would have done so easily, but now his hair was gray and his skin was as wrinkled as his member. He couldn't make two payments in one day, no matter how hard he—or I—tried. The hour expired, and so did he."

Raymond was flushing a deeper red than all the rubies in his treasure trove. "Uh... how did your bottle end up in the graveyard?"

"My master was walking through the graveyard when payment

came due," Kaden said. "I suspect the startled passers-by had an impact on his inability to pay."

"I...see." Raymond fought thoughts of Kaden extracting payment in the cemetery where Raymond used to work, or in Central Park, or on top of the Reilly Building, or...

To distract himself, Raymond asked, "What happened to the two souls?"

Kaden looked away. "They fed me. Still do. They make me stronger, and bind me more tightly to the bottle. It's not power that I ever asked for."

"Oh. Uh... I'm sorry," Raymond said.

"But now I have you for a master." Kaden smiled, looking almost shy. "I find myself hoping you make no mistakes. You are kind and have found ways to create good in this evil world." He touched Raymond's hand, and Raymond's heart made a feathery flutter in his chest. "Is it all right to hope we'll be together for a long time?"

The word *yes* was already trying to leap from Raymond's mouth. He caught and strangled it before it could get away. Having congress with a man was a sin. Using magic was a sin. Having daily congress with a man who used magic must be an abomination. But Raymond hadn't intended to do any of it. He had opened Kaden's flask in the cemetery out of curiosity, not remotely suspecting he was entering a contract. It couldn't be a sin if he was forced. God wouldn't damn him to an eternity of torture over something he hadn't actually done. Well, he had done it. Daily, in fact. But only to survive.

Except he'd also benefitted greatly from the bottle, and...he couldn't deny the pleasure Kaden brought his body—or his soul. With Kaden's confession came a flood of forbidden thoughts, thoughts of spending every day with Kaden, and going to bed with him every night. Of walks under a silver moon and a gold-drenched sun. Of Kaden's hard body and soft mouth. Of his wicked wit and slow smile. Those pleasures were great sins indeed.

"Look," Raymond said, "I just need to...talk with one of the priests for a little bit."

"About what?" Kaden pressed.

A little ire rose now. Kaden was only concerned about his

magic and extracting payment from Raymond. "It's none of your business," he said waspishly.

"Everything you do is my business," Kaden said. "You're my master."

"Stop calling me that!" Raymond snapped. "How many times—?"

"I'm your servant," Kaden said, "not your slave. We djinn have the power to fulfill wishes in whatever manner we want, did you know that? We can hold back information that the master might need. We can fulfill the wish so literally that it kills you—or makes you wish you were dead. When you wished for that roomful of rubies, I could have dropped them on your head. When you wished for the mountain of money, I could have stolen it from a hundred banks and led the police to you. When the time for payment arrives, I could stay silent so the deadline catches you unawares. But I do none of these things. Instead, I grant your wishes in the way you want."

"And why is that?" Raymond demanded.

Kaden leveled him another electric stare. "I have wishes of my own. You know what you do to me every time I perform for you."

The confession was too much. The black slick of guilt oozed over Raymond, suffocating him and stilling every other thought.

You have to be a good boy, or no one will want you.

He needed help, and he would take it. Now. Raymond yanked the stopper out of the bottle. "In."

The hurt look on Kaden's face before he was forced into smoke and sucked into the bottle stayed with Raymond even after he shoved the bottle into his coat pocket and heaved open the giant cathedral doors.

Walking through the great cathedral was strolling through a jewel box. Sparkling stained glass windows of saints and reformed sinners and Lord Jesus and Mother Mary cast shards of multi-colored light across every surface. The enormous nave, easily able to house a thousand or more parishioners, was supported by dual rows of pillars that set off the equally cavernous aisles that ran along the outer walls. But the space wasn't empty. It was filled with sumptuous hangings, intricate and life-like statues, spiral staircases that climbed to the vault, and two proud pipe organs raised brass fingers toward the vault. The second one, the biggest in America, had only recently been erected, and it took an entire team to work the bellows and play it properly. No one knew that Raymond had anonymously donated most of the funds to pay for its installation.

Raymond emerged from the narthex into the nave and automatically dipped his fingers into the holy water basin by the door and crossed himself. Perhaps forty or fifty people were wandering about the cathedral or kneeling at the pews or lighting candles at one of the many altars.

"Raymond, my boy!" Brother—now Father—Lawrence bustled down the aisle, his black surplice and cassock cut too narrow to billow properly. His gray hairline was receding now, and a spiderweb of wrinkles creased his long face, but he was the same man who had become Raymond's father in all but name during those years at the orphanage. Raymond felt a rush of affection along with the usual guilt. He also felt relief. Kaden had said that priests had power of their own, and Lawrence was the best priest Raymond knew, better even than the archbishop, as far as he was concerned. Raymond smiled and offered his hand.

"Father!" he said as they shook. "I'm glad you're here."

"Where else would I be?" Father Lawrence gestured at the great pillars holding up the vault. "But you—it's been months since I've seen you at mass, and you left your job at the graveyard."

He leveled a look at Raymond, who flinched and looked away, as he always did in the face of Lawrence's looks. "Things have gotten...complicated."

His heart was beating fast and his palms were sweating, just as they had when he was a boy and Lawrence caught him in a childish lie or deed. Lawrence had doled out few cuffs on the ear and almost no switches on the posterior, instead preferring to hand out treats and pats on the shoulder. But his disapproval became all the more distressing for its rarity, and Raymond dreaded what was coming, even as he looked forward to getting help.

"Something is troubling you," Father Lawrence said, and Raymond only nodded. Lawrence could always see straight through him. "You know where the confessionals are, my son."

Raymond glanced at the booths, with their flimsy curtains and wooden screens the only separation between him and the rest of the parishioners. "Could we go somewhere more private?"

Lawrence gave a nod, unflappable as ever, and for that Raymond was grateful. "How about the vestibule?"

The vestibule, where the priests and altar boys dressed for mass, was deserted. Racks of varicolored vestments lined the walls, and the place smelled of incense and old silk. Lawrence took up a heavy wooden chair and gestured for Raymond to take the one next to it. Both men sat facing forward, each not looking straight at the other. Raymond set the bottle on the floor near his feet. It twitched once and went still. Lawrence didn't notice.

Raymond crossed himself. "In the name of the father, the son, and the holy spirit. Amen."

"Amen," agreed Father Lawrence from his chair. "What brings you here, my son?"

Raymond paused, not sure how to begin. The bottle remained on the marble floor, heavy and still. Finally, Raymond said, "I found a genie."

There was a pause. Raymond kept his eyes on a cross embroidered into a purple stole hanging amid the vestments. Finally Lawrence said in a neutral voice, "A genie."

"He actually calls himself a djinn," Raymond said. "He lives in a bottle and grants me wishes. Just like those new stories from the Orient."

Another pause. "My son," Lawrence began, "I don't think you're quite—"

To forestall further debate, Raymond yanked the stopper from the bottle. Orange smoke solidified into Kaden next to Raymond's chair. His face was set hard.

"Master," Kaden said tightly, "what do you wish?"

Raymond firmed his resolve. "Back in the bottle."

Kaden fled back inside. Raymond replaced the stopper and glanced at Father Lawrence. He was sitting perfectly still in his chair, his face frozen in an expression Raymond associated with careful thought. But his fingers were white on the arms of his chair.

"I had no idea what it was when I opened it," Raymond said, "and now I have to make a different wish every day, or I'll lose my soul."

"Your soul," Lawrence repeated faintly.

"There's more." Raymond's throat was dry. "I have to pay for every wish."

Lawrence remained unflappable except for the pale fingers gripping his chair. "In what way, my son?"

Face red with shame, Raymond forced himself to explain. The bottle sat immobile at his feet. When he was finished, he stared at the floor for a long time. Silence filled the room. At last, Raymond said in a small voice, "Am I going to hell, Father?"

Yet more silence. Crushed under the weight of disapproval and disappointment, Raymond forced himself to look up. Father Lawrence's face was a mask of fury over his black vestments. Ice crawled over Raymond's skin, and he wanted to crawl under his chair like a child and never emerge. He flinched and looked away.

"This...thing," Lawrence said in a deadly, measured voice. "It forced its magic on you? You didn't ask for it?"

"I just opened the bottle," Raymond said.

"Have you tried to rid yourself of it?"

"I dropped it out a window, and it bounced instead of breaking. I threw it into the ocean down by the docks, and it was waiting for me when I got home. Nothing works."

Lawrence remained absolutely still in his chair. His eyes tracked across nothing. It finally came to Raymond that Father Lawrence was angry, but not at Raymond. Lawrence was angry at Kaden.

"God doesn't condemn those who sin without knowledge," Lawrence said at last, and he made the sign of the cross over Raymond. "You have confessed everything to me, and you are forgiven, my son."

Relief washed over Raymond in a wave. "Thank you, Father. Thank you."

"But the demon that did this to you—to one of my boys?" Lawrence continued. "We'll send it back to hell."

Raymond shifted in his hard chair, suddenly less comforted. "Kaden didn't come from hell, Father. He—"

"So it has a name!" Lawrence exclaimed with a clap of his hands. "That's good! That's very good! It'll help." He got up now, and paced the vestibule with a mixture of agitations and excitement. "I have sources to consult, books to check. We'll make this right in the end. Do you understand?"

"Yes, Father."

"You did the right thing in coming to me before it was too late. The church never forgets her own," Lawrence said, rubbing his hands with brisk energy. "Go home, now. I'll make the preparations and gather what we need. When everything is ready, I'll send word to you at—where are you living now?"

Raymond told him. With an absent nod, Lawrence bustled him through the vestibule door, down the aisle, and out the cathedral. He gave Raymond another blessing in farewell and swung the great door shut with final boom.

Conflicting thoughts and ideas swirled through Raymond's head on the walk back to the Reilly Building. It didn't come to Raymond that he had left the bottle behind until he was halfway home. But he only shrugged, and when he arrived in the apartment, the bottle was waiting for him on a table in the cluttered living room. Raymond ignored it and went into the master bedroom. The nicked and battered bottle was already on the windowsill, gleaming like an flawed emerald in the dying sunlight.

We'll send it back to hell. A new kind of guilt pressed Raymond down. Kaden wasn't a demon. He was a man, trapped by circumstances just as much as Raymond was. It wasn't a sin if you were forced, and the curse forced Kaden as much as it forced Raymond. With shaky hands, Raymond opened the bottle. Kaden appeared in a rush of smoke, his face both fearful and furious.

"What did you do, master?" he demanded. "All I ever wanted was to serve you!"

"Don't call me master."

"I can't stop. Master. The bottle requires it, just as it forces you to make wishes and payment." Kaden paced the room like Father Lawrence, though Father Lawrence never looked so handsome or moved with such easy energy. "What will that priest do to me?"

We'll send it back to hell.

"I don't know," Raymond said. Now that he was away from the church and Kaden was out of the bottle, Raymond found his earlier resolve fading. "Look, maybe Father Lawrence can break your curse."

"I don't trust a priest to break anything but my spirit."

"Father Lawrence isn't like your priest. He's a good man," Raymond insisted. "He raised me. He's kinder than anyone I know. He'll help us."

Kaden halted his pacing and stood in front of Raymond, so close Raymond could feel his breath. "He'll help *you*. He doesn't care about me." His voice was skin sliding over soft sand. Kaden leaned closer. Raymond couldn't move, couldn't think, couldn't speak. He trembled just a little. Kaden was every promise, every wish he had ever made, and Raymond trembled with the effort of holding himself back. It was wrong.

Kaden whispered in that soft desert voice, "Can you trust me?"

Raymond wanted to say he didn't, but his head nodded of its own. "With anything." And even as he said the words, he knew them to be true.

"Then make a wish, master." Kaden leaned closer still. "Make that wish you've been waiting for and wanting. I promise I'll grant it, and not because I have to."

"I..." Raymond's heart sang in his ears, and his body throbbed. He was a spark, a bit of flame, hungry and eager to burst into brightness. "I wish..."

Be a good boy, or no one will want you.

"What do you wish, master?"

"I wish," Raymond said in a husky voice, "that you would kiss me. The way you want to."

Kaden kissed him. It was long and languorous. Kaden's mouth was hot, almost scorching. His tongue flicked across Raymond's lips and pressed inward. Raymond accepted it with a small groan. The world snapped into shocking clarity, and in that moment, Raymond had everything he had ever wanted. The piles of diamonds and heaps of emeralds that filled the other rooms were trinkets. The treasure was Kaden. This internal confession lifted a burden Raymond hadn't known he was carrying, and he almost wept with the relief of it. Kaden had brought him home.

When at last they parted, Kaden pulled Raymond to him and stroked his hair. "I hope I filled your wish, master."

Raymond closed his eyes and let himself inhale Kaden's

slightly smoky scent. His muscles were loose, and his groin was tight. "In every way."

"You worked enough magic on me for a thousand djinn," Kaden replied. "A hundred thousand."

They embraced again. Raymond felt Kaden's urgent tightness against his own. But he pulled back again. "So what do we do now?"

"That's pretty obvious." Kaden's hand drifted low, and Raymond gasped. "So's this."

"I meant," Raymond said, "what do we do about us?"

Kaden moved his hand, sending thrills through Raymond's entire body. "We have time to figure out later. Right now, in this moment, you have to pay for that wish you just made. Or do I have to take your soul?"

"I think I'll keep it, thank you."

"I'll give you mine in return," Kaden said. "Just make the right wish. Can you manage yet another?"

Raymond's aching groin twitched under Kaden's palm, and he exhaled slowly. "I think I could manage three or four more wishes today."

Kaden led him to the bed. "You know, you're required to pay me, but afterward I can choose to pay you."

"Really? How?"

"Let me show you."

A pounding at the front door snapped Raymond awake. He disentangled himself from Kaden and scrambled out of bed. The pounding continued. Raymond yanked on a shirt while a naked Kaden sat up and rubbed bleary eyes.

"What ungodly creature is making that noise?" he demanded.

"You better get back in the bottle," Raymond said. For a moment, Kaden looked like he wanted to argue further, then he dissolved into a smoky cloud that rushed into the bottle on the windowsill. The stopper popped into place.

Raymond dashed barefoot down the hall to the pounding door. "Coming!" he called, and drew it open. Father Lawrence stood there, looking stricken. He had a black-handled bag in his hand and was wearing a purple stole with his black cassock.

190

"Thank god!" he said in obvious relief. "I was afraid something terrible had happened to you since we spoke yesterday. Is it still here?"

"It?" Raymond asked, confused.

"The demon. I've been up all night preparing." Lawrence pushed past Raymond and went down the hall. The green bottle on the windowsill was visible through the open bedroom door. "There it is! Did it force itself on you again?"

Raymond was still trying to get his scrambled wits together. "Not exactly. It—he—isn't—"

"Good, good." Father Lawrence dropped the bag on the messy bed, popped it open, and pulled out a book bound in black, an aspergillum of holy water, a corked bottle of salt, a heavy brass bell, and a silver crucifix. He acted like he belonged here, like it hadn't occurred to him that anyone might object. His confident, powerful presence filled the room as it had when Raymond lived in the orphanage, and a long childhood of obedience to the only father he'd ever known made it difficult for Raymond to challenge him.

"What are you doing?" Raymond said.

"Banishing your demon, of course. Don't worry, my son. In a moment, you'll be free of it. Satan has no power over one of my boys!" He gingerly picked up Kaden's bottle, set it in the center of the floor, and used the salt to draw around it a quick circle perhaps five feet in diameter.

"Father." Raymond took his arm. "Things have changed. It's not what you think."

Lawrence turned startled eyes on him, and for the first time, Raymond noticed they were the same electric blue as Kaden's. "I can sense the demon's essence within you, my son."

Raymond thought back to what he and Kaden had done last night, when he had paid Kaden in new ways, and Kaden had paid him in return. His earlier joy vanished, and the guilt returned.

"The demon's influence is getting stronger, my son," Lawrence continued. "You don't understand what you're saying."

Raymond began, "Kaden isn't—"

Lawrence snatched up the aspergillum and flicked it at Raymond. Cool holy water spattered his head. At the water's touch,

Raymond's voice died. He struggled to speak, but no words would come. In fact, he couldn't even move.

"The power of god compels you," Lawrence said, and he chanted in Latin, which years of church schooling let Raymond understand. *"Merciful God, accept our prayer that this servant of yours, bound by the fetters of sin, may be pardoned by your loving kindness."*

Raymond fought, but still couldn't move. Sweat broke out on his face, mingling with the holy water, and his heart raced in shock and surprise at the priest's power. But in a world where an imam could curse with a word, why wouldn't a priest have any less power? Especially over a man who now had the essence of a djinn within him.

Lawrence touched his shoulder. "With god's help, you'll be saved, my son."

While Raymond watched in growing fear, Lawrence opened the black book to a particular page, then swung the aspergillum to fling holy water over the bottle. *"The power of god commands you to show yourself, demon Kaden!"*

The bottle wobbled within the salt circle. It tipped over and spun in place, whirling faster and faster. Kaden was fighting the command. Raymond still couldn't move, couldn't help. Lawrence made another command in Latin, and the stopper popped free. Smoke boiled out and coalesced into a naked Kaden. His feet hung above the floor, his toes pointing downward. His arms were flung wide. Every muscle was etched across his dusky skin, and sunshine poured from his eyes and fingers. It was the most breathtaking sight Raymond had ever seen.

Father Lawrence paled and backed up a step. "Satan disguises himself as an angel of light," he whispered. He swung the aspergillum yet again. Holy water spattered Kaden, who howled in agony. The light wavered. Pain tightened in Raymond's gut as the essence Kaden had shared with him reacted to the water's touch.

"Leave this place, cursed one," Father Lawrence commanded in Latin. *"By the Blessed Virgin, I command you. By the blood and body of Christ, I command you. By your own name Kaden, I command you."*

"Master!" Kaden, still hanging in the air above the bottle, reached toward Raymond, but his hands rebounded from the boundary of salt on the floor. "Master!"

"He is not your master," Lawrence intoned. "God is. He commands you to leave this place!" He set down the aspergillum and picked up the bronze bell. It rang, and the harsh sound clanged through the room. Raymond tried to cover his ears, but still couldn't move.

Kaden burst into flame. The fire blazed outward in a rush of heat that flapped Lawrence's cassock and stole, but the flames themselves halted at the circle of salt. Lawrence stepped forward. He reached across the boundary into the flames and struck the bottle with the bronze bell.

The flames vanished and the bottle cracked. A ghostly form puffed from the glass, and Raymond had time to make out the misty form of a man in a Bedouin robe before it twisted into nothing and vanished. It came to Raymond that this was Kaden's first master, freed from the bottle. When the spirit evaporated, Kaden's light dimmed by a third. Fear and frustration made Raymond try to claw the air, but the water held him in an iron fist. He tried to speak, get Lawrence's attention to beg him to stop, but the words wouldn't come, and Lawrence paid him no heed anyway. The man was trying to help, but, oh god, he was killing Kaden, piece by piece, and Raymond couldn't stop him and Lawrence didn't know what he was doing.

"*Leave this place, Kaden!*" Lawrence struck the bottle a second time. It cracked further, and a second misty spirit, this one of an overweight, older man, wisped away. Kaden screamed again, and his light dimmed more. The sound of Kaden's suffering tore Raymond's heart through his rib cage. Desperate sweat coursed down his face. He struggled and fought to move, but he had no power.

"Master!" Kaden screamed. And then he cried, "Raymond!"

The sound of Raymond's own name, spoken by Kaden for the first time, rang through Raymond, struck him like a hammer ringing on an anvil, reached through him with hands of thunder, commanded him with an electric power that jolted his own soul.

Father Lawrence raised the bell a third time.

"Raymond!" Kaden cried again. "Raymond!"

For a spirit-shattering moment Raymond was connected with Kaden. He felt the raw energy of the djinn, of the wishes Kaden held within him, of the fear and sorrow and loneliness. Of the adoration he felt toward Raymond himself.

With a shout, Raymond burst free of his watery bonds. He lunged forward and caught Father Lawrence's wrist just before the bell would have struck the bottle.

"No!" Raymond's voice boomed with a power he had never felt before. "No, you won't!"

Lawrence's wrist was covered in sweat. He stared at Raymond with those strangely blue eyes. "My poor son. You don't know what you do."

"I do know," Raymond said. "You can't have him."

Lawrence straightened. "Why, my dear boy?" he asked.

Raymond hesitated a long moment. Above them, Kaden hung naked in the air, his light dimmed, his expression filled with hope. Raymond ached to hold him.

"Because I love him, Father," he said simply. "I love him."

Lawrence looked at him for a long moment with all the weight and power a father could muster. For the first time in his life, Raymond returned his look without flinching.

At last, Father Lawrence nodded. "I understand, my son."

Raymond exhaled heavy relief, an expression Kaden copied. "Thank you, Father."

"You must have my blessing," Lawrence continued. "One that will last all your days."

"Thank you," Raymond repeated. Relief made his bones weak. "I didn't expect you would—"

Lawrence whirled in a blur of movement. Before Raymond could follow what had happened, the bell flashed down and smashed the bottle.

Kaden flung his head back with a scream that shattered the windows and blasted the blankets off the bed. Raymond and Father Lawrence were flung to their knees. The ceiling and the floor creaked and groaned, and shadows swirled in the corners.

"What have you done?" Raymond shouted at Lawrence. A wind whirled hungrily through the room, and the two men clung to each other for balance. "Jesus! What have you done?"

"I saved you!" Lawrence shouted back. "You're free!"

"I never wanted to be free!" Raymond pushed Lawrence aside

and scrambled to his feet. The wind ripped around the room, carrying books and sheets and other debris. Kaden hung in the center, arms still outstretched. He howled his pain, and his pain became Raymond's. His body flickered and thinned, spreading itself like the other spirits. This couldn't be happening. Only moments ago, they had inhabited a paradise they'd built together. Only moments ago, Raymond had found the strength to say with his voice the words from his heart. How could god be so cruel? Raymond flung out a hand to Kaden, but the salt circle was unaffected by the wind and it pushed Raymond back. Kaden's shape was transparent now, thinning in the wind.

"Kaden!" Raymond yelled. "Oh, Jesus! Kaden, don't leave me!"

"He's gone," Lawrence said from the floor. "God has saved your soul."

It's not always a bad thing to give up your soul.

Kaden's words flicked through Raymond's heart and mind. He caught Kaden's fading eyes again. They showed his soul.

We djinn have the power to fulfill a wish however we want.

Kaden was almost gone now, a bare flicker of light in the salt circle. The wind was dying, and the ceiling stopped its groan. Father Lawrence managed to retake his feet.

It's not always a bad thing.

Realization shocked Raymond with lightning. He knew what to do. But it meant losing everything he had, everything he knew. How could he give up a lifetime of lessons for something the church said was evil?

The last of Kaden's form faded, leaving only a tiny whisper on the air. Raymond stiffened.

You have to be a good boy, or no one will want you.

Kaden wanted him. No matter what anyone else might think, Raymond had been good for Kaden, and Kaden good for Raymond. Raymond was good. This was good. No matter what the church taught, good could never be evil. And now he was letting it go.

If he had to choose between Kaden and the church, there could only be one choice. With a final, silent prayer, Raymond shouted two words: "I wish!"

The whisper in the air paused in the act of fading and hung there, as if hesitating.

"What are you doing?" said Father Lawrence.

"I wish!" Raymond shouted again. "Kaden, can you hear me?" Raymond paused, then pushed the words out. "I wish for you to take my soul!"

"No!" Lawrence whispered.

For a horrible moment, nothing happened. Raymond's heart stopped in his chest, dead as a stone. He was too late. Kaden was gone. Then he felt it. A rush of air and light and thrill. It streamed from his body and swirled around the circle, sweeping the salt and broken bottle glass away. The stream from Raymond's body outlined the last tiny bit of Kaden's form, limning it with sunshine and fire, feeding it. Fulfilling it. Kaden grew solid and heavy, with a look of ecstasy and wonder on his face. His feet drifted toward the floor, and when they touched the wood, his knees buckled and he collapsed. Raymond knelt next to him and took him in his arms, the holy water and salt circle no longer an impediment. Kaden's naked skin was warm.

"You did it," he whispered. "You rescued me."

Raymond's throat choked under flooding ecstasy of his own. Kaden was alive and in his arms. He never wanted to move again. "I was going to say the same thing about you."

Droplets of cold water splashed across them both. Father Lawrence intoned desperately, "*In the name of god, demon Kaden, leave this place!*"

Raymond closed his eyes. In the last few seconds, he'd forgotten all about Lawrence. Now he had no idea what to—

"It's all right, sir." Kaden came to his feet with an audible snap of joints and creak of tendons. Mortal tendons. "It worked. You saved me. Saved *us*."

Lawrence paused, the aspergillum caught in mid-flick. "What did you say?"

Still naked, Kaden caught the startled priest in a bear hug while Raymond watched with his mouth hanging open. "How can I ever thank you, you dear, dear man?"

Flustered, Lawrence pushed Kaden away. "How did I—?"

"Your faith and your power broke the curse!" Kaden took a

deep, shuddering breath and grinned his charming grin. "I was a mortal man cursed by an evil priest. Now I'm a djinn saved by a good one. You gave me my mortal life back."

Raymond came forward now and shook Father Lawrence's bewildered hand. "That was amazing, Father. Truly amazing!"

"The glory is God's," Lawrence said uncertainly. "But I could have sworn I heard you say to him—"

"Look!" Kaden took the aspergillum and dashed holy water on his own hand, then on Raymond's. "The evil influence is gone. I'm free. We both are."

Lawrence settled himself and gave both of them a long look. Raymond met it without flinching. At last, Father Lawrence nodded carefully and took back the aspergillum. When he spoke, his voice was heavy with new knowledge. "It's all clear to me, my son. My sons. I'm happy I could help you both through the glory of god. Everything has gone according to his plan, and who are we to question it? You have my blessing. But perhaps something to cover yourself with?"

While Kaden hastily wrapped himself in a battered blanket, Lawrence packed up his things and, with another brisk nod, headed for the door. "I'll expect both of you at mass on Sunday. Maybe you both can buy me a drink afterward."

"We will, Father," Raymond said, and meant it.

Lawrence left. With a small whoop, Raymond caught Kaden in his arms again and whirled him around the devastated room. It was the finest moment in Raymond's world.

"I gave credit to the priest, but it was your wish that saved me," Kaden said impishly. "Once the bottle broke and I lost myself, your soul gave me strength to find myself again."

"I have no soul now?" Raymond asked, suddenly uneasy.

"I took your soul, but you've had mine since the moment you opened that bottle. I think it evens out."

And Raymond realized he was right.

"So," Kaden said, "To repeat your earlier question, what do we do now?"

Raymond spread his hands. "We have an apartment filled with gold, money, and jewels. We can do anything we want."

"Then I want to do this." Kaden kissed him. "Thank you. My

heart. My soul. My Raymond."

"Not master?"

"Never again."

And Raymond's free and happy laughter filled the world.

AN INTERRUPTED BETROTHAL

by Lawrence Watt-Evans

The arranged marriage that turns into a love match may be a staple of romance novels, but surely it is the exception rather than the rule. While historically marriage functioned primarily as a business contract to preserve property, make political alliances, and so forth, the realm of "lace and blade" fantasy operates under its own rules, rules that often call for a certain amount of deviousness.

Lawrence Watt-Evans, who is inordinately fond of pink flamingos, has been a full-time writer for almost forty years, with fifty novels and well over a hundred short stories to his credit, mostly fantasy, science fiction, and horror. He's best known for the Hugo-winning short story "How I Left Harry's All-Night Hamburgers," the Obsidian Chronicles trilogy, and the ongoing "Legends of Ethshar" fantasy series. As of this writing, he lived in Takoma Park, Maryland, just outside Washington, D.C.

Riassa watched from the shadows as the doors of the hall swung open, propelled by a pair of burly, wary-eyed guards. They scanned the room swiftly, taking in Lord Panris and his own half-dozen guards arrayed on the dais, but if they saw Riassa they gave no sign; apparently the first of the spells she had bought worked as promised.

Then the guards stepped to either side, standing with their backs against the doors, and a brightly-clad herald stepped in, trumpet in hand. He did not raise his instrument, however, but instead took a deep breath and announced, in a voice so loud it seemed to fill every inch of the room, "His Excellency Lord Arzam of Barva!"

Lord Panris stirred, straightening where he stood, as his guest marched in. He looked unimpressed—but then, he always looked unimpressed in public. That was deliberate, Riassa knew. Her uncle was too clever to reveal his feelings openly.

Lord Arzam did not look particularly impressed at the sight of Lord Panris, either, but then Riassa saw his gaze wander quickly around the lesser audience chamber, and she thought she saw a little more respect in his expression as he took in the gleaming marble and intricate gilding, the fine tapestries on the walls, and the glittering crystal pendants that adorned each lamp.

As for Riassa, she *was* impressed—Arzam was one of the tallest men she had ever seen, towering over his entourage, but he did not have the rough features or brutish mannerisms that many large men displayed. He stood straight, his shoulders back. His face was strong and handsome, his body perfectly proportioned, his movements graceful. He wore his black hair pulled back in a gold-banded braid that reached almost to the sword-belt at his waist.

Riassa noticed that the leather-bound hilt protruding from that belt was heavily worn; the weapon was clearly not just for show. That worried her slightly, but she did not let it distract her. The plan did not call for any violence, and she had her magical escape ready if she needed it.

She wondered whether her cousin Avinna might reconsider once she saw her suitor, because Riassa certainly found him appealing—but no, Avinna had sworn that she wanted nothing to do with any man, that her interests lay entirely with her own sex, and Arzam was perhaps the most purely masculine creature Riassa had ever seen.

She had no idea what his temperament might be like, though.

"I am here, Lord Panris, as we agreed," Arzam said. Riassa had expected a man of his size to speak in a rumbling bass, but instead his voice was a smooth baritone, and he spoke Kalithian with none of the barbaric accent his envoys had displayed.

"I thank you, Lord Arzam, for coming," Uncle Panris replied. "I know yours are a direct people; shall we dispense with the preliminaries and get directly to the presentation? I am sure you want to see your prospective bride."

Arzam smiled, an unexpectedly open expression Riassa found charming. "It would seem the Kalithian reputation for endless ceremony is undeserved," he said. "By all means, bring her out."

Panris raised a hand, and a waiting attendant drew back one of the curtains at the back of the dais. For a few awkward seconds nothing happened, but then Avinna suddenly emerged as if shoved, as indeed she probably had been. Her head was bowed as she stepped forward to her father's side. She wore a simple but beautiful gown of white silk trimmed with pale beads, and her hair was wound into elaborate curls that framed her delicate features.

She was trembling, Riassa noticed–probably nervous about her upcoming performance. After all, she was about to irretrievably ruin her own reputation.

For now, though, Avinna stood waiting and said nothing.

"Lady Avinna," Arzam said. "I see the reports of your beauty did not exaggerate."

Avinna did not move; her head remained down, and she neither looked at her suitor nor spoke.

"I would be pleased to hear your voice," Arzam added, his smile fading.

"I have nothing to say to you," Avinna murmured; Riassa could barely make out the words.

"Oh? Is there nothing you would ask, nothing you would tell me about yourself? Are you content to marry a complete stranger?"

Avinna's cheeks reddened. Finally she raised her eyes and looked at him.

"I don't want to marry you, stranger or not," she said. "If you would please me, Lord Arzam, then let me be and go home."

Riassa watched her cousin's face, trying to judge whether there might be some trace of interest once she saw Arzam's face and figure–but no, Riassa saw only nervous desperation, the same desperation that had driven the two of them to concoct their scheme.

For a moment after Avinna's words of defiance, no one spoke. Every man in the room seemed frozen in surprise; Riassa looked from one to the next, trying without success to judge what might happen. Then Arzam broke the silence, his tone surprisingly gentle. "You do not know me, girl. Am I so repulsive that you would refuse me without allowing me any chance to prove myself?"

"Yes!" Avinna exclaimed—but then she caught herself. She and Riassa both knew that men did not believe there was any woman alive whose passions could not in time be roused; they had discussed that often enough. For her part, Riassa found it hard to grasp just how thoroughly Avinna detested the idea of letting any man touch her, but she had at last been convinced that her cousin was completely sincere—she had no interest at all in boys or men, but only in women.

And both of them had overheard enough boastful male conversation to suspect that Lord Arzam would see Avinna's lack of interest as a challenge, rather than a disqualification.

"It is not you, my lord," Avinna hastily added. "But I already have a lover, and will have no other." And thus the scheme was launched; Riassa stood ready.

Arzam's eyes widened. He looked to Lord Panris, whose expression was one of shock. "I give you my word, Lord Arzam, I have heard nothing of this before this very moment!" he exclaimed.

"Did you think to ask her, my lord?"

Panris flushed. "I told her I had found her a fine and worthy husband, and she made no such objection at the time."

Avinna turned to her father. "I told you I did not want to marry!"

"But you said nothing of a lover!"

Avinna turned angrily away without answering.

Riassa was looking, not at the principals in this discussion, but at the various retainers. Her uncle's guards seemed to range from amusement to shock, while Lord Arzam's people appeared to be worried, or even frightened. Perhaps their master had a temper?

"It would seem, Lord Panris, that intentionally or not, you have misled me," Arzam said. His voice was calm; if he did have a temper, he was keeping it in check.

"That was not my intent, I swear!" Panris spread his hands. "I had no idea that her objection to the match was anything but adolescent foolishness."

"Perhaps you should have discussed the matter with her more closely before making an offer that would shape her entire life."

"What would you have me do? She is my daughter, and it is

my responsibility to find her a suitable husband."

"She may have saved you the trouble." Arzam turned his attention to Avinna. "Tell me, girl, who is this lover? Where is he? Do you intend to wed him?"

"Yes, Avinna—who is he?" Panris demanded. "Please tell me you have not become besotted with some muscular peasant or handsome soldier."

Riassa tensed at that. She knew her uncle's jab was not random, but a reminder of how his own sister, Riassa's mother, had embarrassed the family. Not that Riassa considered her father an embarrassment; he was brave and strong and a loving parent, and she much preferred him to her noble uncle.

Avinna threw back her head and pointed—not quite at Riassa, but in the right general direction. "He's right there! He's a sorcerer!"

That word, "sorcerer," was the cue they had agreed upon; Riassa released her purchased magic, drew her borrowed sword, and stepped forward, suddenly visible—a reasonably tall figure in men's clothing, a hooded black robe worn loose to hide her face and disguise her shape.

"I am the one who has claimed this woman," she said, speaking in as deep a voice as she could manage.

Several of the men in the room started, and hands fell to sword-hilts as this new arrival seemed to appear out of nowhere, but then Arzam raised a hand. His men froze where they were, and her uncle's guards looked to Lord Panris, who also signaled for calm.

"Who are you that dares intrude here uninvited?" Lord Panris said, his voice trembling—though with rage or fear, Riassa could not tell.

"I am Avinna's sorcerous lover. Surely you know a sorcerer's true name gives one power over him? Then you will forgive me if I do not tell you mine, nor insult you by lying to your face."

"Then you have no noble title, nor renowned family?"

"Indeed, I do not. My power, gained through study, is both greater and less worldly than any derived from birth." She and Avinna had discussed the possibility of claiming some highborn ancestry for their fictional magician lover, but had dismissed it;

Lord Panris knew the pedigrees of every landed family in the region and would spot a lie.

"Yet you think yourself worthy of my daughter?"

"I do."

"And he's the one I love!" Avinna exclaimed, starting toward Riassa.

One of her father's men grabbed her arm and held her. That was not in the plan. At this point in their little act, Avinna was supposed to come to her side. Riassa wished she had anticipated this; a genuine sorcerer would probably have some little spell that could pry the guard's hand away, but Riassa had not included anything of that sort in her tiny magical arsenal.

But then, the trio of spells she had purchased had cost every copper she and Avinna could raise, and more—she still owed the Lornish magician a favor to cover the unpaid balance. She could not have afforded anything more.

"Release her!" Riassa demanded, her heart racing. She raised her sword. She was unsure what she could do if her demand was refused, but to say nothing would make her seem weak.

The guard looked to Lord Panris, but before he could speak, Lord Arzam said, "Wait."

Panris turned to his guest. "What would you have, my lord?"

"If I may, a few questions."

His tone was calm, which was not what Riassa had expected. She had assumed a barbarian lord would be enraged to have his betrothal disrupted this way. She let her blade down a little. "Of whom do you want your answers, sir?" she asked.

"Of our host, O nameless magician—at least, for now." Arzam turned back to Panris. "My lord, our negotiations were conducted through intermediaries, so perhaps I have misunderstood some points. I would like to clarify them."

"Lord Arzam, this is not the time or place..."

"It is *precisely* the time and place," Arzam roared, interrupting Panris. His right hand was closed on the hilt of his sword, and the sudden bellowing after his previous calm was shocking. "You appear to have brought me here under false pretenses, and I will have this matter clarified now. You may have issues to straighten out with your daughter and this young man, but you are not going to waste my time with them until our own situation has been clarified."

Riassa was impressed with both the volume of the Barvan's voice, and his command of Kalithian.

Panris frowned, but before he could reply Arzam continued, "My understanding was that you were offering me a beautiful virgin bride to seal the bond between our two lands. You were quite definite in your description, were you not?"

"Yes!" Panris said. He was about to say more, but again, Arzam interrupted.

"I can see that your daughter is beautiful," he said, "unless you have availed yourself of a glamour–perhaps this young man provided that, as part of some elaborate performance?"

"No!" Panris exclaimed, as Riassa burst out, "I have not..."

"But is she a virgin? The existence of this alleged lover casts doubt upon it."

Again, Panris and Riassa both spoke at once. Arzam held up a hand, then pointed at Riassa. "What do you say, sir? Has this young woman known a man's company?"

"I have shared her bed," Riassa replied. Which was true; the cousins had innocently spent many nights together as children. This was the very heart of their plan; Lord Arzam was now supposed to reject Avinna, dismiss her as unworthy of him.

For a moment Riassa thought it was working, as Arzam turned to Avinna, who blushed a suitable shade of crimson. "It's true," she said.

Her father looked shocked. "I didn't... how..."

Once again, Arzam's voice overrode everyone else.

"It would still be to the advantage of both our realms for an alliance to be made, and sealed in some way more binding than signatures on a piece of paper," he said. "Furthermore, I doubt it would enhance anyone's reputation save perhaps that of our magician friend, were I to yield all claims and let these lovers run off together. So if certain concessions are made, I will ignore Avinna's misbehavior and her father's misinformation, and accept her anyway."

Riassa's mouth fell open, and she snapped it quickly shut, as Avinna wailed, "No! You can't!"

"My dear girl," Arzam said, "I most certainly can. I have three good men and my own blade, and your father has six men of his own; can your talented friend there defeat all of us? I doubt it. And if he can, any magic that might strike us down might kill your father, as well–are you so besotted as to want that?"

Avinna threw Riassa a helpless glance. She knew her cousin was not a real sorcerer. The plan had called for her to run to Riassa's side, and the two would then vanish in a cloud of smoke–but her father's guard was holding her back.

And they had not made any plans for what they would do if Arzam did not abandon his claim on her. The plan had been to keep Avinna out of sight until her Barvan suitor had gone home; then she was to reappear, saying that the magician had betrayed and deserted her. Avinna would stay on in her father's palace, disgraced and unfit for marriage–which was exactly what she wanted.

But it had all gone wrong.

"Now, Lord Panris," Arzam said, ignoring both his intended bride and her supposed suitor, "shall we renegotiate the terms of our agreement, in light of this new information?"

Desperate, barely remembering to keep her voice pitched low, Riassa called out, "No! Avinna is mine!" She stepped forward, sword ready.

Arzam's two guards drew their own blades and moved toward her, ready to defend their master, but Arzam waved them back. "So this boy wizard has the courage to fight for his beloved?"

Boy wizard? Perhaps her masquerade was not as convincingly manly as she had hoped. Her size was considered ungainly for a woman, but apparently she was still too slender to pass for a grown man.

But that was not important; her present need was to meet Arzam's challenge. "I do!" she said, desperately hoping that the barbarian lord would laugh, or turn away in disgust, and give up Avinna as not worth the trouble.

Arzam did neither. He casually pulled his own weapon from its sheath and advanced to meet her.

Riassa struggled to hide her trembling. She had been trained to use a sword, but never very seriously; after all, despite her size, she was only a woman. Her two remaining spells were a simple fireworks display intended to show she was truly a magician, and the transporting spell that would carry her and Avinna to safety, and neither of those would help her swordplay. Oh, the fireworks might dazzle her opponent briefly, and the other would let her escape, but she did not want to resort to that if she could possibly avoid it, since it would leave Avinna stranded here. She raised her blade into guard position and stood ready, hoping that Avinna or Uncle Panris would call out to stop the fight.

But neither did. Panris undoubtedly saw this as the simplest way out of an embarrassing situation; if Arzam killed his daughter's illicit lover and married her anyway, everything would be back on course. Avinna—well, Avinna was probably too frightened and confused to think of anything to say. Riassa loved her cousin, but Avinna had never been the most quick-witted member of the family; the plan had been mostly her own creation.

That escape talisman was becoming more tempting every second; her left hand slipped into the pouch holding it.

Then suddenly Arzam closed on her, moving with astonishing speed, far too fast for her to react effectively, but he did not thrust his blade through her heart or belly, nor slash at her; instead he somehow managed to lock blades with her so that the two of them were pressed together, swords crossed between them.

She stood, baffled, chest to chest with the barbarian, unsure what to do next, and very aware of his nearness. Now she could not escape at all; if she triggered the spell while they stood so close, she would take Arzam with her.

"Listen, sorcerer," Arzam whispered, "do you want to live?"

Riassa tilted her head but said nothing; she stepped back, as if forced.

"I couldn't refuse your challenge, nor negotiate openly with you," Arzam continued. "It would look weak, and I can't afford that. But I've no desire to kill you, or to keep you and Avinna apart. Now, we need to make this look good; shift your blade to the right. We'll swing around and lock again."

Riassa nodded, ever so slightly, and then pulled free; in a flurry of steel the blades swept around, clashed, and then they were once again chest to chest.

"I need this marriage," Arzam murmured, speaking swiftly but clearly. "My people—we need this Kalithian treaty. The Olzani are pushing us west, out of our grazing land, and we need wealthy allies and better weapons. My own idiot councilmen won't trust the Kalithians without something more than signatures on a piece of paper, though; they'll probably cut my throat while I sleep if I return without a hostage bride."

"Hostage?" Riassa replied, startled.

"You thought it was a love match?" He pressed forward, and she stepped back again. They were so close his scent filled her head, and his dark eyes filled her vision. "Don't be a fool. Now, yield to me, and we can make an arrangement to suit us all. Avinna and I will stage a wedding, but if she doesn't want me I won't touch her—the two of you can do as you please, if you're subtle about it. I can take you back as my new court magician. Fling your sword aside and raise your hands, and we're done."

For a moment Riassa seriously considered this offer, but an instant's thought told her it could never work. She was no magician, and did not want to be Avinna's lover.

But another thought struck her.

She felt Arzam tensing, and there was another staged flutter of their blades, this time without any spoken prompting. When they had again locked into position she whispered, "I can't do that. I'm sorry. But there's another possibility."

"What?" Arzam grunted, as he pressed her back another step.

"Avinna has a cousin, a year older than herself. Her name is Riassa, and she *is* a virgin, if not a beauty. I think she might be more cooperative. She's not a lord's daughter, but she's of noble blood."

Arzam blinked, smiled, and then stepped back, breaking away from his opponent. "What sorcery is this?" he shouted. "I cannot touch him!"

Riassa saw this as her best chance; she thrust her left hand deeper into the pouch and squeezed the transporting talisman. Smoke swirled up around her.

When the smoke cleared she was in her own bedchamber. Avinna was not with her, but that no longer mattered; she dropped her sword and quickly stripped off the bulky garments she had been wearing. Pulling on her nearest dress she hurried out into the corridor and down the stairs, only realizing halfway down that she was still wearing men's boots, and not her slippers. She straightened her skirts and ran on, hoping no one would notice.

The doors of the lesser audience chamber were still wide open; she ran in without pausing, rushing past too quickly for the guards to react.

Lord Arzam was standing before the dais, saying, "...saw what he did! Who's to say he could not transport himself into my bedchamber thus, and cut my throat before my guards could stop him?"

"Uncle!" Riassa called, as she came skidding to a stop at Arzam's side. "I saw a man flying!"

One of Arzam's guards grabbed her from behind; she did not resist.

"Riassa?" Lord Panris said.

"Uncle, truly, he was flying! I saw him soar off above the stables!" Her bedchamber's one window overlooked the stables.

Arzam turned to her. "Was he dressed in black, with a long sword?"

"Yes!" she said. "Did you see him, too?" Then she blinked, and attempted a curtsey that was severely impaired by the strong hold on her arms. "My apologies, sir; do I know you?"

"I am Arzam of Barva," he replied, with just a trace of a bow.

Lord Panris sighed. "Lord Arzam, may I present my niece, Riassa ter-Vallez?"

"I am honored," Arzam replied, bowing a little more deeply and meeting Riassa's eyes. He smiled. Then he turned back to Lord Panris.

"My lord," he said, "why did you not tell me that your home held *two* remarkable beauties?"

"What?" Panris said, clearly caught completely off-guard. Riassa suppressed a smile; she knew that her uncle had never considered the possibility that anyone might think her beautiful; she was too tall, her shoulders too broad, her features too pronounced. He preferred the petite delicacy of his wife and daughter. Riassa realized that Arzam's question was just flattery, but she still enjoyed hearing it.

"Her husband is a lucky man," Arzam continued.

"I am not yet married, my lord," Riassa said, casting her eyes demurely downward. She had suggested herself as an alternative entirely for tactical reasons, to save Avinna from a fate she dreaded, but now that it appeared about to be realized she felt her heart beating faster, not with fear, but with anticipation.

"Why, then..." Lord Arzam smiled again, that wide-open smile she had admired before. "Lord Panris, I believe I see a happy solution to all our problems! If you will simply substitute her name for Avinna's in every agreement, I think we will all be pleased." He turned to Riassa. "Assuming, of course, that she will have me."

Before either Panris or Riassa could respond, Arzam went down on one knee, snatching up Riassa's hand and freeing that arm from his guardsman's grip. "Riassa of Kalithia," he said, "will you marry me?"

"It's ter-Vallez," Riassa said. "And I will certainly consider it."

It was three days later, on the ride back to Barva after the negotiations were concluded, when the two of them were alone in the carriage, that Riassa was finally able to ask, "When did you know it was me?"

"The moment I looked in your eyes," Arzam replied. "It's fortunate no one else had seen the 'sorcerer' at close range." He hesitated, then asked, "Were you really Avinna's lover?"

Riassa blushed and shook her head. "Not beyond a few silly games when we were children, though I think she wished there were more."

"You prefer men?"

"Very much so."

"Then...I will not press you, and I am willing to accept whatever you decide, but will this be a marriage in more than name?"

"I certainly hope so." She smiled as she leaned toward him, ready for her first kiss. "And won't it make a fine story to tell our children, when they ask how we met?"

WATER BOUND

by Julia H. West

When Julia H. West was in college studying anthropology, people asked her, "What will you do with your degree?" She always replied, "Write science fiction and fantasy." She enjoys finding interesting cultural and mythical tidbits for her stories. In creating Vlazantzar she mixed the notion of djinn who live in water pipes with the idea of a demon who rests on uncovered water at night and blinds those who drink from it. The water-filled tunnels beneath Kindah are modeled on underground desert aqueducts called *qanats* first built in ancient Persia.

Julia lives in West Jordan, Utah, with a husband and two daughters who also write science fiction and fantasy. They share the house with numerous benevolent cat overlords who occasionally try to write stories, but the humans never understand or appreciate it when they find such gems as "4rteffffffffdd," "jweqqqqqa," or "zsxd]" in the middle of a manuscript left open on the computer. (By the way, if you speak Cat, perhaps you can translate those offerings, as they are actual bits copied and pasted from the Writings of Cats.) Julia's website is at http://juliahwest.com.

Old Reau the water seller was blind, and perhaps mad; it was whispered that she talked to water. But those who watched her in the bazaar of Kindah to see if this was so found her sitting on her mat, silent, her face lined with sorrow.

"O water, why did you blind me?" sixteen-year-old Reau asked as she lay on her pallet in the water room, watching the unnatural colors that swirled, as always, before her eyes.

The voice of water, which had been murmuring of running through the streets of a king's city, stopped abruptly. All was so still in the water room it seemed Reau was alone in the world.

Then, in a distant voice, water asked, *Do you hear me, oh human?*

"I have heard you for years. You talk of mountains and oceans, lakes and farmland, cities and armies. Things I have never seen, and never will see, for you stole my sight."

*Ah! *You* are why I was compelled to stay here, beneath the burning desert sands.* Reau had never known water to sound excited before.

"You are water. There has always been water beneath Kindah."

Ah, young human. I am not water. I travel in water. I exist in water. But I am something other.

"Demon!" Long ago there were demons in the desert, but most were driven from Kindah by the wizard Zahid.

I am not a demon. A long silence from water, then, *I do not *believe* I am a demon. I exist in water. I travel and learn much. I try not to harm living things.*

"Why, then, did you harm *me?*" Reau cried, forgetting to whisper lest she wake others in the house. "I'm blind! I can't sell water, or head the House, or serve on the city council. I am a burden to my family."

May I come to you? Water—or not-water, as it insisted—sounded oddly humble.

"To complete what you started?" Reau said, now hot with anger. "To kill me, and erase this blot from my family?"

I do not understand how I have harmed you, said not-water. *I must inspect you, as I have inspected many things in this world *without killing them.** Now not-water sounded almost as angry as Reau was.

"Do it, then," said Reau, beginning to be interested in not-water. She had listened to it for so long that, once she forced her anger down, she found herself eager to meet this creature, demon or not.

I am in the pipe. Open the spigot, that I may escape.

Reau pushed herself to her feet, felt her way to the pipes, and found the spigot.

Turn it slightly, so no water is wasted, instructed not-water. *Put your hand under the opening.*

Reau did as she was told. Hunching her shoulders and squeezing her already-sightless eyes closed, Reau held her hand under the spout.

Something touched her. Not hot, not cold, neither slippery nor scratchy—as impossible to describe as the colors that moved behind her eyelids. She stood motionless, letting the strange thing flow along her fingers, cup in her palm like water but with more weight. Colors rippled behind her eyelids in slow undulations, and something like a sigh ran along her skin.

It flowed from her hand to the pipe. *Close the spigot.*

She did so. What had not-water discovered?

Not-water was quiet for so long that Reau thought it had decided to stop talking to her. She'd been rude to it, after all. Then it spoke, its voice subdued, as if dismayed. *When you filled the jar that morning four years ago, I rested in the pipe, not expecting to be disturbed. You startled me, and I...interacted with you. It was instinctive. I did not know I could do it.*

"What did you do?" Reau didn't understand not-water's explanation.

I changed your body.

"What? How?" Reau touched the hand where not-water had rested. It seemed the same as always—smooth skin, bumps of knuckles and wrist just as they had always been.

*Your body works differently now. You have not lost your sight; it has changed. Do you see colors? Bright and moving? Those are warm things—living creatures, or material that has been heated, like food over a fire. But your mind cannot interpret what your eyes see."

"I still don't understand. I can see?"

"Hold your hand up to your face. Do you see moving colors?"

She did. An elongated purple mass, shading to blue, then to other colors she had no names for. She moved her fingers. The mass changed shape, the colors rippled and changed, but nothing there looked like a hand.

You must train your sight.

Reau moved her hand again. Did the shape of the colors look like a hand moving? Not that she could tell. "Why can I see colors with my eyes closed?" she asked.

I do not know.

In the tales Reau had heard of demons they were bloodthirsty, greedy, loud, and sure of themselves. If not-water was a demon, it was an insecure one. "It's not just my vision that changed. Why did I stop growing taller?"

There was enthusiasm in not-water's voice when it answered, *That change was truly an improvement.*

"How can it be? Though I'm a woman grown I'm shorter than the children!"

You are more solid. Your strength is many times that of other humans your size. Your speed has also improved. This I imply from feeling the changes in your body, but I witnessed neither in your actions.

Reau felt her way back to her pallet. "What must I do?" she whispered as she lay down. Her head ached from all she'd learned this night.

Train your abilities, said not-water. *I am tied to you until you achieve your potential. Only then will I be free to return to the greater world, where water is not so scarce.*

Before sleep claimed her, she asked, "Do you have a name? I can't keep thinking of you as water—or not-water."

Not-water chuckled; or perhaps it was just water gurgling in the pipes. *Among my kind—though it has been decades since I have seen another of my kind—I am called Vlazantzar.*

Vlazantzar. As Reau slept that name swirled, with un-named colors, through her dreams.

Old Reau the water seller was blind, and perhaps mad. She certainly was not a normal woman; though small as a child, she lifted the largest water jars with ease.

As Vlazantzar told Reau of a city high in the mountains, where water was so cold it became solid and children slid on it, it insisted she practice using her sight. *You have let your eyes become confused, not using them properly for years.*

So she stripped off her sleeping tunic and concentrated on her chest and stomach. Her body was larger than her hands or feet, and warmer. She stared at the shifting mass of colors and tried to imagine what she knew from feeling was there; swell of hips and stomach, tuck of waist, curve of breasts. But the colors refused to be anything but colors. Finally, stomach churning with nausea, she reached for her tunic, to pull it back on.

Wait, said Vlazantzar, stopping its description of a fountain—water shooting into the air and falling, free for anyone to take, into a basin below.

"What?" Reau asked sulkily. She'd expected to see immediately, now that she knew she could.

There is other training you must do.

"Ahhh!" She'd forgotten her other 'abilities,' as Vlazantzar described them.

It is easier, for this training, to leave the tunic off.

Reau wondered how Vlazantzar knew of her undress. She'd said nothing when she removed her tunic, and made no noise when she reached for it. Could it *see* her, from its home in the pipe? She didn't have time to ask, for Vlazantzar began explaining, move by move, a training exercise to strengthen her muscles and make her more limber.

This went much better. In the water room, unless she blundered into pipes or a jar, there was room for her to move around without bumping into things as she did in other parts of the house.

"It's like dancing," she panted. "It's fun."

You have done well, for a beginner, Vlazantzar praised her. *I have seen this very training practiced by warriors of Kittima. Once you have mastered this, I have other moves I can teach you.*

Though Reau was now panting, sweating, and exhausted, and the rest of the house so quiet that all must be abed, Vlazantzar would not let her rest. *One more thing you must practice,* it said. *For strength.* Then it had her lift water jars. She'd not been allowed near water jars since she'd been blinded, so she didn't know how much she could lift. Then, of course, it had been smaller jars, easy for a twelve-year-old to carry when full.

Carefully, for the jars were valuable, Reau lifted the smallest jar. As she'd expected, it was easy. She went along the row to larger jars. None of them, even the largest, was any challenge to her— empty. Full of water, they were far heavier.

When you have trained your sight, you can fill the jars,

215

Vlazantzar told her. *For now, sleep. I, too, shall rest.*

Reau slipped into her tunic and lay down on her pallet. "Vlazantzar, do you sleep?"

I do not know if what I do is like your sleep. I lie quietly, not moving, as do you. I rest my mind. Is that how you sleep?

Reau frowned into the darkness. "Yes, but I also dream. Things that never happened to me appear in my mind."

Do you see the future? Or witness faraway events? I did not think humans had those faculties.

Sometimes Vlazantzar used such hard words. "Our minds create stories from what we have known or heard."

Vlazantzar was quiet for a long time. All Reau heard was the gurgling of water in the pipes. When she had nearly drowsed off, thinking it was resting now, it said, *Human storytellers, who craft tales of things that have never been, fascinate me. That is something I cannot do. My mind differs from yours in many ways, and this is one of them.* It paused for a moment. *Rest now. Tomorrow you will train again.*

For many days thereafter Reau trained under Vlazantzar's tutelage. In the darkness of the water room, she easily crouched and whirled, leapt and kicked, as she knew where everything there was. But during the day, the jumble of colors behind her eyes confused her, and she was nearly as clumsy as when she was first blinded. All efforts to train her new sight failed.

Vlazantzar pondered the problem. It had Reau open the spigot again, inspected the changes in her body, and assured itself that her eyes had no defects.

You should be able to see, it said after it returned to its home in the pipes. *I have discovered no damage.*

Sulky again, Reau said, "How can you know that? I've trained for weeks now, and I've improved at everything else. But I can't even see my own hand. I think you're wrong. My eyes don't work. I'm just blind, and will never be anything more."

I. Know. What. I. Know. Do not question me!

Reau had never heard Vlazantzar angry before. Not really angry, like this. Its normally pleasant, faint voice suddenly roared, and though she covered her ears with her hands, it rang through her head. She dropped to her knees, certain Vlazantzar *was* a demon, for surely no other creature could fill her head with such thunder.

She crouched, arms wrapped around her head. When she heard no further comment from Vlazantzar, she wondered if she was now deaf as well as blind. *Perhaps Vlazantzar should have killed me, after all,* she lamented. *Perhaps it will leave me now. In all these years, it's been my only friend.*

Tears began to roll from her eyes and drip onto her knees.

After a long time, during which the only sound was her weeping, *Young human?* said Vlazantzar in a subdued voice. *Forgive me. I forget my strength.*

"I'm sorry," Reau sobbed. "I shouldn't doubt you. I'll try harder. I'll do what you tell me. Only please, please don't leave me."

I cannot leave you, Vlazantzar said. *I must train you.*

Reau tried to calm herself, scrubbing at her eyes with the back of her hand. She pushed herself to her feet. "What should I do now?" she asked, voice still quavering with unshed tears.

Patiently Vlazantzar described the next moves she should practice.

Months passed. During the day, Reau concentrated on her hearing, trying to overcome the nausea caused by the colors crawling in her sight. She listened to see if people were in a room before entering; her sister and brothers found it amusing to move furniture into her path to trip her.

One day her mother called for her. Reau entered the parlor, feeling her way to where her mother sat in a heavy carved chair, and heard, "Reau Elu-Eus."

"Mother," Reau answered. She had not been disowned—she was still a daughter of House Elu-Eus, so she had that right.

"Next week your sister Jenar will marry. Everyone in the household will attend the wedding feast—yourself included. We don't want people talking, inventing stories about House Elu-Eus. So you will sit with the family, but you will not talk to anyone. Is that clear?"

"Yes, Mother." Reau knew better than to ask what she should do if someone approached and asked her a question.

"You will be dressed for the occasion. Attend me here tomorrow, and your attire will be fitted."

"Thank you, Mother."

Reau was not misled into thinking this would change her status in the household. She was still the useless beggar in her own family, dependent on others for everything. But for the first time in years, she would be able to do something besides drift around the house that she would have inherited.

As Elu-Eus was the pre-eminent House of water sellers, the heir's wedding was an extravagant affair. So many guests had been invited that the wedding feast was held in Kindah's largest walled garden. Four servants were detailed to watch and assure Reau did nothing to shame the House. Now they herded Reau and her younger brothers through the streets of Kindah to the feast.

In her new finery, which a servant had described to her in a shy whisper, Reau stepped out of the house. It was the first time she had been outside since she was blinded, and the feel of the sun on her face, even through her veil, lifted her heart. She turned her face upward to where an opalescent blaze, emitting streamers of colors she had no names for, warmed the sky.

Reau didn't realize she had stopped until a servant whispered, "Come along. We can't tarry." A gentle hand on her back guided her forward.

Her vision was a riot of color. It shifted, changed, flowed in a sickening storm such as she had never experienced before. Closing her eyes didn't help—the colors were still there, changing with every step she took. She gulped back nausea, glad she had eaten nothing this day.

If she looked down, the colors did not squirm so. Since the servants led her, it didn't matter that she stumbled along, head bowed.

"Step up here," the servant told her, speaking loudly over the noise of the crowd.

Reau could tell they approached the doorway to the garden; the clamor about her sounded different than between building walls. She was determined to enter with dignity, as befit a daughter of Elu-Eus, so raised her head even though the colors immediately swirled sickeningly.

The servants led Reau to her place at the feast, helped her sit on the rug and arrange her skirts, and knelt on either side of her.

In the garden the colors, not so bright, were still disorienting. As Reau sat through speeches and cheering, the servants quietly directed her hand to her cup and described the food placed before her. She ate very little—sipping her drink and nibbling bread and dates.

As she listened idly to discussions around her, feeling the sun slowly moving across the sky, the colors became less overwhelming. By the time the sun sank behind the high walls around the garden, Reau began to enjoy herself. The laughter, talking, smell of food, and green scent of plants—all were so different from the life she had led, trying to be invisible, for the last four years.

Then one of the servants beside her gasped, and Reau turned her head toward the girl. "What is it?" she asked, but received no answer. The talking and laughter faded, and someone let out a short scream, cut off quickly.

Reau squinted as she tried to hear what was going on. The colors in her vision swirled, then settled. She perceived a shape, more human than the usual clot of colors. A head, two brighter eyes, a gaping mouth, and arms like flickering flames. Reau still faced the servant; could this be her?

The girl backed up—Reau felt that. Reau turned her head to follow, and saw the arms rising to block the bright color of the mouth.

Then the uneasy quiet erupted into chaos. Men shouted, women screamed, but no words Reau could understand. She turned away from the servant and saw masses of bright colors, but more discrete than what she usually perceived. Bodies, heads, the brilliance of eyes and mouths—all moving, running away from the center of the garden. In the midst of them something brilliant, radiating opalescence as the sun had.

Even over the hubbub, Reau heard strange hissing. Even over the odors of food and plant life, she smelled acrid burning. There, in the middle of the wedding party, something Vlazantzar had described to her—a firepot, about to explode.

Though Vlazantzar seemed horrified by weapons and killing, it had spoken of battles, and part of its account detailed firepots and their use in battle. Its description had been good; Reau knew that in a matter of seconds the firepot would explode and many people would be killed or horribly injured.

Reau felt for the nearby water pitcher, seized it, and pushed herself to her feet. Led by the scintillating color in the midst of screaming wedding guests, she ran. Months of practice let her body move around running people without her thinking about it.

The hissing intensified, and Reau flung the water straight into the center of the "opalescent brilliance, which vanished, becoming a dull coal of brownish red—the first 'normal' color Reau had seen in years.

Someone left the mass of moving bodies and crushed the remains of the firepot to nothingness. She sank to her knees, trembling with the realization of what could have happened.

Reau went back to Elu-Eus house in her mother's litter. There the servants washed her hands and face and helped her doff her wedding finery. Back in her accustomed trousers and shirt, she sat on a cushion in the parlor, awaiting her mother.

In the cool, dim house she could make out the servants better than she had perceived people in the warmth of the garden. The slender oval of a servant girl's face, eyes and mouth oddly bright. The large body of one of the family's guards, standing unmoving beside the door. The blaze of her mother's little dog, asleep on the carved chair. Finally she had learned to use her sight. What had caused the breakthrough? The excitement of the wedding? Focusing on something besides trying to see? The sheer number of people present? Being outdoors? She didn't know, but it had happened at an opportune time.

The house's quiet was broken when the wedding party returned. Subdued chatter—except for her sister. Jenar was furious that her wedding feast had been spoiled. She demanded to know what had happened, who was responsible, how the guards had allowed the attacker into the garden.

Reau leaned against a cool stone pillar. She was exhausted. Had this been her wedding, would she have acted like Jenar? Would anyone have had the presence of mind to do what she did?

Finally, the noise died down. Jenar and her new husband had

retired to their wing of the house.

The parlor door opened. Reau pushed herself to her feet, staring up at her mother. She looked strange, with her thick black hair a subdued purple-blue flame, the smooth brown oval of her face shining gold, black eyes glowing a color somewhere between red and amethyst.

"Reau," her mother said. "You saved us all." There was gentleness in the voice that could be so imperious.

"Someone had to. The water was near me." Reau did not want to describe what she had done.

"But how could you tell where to throw it, how to get there?"

"Perhaps the water told me. Water has talked to me for years." Reau wasn't sure why she said that. It sounded mad. But if she described the reality, how she'd *seen* the iridescent mass, that would sound mad too. And she didn't want to tell her mother anything of Vlazantzar, and what Vlazantzar had done to her. She pictured guards marching to the water room, tearing pipes out, demanding...what?...of the being.

"Of course it has." Her mother's voice changed. "You sleep in the water room, why should not water talk to you?"

Now she's patronizing me. Reau had heard that tone before. Just as well.

"Can you understand me, when I tell you that enemies tried to kill as many as they could of House Elu-Eus at the wedding?"

"I thought that might be what happened. Do you know who did it?"

"No." Her mother snorted and shook her head in frustration. "But we will soon. I have sent men all over Kindah, searching for answers." She started pacing, a nervous habit she would never let anyone else see, for she felt it betrayed weakness.

"I am confident you will find them soon, and they will be punished."

Reau's mother smacked a fist into her other palm. "Oh, they will be punished. They will die screaming, and their families, and their servants, and their—"

She broke off as the door opened once more. Reau turned, and saw it was her father. Tall, stooping, his mass of curls glowing an improbable orange red. He stepped forward and took Reau's hands. "Thank you for saving us, daughter," he said, voice soft. She wondered if he even knew of her blindness. He paid little attention to anything not in a scroll.

"She says water told her what to do," her mother supplied sarcastically.

"That makes as much sense as any other explanation. We are water sellers; why should water not speak with us?" In the glowing oval of his face, his mouth turned up in a smile.

"Don't be daft," Reau's mother said. She was often short with Reau's father, especially when he expounded some new theory.

Reau's father still held her hands. He squeezed them. "Don't worry, Reau. Whoever it was, they won't get another chance at the family. That was a particularly clumsy move, messy. They tipped us off, so now we're aware of the danger."

"I'm not afraid, Papa." Her hands glowed where his gripped them.

"Good girl." He let go of her hands and patted her back. "Off to sleep now. I'm sure you're exhausted after such excitement."

"Yes, Papa."

Reau bade her parents good night, and the servant led her out of the room.

Alone at last in the water room, she waited a long time for the household to quiet. What if her mother set someone to listen, since Reau had said water talked to her? She lay on the pallet, moving restlessly, not daring to say anything to Vlazantzar.

Finally, Vlazantzar said, *There was a great commotion tonight.*

"Can you tell if there's anyone near?" Reau whispered.

I know where everyone is, and what they are doing. Your parents are arguing in your father's study. Your sister and her husband are already asleep. One of your brothers—

"No one has been set to listen?"

No. All is as usual, now that the disturbance has abated.

"Oh, Vlazantzar, I hope I haven't been stupid." Reau told him about the wedding and how she'd extinguished the firepot. Then she described her conversation with her mother.

She disregards you and what you say.

"I hope so."

You have good news for me as well, Vlazantzar said. *Sometime during the day, with all its excitement, you have learned to better control your sight.*

"Yes!" She spoke too loudly, and clapped a hand over her mouth. Odd that she could see it now, slender and green-blue. No longer writhing colors shading one to another.

That will make your training much easier, Vlazantzar said. Satisfaction colored its voice. *Shall we begin—or are you too tired?*

"Training saved my life today. I'm not too tired."

Vlazantzar described a new move, and Reau tried it, reveling in the smooth motions of her body.

Old Reau the water seller was blind, and perhaps mad. She sat in the Elu-Eus water stall, eyes closed, head moving as if she watched the crowd for someone.

Your water supply is dwindling, Vlazantzar told Reau a few months later as she settled on her pallet in the water room.

She sat straight up, hands clutching the straw of the pallet. "What? What do you mean?"

There is much less water in the cavern below than I have ever sensed.

"It's the height of summer. The spring rains in the mountains to the north are long past." Vlazantzar had explained where the water for the Elu-Eus well came from.

I have been here for years. The water level remains constant through the seasons. But now...it is distressing.

It *would* be distressing, for a being who existed in water. But House Elu-Eus would also be distressed. Their livelihood, their seat on the council—both were completely dependent on the water drawn from their well.

"Has it been this way for a long time, and you just now thought to tell me?" Reau asked.

No. Two nights ago, all was well. Last night, the level seemed low, but I thought nothing of it. But tonight there is much less water. It was silent for a time, then said, *In the passages below, water barely wets the floor, where usually it rushes nearly to the ceiling.*

"How could it change so much overnight?" Reau asked.

That is out of my experience, Vlazantzar admitted. Since its experience was vast, that troubled her.

"What can we do?"

I do not know.

"Should I tell my family?"

And have them taunt you for talking to water? Her younger brothers had learned of what she told her mother, and teased her constantly. *They will discover soon enough for themselves.*

That was true. The next morning, when her family gathered to fill jars in the water room, Reau stood outside the door, watching. Jenar filled the smallest jars and handed them to the youngest boys. When she started filling the next jar, the water's flow trickled to nothing. Reau couldn't see this, but she heard when the water stopped splashing into the jar, and the very bad word Jenar said. Jenar murmured, "Is there something stuck in the pipe?"

Soon the older members of the family gathered in the water room. They disassembled the pipes, then the pumps, then put them back together. Still no water. As they argued, fear in their voices, Reau faded back into the living rooms.

The water was gone. What could they do? Without water the family had no income. Mother, of course, had saved money, but that wouldn't support the family for long. All Elu-Eus had ever done was sell water. Reau supposed her younger brothers could be apprenticed to someone, but Jenar...Jenar would never take another trade. The family would be dishonored. They would have to leave Kindah.

Huge stone cisterns beneath the house held emergency water reserves. Elu-Eus family could sell water in their stall for many days. But after that...

Once everyone left the water room, still arguing, Reau crept back. She sat in the cool darkness, already imagining it was warmer, drier than before.

"Vlazantzar," she whispered. "Can you hear me?" It must have fled when her family disassembled the pipes. Had it come back?

Reau. The voice was faint, wavering.

"Vlazantzar, help me. You can see the water. Have you traced it back?"

There is an obstruction.

"Obstruction? What kind?"

It is manufactured. Someone has deliberately cut off your water.

Reau gasped. How could anyone do that? *Why* would anyone do that? Then she remembered the firepot at the feast. "Could it be whoever tried to kill us?"

That is a possibility.

Reau asked slowly, "Can a person get through the passages where water normally flows? Could I go down and unblock the water?"

It would be dangerous. There is nowhere for you to go, once the obstruction is cleared, before water fills the passageways again.

"But would I fit?"

Vlazantzar's voice sounded reluctant. *You would, Reau.*

"I'll go down and see— But *will* I be able to see down there?"

You should be able to see almost as well as you can in the water room.

Reau knew that the round stone she had slept on for the last four years covered the old well. Elu-Eus family had drawn water from the well until, in Reau's grandmother's day, pumps were installed. The stone was huge and heavy; it had not moved even when she leapt on and off it during training.

Now she ran her hands along its edge. It was thick as her arm, a circle wide as her father was tall. "Vlazantzar, how strong am I?"

It is impossible for me to ascertain that, it said, voice still faint and wavery.

"I need to move the cover off the well. Can I do it without hurting myself? You said I am much stronger than a normal human."

Reau! Was that panic in Vlazantzar's voice?

"Don't worry. I'll be careful."

Reau had never heard of anyone moving the cover for the well. But she saw nothing fastening it down. Did the cover's weight hold it in place?

She spread her arms out, hugging the curve of the stone.

*Reau, will you traverse the chilly caverns below the city in thin trousers, barefoot? You have never known cold. I suggest you

225

dress warmly.*

Reau blinked. She had not thought, when Vlazantzar described the water passages, that they would be uncomfortable. What could she wear? She had leather sandals she'd not worn since she was blinded. They would have to do; her only other footwear was the silk slippers she had worn to her sister's wedding.

She kept her clothing in a box against the water room's wall. She opened it, lifted out the pretty things she'd worn to the wedding feast and laid them aside, then took out her sturdiest trousers. Those went on over the trousers she already wore. A heavier shirt and a vest she hadn't worn for years. Even in the coolness of the water room, she was uncomfortably hot in all that clothing.

"I'm dressed more warmly," she told Vlazantzar. She knelt beside the stone cover.

In training, Reau had never been able to test the full extent of her strength. Trying to move the cover was a worthy challenge. Though she lifted with her arms all along the edge, the stone did not move. She shifted her stance. Putting one foot on the ground, knee bent to give herself more leverage, she pushed the stone with the big muscles of thighs and shoulders.

When the stone remained immobile, Reau used more force than she'd ever anticipated needing. She closed her eyes, gritted her teeth, and shoved.

The stone moved. Slowly, a finger-width at a time, it grated across the well's rim. She was certain the sound of its passage was so loud someone would rush in to investigate. But no one came, and still she pushed, though sweat ran down her face, and shoulders and back burned with the effort. Damp air wafted across her face to cool it.

Reau was slender, only as tall as a twelve-year-old. She pushed the stone until there was space to fit her head and shoulders through, then stopped to rest aching muscles. "I opened it, Vlazantzar," she said. There was no answer. She leaned against the well's edge, waiting. Perhaps it was inspecting the obstruction. Always before it had answered her. Where was it? "Vlazantzar?" Nothing.

Taking a deep breath, Reau pushed her head through the gap.

She could get a rope, tie it to pipes in the water room, and let herself down into the well. But she needed to know how deep it was.

The inside of the well shone purest amethyst. Reau blinked, trying to get past the color and see the details. She slid farther in, until head and shoulders were both inside the damp-smelling cavern.

When the well's interior came into focus, she took another deep breath, feeling the stone tighten around her chest. The well's rim was mortared stone. She'd seen it, without really noticing, for years. But what she had not known—perhaps no one in her family knew—was that stone steps spiraled down the inside of the well. She would need no rope. "Vlazantzar?" she asked tentatively. No answer.

Putting her feet on the lip of the well, she placed her shoulders against the cover and pushed it far enough to the side that she could reach the stairs. Then, holding tightly to the rim, she touched the top step with one foot.

The stone was dry, the wall of the well cool against her hand. Slowly, feeling for each step, she descended. The depths of the well roiled with purples, blues, and colors she knew no names for.

When her head was below the level of the well's lip, she shuddered, feeling she had passed into a realm beyond her control. "Vlazantzar?" No answer.

Down and down she spiraled, one hand on the wall, each step careful and controlled. The air became more moist, and the walls shone with pink iridescence. The steps beneath her sandals were damp but not slick.

In the purple-blue depths of the well, Reau was certain she was below the level where water usually stood. The steps were rounded, as if water flowed along them, wearing off tiny particles year after year. The air moved slightly, and hairs on Reau's arms rose at the chill, even through the sleeves of her heaviest shirt.

Then the endless step down, step down, step down ceased. Reau's sandal met stone floor and splashed. She drew her foot up and paused on the last step. "Vlazantzar?" she called into the oddly echoing passageway.

Still no answer. She'd expected, once she was closer to

Vlazantzar's domain, that it would return to her. She found herself blinking back tears. For months it had been her only friend and companion, her helper and teacher. To have it disappear so suddenly, without explanation... Could a being like Vlazantzar be killed? Or had it left because the water was gone? Then why had it not bade her farewell?

She took a deep breath, wiped tears from her cheeks with her sleeve, and stepped into the puddles that were all that was left of the Elu-Eus water supply.

Water dripped everywhere. Reau, desert born, had never experienced the like. In this passage all was chill and damp. The walls shone deep purple, the blue of the sky just after dusk, or in places a green so dark as to be almost black. The footing was treacherous—ridges ran along the floor so she had to step carefully.

Reau had thought to be guided by Vlazantzar once she set foot in the water passageways, so had not asked it to describe the route she must take. Now she splashed, shivering, through the underground corridor, peering closely at every change in color to see if it signaled some branching passage.

Then ahead she saw shifting, flickering colors—pink and purple and gold. A person down here in the cold damp with her? Vlazantzar suspected Elu-Eus's water had been cut off—could this be the person who did so?

She stopped, aware that in the darkness she could see, but one without her odd gift could not. If she did not splash, this other person should not know she was here. She backed up almost to the passage wall, breathing quietly, though she didn't expect to be heard above the intermittent drips.

A voice echoed oddly through the passage. "Reau?"

For years she'd heard this voice, though it was now distorted by water drips and muffled by walls. Impulsively she called, "Vlazantzar?"

Whoever was ahead, flickering purple and gold, turned and ran toward Reau. Feet splashed in pools. Breath rasped, as if the person had run far and was almost at the end of endurance.

Reau held still. The voice had sounded like Vlazantzar, but it was a creature of water—not a man who ran, and splashed, and called her name yet again.

He stopped a few arm's lengths from her and stood, panting. "Reau. I manifested in the wrong passage, and it has taken far too long to find you." It *was* Vlazantzar's voice, coming from the mouth of a short young man. Unlike most people, whose colors remained fairly stable, his flickered along his body, golds and purples and pinks intermixing with colors that were not so ordinary.

"How can you be Vlazantzar?" Reau faltered.

"My kind can take human form, but rarely do. It is so limiting! I can hardly see you, much less what's happening above the ground."

He stepped closer, and Reau realized he was scarcely a hand's width taller than she. He had curly hair—at first glowing golden, then streaked with amethyst, then dripping pink. His face was round, with a turned-up nose and wide mouth. He grinned. "Not quite what you expected from one of my kind?" he asked.

"I...never expected you to...look like one of my brothers," she gasped.

"I don't know what my physical form looks like to human eyes," he said, suddenly serious. "Do you find it pleasing?"

"I...yes, I do."

He reached for her hand. "Come, we must hurry."

Reluctantly, she took his hand. It was warm as any human's. His grip was strong, and he squeezed her fingers reassuringly before saying, "Follow me."

They splashed through the passageway. Vlazantzar bumped into walls and tripped over ridges in the floor. "Can't you see like I do?" Reau asked. "I thought—"

"I was too hasty assuming human form," Vlazantzar said, panting. "I forgot to specify what attributes were required."

"I can see," said Reau. "Let me lead, and save you from hurting yourself." Would he be angry at this suggestion? How could a mere human lead a being such as he? But he acquiesced eagerly.

After a long time splashing through cold, damp caverns, Vlazantzar said, "Quiet. We approach the obstruction."

Reau stopped, shivering, trying to keep her teeth from chattering. Ahead was a jumble of colors—pale, different from the dark iridescence of cavern walls. "I don't see any people," she said. "What should we do?"

"Before I took human form, I explored the obstruction. It is a wall built of stone which diverts the water to another passageway."

"We can move the stones, and Elu-Eus will have its water back." Reau set off purposefully through knee-deep water toward the pale jumble of stone. Since she still grasped Vlazantzar's hand, she could feel how reluctantly he followed.

Water trickled through the wall—which was built from old paving stones and worked stone from house or courtyard walls—in several places. Reau scrambled up, easily finding finger and toe holds, 'til her head brushed the damp stone ceiling.

Vlazantzar followed more slowly. Still getting used to his human body? "What will happen if I pull these rocks out?" Reau called.

"The wall could collapse and sweep us both away when the water is released," said Vlazantzar. "I do not know this for certain; I am no engineer. I have watched walls being built, but never done so myself."

Reau took a deep breath. Should she take the chance? Was she willing to sacrifice her life for House Elu-Eus? For her mother, who condescended to notice Reau only when it benefitted the House? Her father, who barely noticed she existed? Her sister, who gloated over the fact that *she* was now heir? Her brothers, who teased and tormented her? They would never even know what she'd done. Vlazantzar had warned her, back in the water room, that this could be dangerous. Yet she had come. She'd decided *then* to take the risk.

Reau reached for a paving stone jammed in at the top of the barrier. It came out easily. She dropped it—being careful not to hit Vlazantzar, who was still below her—and heard it splash into the water below. Hardly exerting her strength, she pulled out another stone, then another.

Water spurted out of the gap she was forming, but the stones Reau stood upon held firm. She removed stones and dropped them. Vlazantzar, when he joined her, did the same. Soon water flowed, deep indigo with glints of purples, greens, and blues, through the hole they created, and splashed down into the cavern below.

Vlazantzar began talking, in the monotonous tone he had used when recalling bygone experiences. "A sailor fell from his ship into the ocean. Curious, I watched him. He kicked his feet, and swung his arms, first one, then the other, over his head and then back toward his body, cupping water with his hands. Thus he stayed above the ocean's surface and propelled himself back to his ship." He stopped abruptly, then said with far more expression in his voice, "Reau, you have worked with water all your life, but do not know the power wild water exerts. I never thought to have you practice moves to keep you above water, should you fall in, for in Kindah that was an impossibility."

"My thanks, Vlazantzar," Reau said, never pausing, though her shoulders ached. "I'll remember your instructions, should the need arise."

"We may both need to practice this maneuver, since the water in the cavern is now too deep to wade through."

"I see." Reau tamped down panic building in her chest.

Soon Reau and Vlazantzar had to move farther along the wall, away from the rapid flow of water escaping through the sizeable hole they'd created. The colors in the water reminded Reau of when she had first been blinded—ever moving and changing, never the same twice.

Reau's four years of training her hearing to compensate for sight had sharpened her ability to separate sounds. She was certain she heard a noise differing from the rush of water. "Vlazantzar, I hear something."

"Curse this body and its inadequate ears," he replied. "I hear nothing but water."

"To the right, where this barrier meets the cavern, most of the way up the passage wall." At that moment she saw the unmistakable writhing opalescence of flames, and the moving shapes of human bodies. "It's people with torches."

"Ah." Vlazantzar sighed. "I had hoped it would take much longer before they noticed the water level receding on the other side of the barrier."

Rushing water echoed through the cavern too loudly for Reau to make out anything the people—three of them—were saying.

After a time, the colors of flame and human bodies disappeared, leaving only the deep blues and greens of the cavern walls.

"There's an entrance into the water cavern. We can find out who built this," Reau said.

"Reau, no!" Vlazantzar moaned. "It's too dangerous. Go back to your house and tell your mother. Have her send strong men with spears."

"No." Reau was surprised at how much emphasis she put into that word. "We mustn't let others know of the water caverns below Kindah. If everyone knew, everyone could make their own wells, and House Elu-Eus would be ruined. I'm strong, and you've trained me. I'll stop these water thieves."

Vlazantzar made a strange noise. Reau turned to look at him. His face twisted with emotion. He moved closer to her and awkwardly pulled her against him. She felt his heart pounding, and his warmth eased her shivering. "Reau, I have lived a long time, and seen much. Always before, even when I took human form, I was simply an observer. This time...I cannot explain what has happened. We have become connected in a way I do not understand. But I feel more for you than simply the urge to free myself from the bond that held me here. You are strong, but you can be easily broken. I had forgotten how fragile these bodies are. I have trained you, yes, but you have never used your training against enemies. I have seen many things, but have not *done* many things. I observe. I remember. But I do not *do*. And...I do not want you killed."

"Then this is how we differ, Vlazantzar," said Reau, though his words started an odd fluttery feeling somewhere in her stomach. "I must do this. Are you coming with me?" She gently freed herself from him and started edging along the stone barrier before he answered.

"I will come." He spoke so quietly his words were hard to hear over the echoing rush of water.

In the cavern wall, near the ceiling, was an ancient wooden door, water-soaked and rotten. The metal holding it together was rusted nearly away. Yet it had obviously held together when opened recently, so Reau stepped onto a stone ledge at the base of the door and reached for the handle.

The door opened with a screech of rusty hinges. Reau rushed in, with Vlazantzar close behind her.

The three men sitting on muddy piles of stone turned startled faces toward Reau and Vlazantzar. Then they pulled knives from their belts and leapt to their feet.

Before fear could slow her, Reau launched into a training move Vlazantzar had taught her. Running crouched, she butted the first man in the stomach, sweeping her arm up to knock his knife away. Startled when the move worked so well, she was bowled over when the next man swung a fist at her.

From the gritty floor she reached out, grabbed his legs just below the knees, and wrenched him from his feet. As he fell she jumped up and butted into the third man as she had the first.

The fight didn't last much longer. The second man had hit his head on a stone as he fell, and lay groaning on the floor. When the first man scrambled to his feet and tried to hit her, she planted a foot in his groin, a move Vlazantzar had told her was very effective against men. Considering how the man collapsed, curled in a ball and moaning, Vlazantzar was correct.

The third man backed into a corner behind some stones and said, "Don't hurt me, child. I didn't do anything to you!"

She recognized his voice. It was Aquel Bishah, son of one of the other water sellers in Kindah. When she was young she had been promised to him. His mother had broken the betrothal when Reau was 'damaged.'

"How can you say that, Aquel?" she snarled at him. "Taking all the water from Elu-Eus. You have hurt more than me with this action!"

He stared at her, eyes blazing golden and mouth a sickly yellow-green. "Reau Elu-Eus? I was told you were blind, and mad. How...what—"

"*How* and *what* are none of House Bishah's business," Reau spat. "I'm glad that we never wed."

"Had we been, I wouldn't have needed the dam," he retorted. "I'd have been part of Elu-Eus, the leading house of water sellers."

"Elu-Eus does not need small minds like yours. Were you behind the firepot at my sister's wedding, too?"

The way Aquel started guiltily, and one of his friends said from the floor, "Say nothing, Aquel!" told Reau that she had guessed correctly.

"Reau!" called Vlazantzar. She looked down to see the man she had kicked in the groin grab for her leg. Dancing out of that man's grasp, she fell into the arms of the man who had hit his head, who clumsily pulled her against his chest. But she was strong enough to break away. Aquel came around the pile of stone, holding a knife. He threw it toward Reau—and Vlazantzar stepped between Reau and the knife.

As the glittering gold of blood bloomed on Vlazantzar's chest, Reau spun in a move Vlazantzar had made her practice, hitting Aquel with enough force to knock him over the stones to lie in a sprawl on the floor, unmoving.

Vlazantzar sank to his knees, the colors chasing across his body making it difficult for Reau to see his expression. She knelt next to him, and he gasped, "Do not remove the knife. I have seen how that increases blood flow."

"Can...can your kind of being die?" Reau asked frantically. "What can I do to help you?"

"I must give up this body," Vlazantzar said. "The process will severely weaken me. I may have to rest for a long time to regain enough energy to continue my travels."

"I'll take care of you—but I must do something with these murderous water thieves."

"Let me touch them," Vlazantzar said, his voice growing weaker.

Reau was gratified that her strength made it easy to drag the young men—two of them squirming and kicking, trying to escape—over to where Vlazantzar could touch them. When he did they calmed immediately, slumping and shaking their heads as if flies had settled on their faces and they were trying to shoo them. Had Vlazantzar *changed* them?

"Get me back to water," Vlazantzar said, and Reau spent no more time worrying about Aquel and his friends. She picked Vlazantzar up and carried him out onto the ledge.

The water had risen while she fought House Bishah's wayward son and his friends. She knelt on the ledge and eased Vlazantzar's legs, then his torso, into the water. "Does that help?" she whispered, tears rising in her eyes and constricting her throat.

"Reau, I will come back to you," said Vlazantzar, and his body dissolved from beneath her arms where she supported it. The knife clattered to the stone ledge, and Reau was alone.

Old Reau the water seller was blind, and perhaps mad. That happens sometimes to water sellers; Salza Bishah's son and two of his friends were found senseless in the water room, and spoke only gibberish from that day forward.

Soaked, shivering, and sobbing, Reau made her way out of the Bishah house cellars into the heat and sunlight of Kindah. She had been sitting quietly on the mat behind her sister in the Elu-Eus stall for some time before anyone noticed her.

"Why are you here, sister?" Jenar asked, and Reau could tell by the sound of her voice that she was extremely put out to have her impaired sister here in the stall.

"To prove that I can sell water as well as anyone in House Elu-Eus."

"You're blind," scoffed Jenar. "You cannot see to pour the water."

"I'll show you." Reau picked up the largest water jar with ease, and filled Jenar's cup without spilling a drop.

Reau had to repeat the feat for everyone in her family before they believed it was not a trick. "It won't matter anyway," Jenar said glumly. "The water has dried up."

"The water is back," Reau retorted.

"How could you know that?"

"I talk to water."

Old Reau the water seller was blind, and perhaps mad. She sold water in Kindah's bazaar before our grandmothers were girls, and some said she would still be selling water when the world ended.

Most who dealt with Reau could not tell she was blind. As people passed by the blue-and-green striped awning that sheltered House Elu-Eus's water stall, she held up her huge water jar—a feat made all the more impressive because of her small stature—and offered a drink. If they accepted, dropping coins into her box, she poured the water into cup or waterskin, or directly into the mouths of some, spilling none of the precious liquid.

When she had no customers Reau sat on the mat, eyes closed, face turning back and forth as if watching the crowds. Only one person noticed when one day Reau sat up straight, leaned forward with joy lighting her face, and leapt to her feet. She left her stall, raced into the arms of a curly-haired young man, and never returned.

This is the story of Reau the water seller, who was blind, and perhaps mad, but finally rejoined her dearest friend and set off with him to see the greater world..

SEA OF SOULS

by Robin Wayne Bailey

Robin Wayne Bailey's "Sea of Souls" is one of two stories in this anthology that deal with the sea, its perils and its music. Two quite different stories, I might add, whose themes add rich resonances to this eternal theme.

Robin Wayne Bailey is the author of numerous novels, including the Dragonkin trilogy and the Frost series of novels and stories, as well as *Shadowdance* and the Fritz Leiber-inspired *Swords Against the Shadowland*. His short fiction has appeared in many magazines and anthologies with numerous appearances in Marion Zimmer Bradley's *Sword and Sorceress* series and Deborah J. Ross's *Lace and Blade* anthologies. Some of his stories have been collected in two volumes, *Turn Left to Tomorrow* and *The Fantastikon: Tales of Wonder* from Yard Dog Books. He's a former two-term president of the Science Fiction and Fantasy Writers of America and a founder of the Science Fiction Hall of Fame. He's co-edited, along with Bryan Thomas Schmidt, the recent anthology, *Little Green Men-Attack!*

Perilana stood barefooted on the warm, sun-drenched beach and gazed with blind eyes outward over the placid Sea of Souls. The waves stole upon the shore like white-capped thieves as an easy breeze whispered soft distractions in her ear, and although she smiled, she ignored those unchangeable rhythms and listened instead to the shifting grains of sand, the distant call of a frightened seagull and, far behind her, the heartbeats of a hundred men.

A hundred mounted men—and one woman.

Without warning, the seagull gave a panicked cry, and its wings beat furiously as it raced away. The sand rattled, a sound that turned to thunder as a pair of riders charged forward. Steel whisked against leather. *Only two,* she realized, listening closely, *coming fast and drawing swords.*

She drew a deep breath, relaxed, and assumed a defensive stance. The sound of the sea, the gull, the shifting sand and the breeze combined into a harmony. It flowed over and through her. Such beautiful sound. *Music!*

Perilana sensed the soldiers, closer now, swords upraised and cleaving the wind, but she stood her ground and drew the music into herself. Her skin tingled and her dark hair rose up in whipping strands. Then, when she could hold it no longer, she opened her hands and let it back out.

Touched by an unnatural force, the sand rippled outward around her. The riders bore down upon her, oblivious to the ripples. Leaning low over their racing mounts, eyes burning with ferocity beneath their helmets, swords gleaming in the vivid sunlight, Perilana's life seemed lost. Yet, she held her ground and her defensive posture and let the music play over her.

The riders were so close now that she could hear the creak of their armor, the rasp of their breathing. Yet, though it seemed certain that they would run her into the sand, they drew no closer. The horses charged ahead, but they didn't reach her, nor gain any advance at all.

The Queen of All spoke inside Perilana's head. Her tone was regal, but curious, even amused. *What have you done to them?*

Perilana knew the queen was with the rest of her army in the rocks beyond the beach but didn't bother to turn. "They are locked in a single moment," Perilana answered, "riding forever and waving their silly swords, but getting nowhere. And they are completely unaware."

The Queen of All chuckled. *Brilliant!* she said. *I would have never thought of it.*

"That's why you hang back in the rocks, surrounded by your soldiers," Perilana said. "You fear me."

Not today, blind child. The Queen of All laughed. Then, she turned serious. *But I am impressed with your display. Now, release my men, if you will.*

Perilana sighed, knowing she was not strong enough to defy the Queen of All, but though she chaffed, she obeyed. She drew the music back into herself, savoring its sweetness only for a moment more. Then, she released it into the sea.

The two soldiers spurred their horses forward. Perilana felt the harsh breaths of their mounts on her back, and she braced herself. But before either soldier could strike her down, she felt another sudden ripple in the sand and both soldiers, along with their horses, exploded in fine showers of blood.

The Queen of All spoke in Perilana's head again. *Come to my palace at your leisure, child. Take your time—smell the flowers, as you will, and enjoy the sun on your face. But think, also, of your little sister, whose company I am enjoying very much.*

Perilana clenched a fist. "If you hurt her..."

But the Queen of All and all her men only turned and rode away. Perilana listened to the horses' hooves, the jingle-jangle of armor and weapons, the fading heartbeats. But for the soft surge of the waves, all soon became quiet again.

Alone, she ran her right hand over her left arm, down to her wrist, and more tentatively to the fingers. The last two had fused together into a single scaled claw. Her heart sank for a moment as she noted the transformation. Fighting back tears, she cradled her new hand, then flexed it, and tried uselessly to will it to change back again, but the hand was her hand now.

"This is the price," a deep voice said beside her. "Magic always extracts a price, and great magic extracts a great price. No matter how benign and well-intentioned, every spell leaves you open for demonic forces and possession."

Perilana reached out with her good hand to clutch a strong, bare arm. Vaseem's skin felt smooth as sea foam, and he smelled of the sea and sea breezes. When he spoke, his voice carried old echoes of the surf.

"You're not telling me anything I don't know, my handsome Sea Serpent."

Vaseem chuckled. "How do you know I'm handsome? I could look like a fish."

"My eyes are blind, but my mind's eye is sharp," she answered. "In the water, you are a shimmering monster with glittering scales and fins of gold and silver. On land, whatever form you take, cannot help but reflect that power and beauty." She squeezed his biceps, knowing that she was right.

"What if you are wrong?" Vaseem pressed. "What if I appear

to others as something ugly and deadly?"

"Then you are still my friend and protector."

Vaseem stroked her hair, his touch calming. "Don't fall in love with me, Perilana. Our worlds may appear to meet where wave meets sand, but they really are farther apart than even you can imagine."

"I'm not in love with you," she lied too quickly. "But I am somewhat dependent upon you. Take my hand—my *good* hand—and lead me along the shore to the queen's palace. And along the way, if you know of anything in your eternal wisdom that will help me defeat the Queen of All and save my sister without destroying myself."

Vaseem laughed. "Such flattery," he said. "I'm afraid I'm not a fortune teller, Perilana. Just a sea serpent out of water."

They began to walk. The palace stood some distance away up the shoreline. Perilana might have found her own way by listening to the waves and the incoming tide or by the tang of the salt breezes. Hers was a world of sound and scent, a beautiful world, and she had never known another. She was adept at making her way in it.

But she felt glad and grateful to have met Vaseem, although she suspected their meeting was no accident. Only a few months ago, the Queen of All, for no known reason, had come sweeping southward, attacking towns and villages. One of those was Perilana's village. The Queen took no captives, touched nothing of value. But her soldiers rounded up every single man, woman, and child, and drowned them in the sea.

Perilana had escaped only because she was deep inland at the time, in forest country, nursing a sick family with herbs and small healing spells.

Now, the Queen of All, claimed to have Perilana's younger sister. She was determined to find out if it was true, and so she had begun her march to Poseidonis, the seat of the Queen's power.

Perilana stopped suddenly and clutched Vaseem's arm in a tighter grip. The sand vibrated and subtly shifted beneath her bare feet. She listened but heard nothing unusual. "Something lies ahead," she told Vaseem, "but it's too far for me."

Vaseem answered. "Ten soldiers in a line, very far off."

"Yet, you see them?" Perilana pressed.

He gave a low chuckle. "Even in this form, my eyes are not human eyes." He paused. Perilana could feel the muscles tensing in his arm. "I believe they are attempting to avoid the fate of their two comrades."

Perilana felt the new black-scaled claw on her left hand, and she swallowed uncertainly. "If they charge, I can stop them."

Vaseem's hand closed over hers. "Don't be so quick to resort to magic, Peri," he warned. "In your small, nameless village, you might have been safe in your obscurity, but here, so close to this cursed city, demons are everywhere. They have seen you now, and they want you."

"Then, how can I defend myself...!" She didn't finish the question. A strange sound vibrated in the air. It was far away, but swiftly coming straight for her. "Arrows!" she cried, bracing herself, raising her hands.

"No!" Vaseem hissed. He pushed her hands back down, then stepped forward. "Stay behind me!"

The first two arrows flew high, over their heads. Perilana heard the high-pitched whine of the spinning fletchettes in the air. A third arrow flew wide and buried itself in the sand. But seven more struck Vaseem. She heard their impact against his body, then the harsh snapping of arrow heads and wooden shafts, and the broken pieces as they fell to the ground.

"The arrows didn't hurt you!" she said.

"That isn't stopping them from trying again," Vaseem answered. "Stay back!"

A second volley climbed into the sun and then fell earthward again on a fatal trajectory. Perilana listened to the awful song they made in flight, and she began to tremble. She feared unreasonably for Vaseem. Nor was she one to cower behind another.

The soldiers aimed better this time. All ten shafts struck Vaseem. All ten shattered into fragments against his body.

"Third flight," Vaseem warned. "They're persistent."

Perilana growled suddenly. Angry and anxious, she stepped away from her friend. Before he could react, she took an aggressive stance and raised her clawed hand. The arrows burst into flame, reversed their flight, and plunged right back toward the archers.

Men and horses screamed as they frantically tried to avoid their own shafts. Men fell from their saddles, mounts stumbled. Three found their feet again and raced through the sand back along the shore to safety. The rest of their comrades were not so lucky.

"That was foolish," Vaseem said.

Perilana scowled. "She invites me to her palace and then tries to block my way. What game is she playing?"

"She's testing you," Vaseem answered, "and forcing you to use your magic. Look at your hand."

Perilana bit back the urge to remind him that she could not *look*, but she felt her left hand with her right. The first two fingers were now also fused together into a single scaled and razor-sharp claw. In place of four fingers, she now had two talons. She fought down panic and, without another word, resumed her trek to Poseidonis.

Vaseem walked beside her. "Tell me about your sister," he said to make conversation.

"Her voice is music," Perilana answered, "and she moves like the softest breeze. Her every act is kindness. My parents doted on her, and the village loved her like a treasure."

"But she was not a witch?"

Perilana shook her head. "My mother had some slight ability, but not my sister." She hesitated, lost in a momentary thought. "My mother considered it a secret and a shame. I never shared that attitude. I helped people." She hesitated again. "I just wish I'd been at home when the queen's soldiers came."

"You were where you were meant to be," Vaseem said quietly. "Just as you are where you're meant to be now."

They reached the place on the beach where seven soldiers lay dead, impaled with their own arrows. Vaseem bent down; cloth ripped, a piece of a cloak perhaps, and then he carefully wrapped Perilana's transformed hand. "No one need see it," he said.

But Perilana was listening to something else and turned to face the sea. "Sometimes, I think I hear voices," she said softly, "in the waves and the rush of water over the sand. They sing to me." She touched Vaseem's arm again and leaned her head upon his biceps. "Or maybe I'm just going mad, Vaseem, or in a very strange dream."

Vaseem wrapped his arms around her and drew her close. Perilana listened to his heartbeat, his steady breathing, and felt his warmth. His constant presence these past days comforted her. "I've never killed anyone before," she whispered against is chest. "I killed those soldiers so easily. Almost without thought. And there was no music this time when I used my magic."

"There will be more killing ahead," Vaseem told her. "But none of this is your fault. For some reason, the Queen of All has fixed her eye on you. She will not let go willingly."

Perilana thought about that for a long moment before she pushed away from Vaseem. "Then I am forced to play her game." She started forward along the shore again, and Vaseem followed.

Out to sea, the sky began to darken. Perilana heard the change in the wind and felt the drop in temperature. A moment later, a crackle of lightning filled the air with a low hum, and distant thunder rattled the sky. She didn't fear a storm or rain. She knew the rhythms of the raindrops and reveled in the chaotic tympany of thunder, the whip-lash of lightning. Once again, the world sang to her!

A strong gust blew over the shore, nearly toppling her, but Perilana stood her ground and savored the salty breeze. When the rain came down in sharp, pelting drops, she lifted her face to it. But also, carried on the storm, she heard voices, the same voices she had heard before in the sea foam, but those were distant and these seemed very close. Still, she could not decipher the words or the language. Maybe they were many languages. She couldn't be sure.

On impulse, she cried out to them. "I don't understand! What do you want?"

But the voices faded away again as the storm gained power.

Suddenly, Vaseem dropped a wet cloak over her shoulders. "I ran back to the soldiers and snatched these for us. They won't keep us dry, but they may keep us warmer."

Perilana recoiled and shrugged the garment off. "*Ugh*! Dead men's clothes!"

"Then we need to find some shelter!" He picked her up, and for the first time, Perilana got a real hint of Vaseem's size and strength. Turning his back to the sea, he headed inland, sheltering her with his body as much as he could. He had kept one of the soldiers' cloaks for himself, and she could smell its burned edges. He had also taken a sword and wore it now strapped around his waist. She heard the leather scabbard slapping against his thigh. She heard a new sound as well, the hammering of rain on the leaves of trees.

"It's only an oasis," Vaseem shouted over the howling wind. "But I see rocks, too. They'll protect us."

He carried Perilana a little further and then set her down with her back against a boulder. The rocks blocked the force of the wind, but lightning crackled wildly overhead, and the thunder nearly deafened. "Wait here," Vaseem instructed. "I won't be far."

She leaned back and hugged herself, admitting privately that she'd been too hasty to discard the fallen soldier's cloak. Too late now. Lightning crackled above the oasis, and a tree limb splintered and crashed down. Then another tree limb came down. A third followed it. Perilana listened uncertainly as Vaseem dragged the limbs across the sand and rocks. She tried to envision what he was doing. Then something fell above her, and a thick shower of raindrops made her recoil and shiver. She recognized the rattling of leaves and the wet plant smell. Vaseem reassured her as he piled a second branch beside the first and then the third on top of both.

The lean-to shelter completely blocked the wind, and although water continued to drop through the leaves, it was not the stabbing storm-driven rain. Vaseem crawled in beside her. He wrapped her in the cloak he wore and then held her in his arms against his body. "I wish you could see it, Peri," he said as he hugged her, "the way the wet edges of the leaves glimmer in the lightning."

Perilana felt the new shape of her left hand and shivered. "What a strange moment this is," she said. "I'm in a fight for my life—for my sister's life—and yet, right now, chilled and soaked to the bone, I feel at peace beside you."

"When I first saw you on the beach, you looked sad and broken. I could feel that sadness, and I was glad you could not see the bodies of your people bobbing on the surf, washing up on the shore."

"You helped me bury as many as we could."

They grew quiet for a few moments. Perilana listened to the rain on the leaves, to the thunder and lightning, to the beat of

Vaseem's heart as she snuggled closer. She had always thought of her blindness as a gift. It allowed her to hear the world as few others did, as music. But now, for the first time she could remember, she wished that she could see, that she could know what Vaseem looked like.

The thought disturbed her. Suddenly, she pushed away from Vaseem and turned her mind to other things. "I should have seen it," she said. "I should have thought it through. The Queen of All killed all those people, not just in my village, but all the others along the coast, because she was looking for me. That's why she spared my sister, to use her as bait."

Vaseem sat up. "I've watched you many times, Peri, long before you realized my existence. I watched as you practiced by the shore, casting spells over the water, growing stronger as you grew up. I saw how you helped your friends and neighbors, healed and helped them when you could out of goodness and kindness. I saw your heart and swore to myself that I would always protect you." He hesitated before continuing. "I will not let you come to harm."

"Why, Vaseem?" She wanted him to say something.

Vaseem drew a deep breath and let it go. "Because you are something rare in this world. I nick-named you *Peri* for a reason. You are genuinely good, child, with no evil in you."

It wasn't quite what she wanted to hear, but for now, it cheered her. She unwrapped her left hand and held it up. "But for how long? If I'm to be possessed, how long can I remain good?" She touched Vaseem's arm for reassurance. "She wants my power. I feel it. And once she takes it, I will not be the same."

She crawled from beneath the lean-to and stood up in the rain. "We should go to Poseidonis.

Vaseem stood up beside her. "Are you so eager to fight?"

Perilana pursed her lips as she turned her face up into the storm. The rain stung, but it also invigorated. She thought of her sister, her villagers, the voices in the sea calling to her. To join them? Or to avenge them?

Vaseem's question echoed in her head. "Yes." She answered.

Vaseem caught her hand and led her out of the oasis and back toward the sea. Night had come over the land, and continuous lightning set the air to tingling. She felt it like an itch on her skin, heard it like wild music. She dug her toes into the wet sand and moved at the best pace she could manage. In little time, they made it back to the beach again.

But the music was different. The surf roared in anger, almost savage as it cut away pieces of the shore. The sky shook, and the rain hissed. Through it all came the voices, chanting or singing, she couldn't tell, but speaking to her. "Do you hear them?" she called to Vaseem.

"Hear them?" he answered. He let go of Perilana's hand, crossed the narrowing strip of beach and waded out to meet the waves. The water churned around him as he uttered a brief chant. Then came a loud splashing and thrashing and a cry like none she had ever heard before.

Vaseem suddenly touched her arm. She hadn't heard him emerge from the water or approach her at all. "We should go," she urged.

"It will take me but a moment to dress," he answered.

She gasped. Vaseem was naked. But then, she chuckled. "I guess I don't need to turn around."

Ignoring her comment, he urged, "Let's continue. I find myself as eager for this fight as you. But prepare yourself. We must attack before dawn."

"Attack?" she said, startled. "Before dawn? What did you learn when you went down to the water?"

"Prepare yourself," he repeated, saying nothing more.

Prepare myself? What did Vaseem mean by that? She would do whatever it took to free her sister. She knew her magic and knew her strength. She had restrained herself from the grand spells before, but she knew them by heart. Still, one thought troubled her.

"I've never used my magic for violence," she whispered almost to herself.

Vaseem remained silent, but the voices in the sea sang louder and more powerfully, their music compelling. It disturbed her in a way she didn't understand. What were they saying? What did they want from her? She kept walking and thinking, and she began feeling her new claws. *Prepare myself,* she thought again. *For more of this, for more change. This is the price.*

"Vaseem," she called. "I know it's night, but can you see the towers of Poseidonis?"

"It lies straight ahead," he answered in solemn tones. "Its sheer walls go right down to the shore. Its dark spires have bent and grown crooked under the weight of the sky. Night revolves around it as if it were the center of a vortex. It wears its age like a shroud. I'm glad you cannot see it."

"Your description paints a picture," she answered. She drew herself erect, put aside her fatigue, and waited. Lightning crackled in the air; she felt it tingling on her skin. Without hesitation, she reached out with both hands, visualized seizing the fiery bolts. She jerked her hands downward again and the lighting changed course, striking Poseidonis, rippling along its parapets and spires until stone exploded.

"What have you done?" Vaseem demanded.

"I've announced us," she answered, as the black scales on her hand spread upward over her arm to her shoulder. She had never manipulated so much energy before and it had been easy. She wanted to do it again, but she held back, mindful of the change to her arm, and waited for any reaction from the Queen of All.

"Good," Vaseem said grudgingly. "This is no herbalism or healing witchcraft. This kind of magic can be addictive. You must never lose control."

She barely heard Vaseem. She focused now on her surroundings, feeling the sand with her feet, listening to the wind and the sea. She anticipated the queen's counter-attack before it came, feeling the shift of the wind, its sudden unnatural intensity. Turning her back to the palace, she crouched down. Then, Vaseem crouched over her, shielding her with his body as wave after wave of sand blasted over them.

When the onslaught finally ended, Perilana rose to her feet again, faced Poseidonis, and laughed. She felt certain the queen heard, and she resumed her march toward the dark city. "Take me straight up to the gates," she told Vaseem.

"Confidence is good, Peri," he cautioned, "but not over-confidence."

"I'm committed," Perilana answered firmly. "I didn't choose this fight, but people I loved have been murdered and my sister taken. I will not stand by." She started forward again, and Vaseem fell in beside her.

As they approached the main gate, the portcullis rose. A score of mounted soldiers charged out, weapons drawn, some with torches. Perilana heard the hammering horses' hooves, but the soldiers' heartbeats were a jumble of sound. She couldn't determine their exact number, but she raised her hands to cast a spell.

"No," Vaseem told her. "Leave these to me."

He walked a little way ahead of her. As the soldiers came on, he muttered the same brief chant she had heard once before. The sand suddenly churned and thrashed. The soldiers screamed, horses whinnied in panic as they bucked and threw their riders. The horses fled, but the men were not so lucky. Their screams only intensified amid a loud snapping and popping and crunching of bone.

All became silent. A moment later, Vaseem returned to Perilana's side. "I'm sorry," he said, "but I have no clothes to change into this time."

"We all have to bear hardships," she said. "But you may give the queen a heart attack."

They continued toward the gates, Vaseem guiding her over the remains of the attacking soldiers. The riderless horses that lingered nearby avoided them. Perilana could smell their fear and sweat, hear their uneasy nickering, but she left them alone. Another familiar sound caught her ear, however. "You destroyed your clothing, but reclaimed your sword," she observed.

"It's a pretty bauble," he answered. "I like it."

The creaking of chains and rope told Perilana the gates were opening again, but no soldiers rode forth. She clutched Vaseem's arm and halted, suspicious. Once again, she heard the voices in the sea, but their song was muted and uncertain. Vaseem covered her hand with his own and waited to see what she would do.

"Lead me inside," she said softly.

As they passed through the gates and entered Poseidonis, Perilana felt the pounding of her own heart. She was used to the open spaces of the seashore, the familiar streets of her village and the surrounding forests. But here, she felt at a sudden disadvantage. "Tell me everything you see," she said to Vaseem.

He described the dark streets and the black, empty alleyways, the shuttered shops and broken fountains and the long-abandoned apartments. Here and there, he spied a soldier or an archer lurking watchfully on the rooftops. Perilana listened to what she could, but the city was unearthly quiet.

"Is there no life here beyond her soldiers? No families, no children, no shopkeepers? No dogs or cats? Where are the birds? I don't even hear an insect."

"Stop!" Vaseem warned, clutching her hand. "They're coming."

"What?"

Sharp claws suddenly sank into Perilana's neck and back. Leathery wings beat around her head and face. She tried to shake it off, yank it off, but the claws dug in deeper. "Get off!" she shouted.

A demonic voice shouted in her ear. "Food should not speak. Food should be devoured!"

More bat-like creatures attacked her, attaching themselves to every part of her body, sucking. But they didn't suck her blood—they sucked her soul! She felt herself weakening.

"I'm not food, and I said get off!" Magic surged up inside her and exploded outward, blasting the creatures, who burst into balls of flame and rained down in pieces. Free from them, she thought of Vaseem and heard him some distance off, grunting savagely. She heard the music of his sword as he swung it, the sound of steel cleaving leather flesh and wings.

But the air was full with the chittering and rumbling of demons. Another wave attacked her again, bore her down to the ground. She wrestled and rolled under their weight, unable to think or focus as they sucked her flesh, crawled inside her mind. *Food*, they said. *Succumb!* She was falling into an abyss, a fog, and her soul began to separate from her body. She was losing, losing, lost...

But then Vaseem cried out in pain. Vaseem who was always at her side, always protecting her. His deep voice reached out to her from some vast place, but she focused on it and reeled her soul back in. "I told you, *get off!*

Once again, power exploded from her as a ball of hot, expanding light. Demons shrieked and tried to fly away, but they couldn't fly fast enough. As the light touched them, they burned and died.

Perilana crouched down. Her body stung in a hundred places from teeth and claws, but she covered her face and wept. She had never used her power for her own benefit, only for others, but she needed healing. For the first time, she turned her magic inward. Vaseem's hand fell upon her shoulder, but she resisted him as the magic worked through her.

"Peri?" he said, his tone worried. "Perilana?"

Another moment, and she reached out for his hand and let him help her rise. She did so unsteadily and unsure of herself. Then, she reached up with her left hand to touch his face, and he caught her wrist.

Her white wrist with a normal hand and five fingers.

"You've purged yourself of the demons' influence!" he said. "I didn't know that was possible."

She hugged him. "I nearly succumbed, but you called out to me. I thought you needed help, and that gave me strength. Strength I didn't know I had." She reached out and touched his face again, exploring the shape and texture of it, memorizing the lines of his jaw, his nose. "You told me once not to fall in love with you. But you told me too late, Vaseem."

The soft clatter of footsteps on cobblestone interrupted them. Perilana turned slowly, putting herself in front of Vaseem. She was the protector now. She knew who was coming.

The Queen of All came out of the darkness and stopped with her back to another broken fountain. A sickly light rose up around her, illuminating her tall, black-clad figure and veiled face. She looked straight at Perilana. "Are you warmed up yet?" she asked.

"Where is my sister, Witch?

The Queen of All laughed at that. "Witch?" she said. "You're one to talk. There's more to you than I guessed. When I first sensed you, your magic seemed significant, but small. I couldn't locate you, but I located your mother, who was using her meager power to shield you from me.

Perilana gasped. "My mother?"

The queen folded her arms. "There was more to her than met the eye, child, but she hid her magic, just as she tried to convince you to hide yours. So, I killed her—and decided to test you." She smiled. "You are not a disappointment." She took a step closer and smiled again. "But never mind. If you want to see your sister, I'd hurry. Just make your way to the highest spire at the west corner of the city and climb to the top. There will be no more tests. From this point, everything will be deadly."

"Thanks, but we'll just follow you," Perilana said.

The Queen of All shook her head. "Oh, but I'm not really here." She began to fade away, taking her measly light with her. Vaseem leaped forward and swung his blade, but the figure was truly gone. "An apparition," he grumbled.

Perilana said nothing. "Can you find this spire?" she asked. "Guide me to it quickly." She held out her hand again, and he took it. Together, they moved down the increasingly twisted streets. She stumbled sometimes, off-balance, but when Vaseem asked about it, she answered that it was only the pace. She closed her eyes tightly after that and listened for any breeze, any puff of wind, and heard nothing.

"We're here," Vaseem abruptly said. He tugged open an ancient door. Its creaking hinges and scraping over the floor made an evil kind of music, as did their muffled footsteps as they strode across a stone floor with layers of accumulated pounce. Vaseem placed her right hand upon a cold metal guide rail. "Climb," he told her. The staircase is wide and winding. I'll be right behind you."

They made their way carefully, winding higher and higher in the darkness until they came, not to a chamber, but to an open rooftop ringed with archers. The storm still raged and lightning crashed. None paid attention to the rain. Their eyes were fixed only on the Queen of All. She stood in the center of the roof, cloaked in a shimmering, star-filled blackness, and at her feet, hugging one knee like an obedient pet was a dark-haired little girl–Perilana's sister.

The archers nocked arrows to bowstrings and, once again, the sound of leathery wings beat the air. Vaseem clutched her arm, but Perilana shrugged him off. The Queen of All stretched out her hand, and the little girl rose up to take it. A voice spoke in Perilana's head.

Your sister is mine now. Watch as I take her life while you stand helpless and blind.

"I am far from helpless," Perilana answered. "Come out from

behind your veil and let your men see the crone you've become. What have the ravages of magic done to you? How have you been changed?"

The Queen of All tensed with anger. "I veil myself because no man deserves to see my beauty!"

"I am not a man," Perilana challenged. "Show me, if you dare. Why did you lure me here, anyway? Why did you slaughter my village, kill my mother?"

"Because I intend to take your power," the queen answered in her own voice. "But first I had to make you stronger, and that required incentive." She touched the shoulder of Perilana's sister. "Go to the edge of the roof and stare down at the beautiful waves."

"If you will not remove your veil," Perilana said. "I will."

Perilana made a sweeping motion with one hand, and the veil tore away. The queen shrieked and swiftly covered her face with both hands. "Protect my sister!" she called to Vaseem as the demons plunged out of the sky to protect their queen. At the same time, the archers released their shafts. Perilana fell back into a strong defensive stance and thrust her arms outward. As she had done before, she slowed time almost to a stand-still. The arrows hung in mid-flight. The archers stood like statues. The demons continued to dive, but in an imperceptible slow-motion.

Only the Queen of All was unaffected. "You can't hold that spell forever! I took your measure when you used it on the beach."

"But I'm stronger now," Perilana answered. "You made me so! I'm also smarter."

Without any warning gesture, she broke the spell. At the same moment, she dropped to her knees. The arrows whined overhead and over the head of her little sister. Some struck Vaseem to no effect. But many of the archers screamed and fell backward into the night and to their deaths.

The demons, however, came on.

"Time for a little chaos," Vaseem called. "And perhaps a few allies."

Her little sister was almost to the edge of the roof. Perilana called her name, but the Queen of All stood between them. Without thinking, Perilana reached skyward, seized a bolt of lightning and hurled it at her enemy. The Queen of All waved the bolt away, but it distracted her long enough for Perilana to grab the child. "Didi!" she cried as she knelt to hug her small sibling.

But as she knelt, she heard the sea far below and the now-familiar voices on the waves. And she saw lights, pure white lights singing as they rose upward. For the first time, she understood their song. She watched, transfixed, as the sea gave up its dead: all the victims from the villages, all the sailors whose ships had crashed off the coast, all the suicides, and all the people the Queen of All had ever drowned. This was their time of vengeance. They took form as they flew upward to engage the demons with a fury.

Vaseem saw them, too, and he chanted his own brief spell. Instantly, his human guise fell away. A sea serpent's golden coils snapped and thrashed around the rooftop. Its fins and tail lashed outward, knocking archers into space. Then, just as swiftly, Vaseem took human form again and caught Didi in a protective embrace. "Hello, little one," he said. "I am Vaseem. Do you know the trouble you've caused?"

Perilana stood up. "Queen of All!" she called. "Queen of nothing!"

Her enemy looked up. Her face was black and scaled, misshapen, scarred by magic. So were her hands, and her posture was that of an ancient—or an animal. "I brought you here to seduce you!" she shouted. "After centuries, I am dying, and Poseidonis needs you to take my place, lest it die, too!"

She walked slowly toward the Queen of All. "I will never serve you," she answered. "And I will never serve Poseidonis."

The queen reached out and closed her hand into a fist. Perilana gasped, feeling that hand squeezing her heart. For an instant, she felt weak and dizzy, but she braced herself and with some effort turned the evil spell away.

"All things come to an end, Your Majesty." She raised her hand to the sky. "This is yours."

She brought her hand down, a signal, and all the souls from the sea rushed downward. They seized the queen, carried her upward into the sky, and with lightning to frame the deed, they ripped her limb from limb and cast her pieces into the waves. Then, as one, they continued to fly higher and higher until their light could no longer be seen.

Didi came running to Perilana and clutched her leg. "I could hear you from far away," she exclaimed. "I knew you were coming, but I couldn't do anything. Anything, except obey." She reached into her waistband and drew out a long needle. It flashed in Didi's tiny hand as it slashed at Perilana.

But Vaseem interceded, thrusting out a hand. The thin weapon shattered against his skin. He caught the child and pinned her arms.

"No, no!" Didi cried, kicking. "She told me! I have to obey!"

Perilana looked on, horrified. "What did she do to her?"

"Whatever she did, it can be undone with time and patience. But for mercy's sake, can you put her to sleep? I'm not good with children,"

It took only the slightest enchantment, and Didi fell asleep in Vaseem's arms. He rose to his feet, holding her as if she were his own, but he looked at Perilana and sighed.

"You can see, Peri," he said. "Why didn't you tell me?"

It was her turn to sigh. "I thought it might give me an edge if everyone still thought I was blind. After the first demon attack in the street, when I was at my lowest, I did what I had never done before, and healed myself. I purged the demon influence from my body and I restored my sight. I never wanted to see before. I heard such beautiful music in the world and feared I would lose that if I saw. But to fight this fight, I needed all my senses." She hesitated, then reached out and touched Vaseem's face. "And I wanted to see you. You are beautiful, too, Vaseem."

"We will talk," he promised, "but right now, we should get out of here. There are more dangers in Poseidonis than we have seen, and now, without the queen to rule and control them, they will be free to prey."

With Vaseem carrying Didi, they made their way down the spiraling staircase and fled the city. The gates were still open. What, if anything, might have escaped through them, they couldn't tell.

But once out onto the beach, with a little distance between them and the palace, Perilana stopped and turned to look back. The rain had slowed, but the lightning had not abated. It flashed and crackled, illuminating the bent and twisted towers and spires, the high parapets. A few demons still flew above its walls, she thought. The place exuded evil.

"Such a place must not be allowed to stand," she said to her companion. She knelt down and touched the sand, but her power ran deeper to the very foundations. The ground began to shake and the waters rose.

Poseidonis shivered as if it knew it was about to die. The spires crumbled first. Then the towers. The walls cracked, and the sea rushed in. The dead husk of the city collapsed on itself in a great cloud of dust and smoke.

Perilana reached for Vaseem's hand. "I love you," she said.

Vaseem hesitated. Their worlds were too far apart, he had once told her. But maybe that mattered less now. He gave no response, but he drew her close against his body.

"You're still naked," she whispered.

"Maybe you should turn your back this time."

'TIL DEATH DO US PART

by Pat MacEwen

Pat MacEwen is an anthropologist. She works on bones from archaeological sites and does independent research on genocide, having worked on war crimes investigations for the International Criminal Tribunal, and done CSI work for a decade. Oddly enough, she was once a marine biologist at the Institute of Marine and Coastal Studies at USC. She has two novels out: Rough Magic, a forensic/urban fantasy, and Dragon's Kiss, a YA fantasy about a crippled boy who finds he can talk to dragons but people? Not so much. She writes mystery, horror, science fiction, and fantasy. Her work has appeared in a Year's Best SF anthology. It has also been a finalist for the Sturgeon Award, and made the Tiptree Honors List. Her hobbies include exploring cathedrals, alien-building via nonhuman reproductive biology, and trawling through history books for the juicy bits.

Canterbury
1573 A.D.

SATHYLLIEN:
Where is the 'queen' I wondered? In my current guise, I could not see over the heads of the men surrounding me, nor penetrate the ever-shifting gaps between dancers in the midst of a lively galliard. I must, indeed, pay more mind to my own steps than anyone else's, for I had been partnered with a fat fool of an alderman who could not see his own feet, let alone those he trod upon so freely.

There!

One of her eager young men had seized his chance and his

partner. He lifted her into the air as he made nearly a full turn-about beneath her. Elizabeth herself had made the *la volta* popular in younger days, when the Earl of Leicester was still hale and hearty. But beyond her I could also see the archbishop, frowning at them from the high table. I saw him rise to his feet and bit my lip in annoyance. Would he take it upon himself to rebuke Her Majesty? In public?

He very well might. Matthew Parker was an outspoken reformer and he found such Italian frivolity scandalous. New Religion or no, he did not care for change on other fronts, and he was a suspicious soul. It would not do to let *him* get too close to the object of his current displeasure.

Damn it. The 'queen' had not even noticed His Grace's reaction. Delighted by her partner's audacity, she let loose a peal of laughter that echoed off the stone walls of the Great Hall.

Have a care, I whispered, using the slightest whiff of magic to carry those words to one set of ears, and one only. *We do not wish to offend our gracious host.*

Milady flinched, the elaborate plumes of the pearl-sewn mask she wore shuddering as she resumed the five steps of the galliard's *sinkapace—right, left, right, left, cadence.*

I would have said more, but the fat fool before me abruptly attempted his own feat: in place of the cadence, a tassel kick! I'd assumed the ornaments hanging from his overladen belt were for show alone, given his girth, but no, they were not. He spun about not once but twice, kicked out with his right leg...and struck *me* instead of the tassel.

The chunderhead knocked me into the next pair of dancers. I lashed out in self-defense and hit him squarely with an invisible bolus of power. He flung his arms out and landed upon his own arse like a horse hit by a cannonball.

I went down, too. The impact itself did me no special harm but it startled me. My glamour slipped, and so did the one enveloping the 'queen.' For half a second, those nearest to me got a glimpse of my true self—my hair turning auburn, the pointed tips of my ears in view, and my whole body suddenly grown long and slender. I heard someone gasp at the sight but had no time to fret about it. The 'queen' had resumed her true form as well.

I screamed, long and loudly, voicing my outrage and drawing all eyes away from her. As I scrambled back up off the rush-covered flagstones, I restored the glamour she wore before doing the same for myself. By the time I was upright, we were both once more our public selves. Then, as if to atone for his idiotic clumsiness, the alderman cried out, "Good God!" just before he passed out and fell flat on his back. Fortunately, that took everyone's gaze off me in turn. While others rushed to his aid, I fled.

ROBERT CECIL:

I stared.

What had I just seen?

In two blinks, both the queen and the Countess of Darien *wavered*, like their reflections might in smooth river water, distorted from beneath by the current. I could not make out their faces in any case. White plumes, lace, and seed pearls adorned the headgear of the first, and peacock feathers the second. We all wore disguises, this being the night of the Masque put on by the Kentish Mariners to help celebrate the Queen's Fortieth Birthday.

"Stand aside, boy!" somebody snapped.

My Lord the Mayor!

I bowed my head, meaning to move to my right, but a muscle spasm locked up my back *and* my neck. "Ah! *Damn* you," I whispered through a tight-lipped grimace.

"What?" The mayor snarled at me. "Are you simple as well as a hunchback?" His hard hand took hold of my shoulder. Turning my whole body to the right with painful force, he shoved me into a stone column.

I yelped in protest but was ignored as the Mayor joined in the general rush toward the fallen fat man. Only the Countess moved upstream, ducking her head and glancing about like a cut-purse making off with some hapless merchant's hard-won silver shillings.

I glanced back at the queen but saw nothing untoward. She was still laughing and ringed by her dandies, unharmed in any way I could see. And the Countess?

On her way out of the Great Hall.

What could I do but follow?

SATHYLLIEN:

Upon passing through the arched entrance to the Great Hall, I paused and stepped aside. It would not do to look *too* flustered. Besides, while prisoned in a dancing gown of blue and silver silk, I could barely breathe. The muggy heat of late August did not lend itself to exertion. Nor did I wish to inhale too deeply, for upon that still air drifted a hint of decay. Now, where could *that* be coming from?

There was only a man-high stone wall between me and the kitchens, where a great deal of cooking was still going on. Was it meat I smelled, then? Pork butt, gone off despite being well-salted and smoked? No. Taking another sniff, I was suddenly sure. The source of that faint but foul odor was human.

I turned slowly, scanning the courtyard. To my right, the Great Hall's entrance faced the cloisters. Beyond them rose the square towers of the Cathedral, its pale limestone ablush with the reddened light of the setting sun.

The aroma seemed stronger to my left.

Behind me, a new dance melody rose. It was slower-paced this time—a gavotte. I was in no mood for that. The alderman might recover quickly after so light a blow in return. He might even expect my forgiveness for his misstep. I felt my lip curl up at the very thought. His physical charms included a mouthful of rotted teeth and breath so foul it would knock a crow senseless. He would expect the traditional kiss if I danced the gavotte with him as well. I was not about to accommodate him.

For a moment, I entertained the thought of strangling him with his golden tassels. Then again, that would be such a venal thing to do. Foolish, too. The archbishop would be even further provoked by the alderman's murder. The 'queen' might well be unveiled in the aftermath, just when Elizabeth most needed her privacy.

No, I thought. Better to track down the source of that carrion scent and leave the fat fool to his own devices.

I strolled eastward, turning into a covered corridor that led from the hall to the kitchen courtyard. I had to step aside several times as servants ran back and forth with platters and flagons and trenchers.

I began to circle the kitchens within their courtyard. Damn it. The smoke from the chimneys rose skyward for a good two hundred feet before dispersing toward the east northeast and the city of London. There was no way to get downwind of that aroma, the better to track its source. Still, it did seem to center around the kitchens. It certainly wasn't coming from the Chapter House, the only place where one might reasonably expect to see a body laid out within the Cathedral Close—if one of the monks had passed, for example, and not yet been buried because of the royal holiday. Anyone else would be in their family's care and their dwelling place as well.

There was nothing on the ground or the midden heap that looked remotely human. Should I desist, then? No. Something was wrong. The small hairs rose from the back of my neck as if a thunderstorm were brewing and lightning about to strike. Out of a clear sky? Wait—I could hear buzzing. Not the drone of bees at work, nor yet a hornet's nest. Near at hand, though. Right there, in fact. A blowfly had landed upon my sleeve to investigate a greasy stain.

"Here, now," I whispered to the tiny creature. "Why do you bother with me? Go and find me what I seek." I cast him upward while stroking his six-legged form with a breath of compulsion. I half expected him to circle back to the midden heap and whatever I'd overlooked. Instead he rose higher and higher, going up the side of the building until he'd topped the edge of the slate roof. There his flight path veered left as it leveled out and he passed from my sight.

Frowning, I looked around me. I'd come to the side of the building opposite the Great Hall, where the brick chimney stacks rose but there were no windows. The sound of an axe echoed off the stone walls to my right, where someone was splitting firewood with hard grunts of effort and occasional oaths. From the other side came a woman's voice, yelling something about blood pudding. Neither could see me.

So I gave in to my discomfort. While maintaining the glamour protecting the 'queen' I shed my own and with it my tame, ladylike appearance, complete with an openwork lace bonnet confining my hair, and a Spanish farthingale, and all the other layers of this and that required by the fashions of the day. I straightened up to my full height, which made me at least a head taller than any man in the place. Then, with a gusting sigh of relief, I unfurled my wings. It felt so good just to stretch them out and let them take their natural shape, to waft them back and forth through the warm air while circulation returned and the membranes stiffened. It took but a moment, and then I was overshadowed by their green and gold excess, a butterfly's glory writ seven feet tall.

Once more, I scanned my surroundings carefully, but everyone was still busy elsewhere, and I would be losing the last of the light if I didn't do this now. Therefore I cast caution to the absent wind and launched myself into the air. It took only seconds to climb to the roof's height where I landed as gently as I could on the slippery slates.

My tiny friend was not alone.

There were hundreds of blow flies up there, all eagerly crawling about on...nothing. Behind the chimney stacks, they were most of them resting two to eight inches above the roof, but not *on* it. And here the smell of death was stronger despite stray curls of smoke wreathing it all.

I moved closer, then realized what I was seeing. The flies were clustered so thickly, they formed a living mold of what that had attracted them—a thing with arms and legs and a head. A human shape, but the actual person making it was invisible.

"What midsummer madness is this?" I asked myself, for such could only have been done with magic. No other of my kind should have been present without my permission. The problem vexed me, more than even that of precisely who was dead, and why the body had been hidden *here*, of all places.

ROBERT CECIL:

I stood there, gaping, forgetting to breathe. The Countess of Darien had wings! Not a bird's, but a butterfly's!

I craned my head back despite the hard crick in my neck, the muscles in my bent back drawn as tight as archers' bowstrings, trying to make myself taller, to see what she was doing up there. Who was she, really? *What* was she? Why had she flown up onto the kitchen's roof like that?

I knew my father trusted the Countess. Reluctantly. He'd never explained the whys and wherefores. He'd only told me to keep my eyes open, to avoid her notice, and to bide my time and keep my peace about anything I did discover. To accompany the queen on her progress this year would, he said, improve my education in ways no tutor could. It would help me learn to assess the assets, arms, and intentions of the various nobles hosting Her Majesty as she traveled about her kingdom. For that, he said, was what the queen herself was doing, and being *such* a clever creature, she always did so at *their* expense and not her own. From this too, I should take my lesson.

"And if I am caught out?" I asked him.

"Fear not. You are a child," he reminded me. "She and the queen will both be more accepting of a ten-year-old boy's curiosity than a grown man's improvident snooping."

By that, I was quite sure he meant the Archbishop. I was to avoid his notice, too, not least because there were many churchmen who thought my spinal deformity the Devil's doing and proof of my being His creature.

Very well. But I still had to *see* what was going on, didn't I?

There was no tree handy. There, then. The porch giving entry to the Great Hall rose three stories high, with windows on the upper floors and stone crenellations above that. All overlooked the kitchen courtyard.

I moved as quickly and quietly as I could 'til I'd reached the hallway connecting the kitchen yard to the Great Hall. Then I ran.

It took a bit of doing to cross the Hall itself, dodging dancers and servants as well as the still-irate Mayor. I sought out a stairway leading upward where, oddly, there were neither locked doors nor guards in my way. Soon, I found myself hanging over a stone sill, cranking my head around toward the east. No use. I still couldn't see over the peak of the kitchen's roof.

Up still more stairs, until I burst through a door so small it barely admitted even me, and then I was high enough. Almost. I used finger holds in the stonework and hauled myself still further upward, until I teetered atop the corner where the crenellations along the southeast-facing side met a solid wall along the northwest. The corner stones offered more height and a far more solid purchase for my feet than the crenellations had, but I still couldn't see through those astounding wings of hers. What was it that lay at her feet? What did she study it with such intensity?

Then, as I watched, as the sun set still further, she stood back. She waved her arms as she said something in a low, fell voice. I saw a cloud of tiny glimmers. Will o' the wisps? Or witch-lights? I could not tell.

It mattered not, for the glimmering vanished. In its place lay a woman. Dead. There were crimson stains down the whole front of her golden gown.

"God's bloody backside," I blurted, unthinking, and came near to biting my own tongue in two when the Countess whirled about. She darted looks every which way, then turned her gaze upward until she was staring me full in the face.

I felt my mouth fall open but found no words to express my terror. Then, as she launched herself into the air again, aiming her flight at my high perch, I cried out, "No!" I stepped backward onto nothing and fell, a rock dropped off a cliff.

SATHYLLIEN:

Alighting on the Great Hall's roof, I was fully prepared to do battle, but found my opponent had knocked himself senseless without my assistance. A child, not a man, and even then of smaller dimensions than most. He lay on his side with blood leaking out of his ears—had he cracked his skull? I bent down, examining him, then carefully removed the black domino hiding his face.

Damnation! Robert Cecil, Lord Burghley's son. Why was *he* spying on me?

Silly question. His father had probably set him the task. Between William Cecil and Walsingham, I'd been dancing in circles for years now, protecting Elizabeth in the one way they could not—by means of magic. Lord Burghley suspected my true nature, as did Dr. Dee, but Walsingham had his gaze firmly affixed upon the queen's treacherous cousin, Mary, Queen of Scots. He was welcome to that undertaking. All the better if it kept him at a distance from all things to do with Faerie.

What to do with the boy, though?

The apple of his father's eye, his developing mind was as twisty as his wayward spine. Likely Lord Burghley's successor, despite his being the younger son, for his older brother might be handsome and healthy withal, but there was no spark in him—no sign of his father's legal mind, or his caution, his wisdom, his subtlety.

Therefore, I placed my hands on either side of young Cecil's head. I found the ebbing energy within and bound it in place with a webwork of will. Then I set about stretching the time flow within his body, giving him weeks to heal up even as I directed the flurry of renewed connections within his brain. Otherwise, the lad would have been rendered a simpleton. It required injecting a bit of my own being into the mix, so that he too became somewhat magical. Almost a changeling. I would not have gone even that far but there was a whiff of destiny about this boy. And I needed him.

I used another bit of magic to remove the blood staining his neck, ruff and clothing. Then, as he began to stir, I withdrew from his person. Using Power, I spoke his name.

ROBERT CECIL:

What?

Someone was calling me. My mother? No, but certainly a woman. Her low voice echoed as if we were trapped in a tunnel, deep underground. I struggled with that for a moment, and then gave it up in favor of getting my eyes to open. I found my nose a bare inch from the toe of a woman's shoe. Low-heeled, it was made of leather dyed sky blue and embroidered with a darker blue as well as thread of silver. A courtier's footgear.

Turning my head brought on a wave of dizziness, so I clenched my teeth as my gaze rose past her skirts and a silvered farthingale. As I'd feared, I lay at the Countess of Darien's feet, and less than a foot from the green and gold tip of her wing.

I sat up but could not find my feet. I scrabbled backward, only to collide with the low wall enclosing this square patch of the Great Hall's roof. I could not move in any direction. I was cornered. Doomed.

SATHYLLIEN:

Damn it all. Had the boy done himself some further injury? Mayhap. When I bent down to have a look, his eyes grew huge. He made the sign of the cross, as if *that* would ward me off.

"Are you beef-witted, boy?" Impatience gripped me. I spoke frankly. "If I wanted you dead, you would never have wakened. Nor would you now remember what you have seen."

"Have I...wakened?" he managed to ask. "Or am I dreaming all of this?"

"It is no night *frai*."

"But...*wings*!" he blurted out.

I nodded gravely, flexing them to fan us both for lack of a cooling breeze. "Indeed. And a dead woman."

His dark eyes brightened, though I could not tell whether that came of fear or returning wit. Even magic could not heal a badly battered brain in an instant.

I was reassured, then, when he asked me first, "Who is it? *Who* is dead?"

"Did you not see that yellow gown she wears? It is a cast-off given away by the queen."

"To *whom*?" he demanded, then answered himself. "*Lady Thornhill.*"

"Indeed."

He shook his head and grimaced with the pain it caused him. Still, he spat out a few more words. "It cannot be. I saw the lady below in the Great Hall, dancing. While I was on my way up here. And you—you were already on *that* roof."

As was the late Lady Thornhill's body.

ROBERT CECIL:

The Countess turned and stared at the slate roof she had so lately departed and in such an inhuman fashion. A minute crawled by and then another. The silence pricked me with its claws. "It *was* her. I swear it."

"Was she not wearing a mask?"

"Of course. But Milady's witch mark showed, on her neck. A small red weal, shaped like a leaping trout. I know it well, for she is my mother's friend. And...and..."

Damnation! My sluggard tongue entangled itself so that I had to force my next words out. "...she was wearing that same gown. Golden. Trimmed in black velvet and gilded along either sleeve in the hues of a honeybee."

In a flash, I knew the way of it, even before the Countess turned her gaze back to me. "Aye. Exactly the same. And so will you find her in face and form. In every other aspect, even if you were as intimate with her as a man and his wife."

Silence gripped the both of us for the space of two long-drawn breaths.

Already knowing the answer, I still had to ask of her, "How could that *be*? Were there a twin of the lady's rank and noble bearing, all of England, surely, would know it."

SATHYLLIEN:

Precocious, this boy, but not yet in full command of his faculties. And I needed him. Now. I could not wait upon his full recovery.

"By means of a glamour, of course," I told him. Which he could surely work out for himself, eventually. To make my point in the timeliest fashion, I restored the glamour I'd worn at the start of the masque, first furling my wings until they'd disappeared once more. My clothing shimmered and settled again into silver and blue, all while leaving my hair chestnut brown now, not auburn, and my ears entirely human.

He gaped.

"The queen speaks well of you," I continued. "Was not the recovery of Her Majesty's coronation ring just after the New Year accomplished by *your* hand?" I smiled. "With the help of a cat, I've been told. From a hiding place in the Spanish Ambassador's own private quarters."

He squirmed, discomfited I would wager, by my even knowing of *that* affair.

"You kept that ring from gracing the hand of Mary, Queen of Scots. *And* brought the Earl of Leicester to heel."

Panic bloomed anew at the mention of *his* name. "But...I..." The boy drew back against the wall once more, sweat beading upon his waxen brow.

"Fear not. The queen would never have made me privy to that

266

tale were I likely to share it. Nor will the Earl ever hear from me of your part in the affair."

The panic waned, while his wariness did not. Excellent.

"What it tells me is this. You are a bully rook, a clever lad, and your father's true son. I have need of your talents and your loyalty. We must act to assure the queen's safety."

"The queen!"

I didn't bother to tell the boy which one I meant. Whatever mad scheme was afoot, I did not know myself as yet which one of us was the target. I did know, now, that the false Lady Thornhill had been near at hand when the alderman kicked me, when I'd let slip the glamours disguising my own true form and that of Elizabeth's stand-in. I remembered the gasp of surprise I'd heard as I fell. As I struck back, knocking my partner off his feet.

"Her Majesty," I told the boy, "is not here."

"But..."

"The woman wearing *her* form below is a double of *my* making."

Young Cecil struggled and brought himself upright against the wall. Then, holding one hand to his battered head, he demanded, "Who *are* you, Lady?"

"I height me Sathyllien."

"Sah...thill...yen." He repeated it slowly, his tongue reluctant to shape my name, and winced at whatever that brief effort did to his cracked pate. "Lady...Sathyllien," he managed, "I saw you fly."

"Indeed. In my own land, I am Queen of Air and Light."

"Faerie."

The word was not a question. Still, I nodded and let him digest it, though time was short.

He reached his conclusion and straightened a bit. "Where is Her Majesty, then? And what can I do?" This with a gesture acknowledging his small stature, his hunchback.

"You can carry word to the queen. The real queen. She needs warning, and there are few others either of us can trust, here and now."

He frowned, so I explained further. "She will believe *you*. Especially if you carry my token." I pulled a small enameled butterfly clasp from a pocket within my sleeve, dropping it into his palm. With a whiffet of magic, I made the wings flutter.

His mouth fell open again.

"You can go safely while I cannot." I canted my head toward the door and the stairway that led downward, back to the Masque and the herd of courtiers still vying for the false queen's attentions. "They may think you the devil's spawn, but they fear your father. I would be burned at the stake should they catch me out. And the Archbishop might. He's a canny man in his own straight-laced way."

"Nosy Parker," the boy whispered, naming the threat with a certain familiarity. So, then. He too was wary of the Archbishop, who stood second only to the queen herself within the Church of England.

"The queen is presently at the Crown Inn, on High Street. She has rooms on the first floor there and is using the name of Lady Canleigh. Do you know it?"

"Aye," he replied, nodding. "Sir William Brooke is the lease holder. He is my father's good friend."

"And more," I told him. Now that he was bound to me, I could sense another thread linking the boy to the baron. I did not yet know its nature. "Go you there. Find Her Majesty. Tell what you have seen here. She must be prepared to defend herself should I fail to contain the threat."

ROBERT CECIL:

It was so nearly dark by then, I dared not tarry. I made for the Christchurch Gate while inventing a story to explain my errand's urgency at this hour—the need for an apothecary's potion. Little enough, when all knew how many attempts there had been to assassinate the queen. I could only hope sheer nerve would suffice to gain me free passage.

But when I got there, neither the Archbishop's men or the Queen's Guard took any notice of me. They stood silent, bemused by their own thoughts. Or were they bespelled?

The mere thought chilled my blood as I recalled the peculiar lack of guards on the stairs leading to the roof of the Great Hall. Sudden shudders wracked my bruised back but I bit my lip and kept my peace. I walked between the torpid men just as if I myself were a prince of the realm. Though I braced myself for a challenge, it did not come. None greeted me either, though some among them surely knew me by my short and crooked back, if nothing else.

Wrong. All wrong.

Whatever plot *was* unfolding within the Close, it was already in motion. And so was I, running past the drapers' shops and haberdasheries lining Mercery Lane. I came out where the lane meets with the east end of High Street, where, on the other side, the lane turns into St. Margaret's Street. Almost opposite me, on my right, stood the Crown Inn, the first floor overhanging the street by a yard or more. The ground floor's entrance looked dark and none too inviting but those first floor windows, diamond-paned, aglow with a warm and welcoming light, drew me forth like a mad drunken moth to a candle flame.

I sped out into the street and straightaway was bowled over. Hitting the cobbles hard enough to knock the wind out of me, I could do naught but lay there while someone, a man by his voice, demanded, "God's wounds, boy! What the devil are you playing at?"

SATHYLLIEN:

They were dancing a saltarello when I returned to the Great Hall. I paused in the passageway to watch—it's old-fashioned but vigorous and it lacks the embrace of one's partner that so disturbs His Grace the Archbishop. The pairs still touched, but only by the clasping of their hands as they pranced alongside one another, only parting for some of the spins. I searched out the glamoured 'queen' and found her among them, somewhat breathless but still in fine fettle. Now, then—where was the false Lady Thornhill?

"Behind you," a whisper informed me.

I whirled about.

Golden-gowned, she stood at arm's length, hands fisted on her broad hips, her head canted to one side, revealing on her bare neck the leaping trout of a birthmark young Cecil had noted. She in turn considered my blue and silver façade, and apparently found it wanting. As usual. A golden bird-mask might cover most of her face, but did not fool me. I knew too well the cold curl of *that* lip.

"You," I accused.

'Lady Thornhill' laughed. "Did you think I would never return?"

"Once upon a time, you would have had better sense."

"If you had not come between us, my son would now sit upon the throne. And *all* would be changed thereby."

"No doubt," I replied, sneering. "You would make this small nation, and through it the world, a different place."

"A *better* place! One fit for the fae. A world where the old ways would not be forgotten. Where what is sacred to *us* is not discarded daily. Torn down, destroyed, trampled into the dirt by these foolish metal-mad creatures!"

And there it was—the ancient argument. 'Lady Thornhill' would prevent any real change, always in the name of preserving the life that was. Never realizing that life *is* change. That lack of it leads only to stagnation, decay, and death. A million billion forms of it. And not just here but in Faerie itself.

Anger laid my hand on the hilt of my dagger. It's the delicate weapon of a lady who wields it mainly upon her meat. It did have a steel blade, however, and a wooden grip which did not bite my fingers with the touch of cold iron. It pained me to hold it but that was not the reason I snarled at my fellow fae, giving a wolf's warning.

"Your son does not even know you. Or *of* you," I snapped.

The lip curled further, baring a fang. "I am come to make *that* right tonight."

At my back, the music ended. The dancers withdrew, and a herald began to announce the first of the evening's performances. I paid no mind to that. I kept my eyes on 'Lady Thornhill,' and saw the right hand rise up into the air. Saw the fingers snap. Saw the glamour fall way to reveal a form and stature even taller than my own. Unwingèd, which gave me a different advantage, but armored at the shoulders, the belly and thighs with the thick black keratin plates of giant rhinoceros beetles. At the crotch, a codpiece made of a single living beetle protected the genitals of a figure indisputably masculine.

My kinsman smiled and drew his own weapon—a glowing bone blade four times the length of my own, and enchanted or

270

poisoned, or both, I would wager.

ROBERT CECIL:

I could not make out the face of the man who had knocked me flat. He was naught but a dark silhouette against the twilight sky. When I did not answer, he reached down. He took hold of my arm. He pulled me upright, and then held me so while I struggled for air.

"Sir William!" I managed to squeak.

The man hauled me into the dim light cast by the windows above us.

I tried again. "Sir William Brooke. Lord Lieutenant of Kent."

That gave him pause, being named by his official post in the queen's service. Then, taking my measure, he finally recognized me in turn. "Master Robert," he answered, his tone grave. "What are you doing out here after dark? You'll run afoul of rogues and priggers, even here in Canterbury. Then what shall tell your father? How am I to explain what became of you?"

"I...the queen," I burst out.

"Hush!" he told me, low and urgent. Scowling furiously, he dragged me to the inn's doorway, shadowed as it should not have been if the Crown meant to attract any custom. An armsman dressed in my lord's livery opened the door there. They hurried me through it and thrust me down onto a bench at a table where no one was sitting. The common room was as empty as the street without, save for Sir William's wide-eyed daughter, Betsy. Younger than me by two years, she carried a wine flagon toward the back.

"You will not speak of Her Majesty, not in public. Not tonight," Sir William told me. His lean face was still barely visible as there were only a pair of lanterns alight in the whole room. I could make out his mustaches, curled up at both ends, but he wore a straw hat better suited to a farmer than a soldier save that its wide brim concealed half his face.

"I must," I answered, "for she is in danger."

"Why would you think so? And why would you come *here* to say such a thing?"

"The Countess of Darien sent me."

It did not please him to hear that name. I could tell by the way his mouth tightened, pulling his moustaches down on either side of his long nose until they made a Cupid's bow above his taut lips. So I fumbled at my doublet, retrieving a little leather purse I carried there. Once opened, I turned it upside down. Out fell the token the countess had given me. I caught it in my other hand and offered it to him.

The butterfly clasp would have none of it. As I reached out, it glinted twice and stirred upon my open palm. Then, in silence, it sprang to life and fluttered away from both of us.

"What ho!" cried Sir William. He and his man grabbed at the creature but it rose too high for even the Lord Lieutenant's reach and flitted through another doorway and then up the stairs there.

I followed the two men, wary of their haste and their scabbards as they ran up the steps. When I got to the landing, they'd entered another large room, only to halt while Sir William fell into a deep, sweeping bow, the straw hat snatched off and swung wide as if it were a courtier's velvet cap.

The reason why stood gazing at him in astonishment. The queen! And behind her, Betsy, serving wine to a man I knew not. Young and slender, graced with a child's face, he *sat* in the queen's presence!

"What is this?" Her Royal Highness demanded. "Why do you fracture my privacy?"

Then, even before the Lord Lieutenant could give her an answer, the glittering butterfly flew toward her, landing upon the sleeve of the arm she'd out-thrust to point at Sir William. It settled there, the enameled wings gently fanning the air. The queen stared at it. Then at Sir William, and finally, me.

"Your pardon, Majesty," said Sir William. "The boy..."

"My Pygmy!" She swept toward me, that same imperial forefinger now aimed at my nose.

I fell to my knees as I stammered out my warning. "The Countess of Darien gave me her token. She told me to bring it here that I might also bring you this message. Your Majesty, there's been a murder."

"What?!" cried Sir William. "God's teeth, boy! What are you on about?"

I wasn't entirely sure what to say while the Lord Lieutenant listened, though I knew him for one of my father's closest friends. I glanced aside at his armsman and said nothing more. What if either of them wore a glamour?

"Leave us," the queen ordered. Then, turning back to the young man still seated behind her, she said, "Not you, of course. I think this message must be meant for you as well."

SATHYLLIEN:

I cast off my glamour as well, but still needed a moment to unfurl my wings. So I leapt backward, out of the doorway, glad to be rid of confining skirts. My kinsman followed, lunging with his long bone blade, aiming to skewer me.

Then I'd burst through the remaining dancers and into a large open space at the center of the Great Hall. Voices cried out all around me and echoed off the stone walls. There was a scrabble and scrape of leather-clad feet and a clatter of fallen instruments as the musicians fled. Likewise the servants.

I dared not look at anything beyond my opponent, the glittering tip of his weapon, and his coal-black eyes, but surely I should have heard the Queen's Guard responding by then.

He smiled, no doubt noting the twitch of my ears as I sought some sign of armed assistance. "They are not coming. But have no fear. I have done *them* no harm."

Not for lack of ill will, I was sure. Whatever he had done had been for the sake of his own convenience.

"What is it you hope to accomplish?" I asked, using my dagger to parry his next attack.

"I've told you. I've come here to see the queen. I would have an answer. *I want my son.*"

He feinted left, and as soon as I shifted my weight, he came at me with a vicious backhand slash at my face and then a return blow aimed at my knife-hand. The *scrither* of dry bone across bare steel sent a shiver of dread through both of us but he succeeded only in trimming a splinter from his sword and a long lock of hair from my head. As they fell to the floor, I used the severed tresses to cast a bit of magic at him. The red hair flashed in his face, hot and bright as the muzzle flash of a cannon as I pumped my wings, *hard*, and leaped over his head.

He jinked to his right, came down in a crouch, and thrust blindly at the spot where I no longer stood. Two quick steps brought me back within arm's reach, though not quite close enough that I might plunge my knife into his heart from behind and end this. I managed only to hack at the joint in the beetle armor on his left shoulder, tilted toward me as he thrust with his right hand. The point of my dagger sliced through between two of the layered black plates and scored his skin.

Not a lethal blow, but cold iron cuts deep. Even a minor wound can generate molten agony in the fae. My opponent screamed and flung himself sideways, but he kept his grip on his own weapon. He did not drop it, as I had hoped he would, so as to clutch at his injured shoulder.

Worse yet, it brought him around so that he could see the false Queen Elizabeth where she huddled against the wall, behind a cluster of her young men. Would that we'd allowed any of them to bring swords or pistols to the Masque. They were no better armed than I.

"There you are!" the fae cried out, aiming his long bone blade at her. "Though you are not the one I seek, you surely know where your mistress is."

"Andeill!" I shouted his name, using Power as well as my rage, and the inborn knowledge of relative rank we both possessed. It brought him to his knees.

To the knot-pated courtiers ringing the 'queen' I cried, "*Move*, you fatuous pig swivers! Damn it all! GET HER GONE!"

Then, before Andeill could find his feet, I came at him again, slicing him across the forehead.

He screamed, louder yet, as he flung himself away from me to roll across the floor. This time, he did drop the blade. So I leaped forward to finish him, only to find the Archbishop between us.

"How *dare* you!" the prelate roared.

I pulled myself up, using my wings, and just barely managed to keep from gutting the man with my dagger.

That only lent further force to his outrage. "Are you mad? This is a House of GOD!" Parker bellowed.

It wasn't. Not even a chapel. But I do not go about stabbing priests of any kind. Except Druids. I truly dislike Druids. "Stand aside." I made it an order.

"I will not!"

"Damnation!" I cried. "I'm defending Her Majesty!"

"Ha!" shouted Parker. "Do you think to fool me? I see what you are! *Both* of you!"

He did not. He couldn't. He did not know me by my own face, only that of the Countess of Darien. He certainly did not know Andeill. He knew we were fae. No more, I realized quite suddenly. From the high table, he had not been able to look past the door jamb. He could not have seen either of us drop our glamours in the passageway. I snarled at him, infuriated by his nonsense, only to have this fool thrust a wooden crucifix at me! Where he got it I still don't know for he most certainly wasn't a papist. Invoking the name of his savior, he declared, "*This* is holy ground! We are within the Cathedral Close, and your kind has no power here. No place!"

Not entirely true, but it hardly mattered. I dodged around him and his cross, intent on my target, and found him fled! The fae princeling and his glowing bone blade were gone.

"A pox upon you!" I shrieked at the priest and flew from the hall.

ROBERT CECIL:

"Lady Thornhill," I told the queen, "to whom you gave your golden gown. We found her...bloodied." I stumbled over that last word, realizing *I* had found only the Countess and yet somehow had taken up her cause as my own. To the point of saying 'we.' Why did that word feel right when it wasn't?

I had no idea, but I had to continue. "Her body was hidden on the roof of the kitchens, and... and rendered so it could not be seen. By mortal eyes."

Her brow quirked upward as the queen took my meaning. She glanced again at the baby-faced gentleman, standing (finally!) at her side. To me, she said, "Be frank, Master Robert. Tell me. Do not fear to speak of magic, for I am no stranger to it. Nor is my...companion."

He smiled at the word, amused, I think, and I wondered again who he might be. Foreign, surely, though I could not say why I thought so. Perhaps the French cut of his doublet. As yet, he had not spoken at all. And yet I must, at the queen's command. So I did.

"The Lady's corpse was invisible. Glamoured, until the Countess revealed it." I skipped over how she'd done that along with my fall off the wall. My astonishment. My fright, reborn as I thought of it. "And as I had seen her—Lady Thornhill, I mean— just a moment before, dancing in the Great Hall...not a...a ghost, but a double..."

"An assassin," the queen said, her words edged with ice.

I swallowed another surge of panic. "So we feared. And the Countess sent me to warn Your Grace, so that you might defend yourself. Against...magic?" I could not help asking.

I got no answer. Down below, a loud thumping was followed by a crash and the voices of men, shouting. Was one of them Sir William Brooke? Maybe. But it was not he who came bounding up the stairs and burst open the door to the chambers occupied by the queen. No, that was not a man at all, but a creature of Faerie. His ears were pointed, and so were the toes of his boots, which bore a fang apiece at their tips, while his long hair, coppery-red, flowed down to his waist and moved of its own accord.

He was bloody-faced from a gash on his forehead but came to a graceful halt withal, his weapon drawn—a sword that glowed, whose like I'd never seen before. To the queen, he said, "So *there* you are, goodwife."

Then his black-eyed gaze lit upon the slender young man now one step behind her.

SATHYLLIEN:

I climbed to the full height of the cathedral's towers, from whence I could see the whole of the close, and the gates, though the gloaming offered little light. How to find him, my brother's son? Where was he going? Would he scat back to Faerie and report this fresh failure to his mistress, his step-mother Titania? Or would he now go to earth, find a fox hole and disappear?

Neither, I thought. He would do whatever he must to find Elizabeth. I knew not how, but he would. And I, in turn, could find him. I had drawn his blood. It still dripped from my dagger.

Holding the weapon, point aimed forward before me in the

open air, I used the bloodline we shared to cast about for his soul-scent.

There!

He had already made his way out to the High Street, to the very doors of the Crown Inn. Damn it! How had he got there so quickly? There and in, despite my wards and the guards set by the Lieutenant of Kent. Wishing I'd chosen the wings of an owl instead. I swooped as swiftly as I could toward the inn.

ROBERT CECIL:

"Move aside, boy," the fae told me.

Likewise the queen, though in a more practical fashion. "Master Robert, see to the door. Let no one enter."

"None will come," the swordsman said, smiling through the crimson webwork of blood on his otherwise so-pretty face.

"I am glad of that," she answered tartly. "I need no further embarrassment, sir, where *you* are concerned."

I would have kept my place even so, but just then I caught sight of Betsy, peeking past the broken door frame, tearful, her face all eyes and rounded mouth. The girl had fresh blood on her hands, but I could not tell if it were hers or her father's or someone else entirely. I could not face that fairy sword, but I could get the girl out of here, and perhaps send for help. From the archbishop, or even the mayor?

I made a short bow to the queen and backed away from her and him, whoever—whatever!—he was. On reaching the doorway, I pulled the door to, though it would not latch. I pushed the girl further back, well out of earshot.

"Your father," I whispered. "Where is he?"

"Below," she answered. "He...he breathes, but he does not know me."

"You must go and get help."

"I can't! There's another one down there."

Another...what?

"A goblin," said Betsy before I could ask.

Oh, sweet Christ on the Cross! Was there truly? Or was it a figure of her fright, her imagination? "If you will not go down, then go up!" I said. "Make a light. Try to signal someone. Set fire to the place, if you must!"

She gave me a horrified look but she also slipped her hand into a small cupboard. She produced a fistful of rush lights, and then, glory be! a candle and a flint. I seized the candle, pulling it from its blackened holder, and gave the stick back to her. Then, hefting the hunk of iron in my hand, I sent her off to do her best and turned back to the rooms I'd just left.

SATHYLLIEN:

What was that glimmer I saw? Someone stood on the roof! I landed almost on top of a small blonde child who was lighting one rushlight from another, with more at her feet. She fell back, squeaking like a dormouse while she tried to ward me off with her ridiculous rushes.

"Don't eat me!" she cried.

"Don't be silly!" I shot back, then recognized her—Brooke's daughter. And whatever darkened her small hands smelled very much like blood. "Where is your father? And where is the queen?" I demanded. "Quickly! She's in danger."

"I *know*!"

ROBERT CECIL:

Easing my way past the broken door frame, I held the iron candle stick holder behind me, out of sight. I need not have bothered. The fae had his back turned to me. He was focused on the queen, and Her Grace had flown into a rage. She flung a pewter plate at his head, then pulled pins from her hair and brandished them as she stepped in front of her young companion, her arms spread wide like the wings of a guinea fowl facing a snake.

"He is *not* your son. He is mine!"

I goggled. This...this *Frenchman*? But how was that possible? How could the Virgin Queen be any man's dam?

"You had no right to hide him from me," the fae answered, snarling the words. "I would have raised him *properly*, as the heir to any throne *should* be."

Her Majesty snorted. "He *was*. He grew up in a royal household, a prince in name as well as fact, though not of *this* land. He has wanted for nothing..."

"Excepting a father," the fae spat back at her.

"Is that what you would have been to him?" someone asked behind me. "A *father?*" The Countess of Darien! No! No, it was the Lady Sa...damn it, Sathyllien! She'd entered so silently I heard nothing at all until she spoke.

The swordsman spun about, lunging at her with that glowing blade. I dove sideways, beneath its sweep, but my shoulder gave way as I hit the floor and so I rolled under his feet. He stepped over me to extend his lunge, and I brought the candle stick holder up, cupped in my hand. I shouted something, I know not what, and drove the long wax-coated iron spike on it into the back of his knee, where there was no armor.

The creature let loose an eldritch, bone-shivering scream that cracked three of the window panes as he fell over and clawed at his leg. The Lady kicked his sword away, then yanked me out of his reach as well. I scrambled still further and snatched up a fire poker from the empty hearth. Then I stationed myself in front of Her Majesty, breathless but ready for it when the fae finally managed to yank the spike out again.

"Death take you all!" he shrieked, and somehow climbed back onto his feet. He did not reach for his fallen weapon, however. He raised his bloodied hands instead, palms out, and the very air between us began to shimmer, to redden.

Spotting Betsy once again, lurking just outside the door, I shook my head and mouthed the one word, "Run!"

SATHYLLIEN:

Ah! So *that* was the thread connecting young Cecil to William Brooke—his daughter!

Well and good. The boy had heart, and his courage was all his own. I might have given him some of myself in the healing of his hurts, but I'd only sought to strengthen that which was already there. I had planted the seed of a kin-bond so I could be sure he'd obey me. Nothing more.

Now, I had another such choice to make. I moved to stand beside young François, with whom I did have a kin-bond, though one of second degree. I turned his face 'til his gaze met mine, and I gave him what I could not give a true human—I sent a share of my magical strength, that which made up my wings, and indeed my whole being, his way. It coursed through the bond, through my flesh, pressed to his, through the channel I opened between our two minds.

There was, of course, no time to train him in its use. Andeill's fury now made the lamp lights pulsate with his own heartbeat. I felt his curse reaching its peak as I turned to face him once more. And cried out, "No!"

Not to him, but the girl child, who still had her rush lights. Just as Andeill began casting the geas, she ran up behind him and plunged the red embers at their nether ends into the same wound young Robert had made in the back of his knee. It did not stop him, of course, but it did send the casting agley, so that he missed the queen and the boy altogether while blowing the table apart. And though he struck me and his own son as well, it was not full-on. I shielded myself with my wings. And François?

He fought back instinctively, without instruction, spreading his own hands out in a warding gesture that turned the curse back on his father. Not all of it, or he'd have turned Andeill into a smoking stain on the floorboards.

Almost, as Andeill fell down again, blistered and burnt and keening like a *ban sidhe*, I could feel pity for him. Almost. Then I remembered the slain Lady Thornhill, and all the others he'd gladly kill to have his way. To keep England from changing, and with it the world.

ROBERT CECIL:

Once assured of the queen's safety, I went to Betsy. "Are you all right?"

She nodded.

I told her, "You saved us all."

"As did you, Master Robert," the queen remarked.

I turned and bowed to Her Highness, flushed with pleasure, and more so when I felt Betsy's little hand take hold of mine.

But it wasn't over yet.

The Lady Sathyllien bent over the fallen fae. "Now you know. Your son can defend himself. He will make his own choices."

His answer? A pitiful groaned out, "No."

She shook her head, then told the Queen, "It's your kingdom. Your son. Your decision. Shall I kill him, and end this?"

The queen replied, "Perhaps you should. I need a fully human heir and I cannot marry. Not while I have a living husband. And *he*...is immortal!"

Oh! That explained so many things!

"Can you not simply divorce him?" I asked, and then had to swallow my heart, mortified by my own words, by my daring to question Her Grace.

But the queen shook her head, mournful rather than irate. She looked to the Lady Sathyllien, who said, "As I told you then, once you become the rightful queen. you are the very heart of this land. And the vows you took are magical in nature. Could I break them, I would not, for your people would pay the price as well."

"And he...he is royal," Her Majesty muttered. Something I knew had stayed her hand where her cousin the Queen of Scots was concerned, much to my father's displeasure.

"So, then?" the Lady inquired.

Still Her Majesty dithered. "He did save my life, as he promised back then. When my sister and Phillip of Spain were set upon my execution." She turned aside and caressed the young Frenchman's beardless cheek. "And without that marriage, I would not have you. Even though I've been forced to keep you hidden and cannot acknowledge you even now...I would not undo that. Not for anything."

The young man, somewhat singed around the edges, spoke for the first time, and yes, with a French accent. "Yet if you do kill him, you will be freed of the constant peril." He paused. "Free to marry again without breaking your vows."

"And repeat my father's worst mistakes? I think not. I will find some other solution." She turned to the Lady, decisive now. "Let him live, but not in England. Nor in France. Let him go back to Faerie and *stay* there!"

The Lady smiled, well pleased, I think. She told Betsy, "I'll see to your father when I return."

Then she bent over the fae and brought her great green and gold wings around to enclose them both. Something twinkled, then flashed, lightning bright. I had to shield my eyes and when I could see again, they were gone.

The queen let out a sigh of relief. "I am so sorry," she told her son. "We have so little time together, and now it's been cut even shorter than usual."

"Have no fear. I will come again, Madame.. Perhaps this time as myself, as the Duc D'Alençon." He smiled, an expression full of whimsy. "I could, perhaps, come to you as a suitor, *n'est-ce pas?*"

What? I blinked and felt Betsy squeezing my hand as she fought to control a fit of giggles. I nearly joined in. To be a queen and courted by one's own son? Scandalous! Whatever would the Archbishop think?

But Her Majesty merely laughed and embraced him. "Whatever you like, my little Frog."

FIRE SEASON

by Anne Leonard

For the final story in an anthology, I look for a tale that leaves the reader with a lingering sweetness, even if there is a bit of heartache, too. Anne Leonard's "Fire Season" fulfills both admirably. It's like a morsel of deep, rich chocolate on a satin pillow. Sweet dreams!

A lawyer and mediator, Anne Leonard is the author of the fantasy novel *Moth and Spark*. She also has an MFA in Fiction Writing and a PhD. in English literature. "Fire Season" was first drafted after a visit to Istanbul and substantially revised after wildfires burned through many communities near her home. She lives in Northern California with her family and two cats.

Ash floats softly down like snow. My eyes are swollen and stinging from smoke, my throat raw. The sky is a murky yellow-grey, the sun a dull copper through the haze. I am taut with readiness. I was one of a dozen people to climb the fire tower at dawn when the wind blew into the village with the smell of burning on its back. From the tower we saw blackened hillsides and billowing smoke. The flames seemed to have turned north, away; if they continue on that path, they will burn themselves out in the canyon lands. We are not fleeing yet.

It is autumn, the hot dry time of year when fires are common, and my neighbors speculate about the causes: a hunter's careless fire, dry lightning, a wind-carried ember. I say nothing. I know what caused it—my lover, the djinni.

I met him in a bazaar in a city in another country, where he was selling olive oil. He had five varieties; he drizzled a little of each onto a platter and gave me bread to taste them with. One was light, almost grassy, round in my mouth like good wine.

"That is for summer cooking," he said. His hair was as dark as mine but with a wave to it. His skin was a warm gold-brown, his

283

lips narrow, his eyes an intense black. I could not tell his age–his eyes were far older than his features. Looking at them, I thought of glistening coal, obsidian, onyx. Hard and ancient and reflective. He was handsome, with a lovely voice. Desire, which I had put aside for a long time, flickered in me.

"Thank you," I said. "How much for one of the smaller bottles?"

He named an absurd price. I laughed at it and offered something much too low. I had the advantage in haggling, because I could take as much time as I wanted while he needed to sell quickly, and I pressed it. The numbers flew back and forth. We were very close to something fair and in the middle, when impulse seized me.

I said, "I'll buy at that if you come have dinner with me when I use the oil first."

It surprised him, but he was quick on his feet. "Done! And I promise you it will be the finest meal you have ever cooked."

He arrived at the agreed-upon time, carrying roses and a small volume of poetry. His name was Azhif, *firelight*, the opposite of my own Rahit, running stream. I lived in a small but well-made flat which overlooked a courtyard garden. The willow in the center was tall and old, and the early evening light on its upper branches had the same green-gold glow of the olive oil. I had dressed carefully and wore the sandals which set off my feet to the best advantage.

We had cucumbers, goat cheese folded into flaky pastry I had cooked with the oil, nectarines. I don't remember what else. We took wine to the garden with us and sat on the grass under the willow, and he read me poetry. Not love poetry, which would have been precipitous, but poems about beauty and friendship and hope. His lashes were long and dark as he bent over, looking down at the page.

When it grew too dark to read, he shut the book, and we sat silently while night purpled around us. I looked at him and saw the flame in his eyes.

He took my hand. We kissed. Then I knew he was not human. He shifted under my touch like the being of fire that he was. He was heat, light, motion. There are no words to describe the reaction of my body. I was transformed.

The mistake, it turned out, was not falling in love with him. It was letting him fall in love with me.

How can I tell the wonder of those first weeks? I can't. No one can ever tell happiness.

He said, "All things are fire, even water, because without fire there is no life, no movement."

"Love is movement," I said.

"Love is fire."

That winter, my father died. I am the only child, and I went back to the village where I had grown up to hold his funeral, pay his debts, and sell his animals. The farm house was small and old; the roof leaked and dust was thick in the rooms my father no longer used. I swept and cleaned and hammered, and somehow the silence of the country folded around me so that returning to the city was fearsome.

I wrote Azhif, and he came. He brought small and beautiful things which enlarged and warmed the house: copper statuettes, books with covers calligraphed in gold, crimson teacups that seemed to blaze where they rested. Winter was held at bay. Azhif and I drank tea in the morning while looking over the fog-covered land. When he touched the window glass, steam rose from the condensed moisture.

We loved each other madly. We made love on the kitchen table and the stairs and behind the goat shed. I was never cold. Once when rain fell in torrents, we climbed the slippery wooden steps of the fire tower and took each other on the damp floor. The rain that landed on my bare skin was warm as a summer sea. We were scarcely two separate beings, constantly touching, hands and lips on breast and thigh and cheek. I was replete. Replete and burnished.

And in my joy, my pleasure, I failed to notice what was happening to Azhif. He was separate from his kin, from the place that had been his home for years uncountable. One night I lay close to him and put my hand on his chest. His skin was warm.

Warm, not hot. I kissed him, and where usually I felt only flame I felt the pressure of his lips and tongue. He was cooling.

Looking at the thick columns of smoke in the distance, I consider now—I have often considered—whether I should have said nothing. Would things have turned out differently? Inhaling the smoke, I think that silence would have set a secret between us, and secrets kill love faster than anything else.

I run my hand along the rail and by touch find the scorch marks from Azhif's fingers. I place my own fingers over the marks, but they are only burned wood. Nothing of him lingers. I imagine being among the flames, feeling the hot smoky air against my skin, hearing the hiss and crackle of dry wood burning. I never knew I wanted that.

I waited over a day to speak to him. It was evening, rain falling softly, the room cozy with the fire in the hearth. He was reading. I had been tense all day, worrying about this. I gave him his usual after dinner glass of wine and said, "Azhif, we need to talk."

He looked up. For a moment I thought he seemed older, lines on his face. He moved and the illusion vanished. "What about, my love?"

I sat down opposite him and put my own glass on a side table. I said, "Two nights ago, when I touched you, you were cooling."

"Impossible," he said. "Fire is who I am. It cannot be expended or used up as long as I am alive."

"Then maybe you're dying," I said.

"I am not dying."

"How old are you?" I asked. "Really?" It was a thing we had never talked about.

He was always confident and self-assured, but the question caught him out. He kept his eyes on his glass as he answered.

"I've lost count."

"Two hundred? A thousand? Ten thousand?"

A log shifted in the fireplace, sending up a shower of sparks. Rain tapped on the windowpane.

"Not quite a thousand, I suppose," he said at last. "What does it matter?"

How many lovers have you had? I thought, but I had the sense not to say it. "How long do djinn live?"

"We die if we are slain in combat or by magic. Otherwise we do not age. I have known other djinn who have lived six thousand years. I am young. Rahit, I'm not cooling. You imagined it."

I didn't. I was too cowardly to say the words. I drank my wine, dismissing the topic, and sat watching him with lowered eyelids. It was terrible, in all senses of the word, frightening and magnificent, that he was so old. That I slept with someone who had seen so much history. That he loved me. Because I had no doubt of that.

He continued to lose heat. I saw the evidence in the absence: the lack of steam from his footsteps when he walked barefoot on the wet porch, the ordinary feel of metal things he had touched, the loss of incandescence when we made love. That he could control his fire, I knew, or he could never have lived in a human world, but he had been less careful around me. Now when he kissed me, I felt the blood pulsing in his lips.

The winter rains ended and the trees bloomed and leafed. The days grew longer. Azhif and I took our meals outside more and more often. Grass which had been green turned brown, then gold, with sun. His cooling was harder to tell as the world warmed. His eyes had lost their flicker, though.

One morning I slept late. When I looked out the bedroom window I saw him standing by the goat shed, and his posture was that of despair.

He came in, and I said, "Azhif, it's time you go home. It's damaging you, to be here."

He was angry. "Do you love me for myself?" he said. "Or for my fire?"

"You can't separate it that easily," I shot back.

"Are you banishing me?"

"If you will have me, I'll come," I said. "This house, this place, they don't matter."

"They do to you," he said. "You're happier here. You breathe more."

"I've left it before. I can leave it again."

He sighed. "I'll make arrangements," he said.

287

The hills in the north give way to broken, tree-less land, all rock with a bit of scrub. There are wild animals—mountain goats and crows and snakes and mice—but no people. When the fire reaches that far, it will die. It will not even smolder. In that land, flame has no fuel.

Azhif is settled there, somewhere. I imagine that at night he looks at the stars and tells himself the stories about them which everyone else has forgotten. Perhaps he sits on the sandy bottom of a canyon and waits for an animal to approach him. He might read by candlelight or even by the glow of his own fingers.

Or perhaps he walks in this fire, exultant, watching the flames rise in his footsteps, touching the dry leaves of the trees and making the fire dance and swoop as it tears along the limbs. The wind bears to me the gift of his hot breath.

Azhif had shown no signs of leaving, and finally I confronted him. I waited until night, when I could look up at the dark ceiling.

"I need you to go," I said. "I can't stand to watch you withering like this." His face was that of a middle-aged man, and when he left the bed in the mornings the sheets were cool.

For a long time he was silent. I was afraid to touch him. I knew that he was angry, that he would leave, that I had drawn a knife I couldn't sheathe.

"I can't go back," he said. "Not with you. I am outcast."

"By your people?"

"Yes."

"Because you took a human lover?"

"Because I stayed with you," he said. "A night, a week, a month, that would be of no account. But I left my home and followed you here, and for that I am exiled so long as I am with you."

"Did you know that would happen?" I was ready to be furious with him, and also full of grief. I didn't want him to make so great a sacrifice for me.

"When you asked me to return, then they told me."

"Leave me, then," I said. It hurt. "You're dying. Go back."

"Not dying. Merely becoming mortal." His hand clasped mine.

"To love a human is to become one."

"Why me?" I asked, afraid that at any moment I would start to cry. "In a thousand years of life, why am I the human you give everything up for?"

"There is no everything, there is only you, Rahit, and I love you."

Not so much, not so much, please not so much. I couldn't say it.

He turned onto his side and pressed close to me, his arm across my chest. He kissed my forehead, light and cool as a butterfly.

"Let it be," he said. "I've lived long enough to make many mistakes, often more than once. This is not a mistake."

I did cry, then, and after a long while fell asleep. I woke once. He was gone from the bed. I listened for the sounds of him in the house and heard only silence. When I could bear it no longer I got up and went to the window.

He sat naked on the grass, facing the hills. He glowed dull orange, like an ember. It was more heat than there had been in months. We would never, not even when the universe wound down, be of the same kind.

It was not a bar to love. But it might be a bar to happiness.

Let this not be the last, I wished, let this not be the last.

Late summer arrived, fierce and hot. Around us the world dried and dried. The air smelled of dried sage. The sun bleached and cracked the bare earth. Hornets came out of their nests and droned near anything moist. Frogs went silent as their wet places dried up. It was too hot to bake and too hot to eat; we lived on water and fruit and the lettuces we rescued from wilting in the garden. The light was hard and white.

Azhif spent most of his time outside, reveling in the furnace of sun. He wore no shirt or hat. He sweated only a little. When he was inside, we rarely spoke. I wished he would go home, where he could have what he needed. The space between us thickened with the need for change.

One night, after a particularly hard day where I had simmered alone in anger and grief, he asked me to climb the fire tower with him. I went, unhappy, aching for something more. I could not pinpoint the moment where everything had gone askew, but I knew I could not endure much more. One of us would have to leave. I hoped we could do it while we still loved each other.

He pointed at the heat lightning flashing on the horizon and said, "People used to say that was caused by dancing djinn, our feet striking the floor of heaven."

"Was it?"

"Only sometimes." I could not tell if he was joking.

We were silent. "This can't go on," I said at last.

"I know." He inhaled, a very human noise of nervousness. I remembered haggling with him, when I had thought he was just a handsome young man. He said, "I have made a bargain with my folk. I can burn again, and stay with you. But there's a cost."

"What?"

He put his hand on the rail, and grey smoke threaded upward. "We can be together only during the rains. The rest of the year, I burn, and parts of the world burn with me."

"Will you go home?"

"Home is with you," he said. "Always. What burns will be close." He turned and kissed me, and it felt like the first kiss, heat inside and cool darkness around and our bodies as ephemeral as air but powerful as wind. The gold light was back in his eyes.

"Let the world burn," I said.

I climb down from the fire tower. When it is wet he will return. He will leave his warmth on the sheets and read poetry aloud to me in his beautiful voice.

The fires he starts are not born of malice. They are simply the signs of his passage, the trace of his being, like steaming footprints on the porch.

I know I should be consumed with guilt. The smoke, the destruction, the fear, they are my fault. But if he had not caused them, something else would have. It is fire season, after all.

ABOUT THE EDITOR

Deborah J. Ross is an award-nominated author of fantasy and science fiction. She's written a dozen traditionally published novels and somewhere around six dozen pieces of short fiction. After her first sale in 1983 to Marion Zimmer Bradley's *Sword and Sorceress,* her short fiction has appeared in *F and SF, Asimov's, Star Wars: Tales from Jabba's Palace, Realms of Fantasy, Sword and Sorceress, Sisters of the Night, MZB's Fantasy Magazine,* and many other anthologies and magazines. Her recent books include Darkover novels *Thunderlord* and *The Children of Kings* (with Marion Zimmer Bradley); *Collaborators,* a Lambda Literary Award Finalist/James Tiptree, Jr. Award recommended list (as Deborah Wheeler); and *The Seven-Petaled Shield,* an epic fantasy trilogy based on her "Azkhantian Tales" in the *Sword and Sorceress* series. Deborah made her editorial debut in 2008 with *Lace and Blade,* followed by *Lace and Blade 2; The Feathered Edge: Tales of Magic, Love, and Daring; Mad Science Café; Stars of Darkover* (with Elisabeth Waters)*; Gifts of Darkover; Realms of Darkover;* and *Masques of Darkover,* and other anthologies.

CPSIA information can be obtained
at www.ICGtesting.com
Printed in the USA
BVHW042245020420
576765BV00008B/249